the raptor virus

frank simon

a novel

the raptor virus

BROADMAN & HOLMAN PUBLISHERS

nashville, tennessee

0-8054-2339-7

Published by Broadman & Holman Publishers,

Nashville, Tennessee

Dewey Decimal Classification: 813

Subject Heading: NOVEL

Library of Congress Card Catalog Number: 00-068884

Library of Congress Cataloging-in-Publication Data

Simon, Frank, 1943-

    The raptor virus : a novel / Frank Simon.

    p. cm.

    ISBN 0-8054-2339-7

    1. Women computer programmers—Fiction. 2. Chinese—Washington (State)—Fiction. 3. Computer viruses—Fiction. 4. Seattle (Wash.)—Fiction. I. Title.

PS3569.I4816 R3 2001

813'.54—dc21   00-068884

For John James Simon
P-47 Fighter Pilot

Acknowledgments

I want to thank the people who helped make this book possible:

My wife, LaVerne, first editor and my sweet helpmeet.

My friend and agent, Les Stobbe.

Commander Carl H. Hammert, U.S. Navy Reserve (Retired), for his help in understanding how P-3s make life miserable for submarines. If there are any mistakes, they are mine, not his.

William A. Franklin, Taiwan field chairman for The Evangelical Alliance Mission (TEAM), for sharing information on missions and Taiwan.

Leonard Goss, for his help and encouragement.

Prologue

Friday, June 9, 2000

Hanna Sidwell smiled as she slowly scanned the desolate red-and-green majesty of Palo Duro Canyon. The cool early morning breeze blew strands of her long brunette hair into her face. She swept them back into place. It was June and nearly summer on the High Plains of the Texas panhandle. She thought back to the last time she had been at this exact spot in December 1999, the last year of the twentieth century. She shivered as she remembered what had almost happened when she had accepted that consulting job in Seattle, the "on purpose" Y2K bug that she and Russell Flaherty had worked so hard to fix. The chill drove deeper as she remembered how close it had been.

She glanced at Russell. His eyes were following the far canyon rim. She looked at Scott. Russell's son seemed more interested in the near-vertical plunge only a few feet in front of them.

Russell's lips curved into that smile Hanna loved so much. "So, this is where we met," he said, squeezing her hand.

Hanna felt her pulse quicken. "Close," she agreed with a self-conscious grin. "Actually it was a couple hundred feet that way." She pointed with her other hand, indicating a spot above the yawning abyss.

"Cool," Scott said, drawing the word out. "Dad, can we get a hang glider?"

Russell peered around Hanna at his eleven-year-old son. "We'll talk about it later."

The boy frowned and looked up at Hanna. "That means no," he informed her.

Hanna had to struggle not to giggle. "Well, since I'll shortly be a member of this family, perhaps I can talk to your dad about it."

"Gee, Hanna, do you think so? I mean, Ms. Sidwell."

Hanna laughed but stopped when she saw Russell's expression. "Sorry, but it *is* funny." She turned serious. Here was another detail to be worked out as they planned their future life together as a family. "Russell, I know how you feel about Scott being respectful to adults. But he *is* respectful. He's about the most respectful young man I've ever met. It's what's in the heart that counts."

"I know, I know. We've been through this before."

"Russell. 'Ms. Sidwell' bugs me."

"I know that."

She sighed. "It's your decision. But I'm not Scott's mom, and I'm not an old lady either."

She watched his eyes. The stern disapproval began to change subtly. She saw he was struggling not to smile. Finally he shook his head.

"No," he said slowly, "you're certainly not an old lady. Not in the slightest."

"So can't we compromise?"

"Oh? What will you give up?"

She looked into his eyes. "I'll stop bringing it up."

He looked stricken. He turned his head away quickly.

"Russell?" She tugged on his hand. She saw his shoulders shaking. "Russell?"

He broke out laughing as he turned back. Hanna smiled. His sense of humor was just one of the things she loved about this one who would shortly be her life partner.

"Deal?" she asked hopefully.

He shook his head. "Deal." He looked past her to his son. "You may call Ms. Sidwell 'Hanna,'" he said.

Scott was clearly embarrassed. "Uh, thanks Dad." The boy looked up at his benefactress and grinned. "Thanks, Hanna."

"You're welcome, dude. Now, I've shown you guys Palo Duro Canyon, but I need to get back to Hereford. You two can relax with my folks, but I still have things to do before tomorrow." She looked at Russell. "You did remember everything, didn't you?"

"There wasn't that much. Let's see: there's me and Scott and our rental tuxedos." He glanced at his son. "I did pack those, didn't I?"

He sidestepped the expected elbow.

"He packed 'em," Scott said.

"Yep," Russell continued. "I think we're all ready. Scott looks real cute in his tux."

Hanna saw the boy's look of irritation and the fact that his father was completely unaware of it. "I'm sure he's quite handsome in it, just like *my* man."

"You'll see tomorrow," Russell replied.

They walked back to Hanna's Ford Explorer. Russell held the driver's door for his wife-to-be while Scott clambered into the backseat. Russell walked around and got in on the passenger's side.

Hanna drove down the rutted dirt path to the farm-to-market road and turned right. She tilted the rearview mirror and glanced at Scott. "So, what do you think of the Texas panhandle?"

"It's cool!" he said. "It sure is different from home. I've always wanted to see the desert."

"Well, this really isn't a desert. We're in the South Plains, an extension of the prairies of Kansas and Oklahoma. But it is dry, compared to Seattle."

A lithe tan shape loped across the road ahead as they neared Interstate 27 north of Happy, Texas.

"Wow, that dog must be lost," Scott said. "There are no houses nearby."

"That was a coyote," Hanna said.

"Really?"

Hanna saw his wide eyes in the mirror. "Would I kid you?"

"Sometimes."

She laughed. "Well, I'm not now. That really was a coyote. We have all kinds of critters you don't have back home—roadrunners, rattlesnakes, prairie dogs."

"Wow! Can you show 'em to me?"

"The coyote you've seen. Roadrunners and prairie dogs I think I can manage. But the rattlesnakes I'd just as soon leave alone, if you don't mind."

"I second the motion," Russell observed.

"Aw, Dad. It would be so cool to see one."

"Not if it struck you," Hanna said. "Besides, I know Mom and Dad have a lot planned for your visit with them. You won't be bored, pardner."

"You mean while you and Dad go on your . . ."

Hanna smiled. "I think that's the general idea." She paused, watching his eyes in the mirror. "That OK with you?"

"Yeah."

"Thank you, Scott."

"Where are you two going?"

"Didn't your dad tell you?"

"No. Said it was a secret."

Hanna glanced at her fiancé.

"Well, it started *out* as a secret," he said. "But I got persuaded that I might want to change my mind."

"She got it out of you," Scott said.

"That she did. Ms. Sidwell can be quite convincing when she sets her mind to it."

"You're treading on dangerous ground there, pardner," Hanna said.

Scott sat forward as much as the seat belt would allow. "So?"

"We're flying to Hawaii," Russell said. He reached over and squeezed Hanna's hand. "Our honeymoon night will be at the Mark Hopkins in San Francisco. Then we fly to Honolulu. After a few days there, we'll see Maui, Kauai, and the big island of Hawaii."

"Cool!"

"Way cool!" Hanna agreed. Her eyes darted to the dry brush beside the road. She put her foot on the brake and slowed down. "Scott! Look over by that clump of cactus. See that big brown bird with the long legs?"

"Wow! That is *some* herky bird."

"That's a roadrunner. Watch what he does."

The bird snapped its head around, looking at the approaching car. Then it sprinted off in the same direction as if in a race, dodging in and out of the clumps of weeds, its legs a blur of motion.

"Look at him go!" Scott said. "Can't they fly?"

"Sure they can, but they'd rather run. That's why they're called road-runners."

The bird angled suddenly away from the road and was soon lost among the stunted brown vegetation.

"Is that why you named your business Roadrunner Consulting?" Russell asked.

Hanna turned her head slightly. She saw the gleam in his eyes. "Meaning?"

"I had a hard time convincing you to come to Seattle to check my company for Y2K compliance—said you didn't want to leave Texas. I don't know, roadrunners reluctant to fly. . . ."

"I get it! Well, I accepted, didn't I?"

"Yes, but it took some doing. And I sure am glad you did. I wouldn't have met you otherwise."

"And we'd all be learning how to do without electricity."

"That, too. But the first is more important."

Hanna glanced into the rearview mirror at Scott. "Getting too mushy up here for you?" she asked with a grin.

He smiled and shook his head. "Nope. I'm glad you're marrying my dad."

"Thanks, pardner. Maybe I can bring some life to this family."

"Sounds great to me."

"What do you mean by that?" Russell asked.

"Oh, doing new things, like learning to hang glide."

Russell shook his head. "I don't want to think about that. I still can't believe you'd jump off a cliff with that thing."

"Russell, it's perfectly safe as long as you know what you're doing—and are careful."

"I still remember how far down it was."

"We'll talk about it later."

"Aw, Dad," Scott broke in. "Hanna can teach you."

"That's enough," Russell said, firmness coming into his voice.

Hanna turned north and drove up the eastern shore of Buffalo Lake before angling west again, entering Deaf Smith County on U.S. Highway 60. Scott sat up as they passed the municipal airport outside of Hereford.

"That where you learned to fly, Hanna?" he asked.

"That's it. Learned in an ancient Cessna 150."

"Wow! Did you have to spin the propeller by hand to start it?"

Hanna frowned. "It wasn't *that* ancient."

"Oh."

Hanna giggled. "I bet you think I fly in an open cockpit wearing goggles and a long scarf—you know, like Snoopy."

"Not after playing F-15 with you," Scott said.

Hanna remembered the Jane's Simulations game they had played back in Seattle.

"You're pretty good yourself. Are you making any headway teaching your dad?"

"I've tried it a time or two," Russell said before Scott could answer.

"And?" Hanna prompted.

"I'm beginning to get the hang of it. I just don't get much time to practice."

"I see. Well, perhaps I can help. With two trainers, you should come along quite nicely."

Hanna turned north off the highway and drove through a recent subdivision of large ranch-style homes with green lawns and well-tended shrubs and gardens. Modest-sized trees, mostly oaks, provided welcome shade, hinting of the coming summer heat.

Hanna parked on the street. They got out and walked toward the shelter of the front porch. Curtis Sidwell opened the front door and came out. He was of medium height and had a solid build that was not in any way soft. He wore jeans that appeared new and a crisp tan western shirt with pearl buttons. He carefully settled his wide-brim hat on his head and started down the walk.

"Lookin' real *GQ,* Dad," Hanna said.

"What?"

"You look very handsome."

"Oh. Thank you." He turned to Russell and Scott. "What did you guys think of Palo Duro Canyon?"

"It was awesome!" Scott said.

"It's beautiful," Russell added. "You wouldn't think anything that big could be anywhere around here."

"It surprises most visitors, what with everything else being so flat. Glad you enjoyed it." He walked back to the house with them and held the door.

"Was Mom able to fix the zipper?" Hanna asked as she went through.

Curtis winked at Russell. "She fixed it. Don't worry. You're going to look great. Besides, your mother knows about safety pins and such."

"But . . ."

"Everything's under control."

Hanna saw he was still smiling, but it was vying with his familiar "that's enough" expression.

"Yes, Dad," she said finally.

Curtis turned toward the back of the house. "Come on, Scott," he said. "Let's mosey on back to the kitchen and see if any of that lemon pie is left. Want some?"

"Yeah." The boy hesitated, then glanced at his father and grinned self-consciously. "I think we're supposed to leave you two alone."

"I think you're very perceptive," Russell said. "Now, be gone."

"Yes, sir." Scott dashed after Hanna's father.

Hanna watched him go, admiring his energy.

"I bet you were just like that as a boy," she said, now that they were alone.

Russell shrugged. "I guess." He paused. "I'm glad you and Scott hit it off so."

"Me too. You have a wonderful son, Russell. I'm looking forward to sharing my life with both of you." She smiled at the twinkle she saw in his eyes. "But especially you."

He pulled her close. She watched in anticipation as he tilted his head.

The familiar electric tingle raced down her spine as he kissed her gently. She leaned forward and returned it with feeling. Her knees grew weak as she saw how much his emotions matched hers. She was breathless when they broke.

"I love you," he said in a husky whisper.

"And I love you." She looked into his eyes, admiring what she saw there.

* * *

"What else can go wrong?" Hanna said. She knew tears were near, and she didn't want that. Not now.

"Calm down," Carol said firmly. "This safety pin will work just as well as the zipper. There. Looks just fine."

"It's not only the zipper, Mother. First the Flahertys' plane was late. They missed the rehearsal, and we *all* missed the dinner party."

"That couldn't be helped, dear. They're here now. You and Russell will be just as married as if everything went fine—which it never does."

Hanna turned and walked to where her bouquet lay on the table. She fingered the delicate blossoms.

"But I wanted everything to be perfect," she said. She looked down. "This dress has been nothing but trouble, and the service is about to start, and we don't have a wedding cake. What happened to the caterer?"

Carol rushed over and gathered her daughter into a gentle hug. "Hush now, dear," she said gently. "Don't you worry. I don't know what happened to the caterer, but I have some friends working on it."

Hanna stepped back. "But . . ." She stopped when she saw the unshed tears in her mother's eyes.

"Honey, in a few minutes, your father is going to walk you down the aisle and give you to Russell." She dabbed at her eyes with a handkerchief. "Listen, dear. You're marrying a fine man. That's what's important, not all these piddly little things."

Hanna looked down as she felt the heat of embarrassment. A glimmer of a smile came to her face as she thought about it. "I think the guests might wonder where the cake is," she added softly.

Carol grinned as she swatted at Hanna with her handkerchief. "I *said* we were taking care of that."

"What do you think happened?"

"Who knows."

Hanna's lips curved into a wry grin. "Suppose she got asphyxiated when she drove past the feedlot east of town?"

Carol laughed. "There are plenty of feedlots around Amarillo, dear."

Hanna nodded. "Yeah, that's right. I suppose we'll find out later."

"Yes, and by then it won't make any difference, will it?"

"No, Mother, it won't."

Hanna jumped as a knock sounded at the door. Carol opened it a crack.

"Time for you to take your seat," Curtis said softly. He looked past at his daughter. "How's my princess?"

"Fine, Dad." Hanna was surprised to find she meant it. A peace had descended over her.

Curtis grinned. "I'll be back after I deliver your mother to an usher."

"Thank you."

Carol went out, and the door closed. Hanna could hear the faint strains of the organ playing "Sheep May Safely Graze."

A few minutes later the door opened again. Curtis smiled, looking a little uncomfortable in his tuxedo but beaming nonetheless.

"It's time," he said. He extended his arm.

She took it, and he escorted her through the hallway outside the sanctuary, stopping before the open doors. Hanna felt a quick stab of fear. She looked down the long aisle. The music stopped, and a moment later the wedding processional began. Her heart skipped a beat when she saw

Russell standing there before the minister. His eyes found hers and seemed to pull her forward. Hanna felt a warm glow as she saw that smile she loved so. She could hardly breathe.

With a peal of organ trumpets, the processional began. Curtis and Hanna started their solemn march toward the waiting groom. Hanna felt her eyes sting as she approached. It seemed to take forever, but at last she was there. The minister said something, and her father replied. Then Russell took her arm, and they turned to face the minister.

Hanna had to force herself to concentrate on the ceremony. She exchanged her vows with Russell. Then came the electrifying moment when he slipped the ring on her finger, and she placed a wide gold band on his finger as they repeated their vows.

The minister concluded the ceremony and turned to Russell. "You may kiss your bride."

Hanna heard the congregation grow very quiet. Russell turned toward her and gently lifted the veil. With love in his eyes, he leaned forward and kissed her. Hanna's heart raced, realizing she was now a wife. She smiled at her husband as he drew away, obviously a shorter kiss than usual.

"Ladies and gentlemen," the minister concluded, "it gives me great pleasure to introduce to you, Mr. and Mrs. Russell Flaherty. They have asked me to invite you to their reception, which will take place in the fellowship hall immediately after the service."

The organist began the recessional. Russell took his bride's arm, and they started up the aisle. Hanna struggled to keep her emotions under control as she saw the faces of her relatives and friends. She glanced at her husband. He was hers now, until the moment death would part them.

* * *

The key refused to turn. "Blasted security!" The AT&T technician grumbled.

He tried several others until he finally hit on the right one. The bolt opened with a heavy metallic click. The man pushed open the sturdy steel door, flipped on the lights, and entered. He wrinkled his nose at the pungent odor of ozone. He closed the door and quickly scanned the room, then glanced down at his work order. He nodded to himself as he mentally checked off his tasks: perform routine diagnostics and reset the switch's internal clock. Nothing tough about that.

He looked up from his clipboard and spotted the control console in the corner. Electronic cabinets lined the walls and formed steel islands, joined together by thick bundles of black cables. The man thought about the thousands of long-distance voice and data connections coursing through this room, all controlled by this digital tandem switch. He wondered what would happen if he brought the switch's computer down rather that performing the scheduled maintenance; all those important calls, all that vital data, cut off instantly. The technician quickly shook off that thought. No, it wouldn't be any fun to be out on the street looking for a job.

Arriving at the console, he ran through the diagnostics quickly, noting a few minor alarms that didn't really mean anything. The switch was performing its tasks to its usual digital perfection. The technician made a few notes on his clipboard, then glanced at his digital watch, which he had set to the National Institute of Standards and Technology WWV time recording that morning. The switch was less than a minute off, but his bosses wanted the time exact.

After punching the key sequence into the console, the technician entered the date and time and waited until his watch ticked over to the new minute before hitting the enter key.

Minor irritation furrowed his brow as he reviewed the time entry. The time was right, but he had miskeyed the date. Instead of 6/10/2000, he had accidentally keyed 6/10/2200, what he called a "fat finger." He cursed as he hurried to correct the entry, knowing that thousands of calls were receiving incorrect date stamps. What the billing programs would make of that he didn't know and didn't want to know.

The man paused in his rapid keying when he heard a sharp snap behind him, followed immediately by the unmistakable sound of cooling fans shutting down. He turned slowly, his eyes wide. He groaned as he saw white smoke pouring out of the ventilation louvers. An alarm horn started sounding, telling him the switch was out of service, something he understood only too well. *Did I do that?* he wondered. He dismissed the thought immediately, knowing it *had* to be a coincidence.

He looked down at the now-dead console. He decided quickly he would say nothing about keying in the wrong date. Hopefully the chaos caused by the massive disruption in long-distance service would mask his error. His beeper and his mobile phone went off at the same time. He sighed. He knew what that was about.

* * *

Hanna struggled to keep up with Russell's long strides as they made their way arm-in-arm through the corridor to the fellowship hall. She clutched his arm tighter. The photographer had beaten them there and was off in a corner attaching a strobe to one of his cameras.

Hanna's eyes went to the wedding cake like a magnet. There it was, three tiers and beautifully iced, but she knew it wasn't the one the caterer had promised; it didn't look like the picture. She guided her husband toward the table and looked closer. The icing was far from professional but had obviously been applied with love—and quickly. And the bride and groom looked a lot like Barbie and Ken. Despite her earlier anguish, she smiled.

"What do you think?" she asked. She watched him as a grin lit up his face.

"I think it looks awesome, Mrs. Flaherty."

She giggled. "That's going to take getting used to."

"I guess, but won't it be grand?"

She looked him in the eye. "Yep."

1

HANNA SCOOTED HER BLACK LEATHER SWIVEL CHAIR AWAY
from her twenty-one-inch computer monitor and turned toward the windows. She felt comfortable and snug inside what she called the executive headquarters of Roadrunner Consulting, not incorporated. This one room dedicated out of the three-bedroom apartment didn't accommodate what her house in Hereford had, but it sufficed. And Russell and Scott certainly made the loss of space worthwhile. Still, it would be nice if the Flahertys decided to buy a house, she thought. Maybe 2002 would be the year for that.

She watched as the slanting rain pelted the panes, distorting the second-story view of the park across the street, turning the trees into dull green blobs. *Typical day in May,* she thought. For a moment she longed for the arid climate of the Texas panhandle, but only for a moment. Although it had taken getting used to, she found she enjoyed the riot of green, growing things in Seattle and the beautiful majesty of the mountains and Puget Sound. The scenery was well worth the frequent rain. Besides, her place was with her husband, and her consulting business was a lot more portable than Russell's work as maintenance manager for Western Washington Utilities.

The background sounds, which she had been ignoring, suddenly climaxed with a loud explosion. "Aw! Lucky shot!"

Hanna jerked around at the sudden outburst and saw Scott scowling into the monitor attached to the test computer. Although that computer was dedicated to trying out new peripheral boards and software, young Mr. Flaherty had more or less appropriated it for his computer games and Internet research. Not that Hanna minded. She got up and came over to where she could see. She glanced at the F-15 fighter simulator's score.

"Whoa, pardner! Looks like you landed face down in the feedlot."

Scott peered at her suspiciously. "What?"

"Remember that big feedlot outside Hereford?"

The boy wrinkled his nose as he remembered the colossal bovine mess and smell. "Ew, gross!"

She tousled his hair. He grinned as he smoothed it back in shape with his hand.

"You playing Brian?"

"Yeah. He's getting good."

"You both ought to be experts, as often as you play."

Scott smirked. "*I* am, at least."

"Are you bragging?" Hanna saw that the question registered on him, and in a good way. She was grateful for the loving relationship they had despite the fact she was not his mother. He knew she loved him for who he was. He was growing up, which would present its own set of problems before long, especially since he was now officially a teenager.

"Dad gets on me about that too," Scott said.

She held his serious gaze. "I'm not getting on your case. I just want to see you develop into the fine young man I know you can be. Like your father."

He shrugged and looked down. "If you say so."

"Scott. Look at me." She waited until he did. "You know I care what happens to you. And you know I'm a straight shooter."

After a few moments he nodded. "Yeah. I know." A sheepish grin came to his face. "Thanks."

She tousled his hair again. "You're welcome, pardner." She saw the look in his eyes that indicated his nimble mind had jumped track. She mentally braced herself.

"Hanna, have you talked Dad into taking hang gliding lessons yet?"

She glanced toward the door of her office, wondering if the elder Mr. Flaherty were in earshot. "Not yet," she whispered. "But I'm working on it."

"You gotta do it! I wanna learn, but he won't let me."

"He's thinking of your safety."

"But it *is* safe. You said so."

Hanna laughed. "So now I'm the authority on hang gliding." She paused. "It's safe, as long as you know what you're doing and you don't take chances. But whether you can take lessons depends on your dad."

"Yeah, but you have a say, don't you?"

She struggled not to smile as she looked into his pleading eyes. "Yes, I do. Your dad and I talk over important decisions, and we pray about them. We generally arrive at an agreement. When we don't, we either wait, or I trust Russell to decide for us."

"But . . ."

"Patience. I think he'll come around."

Scott sighed. "I hope so. I'm dyin' to learn."

"That's exactly what we're trying to avoid."

"Aw, you know what I mean."

"Yes, I do. Sit tight, and let's see what happens."

Heavy footsteps sounded in the hall.

"Happens about what?" Russell asked as he entered the office.

"We were talking about hang gliding," Hanna replied. She saw his almost imperceptible hesitation as he glanced toward Scott.

"Ganging up on me, huh?"

The pain was evident on Scott's face. "Dad! It would be so cool!"

"I'm not convinced it's safe."

"Aw, Dad. Hanna wouldn't do it unless it was OK."

"That's enough. Have you finished your homework?"

"I can do it tonight—or tomorrow."

"We're going to the McCluskys tonight, and tomorrow's Sunday."

"But . . ."

"Right now, Scott."

The boy scowled for a moment, then got up and stomped out of the room.

Russell frowned and shook his head. "I don't know what gets into him."

"Russell?"

She saw his eyes narrow suspiciously.

"What?" he replied.

"Were you a perfect little kid?"

"You gonna read me my rights?" A faint glimmer of a smile came to his face. "No, of course I wasn't."

"Seems to me you turned out nice."

"I guess, thanks to my folks."

"Uh-huh. And you have a fine son who is going through the normal problems of being a kid. And he's entering adolescence. Remember what that's like?"

Russell groaned. "Yeah." He shook his head. "I don't even want to think about it."

"Don't lose heart. You're doing fine."

He smiled. "I'm trying. I appreciate your help in all this."

"I'm glad to help. I can never be Scott's mom, but I love him as though I were."

"I know. And I know *he* knows."

Hanna shrugged. "Can't hide something like that."

His expression changed subtly as he thought that over. Hanna could tell something else had intruded. *Like father, like son,* she thought.

"Dear," he began slowly, "there's something about you I've never completely understood."

"Oh?"

"This hang gliding thing. What made you want to do it? I mean, it seems almost as extreme as skydiving."

"I considered skydiving," she said, trying to keep from smiling as she saw his look of horror.

"Really?"

"Really. But then I tried hang gliding and decided to give the other up."

"I'm glad," he said in obvious relief.

"And that brings us back to hang gliding," she said with a mischievous grin. "Why don't you consider giving it a try? It's lots of fun, and I wouldn't do it if I thought it was dangerous."

"I don't know."

"Remember when I came up here in ninety-nine?"

"How could I forget?"

"You introduced me to sailing, something I'd never done before. I loved it. And sailing is similar, in some ways, to flying."

He shook his head. "But it can't be as safe when you consider what you're doing and what could happen."

Hanna struggled to maintain her composure. "Russell! More people die in boating accidents than from hang gliding."

"Not as many people hang glide."

"It's still a safe sport, as long as you're careful. Why don't you give it a try? I think you'd like it. It's something we could do together as a family."

She was surprised to see a sheepish expression come to his face.

"I'd kinda like to," he admitted, lowering his voice. "It looks like fun the times I've watched you. But I don't want Scott doing it, and if *I* do, I wouldn't feel right not letting him."

"Why, Russell Flaherty. So that's what's been bugging you." She paused. "I understand your concern, but I don't think you're being fair to Scott. Hang gliding is similar to rock climbing or those confidence-building courses. Yes, it can be dangerous if you don't know what you're doing. But you have at your service an expert instructor."

"And modest too," he said with a twinkle in his eye.

"Of course," she agreed. "Want to give it a try? We could get another glider. I could teach you and Scott. And don't worry. Scott listens to me. You know he's a responsible kid, and this would be strictly supervised."

She watched as his mental gears ground away at her argument. On the one hand she wanted both of them to enjoy the thrill of the sport she enjoyed so much, but she did understand Russell's concern for his son.

Russell sighed. "I guess I am being overprotective, and that's not a good thing. OK. Summer's coming up. Let's give it a try."

"Yes!" Scott shouted as he raced in from the hall.

Russell whirled around. "What were you doing out there?" he demanded.

A stricken look came to the boy's face. "I was coming for my calculator. I left it in here."

For a moment Russell was silent. "Scott," he said finally. "I'm sorry. I thought you were spying on us."

"Yeah. Well, I wasn't."

"I was wrong, son. Forgive me?"

Scott nodded. Hanna could tell the momentary hurt was passing as Russell hugged his son.

"So, Hanna finally talked your old man into it," Russell said as he tousled his son's hair. "Just how long have you two been plotting this?"

"We weren't plotting," Scott replied as he smoothed his hair. He glanced at Hanna and grinned. "But she's good, isn't she?"

"Good *and* persistent."

"I prefer 'goal oriented,'" Hanna replied.

"Whatever," Russell said. "So, I guess we need to plan this out—find a hang-gliding shop, decide on what to get, research places to practice, that sort of thing."

"Way ahead of you, Orville. I've already done all that. Cascades Hang Gliding and Paragliding has a Wills Raven with your name written all over it." She glanced at Scott. "Yours too. All we have to do is go pick it up."

"Pretty sure of yourself, weren't you?"

"Oh, I thought you'd come around."

"Can we go get it now?" Scott pleaded.

Russell glanced at his watch. "Not today. We've got to get ready to go to the McCluskys. Besides, you've got to finish your homework."

"But, Dad."

"Grab your calculator and go."

Hanna saw the conflicting emotions flash over Scott's face. The joy of his father's decision to try hang gliding, which opened the way for him to participate, mingled with irritation at having to return to his homework rather than looking at hang gliders. His departure, though in protest, was clearly less tumultuous than his earlier exit.

Russell shook his head. "Public enemy number one twice in one day. How lucky can I get?"

"Hang in there, Pops," Hanna said. "You're doing fine—and so is your son."

"Thanks. 'Preciate your encouragement."

"Well, I think I can do better than that."

She saw the twinkle in his eyes. "Oh? And what did you have in mind?"

"Just this."

She leaned forward and kissed him, gently to see if he was paying attention. He was. He pulled her close, and the rapid beat of her heart shifted into a gallop. Joy welled up within her as she felt herself responding to his embrace.

"I can tell you meant that," she said after a bit.

"Yes, I did. But there was ample provocation."

"Oh?"

"You know what I mean." He paused. "I thank God for you, Hanna. I'm so glad he brought us together."

She smiled at the warm glow this brought her. "I am too, Russell. Sharing my life with you—and Scott—truly is an answer to prayer."

Hanna examined his face with her fingertips in a proprietary way. She stopped when she heard a sound in the hall and turned to see Scott grinning at them.

"Forgot something else," he said as he hurried over to the computer table and grabbed his ruler. He paused at the door on his way out and turned. "Uh, you two can carry on." He disappeared.

Hanna looked into Russell's eyes. "You heard him."

"Yes, ma'am." He leaned forward and kissed her.

* * *

Zhu Tak-shing shifted nervously in his chair as he looked down on the control room located a few blocks from his Kowloon manufacturing plant. He peered through the one-way windows at the tiers of consoles arrayed below him, facing a panoramic world map as large as a theater screen. The cities of the world stood out clearly, linked by orange lines representing telecommunications links and red ones for the power grids.

A countdown clock in the map's upper right-hand corner reached the one-minute mark. A loud Klaxon sounded. Zhu leaned forward. Every operator was in place. It reminded Zhu of pictures he had seen of the Johnson Space Center's Mission Control.

Zhu jumped as the door behind him opened with a loud click. He tore his eyes away from the clock and saw Jiang Ling enter the dimly lit observation booth as if he were only a little late for a matinee. His boss had ordered the demonstration but apparently attached little importance to it.

"Ah, I see I am just in time," Jiang said as he eased into the chair beside his technical director.

"Yes," Zhu said through clenched teeth. "Per your instructions, the test is underway."

"Everything is normal in Chongqing?"

"For a few more seconds, yes."

"I still find it hard to believe that a handful of sabotaged chips can devastate an entire country."

"You will see for yourself."

The countdown clock reached zero and began to count upwards, as if timing a mission, which in fact it was.

Jiang turned. "Nothing happened!" He pointed toward the elaborate map. "The telephone system is still up."

"The map is not real-time. All telecommunications in Chongqing are down. I'll stake my life on it." A chill ran down his spine as he considered this could literally be true.

All the orange lines linking the city to the rest of China winked out.

"There," Zhu said pointing.

"So, they can't use their telephones. What happens next?"

"It's not only Chongqing. We have cut off communications to much of central and western China. And very shortly their power grid will fail, leaving around thirty million people without electricity."

"Why would it affect the power?"

"The power transmission control centers require telephone lines to operate. Without them the interconnections will trip, and there isn't enough generating capacity near the city to sustain the load."

"How soon?"

"I'm not sure. Within minutes, probably. This will shut down the hospitals since they don't have emergency power. All traffic lights will fail, the airport will shut down, and the trains will stop running. The water and sewer systems will quit. Within a day or so, if we let it go that long, trucking would cease for lack of fuel. And how long would the people last with only a week's worth of food in the markets? It's impossible to say whether more people would die of starvation or the riots. People fleeing the city would strip the countryside and all the towns and cities within reach. Imagine the effect on an entire country, not just one city."

Jiang nodded. "And no way to repair it."

"That's right. Since all the replacement chips have the same defect, there's no way to get the switches back up—at least not for a long time. And by then our enemies are back in the dark ages."

"Where they belong!" Jiang said with feeling.

Zhu nodded. "As you say."

"Don't you agree?"

"Yes, of course," Zhu said after a barely perceptible pause.

They watched the map in silence. Although he had been expecting it, Zhu still jumped when the red lines representing the power grid winked out.

"There," he said. "From this point it is simply a countdown to chaos. You've just seen the Raptor Virus in action. *We* can overcome it because we've got the correct repair parts."

"How long to restore everything?"

What do you care? Zhu thought to himself. "A few hours. Our technicians are already entering the switch rooms to start repairs. Per your instructions, we will not bring the switches up for another twelve hours so we can more fully study the effects."

Jiang nodded. "Good. I regret the inconvenience to those in Chongqing, but we must think of the greater good to our nation."

"Of course."

* * *

Zhu jumped when the phone rang. He shivered as he reached for the handset, since he had left explicit instructions not to interrupt as long as Jiang was in the control center.

"Put it on the speaker," Jiang ordered, his voice soft but sheathed in steel.

Zhu nodded and pressed the button. "Yes, what is it?"

The technician's voice seemed painfully loud in the confined room. "Sorry to bother you, but we have a problem."

"What is it?"

"We've had two disturbing reports from the repairmen so far. They say they can't fix the switches."

"What!" Zhu stammered, his voice rising. "Why not? What's wrong?"

"The damage is greater than they expected. Smoke was coming out of the switches. They replaced the defective chips and started the emergency generators, but the units refuse to come up."

"That can't be!"

"They have tried everything they can think of. We suspect the power supplies are bad, but it could be more than that. There aren't any spares, so they don't know for sure."

"So it may take more than power supplies."

"Yes."

Zhu rested his head in his hands. "And if any of the other boards are bad, that will *further* delay repairs." An icy chill stabbed him in the pit of the stomach. Chongqing was going to be without phones and power for a lot longer than twelve hours.

"That is true—just a minute."

Muffled sounds came from the speaker; then the technician came back on. "More reports. It looks like all the switches have the same problem."

Zhu uttered a sharp curse. "We have to replace the entire switches. Where are the closest spares?"

"Right here. We have some in Kowloon and Hong Kong."

"None closer to Chongqing?"

The man paused. "No. The mainland cities have very little in the way of spares. The infrastructure is spread too thin."

"What is he talking about?" Jiang demanded.

Zhu jabbed the mute button. "Chongqing won't have phones or power until we replace all the burned-out switches."

"I thought only the chips needed replacing."

"Apparently the virus caused other boards to fail. We've seen it happen before in our testing."

Jiang pushed back in his chair and glared at his subordinate. It took all of Zhu's self-control not to shudder.

"Find a way to fix it!" Jiang said as he got up.

Zhu stood. "I will. Can you authorize me military transportation?"

"I will let you know," the man said as he stormed out.

* * *

The engineer cursed and placed a hand on the engine's throttle. The express train from Chengdu to Chongqing was already hours late. The engineer had been looking forward to getting home for several days now, only to be thwarted by a seemingly endless series of mechanical glitches. Now the signal lights were out. *What next?* he wondered.

Rain pelted off the windshield as the engine continued to plow through the combination of rain and fog on its approach to the mountain city. By regulation the engineer knew he was supposed to stop. But the last signal had been green, and the track was supposed to be clear all the way into the station. The thought of sitting in the engine cab for however long it took to fix the signals was almost more than he could bear. They were only a few miles from the station. He could always say he had passed the last signal before the failure. Who would know? He glanced at his assistant.

"Are you going to stop?" the man asked.

"Do you like your job?"

The look of shock on his face was obvious. "Yes, of course I do."

"And you understand the engineer is in complete charge of the train?"

The man nodded.

"Good. Remember that, and I will make sure your future is assured."

"Please forgive me."

"We will say no more about it."

The wheels screeched as the train rounded a curve. *Not long now,* the engineer thought. He reduced power a little, preparing for the approach into the city. A spark of red light pierced the murk up ahead.

"What?"

The engineer leaned forward, his eyes wide in disbelief. He jerked the power off and slammed on the air brakes as the express bore down on the bedraggled figure signaling frantically with a flare. The man ran for his life as the engine roared past. Then the engineer saw it—a stalled train blocking the track. He needed no glance at the speedometer to know they would never stop in time. His scream joined that of the tortured wheels sliding over the wet steel rails.

A split second later the engine plowed into the car ahead. The impact lifted the rear car of the other train and shoved it to the side. The engine's nose collapsed backward, pulverizing both men in the cab instantly. The rear passenger car bounded aside and rolled even as the engine rammed into the next car. Each succeeding car flew off the track as if each were part of a giant zipper. Finally the engine jumped the tracks and began gouging a deep furrow in the muddy earthen embankment. The trailing cars derailed and started colliding randomly with the other train. Finally it was over, and the cries of the injured could be heard over the wind and rain. Dazed and injured passengers staggered out of the wreckage, looking for help that was not to be found.

2

RUSSELL PULLED HIS WHITE FORD MUSTANG INTO THE McCluskys' drive and stopped. The large one-story house looked like a snug harbor after the soggy drive from the apartment. Hanna opened her door and leaned forward so Scott could dash out into the drizzle and up to the front porch. Russell reached into the backseat for a large blue golf umbrella.

"Master Scott may be able to dodge between the raindrops, but I think we'll use this," he said.

He got out, opened the umbrella, and came around for Hanna. Together they hurried to the porch. A middle-aged man with reddish-brown hair held the door for them, his friendly blue eyes following them as they approached. Hanna hurried inside while Russell shook out the umbrella and folded it.

"Hey, Jim," Russell said, as he stepped through into the entryway and took Hanna's hand. "How's everything at the lawyer place?"

"Fantastic. Been thinking of changing the firm's name to 'Lawsuits 'R Us.' Everything OK at the power monopoly?"

"You bet. Made it through Y2K without sending us back into the dark ages. Now if we can just convince the regulators we need a rate increase."

"Uh-huh. Just one problem after another." He turned to Hanna. "But what I really want to know is how Hanna's doing." His eyes took on a mock-serious expression. "He been treating you right?"

Hanna laughed as she squeezed Russell's hand. "Yup."

"Just 'yup'?"

"Yup."

"These Texans don't say much, do they?"

Hanna watched her husband as he considered his reply.

"Think I'll plead the fifth."

Jim nodded. "Wise choice. Shall we see what Fran's up to?"

They followed a set of wet footprints until they turned off. Sounds of computer mayhem drifted out.

"Sounds like Scott and Brian are going after it."

"Yeah," Jim said, "and Amy's in there too, right in the big fat middle of things."

"Equal opportunity," Hanna commented.

"You bet," Jim agreed.

They entered the den. A short, thin man with sandy hair got up from a huge lounger, dropping the crossword puzzle he had been working on. Jim continued on around the corner and into the kitchen. They heard him open the refrigerator and start rummaging around.

"Paul," Russell said, shaking his hand. "Glad to see you could make it. You sounded doubtful last time I talked to you."

"I have been busy," Paul Parker admitted. "This freelance work for my former employer, who shall remain nameless, has soaked up most of my time."

Hanna saw the tension lines around his eyes. "Anything you can talk about?"

Paul scratched his buzz-cut hair. "Not a lot. I'm doing research related to the Y2K bug you found."

Hanna frowned. "But we're well past that now."

"We're still looking into the deliberate aspect of that incident."

"Oh. You mean cyber terrorism."

Paul nodded. "You're on the right track. But really, I can't say any more about it."

"Or you'd have to shoot us?"

Paul grinned. "Something like that. So how are you and Russell doing?"

"Great," Hanna replied, squeezing Russell's hand.

"I can see that. I'm glad for you both."

"You are still working at Blue Water Yachts, aren't you?" Hanna asked.

"Oh, yes. That's still the day job. Matter of fact, I'll be taking out a new ketch for sea trials in a few weeks. Big boat and I *mean* fancy. Looking forward to it after all this drudgery. Would you two like to come along?"

Hanna and Russell traded glances. "Appreciate the offer," Russell said. "I'd love to, but let us discuss it. We've got our summer trip coming up soon."

"And some training sessions," Hanna added. She saw her husband's look of discomfort.

"Training sessions?" Paul asked.

Russell cleared his throat. "I agreed to try hang gliding."

"Really? She finally talked you into it?"

"*Yes,* Paul, she *finally* talked me into it. Somehow I get the feeling there's this huge conspiracy to get me on crutches."

"Hold on there, pardner," Hanna said. "None of my students end up on crutches."

Russell grinned, but it was a little weak. "That a promise?"

"Sure is."

"Sounds like fun," Paul said.

"I'll let you know," Russell replied, not sounding too sure about it.

The door to the garage opened, and Fran McClusky hurried in with several plastic bags of groceries. Her sandy blond hair showed the effects of the dreary rain, but her blue eyes didn't.

"Here are the buns, relish, and barbecue sauce," she informed her husband.

The thumping and thrashing came to an abrupt stop. "Thanks, dear. I'm almost ready to start cooking."

Hanna looked toward the kitchen just as Jim trundled out with a large tray of hamburger patties. "You're going to cook outside in this weather?" she asked.

Jim grinned at her. "You bet. I love a challenge." He opened the sliding glass door and stepped out onto the redwood deck, placing the tray on a table under the eaves. He opened an umbrella, picked up the tray, and continued on past the picnic table to the propane gas grill. He raised the cover and started placing the patties on the grate while struggling to hold the umbrella under his arm. The rain streamed off the umbrella's panels, splattering on the wood deck and forming dark blue circles on the legs of his jeans.

"Doesn't seem to bother him," Hanna said.

Fran only shook her head. "Times like this, I don't claim him," she said with a laugh. "He seems to think the weather is an enemy, and he's not going to let it get the better of him." She paused. "Is Russell like that?"

Hanna turned to her husband.

"I'm curious to hear this," Russell said.

"Not about weather. But he has his own idiosyncrasies. I suspect all men do."

"Paul, come to my aid."

Paul held up his hands. "Don't drag me into this. I'm just a happy bachelor."

"That may not last," Russell said. "Hanna and the rest of the females at the church are gunning for you. They seem to think you'd be happier with a mate."

"Russell," Hanna said, "how can you say that?"

"It's true!"

"Well, we're only thinking of Paul."

"I'm biting my tongue."

Hanna giggled. "Good!"

"Have you asked Paul about this?"

Every eye turned toward the middle-aged bachelor.

"I haven't," Hanna admitted. "Have we been that obvious?"

Paul grinned sheepishly. "Well, yes." He paused for a moment. "I appreciate your concern, and I *would* like to find the right one for me. But it's a serious decision. I sure don't want to make a mistake."

Russell nodded. "I understand that, and I agree." He looked at Hanna, and her heart skipped a beat as she saw the look in his eyes. "God blessed me with two wonderful women. Linda . . ." He cleared his throat. "And Hanna. I can tell you, it's worth waiting for the right one."

Hanna's heart warmed as she saw Paul's approving look. "I can see that," he said. "The Lord's blessed you both wonderfully."

Squeaking shoes sounded in the hall. Scott flew into the den only a little ahead of Brian, with Amy close behind.

"When's dinner?" Scott asked as he slid to a stop.

Hanna eyed him suspiciously. "Who won?" She saw his eyes dart to Brian, then back at her.

"Uh, he did," he admitted. "But he is *so* lucky. I'll get even after dinner."

"Is that luck or skill?" Hanna probed.

Scott's forehead wrinkled. "I'm ahead on total wins."

"You are not!" Brian shouted.

"Brian!" Fran interjected. "Behave yourself. Scott is your guest."

"But . . ."

"No buts."

"Scott, it's not nice to brag," Russell added.

Hanna watched the boy. She could tell he wanted to protest, but he restrained himself.

"I know," he finally admitted.

"You and Brian are friends, and that's worth a whole lot more than who's winning."

Scott looked at his friend and grinned self-consciously. "Yeah," he said.

The sliding glass door rattled on its tracks as Jim came in. "Here's the first batch," he said. He stamped his feet on the mat, then carried the platter over to the table. "Let's get started before the flies get it all."

They held hands while Jim said the blessing. Then the adults sat down at the breakfast room table while Scott, Brian, and Amy took their places at the card table.

"You sure you don't mind cooking in the rain?" Hanna asked.

Jim shook his head. "Not at all. Adds to the challenge." He speared a thick patty with his fork and lifted it to his plate. He grabbed the squeeze bottle of mustard and proceeded to doctor his hamburger. "You having onion?" he asked without looking up.

"Yes," Fran replied.

"Good." Jim lifted a huge slice of onion to the mountain he was building and carefully set it in place. Next came the top of the bun. Jim picked up his sandwich, squeezed it a little, and took a healthy bite. "Mm, that's good," he said as he smacked his lips, "if I do say so myself."

The kids attacked their burgers, chips, and soft drinks as if they were an extension of the video games they had been playing earlier. But the adults weren't that far behind. Jim and Fran made sure seconds were available. From the card table, three pairs of eyes focused on the kitchen.

"What's for dessert?" Brian asked finally.

"You *can't* hold any more," Jim commented.

"Sure I can." The boy beamed his confidence.

His father shook his head. "Wish I could eat like that."

"You do," Fran observed as she got up.

"I don't recall asking for your affidavit," Jim said as he pushed away from the table.

"I'm *amicus curiae*."

Jim shook his head. "Friend of the court, huh? What did I do to deserve this?"

"Get the ice cream."

"Yes, dear."

Fran removed the lid from the pound cake and started cutting thick slices. Jim opened the freezer and pulled out two half-gallon containers of ice cream and set them on the counter.

"Sorry about the ice cream, but the supermarket was out of my favorite brand," Jim announced as he pried the lids off.

Hanna's head spun around. "Jim McClusky, that happens to be Blue Bell! There isn't any better ice cream anywhere."

Jim looked doubtful as he examined the label. "You sure? A little girl leading a cow—not very imaginative packaging. Wonder where this stuff comes from, anyway?"

"Brenham, Texas. You're lucky they ship to Seattle. You can't get Blue Bell just anywhere."

"Hm. Well, it will have to do." He glanced at the label again. "We have chocolate-covered cherries and strawberry cheesecake." He looked up. "What'll it be?"

He got about equal requests for each flavor. He scooped generous portions into large bowls and served them while Fran took care of the cake. He sat down and tasted a dollop of chocolate-covered cherries.

"It's OK, I guess," he said.

Hanna looked across the table. "Paul. Aren't you going to help me?"

He grinned. "You seem to be doing all right by yourself." He looked at Jim. "But Hanna's right. Blue Bell *is* the best there is, if you'll accept the word of a transplanted Texan. Not to mention any names, but you can keep your designer ice creams."

"I'll take it under advisement," Jim allowed.

Paul looked back at Hanna. "Speaking of things Texan, where exactly are you guys going on your vacation?"

"First stop is Hereford."

"Cattle country."

"Yep. Visiting my folks and my brother and his family."

"And drying out."

Hanna laughed. "It *is* a little more arid there this time of year—actually any time of year."

"Where to after that?"

"Then we're going down to Fort Davis, McDonald Observatory, and on to Big Bend." She glanced at her husband. "The only places Russell and Scott have seen are Amarillo and Hereford."

"How deprived."

"You bet. There's lots to see and do."

"Will you be camping out?"

"Yep. And we're taking the hang gliders along."

"We are?" Russell asked.

"Yes, dear. You'll pick it up in a hurry. A few lessons here and the rest in Big Bend."

Paul glanced at Russell. "You two *do* talk things over, don't you?"

Russell cleared his throat. "I only agreed to try it today. I thought we were going to take this easy."

"Oh, we are," Hanna assured him. "You're such a good sailor, you'll have no trouble with hang gliding. After all, look who you have for an instructor."

"Hm, what can I say to that?"

"I think you've said about all you should," Paul said. "So where else are you going?"

"After we leave Hereford, we'll go through Abilene and Fredericksburg and spend the night in San Antonio," Hanna said. "Next day we'll tour the Alamo and the River Walk and see some of the old missions."

Paul grinned. "Gotta see where John Wayne did his thing."

"Paul, this is serious."

"Excuse me."

"Then we hop on I-10 and head out to Fort Stockton, Fort Davis, and the Davis Mountains."

Paul nodded. "Good camping 'round there, I've heard."

"You've been to Big Bend, haven't you?"

He shook his head. "Nope. Wanted to but never made it. Remember, I left Texas after I graduated from Tech. Made a few trips to Padre but never made it down to Big Bend."

"You really should. It's beautiful."

"I'd like to sometime."

Hanna basked in the relaxed glow of fellowship as the conversation swirled around, taking them along unpredictable paths. Scott, Brian, and Amy disappeared in search of action, leaving the adults to their interests. All too soon it was time to go. Russell stood and called for Scott.

"I've enjoyed this," Paul said, clearly meaning it. "And your vacation really does sound like fun."

"Hope so," Hanna replied.

Paul hesitated. He glanced around, but young Mr. Flaherty had not yet made his appearance. From the look in the father's eyes, that was about to change. "Hanna, I'd like to ask you a question—strictly off the record."

"Having to do with . . ."

He nodded. "Yeah. That which I can't talk about."

"Shoot."

"How vulnerable do you think we are to cyber terrorism?"

Hanna took in a deep breath and let it out slowly. "From what I've read and seen—very."

Paul's face sagged. "That's what I thought. How bad do you think it could be?"

She waited quite a while before answering. "Worse than anyone predicted Y2K would be."

"That's pretty grim."

"Yeah. Why do you ask?"

He shook his head emphatically. "Can't tell you."

3

"SO, THIS IS THE PLACE," RUSSELL SAID, AS HE PULLED Hanna's Ford Explorer into a parking place in front of Cascades Hang Gliding and Paragliding.

"Yep," Hanna confirmed.

"Wow!" Scott said, wedging himself between the two front seats so he could see through the windshield. "They've got a parachute in the window."

"That's a paraglider," Hanna informed him.

His face scrunched up in wonder. "What's that?"

"It's like hang gliding. It came along later but has really caught on. Instead of a glider with a rigid frame, you use a special parachute designed like a wing."

"So which one is better?"

Hanna laughed. "Depends on who you ask. But since you're asking me, hang gliding is." She looked over at her husband. "Ready to go see what you're getting into?"

"Yes, I am. Now that I'm committed, I'm looking forward to it."

He got out and came around to open the door for Hanna. His son bolted out and beat them to the entrance but waited for them to approach, all the time stealing glances through the windows. Russell reached the door and held it.

Hanna paused inside and looked around. She had visited the store several times, working out what would be best for Russell and Scott. But the middle-aged Australian owner she had dealt with was nowhere in sight. She saw a tall, thin young man standing behind a counter in the back. He had blond hair rubber-banded into a ponytail, and it looked like his face had lost a great war with acne. He looked up from the magazine he was reading. The frown on his face indicated he was not pleased with the interruption. After a moment's hesitation he left his sanctuary and strode down the center aisle headed for Russell.

"Can I help you folks?" he asked.

"Is Ian around?" Hanna asked.

The man's eyes widened. "*You're* a friend of Ian's?" the man asked, his voice rising. "*You're* not into . . ."

Hanna set her jaw. "If you've got a shovel, I'll help you finish the hole."

"What?"

"Never mind. Ian helped me select a hang glider. We're here to pick it up. Oh, and he said he had some information for me on hang-gliding sites near Seattle."

"I see."

"We'll see."

Just when Hanna was sure the man's puzzlement couldn't get worse, it did.

"Perhaps we could check and see if our glider is ready," she suggested. "And if it is, we could pay for it."

"Oh, yeah." He turned around abruptly. "Right this way."

Hanna glanced at Russell and whispered, "If he makes a break for it, you tackle 'im, and I'll do the hog-tying."

She saw the clerk's ears twitch, but apparently his course was well laid in. He made good time to the workshop in the back of the store and carried on through without further navigational problems. The three Flahertys stopped at the rear counter and waited. A few minutes later the clerk returned with a colorful bundle of red Dacron wrapped around an assortment of aluminum spars and control members.

"Sorry for the delay," he said as he lowered the disassembled glider to the floor. "I didn't realize Ian had put the glider together and checked it. I was looking for one still in the box." He pulled out an unsealed envelope and gave it to Hanna. "He left you this."

Hanna pulled out a thick sheaf of papers and unfolded them. She glanced at the Web site printouts describing local hang-gliding sites and tucked them into her purse. All that remained was a hand-scrawled note written on the back of a packing slip from a glider manufacturer.

Dear Hanna,

Checked out the kite as per our chat. It's top drawer all the way. Although the deltas aren't "where it's at," as you Yanks say, it's a serviceable design even so. If you come to your senses, I also sell several DSFA models. The brain baskets are in a bag by the cash till.

Hope to see you on the slopes and still in one piece.

G'day,
Ian

"Brain baskets?" Russell asked, looking over her shoulder.
"Safety helmets," Hanna replied.
"Oh. Hm. I don't know any sailors who wear helmets."
"Anything else you folks need?" the clerk asked.

Hanna pulled out her MasterCard and gave it to him. "Don't think so, pardner. Write it up, an' we'll ride off into the sunset."

He looked puzzled for a moment. "Whatever." He took the card and started writing up the sale.

"What's a 'DSFA'?" Russell asked.

"It means 'double surface fixed airfoil.' It has a true wing like an airplane. It has much higher performance, but it's also more difficult to fly."

"So what are we getting?"

"Basically a Dacron bedsheet attached to aluminum poles. Not quite as sporty but definitely safer to learn on. People like Ian refer to them as 'billow cruisers.'"

Russell smiled. "Yeah, I can see why. But, that's the kind of glider *you* fly."

"That's right. I believe in being cautious. I've bent a few glider parts in my time, but I've never broken any bones."

"Here you are, ma'am," the clerk interrupted, placing the charge slip on the counter while neglecting to offer a pen.

Hanna's jaw tightened as she considered educating the young man on what she did not like being called. Instead, she pulled a pen from her purse and dashed off a nearly illegible signature. She gave the slip back, and the clerk pulled off a copy and gave it to her as if this were a major accomplishment.

"Shall we?" Hanna asked, turning to Russell and Scott.

"Can I carry it?" Scott asked.

"Sure," Hanna replied. "You'll get tired of it soon enough."

"What?"

"Press on. I'll get the door."

Outside, Hanna supervised as Russell and Scott tied the billow cruiser to the roof carrier.

* * *

Hanna stopped her Explorer, got out, and opened the combination lock. She swung the gate wide while Russell drove the SUV through. After locking the gate, Hanna got back in and put the Ford in gear.

"Ian picked a nice site," she said as they started up the winding road.

"Yes, Blanchard's pretty. I used to come through here on my way to Bellingham when I was in college. Much nicer than driving the interstate. Ian must know the property owner."

"He does. This foothill is about three hundred feet high—sort of a bunny slope." She smiled. "After you two graduate, there's another ridge near here that's twelve hundred feet above MSL." She waited.

"'Mean sea level,'" Scott said.

"Very good," Hanna said. "You *were* paying attention during ground school."

"Of course."

Russell leaned forward to see the colorful gliders riding the wind currents above the peak. Scott offered a running commentary as he looked through his open window.

"Cool!" he exclaimed, not for the first time.

"Only 'cool'?" Hanna asked.

"Way cool!" the boy clarified.

Hanna turned off below the summit into a level grassy area. The Explorer blended in with the assortment of vans, Suburbans, and a variety of SUVs, both foreign and domestic. A few pilots were unloading gliders, but most were up on the slope or in the air. One thin young man with a scraggly beard waved as the Flahertys passed.

"You know him?" Russell asked.

Hanna waved back. "Nope. But hang gliding is sort of a fraternity. Our common love of flying bonds us together."

"Fraternity, you say."

Hanna glanced at her husband. He had that twinkle in his eye that promised trouble. "You know what I mean. You better not get smart with your instructor!"

"Yes, ma'am."

"And don't call me 'ma'am.'"

"Uh, yes, dude."

"That's better."

She pulled into an open place and stopped. The car lurched as a rear door opened then slammed shut. Scott raced up the slope toward the summit.

"Someone's in a hurry," Hanna said.

"I'll say. Wish I could get him to move like that on school days."

"You don't understand. This is important."

"I guess."

"The glider's not going to carry itself to the top—or put itself together, for that matter." Hanna watched his eyes, seeing the obvious interest. But there was also a shade of caution. *Good,* she thought.

"Right."

They got out of the car. Russell undid the straps and lifted the bundled glider down.

"Did I ever tell you what my flight instructor said when I was learning to fly light planes?" she asked.

"Not that I recall."

"'There are old pilots and bold pilots, but there are no old, bold pilots.'"

Russell grinned as he lifted the glider and started up the slope. "I'll try to remember that."

"See that you do." She scanned the gentle incline. "Where'd Scott get off to?"

"Oh, he'll be back when he figures out nothing's happening until we put the glider together."

A familiar shape rounded the hill just before the summit and came rushing toward them.

"That didn't take long," Hanna said.

"Come on!" he said as he slid to a stop. "Everybody's flying but us!"

"Wanna carry the glider?" his dad asked.

"Um, you're doing fine."

"Guess that means I get first flight."

"Aw, Dad!"

"Cool it, you two," Hanna said.

Hanna felt her heart rate increase as she walked briskly up the steep slope, watching the bright gliders sailing along on the unseen ocean of air.

"Notice anything unusual about the other pilots?" she asked.

Russell looked all around. "Hm. Hang gliding must make hair grow out of your face in unsightly wads—the men I mean."

Hanna snickered. "Let's hope it doesn't have that effect on you. No, I meant the absence of pear-shaped people."

"Oh, I see what you mean. No couch potatoes."

"Nope. This is an athletic sport. It requires hiking and running—vigorous running."

"Don't some pilots use tows to get the gliders up?"

"Yep. But *we* won't. That's actually quite dangerous."

"And our instructor doesn't do 'dangerous.'"

Hanna nodded. "That's right. I don't." She looked at Scott. "Now what's the first thing we do?"

"Put the glider together!" he replied.

"Nope. There's something else we do first."

Russell looked toward a pilot who had just launched. "The wind's from the west at about ten knots and steady. Acceptable flight conditions for beginners."

"Right," Hanna agreed. "Check the weather conditions first. If the wind is high or gusty, we don't fly."

Scott frowned. "Oh, yeah."

"We went over this in ground school," Hanna reminded him. "I'm not just flapping my gums, you know."

"I remember now."

"OK," Hanna said. "So who's going first?" She saw the look on Russell's face. She *knew* he wanted to do it, and from her own experience she knew how much. Then a look of concern clouded his expression.

"Scott can."

"Really? Wow!"

"Steady, now," Hanna said. "Let's see you put it together."

He fell to his knees and hurried through untying the straps.

"Slow down," Hanna advised. "Do it exactly like I showed you. Tell me what you're doing and why."

The boy shifted into a lower and more careful gear. He laid out all the structural tubing and unrolled the carefully coiled control cables. He joined all the pieces, attached the cables, and tensioned them. After checking over his work, he stood and looked around at Hanna.

"Very good."

He beamed at the compliment.

"Now prepare your harness and strap in."

"Cool!"

This part was somewhat hurried, but Hanna made sure he did it right. Soon he stood before her, shouldering the weight of the glider and looking like he was under attack by a flapping red bedsheet. His intense brown eyes peered out at her with such expectancy that Hanna almost laughed.

"Sure you can manage that thing?" she asked.

"No problem." He glanced down the slope. "Can I take off now?"

She nodded. "Junior birdman one five echo, you are cleared for immediate departure on runway two seven."

He grinned. "Roger that."

He managed an ungainly turn to face into the wind. After a brief pause he started running down the slope. The triangular wing billowed and filled as it began to lift the dead weight off the boy's shoulders. A few steps later the glider lifted into the air and Scott with it. He gripped the control bar above the crosspiece and swung it to the left. The glider turned rapidly to the right, requiring a quick correction. After a few bobbles Scott was flying parallel to the hill heading north and gradually gaining altitude on the steady breeze.

"He overcontrolled on that first turn," Russell said.

"Yes, but he recovered nicely. He's doing what I told him, as best he can. He'll learn."

Russell shook his head. "I sure hope I did the right thing letting him do this."

Hanna looked into his eyes, seeing the concern there. "I think you did. It's right to take this seriously, because it can be dangerous if you're careless."

"From what I've read, it's not entirely safe no matter what."

"That's correct. That puts it in there with rock climbing, riding dirt bikes, and things like that. The question is, is an experience like this worth a little carefully considered risk?"

"That's the question, all right."

"So what do you think?"

He watched Scott make a careful 180 to fly past the slope in the opposite direction. "I think so. But I'll die if anything happens to him."

She took his hand and squeezed it. She felt a tightness in her throat. "I know. Me too."

Scott made another turn, heading north once more. He was now below the summit and drifting ever lower. Hanna saw him glance back. He started a gentle turn to the left, into the wind. He pulled the control bar back a little and began picking up speed. Despite this his height above the ground increased rapidly as the slope dropped away. He pulled the control bar back further. The hang glider dove through the smooth air currents, the ground farther away than ever. Soon he was over the base of the hill and still over a hundred feet in the air.

"What's he doing?" Russell asked.

"Planning his landing." She paused and bit her lower lip. "But he's forgotten something."

A few moments later Scott pushed the control bar forward, slowing his speed and descent. He turned to the north and began a series of lazy "S" turns as he dropped lower.

Hanna smiled. "He remembered. You can't just dive at the ground when you're ready to land. Come on."

She started down the slope, feeling the wind tug at her hair. Russell loped along beside her as they watched Scott continue his methodical approach to his first hang-glider landing. Lower and lower the brilliant red craft flew, responding obediently to the pilot's commands.

Hanna dodged the bushes and small trees as she selected her path to the bottom. About halfway down she slid to a stop. Russell ran past and had to come back up.

"He's about to start his final approach," Hanna said.

They watched as Scott completed one more north-south run, then turned west into the wind about fifty feet in the air. The hang glider slowed a little as he pushed the control bar forward slightly. He maintained this steady speed and descent until he was about four feet above the ground, where the glider suddenly leveled out.

"He's in ground effect now," Hanna said. "Remember what I told you."

The glider slowed further. Finally Scott pushed the control bar forward as far as he could, abruptly increasing the triangular wing's angle of attack. The craft came almost to a stop as Scott's feet became the landing gear. He stood there as the weight of the glider again rested on his shoulders, and its slight forward momentum brought the nose forward and down. Too late, Scott remembered he was supposed to run the landing out. He started forward but wasn't quick enough. The nose plate plowed into the soft earth, and Scott tumbled forward.

"Not bad for a first flight," Hanna said.

She and Russell resumed their dash for the bottom. Below them Scott struggled to stand up underneath the cumbersome glider. He finally managed and began extricating himself from the harness. He was completely free by the time they reached him.

"So, how was it?" Hanna asked, out of breath from the run.

"It was *way* cool!" Scott said. He seemed almost unable to stand still. Then he settled down, and his wide grin morphed into a serious expression. "What did you think?"

"You really want to know?"

He paused. "Yeah."

She smiled. "For a first flight it was actually pretty good."

His eyes narrowed. "But . . ."

"I think you know what you need to work on. You overcontrolled a little, and you dove at the ground rather than setting up your landing approach. Then you didn't completely flare your landing and run it out, which is why you ended up on your face."

He frowned. "I didn't do *anything* right!"

"Au contraire!"

"What?"

"That's French for 'to the contrary.' You did a lot right. You knew basically what to do for the most part. You'll do better as you gain experience.

Book learning's OK, but some things you learn only by doing." She tousled his hair. "Now let's see how your dad does."

He looked around at Russell, and his smile returned. "Yeah! It's *his* turn now."

Hanna faced her husband. "OK, pardner. Hoist the kite and head 'em up the hill. Scott and I want to see how *you* do."

"Hey, two on one isn't fair."

"Tough," Hanna replied. "Let's go."

Russell lifted the glider and struggled to steady it in the breeze. He turned uphill and began the long trek to the top. Hanna's eyes followed their path upward, rejoicing inwardly at the lush, green beauty all around them. Fluffy white clouds sailed along toward the east like a heavenly armada, moved along by the same power that made the sport of hang gliding possible. High above them a pilot launched himself into the air, strapped underneath a yellow glider with black trim that looked a little bit like a monster butterfly. The pilot made a sharp turn to the north as he searched for lifting currents along the ridgeline.

After reaching the top, Russell began strapping himself into the harness. Hanna watched each step but didn't have to say a word. He, too, had been paying attention during ground school.

"What do you think?" he asked.

"Looks good to me," she said with a smile. Although she was glad to be sharing this sport with her new family, she still couldn't help being concerned, which surprised her. "See you at the bottom."

He hesitated for just a moment. "Right."

He turned and faced downhill, into the wind. He leaned forward and began running briskly, taking care to maintain the proper angle of attack on the glider's triangular wings. A few steps later he was airborne.

At first he showed the same tendency to overcontrol as Scott had. But then he smoothed out as he discovered what minor movements of the control bar could do. He performed a series of figure-eight turns parallel to the ridge, drifting ever lower as he failed to find a lifting breeze. After several minutes he neared the bottom and made his landing approach. He began his landing flare a few feet off the ground, pushing the control bar full forward just as the glider quit flying. He was still moving a little when he touched down but managed to run it out without falling on his face. Hanna and Scott joined him at the bottom. Hanna picked up the newly abandoned glider and began toting it back up the hill. At the top she strapped in and prepared for her flight.

"Do you wish you'd brought your own glider?" Russell asked.

"Nope. I want to see how this one handles. We'll bring both kites out when you and Scott are a little further along."

She checked her rigging and looked up.

"Well, it's the instructor's turn," she said. "I guess I better watch my stuff since you guys did so well. Hate to be shown up by my students."

"What is it that pride goeth before?" her husband asked.

"Don't even think it. I'm not being prideful—at least I don't think I am."

"Blast off." Russell paused a moment, then added, "And take care of the one I love."

Hanna smiled as his words warmed her. "I will, darlin'. See you guys at the bottom."

She felt the familiar adrenaline surge as she turned to face the wind. The wind tugged at her hair as her eyes scanned the downward slope at her feet. Several gliders soared near the peak, but none were close enough to pose a danger. The sky was hers. *Provided I don't flub the takeoff,* she thought. *Wouldn't that be a kick!*

She carefully selected the proper angle of attack and started forward. The first few steps were slow, but she quickly picked up speed. She felt the glider tugging upward as she reached full stride. She gave one final push-off, and the ground dropped away and she hung, fully suspended, beneath the triangular wing. She glanced to the right. *Good. No traffic.* She pushed the control bar to the left, executing a tight turn to the north. *Not bad,* she thought. The glider performed about like hers. Ian hadn't sold them a dog.

She turned closer to the ridge as she slowly lost altitude. Then she felt an abrupt bump. She smiled as the glider regained all its lost altitude and then some. Hanna executed a sharp 180 and reentered the rising air current. After several more passes she was several hundred feet above her launch point. She could see for miles. The rich green of the rolling hills made her heart sing with the aching beauty of God's creation. The thick stands of trees formed accents of darker greens, interspersed with lakes and streams. The cobalt blue of Puget Sound stretched away to the distant western horizon.

Hanna looked around at the hilltop. Scott waved frantically at her, and after a moment Russell did as well, although with a little more decorum. She waved back. Much as she wanted to prolong this flight, she knew her students needed the flight time more than she did.

She turned west to get out of the lifting winds. After several hundred feet she found still air and began a series of lazy eights as her altitude bled off. Within minutes she reached fifty feet above the base of the hill. She pushed the control bar to the left and made a sharp turn to the right, directly into the wind. The ground seemed to come up to meet her as she continued her smooth approach. Nearly down, the glider leveled out as it entered the ground effect. Hanna waited while her air speed continued to melt away. When she sensed the approaching stall, she shoved the bar forward as far as she could. The craft quit flying, and her feet touched down at the same time, with no forward momentum at all. It was, she had to admit, a perfect landing.

"Wow!" she heard a young voice say. "That was some landing!"

She turned to see Scott and Russell running toward her. She quickly got out of the harness.

"That was pretty," Russell agreed. "How long before we'll be able to land like that?"

Hanna savored the moment and was tempted to let them think what they might. But that wasn't helpful, and it wasn't honest.

"I hate to disillusion you guys, but great landings are as much luck as they are skill. I still land on my nose on occasion."

Russell eyed the glider's fluttering fabric wing. "I'm glad I let you talk me into this. I like this a *lot.*"

Hanna grinned. "Knew you would, pardner. Just had to get you to try it."

"Hey, time's wasting," Scott interrupted. "It's my turn."

Hanna saw the intense eagerness in his eyes and had to stifle her impulse to laugh. She attempted a stern look. "Well, start hauling the kite up the hill. Us old folks will be along directly."

"All right!"

He disappeared underneath the glider and struggled to lift it up. Then he turned and started rushing up the hill.

Hanna shook her head. "That boy has more energy."

Russell's expression turned wry. "Yeah, when it's something he wants to do."

Hanna laughed. "Come on, Pops. We can't let your son beat us to the top."

4

THE SWITCH TECHNICIAN LOOKED TOWARD THE EAST
from his rooftop vantage point. Nine stories below waited a failed central
office switch that would remain so until the government provided a
replacement. The man began to wonder if that would ever happen.
Meanwhile, Chongqing still had no telephone service, power, or utilities.
The repairman wrinkled his nose as a stray breeze carried the stench up
from the streets below. His handheld radio kept him in touch with the outside, but this was little comfort. The distant radio operator kept saying the
new switches were on the way, but he had been saying that for five days.

It seemed almost like a war zone. There had been several explosions,
one that erupted into a blazing fire the first night after the accident. The
repairman guessed that a natural gas leak had caused it. This disaster had
consumed a large section of the city, since there was no water to fight it.
The man shivered as he remembered how close the flames had come to
his rooftop post. A sudden rainstorm was all that had saved him.

The riots had begun the third day. For two days shouting crowds had
surged through the inner city, smashing windows and looting stores until
army troops had finally arrived and put down the rebellion with gunfire.

The technician had barricaded his roof access door, hoping no one would be curious enough to break it down. Once, late at night on the third day, the door had rattled several times, but whoever it was finally gave up.

The man pawed through his large canvas bag. He had enough food concentrate for another three or four days. Fortunately, the building had a rooftop tank so there was no shortage of water. The repairman looked toward the east, wondering how long this could go on.

* * *

Zhu Tak-shing suppressed a shiver as he watched Jiang Ling approach. His boss was not smiling, but Zhu did not expect him to. That Jiang had not invited him to his office in Hong Kong said a lot. It was not wise to associate with those out of political favor.

"Welcome," Zhu said with a stiff bow.

Jiang nodded as he entered the other's office. Zhu followed him in. His boss took a chair at the round conference table. Zhu hesitated, then sat beside him.

"How are things in Chongqing?" he asked, afraid to hear the answer.

Jiang tapped on the table for a few moments. "Under control—finally. *What were you thinking when you designed the chip to do that?* It took eleven days for the army to truck those switches there and get everything running again! Do you have any idea the danger you put me in?"

Zhu took a deep breath. "We didn't know the chip failure would cause the power supply to burn up, but complex electronic devices sometimes do that. But if you will examine the original project plan, it says that the Raptor Virus is to cause as much damage as possible, to ensure the devices cannot be repaired. Usually you can't do more than that, but collateral damage *is* part of the specification."

Jiang dismissed this with a wave of his hand. "I could pursue this, but I won't. It's over."

Zhu hesitated but decided he had to know. "Are things getting back to normal in Chongqing?"

"What? Oh, yes, I guess. Fortunately the army was able to restore order. The telephones are working, and power and utilities have been restored."

"Do we know how many died?"

"That is a government secret. However, you have a need to know so you can gauge the effect of your work. We will never know exactly, but the army estimates more than two hundred thousand died in the lawless rioting."

"I am sorry."

"Don't be. Loyal Chinese would not have done that. Do not forget the history of Chongqing. It was Chiang Kai-shek's wartime Kuomintang capital, and our leaders feel the civil disobedience must come from hidden capitalistic longings."

Zhu nodded. "I'm sure you are right. What about world reaction to the . . . incident?"

"Fortunately for us the news reports are limited to the fires and the reported death count, which is far below the actual figure. Official government statements attribute the communications failure to widespread damage from the fire. The army has sealed off the city so there is no way the truth can get out."

"So we continue with Project Dragon?"

"Yes. Fortunately for you, our leaders were impressed by the amount of damage your test caused. Imagine the effect on the United States if they were to lose their entire telephone system."

"That is the plan," Zhu agreed.

Jiang got up. "It is. Keep me informed on your progress."

Zhu stood and walked his boss to the door. He then glanced at his watch and decided to make a trip to Hong Kong.

* * *

Huo Chee Yong heard the approaching footsteps and looked up from the mounds of paperwork strewn about his desk. His eyes widened slightly when he saw who it was but quickly suppressed his surprise. "Mr. Zhu," he said. "How nice to see you." He motioned toward a chair. "Please sit down."

"Thank you," his visitor said.

Huo saw the worry in his friend's eyes. "What can I do for you?"

"We have some critical shipments coming up. They must get to their destination on time. Much depends on it."

"Yes, we are expecting them." He smiled in an attempt to relieve the tension. "I believe Victoria Shipping has given satisfaction in the past."

The other nodded. "Yes, you have. I—my company is grateful, of course. But the consequences of a failure at this point would be . . ."

"Would be what?"

Zhu looked about the crowded room. "Perhaps I would be more assured if I could see your freight operations," he suggested.

"Of course. One of our largest warehouses is a few blocks away on the harbor. It's a pleasant day. We could walk."

Huo stood up and led the way through the narrow aisles between desks and out the front doors. Neither spoke as they hurried down the steps and merged into the living stream of pedestrians. The buildings, so tall near the center of Hong Kong, dwindled in height rapidly as if to meet the bay at the waterline. A Kowloon-bound ferry altered course radically to give a departing containership ample clearance. A large junk was sailing into Victoria Harbor from the west, its orange sails a striking contrast to the opposite shore. Ships of every type, condition, and nationality dotted the waterway, awkward and angular, some tied up at docks but most anchored out.

Huo smiled as he smelled the fresh tang of salt water, only slightly tainted by the inevitable flotsam caking the pilings and docks. He led his guest down a narrow street beside a towering warehouse that occupied two city blocks. Large cargo doors punctuated the long side. Three tiers of dingy windows circled the building just below the flat roof. Huo stopped before a normal-sized door and unlocked the heavy padlock. He opened the door, held it, and followed Zhu in. He closed the door and waited a few moments while his eyes adjusted to the dim interior.

Men struggled with boxes, stacking them up while others applied wide plastic strips like clear cocoons. Huge forklifts roared past with towering cargo pallets, the drivers guiding them into open shipping containers.

"Shall we go up there?" Huo shouted to make himself heard. He pointed to a catwalk along the far wall about thirty feet above the concrete floor.

Zhu nodded.

The two men hurried cautiously through the heavy traffic, which seemed to take no notice of them. Huo started up the steep steel ladder to the narrow walkway where they could see the entire work floor. He continued on until they were near the building's rear corner. Here the sounds, so loud on the floor, drifted into the background.

"Will this do?" Huo asked. He looked into the other's eyes. He had never seen Zhu so tense before.

"Yes, I think it will." He paused and broke eye contact. "We've been friends a long time."

"Yes, and our families."

Zhu finally smiled. "That is right. Going clear back to your grandmother."

Huo sighed as he thought about her. "Yes."

"I wouldn't be here, except for her. Chiang's men would have executed my father if she hadn't helped him escape, and she certainly didn't care for Mao."

Huo smiled. "Yes. Her true allegiance was somewhere else."

"Yes, I know. How is she?"

"As full of life as ever. She's still living in her small apartment in Shanghai. Last time I was there she asked about you."

Zhu's smile took on a wry twist. "I can guess what it was about." He shook his head. "English missionaries—they amaze me."

"Let's be specific. It was one specific English woman—Miss Margaret Jones. Miss Jones came to China to die and to tell whoever would listen about Jesus."

"I did not come to talk about that."

"I could point out that you brought it up. Grandmother loves you as a grandson. And she believes in God because of that missionary. Miss Jones rescued grandmother after her father beat her for refusing to worship the family idol." Huo saw the look of strong disapproval on his friend's face. "But yes, I know you didn't come to see me about that." He paused. "Perhaps some other time."

Zhu cleared his throat. "Perhaps."

"Now tell me what's wrong."

"Remember the talks we had about Lucky Real Estate Partners?"

Huo turned in shock. "The Y2K Bug? How could I forget? If it hadn't been for that American consultant . . .'"

"Yes, yes. You know I was against what our leaders were doing. It was sheer idiocy, but I don't have much to say about what goes on."

Zhu looked down on the floor so far below. He watched the controlled mayhem as the workers prepared their shipments. "You know, something like that might still happen."

"What?"

Zhu continued to stare into space.

"What are you talking about?" Huo repeated.

"I'm working on something called Project Dragon. It's worse than you can possibly imagine."

"What is it?"

Zhu shook his head. "No. I've already said too much. But . . ."

"But what?"

He paused a long time. "If I needed help, would you do it?"

An icy pang stabbed at Huo's insides. "Yes, you know I would."

A weak smile came to his friend's face. "Thank you."

✳ ✳ ✳

Hanna scrolled down the Web page as she read the news account of the fires in Chongqing. There were no pictures, which she thought odd, and not a lot in the way of text. There were a few promotional photos of the city and the Three Gorges, with tourist-style captions that struck an odd chord juxtaposed against the disaster. She stared at the death toll estimate: 20,000. She turned as she heard someone enter her office.

"Hi," she said, standing.

"I'm home," Russell said as he kissed her.

"Mm, so I see. Do I get only one?"

"No, ma'am."

He did a more thorough job, which Hanna found entirely satisfactory.

"That's better. So how was your day?"

"OK, I guess. No one appreciates us maintenance guys until something goes wrong."

"What happened?"

"We had to shut down a generator because of a faulty temperature sensor. Fortunately we had enough reserve capacity to avoid cutting off any power. But incidents like that keep reminding me of how dependent we are on all our electronic systems."

"But the computerized systems are more reliable than what they replace."

"Yes, unless we get hit with deliberate sabotage."

Hanna nodded. "You're thinking about Paul's work."

"It's hard not to." He looked down at her large monitor. "What're you doing?"

"Reading about those fires in Chongqing. Isn't that awful?"

"Yes, it is. It's hard to take in how many people can die when a disaster strikes a large city. What if something happened in Seattle and twenty thousand died? I can't imagine that. Did they say what caused the fires?"

"The report says a natural gas explosion started it, and it spread out of control."

Russell continued to look at the Web page. "Something doesn't add up. Surely the whole city didn't burn. As bad as twenty thousand deaths is, that doesn't suggest complete destruction. I don't think that's enough to knock out all telecommunications and power. Switches and generators aren't all located at the same site."

Hanna shrugged. "Maybe the whole city did burn. The Chinese could be reporting false numbers."

"Maybe. Only they would know."

"Oh, I found out something else interesting in my surfing."

"What's that?"

"Chongqing is Seattle's sister city."

His eyebrows shot up. "Really?"

"Yep."

5

JIANG LING SAT DOWN IN HIS COMFORTABLE LEATHER chair behind a massive mahogany desk, cleared of all paperwork except a one-page report. The uncluttered surface hosted only three other objects on its gleaming surface: a gold pen and pencil set, a large electronic phone, and an exquisite pagoda carved from priceless pink jade. He shifted uneasily as he gazed out through the floor-to-ceiling windows at Victoria Peak. Kowloon and mainland China lay behind him, clearly visible through the windows on the other side of the vast penthouse suite atop this glass-and-steel monument to capitalism in the heart of Hong Kong, now officially a part of the People's Republic of China. His gaze drifted up the beautiful peak named for a dead British monarch, then looked toward the east. Many thousands of miles in that direction rested the paper tiger that he was pledged to destroy.

A frown wrinkled his forehead as he thought of his late brother, Chung Wu. His half brother, he reminded himself, although the untimely death still cried out for revenge, something Jiang looked forward to taking care of. They were still united through the blood of their dead mother. If only Wu had been successful. He would have been, except for the meddling

American, Hanna Sidwell. She should have been eliminated from the beginning. Jiang shuddered. The woman was living in Seattle now, the intelligence reports said. *Could she pose a threat to the new project?* he wondered.

A light winked on his phone. Jiang jabbed the intercom button. "Yes."

"Mr. Zhu to see you," his secretary said.

"Send him in."

He pressed the button again to disconnect. He looked up, and his eyes drifted over the thick blue carpet to the tall wooden door. Jiang adjusted his expensive western suit, although its perfect tailoring certainly needed no adjusting. He shifted slightly as the door swung open on noiseless hinges. His secretary peered in as she invited the guest to enter.

Zhu Tak-shing's stocky form filled the doorway as he strode into the office. Although he was shorter than Jiang by at least four inches, he made up for it by sheer bulk and hard muscle. Zhu's official title was technical director for Hong Kong CyberCircuits, Limited, but what he actually did few beside Jiang knew. The man stopped a few feet from the desk and gave a slight bow without seeming in the least subservient. His eyes, so brown they appeared black, peered down at his boss. Jiang remained seated, smiling stiffly to hide his mild irritation.

"Good afternoon," Zhu said, his voice deep and resonant.

"Yes, it is," Jiang agreed. After a suitable pause he waved a hand toward a chair. "Please, be seated."

Zhu nodded and sat down. "You wished to see me?" the man began.

"Yes. So good of you to come on such short notice." He paused and tapped the sheet of paper in front of him. "Our leaders become impatient. I've already reported two schedule changes on Project Dragon. They want to know when our preparations will be complete."

The technical director's eyes widened. "They will be complete when they are complete. If Lucky Microelectronics hadn't failed, there would be no *need* for Project Dragon."

Jiang leaned forward and pointed. "Are you criticizing the People's leaders? Because if you are . . ."

A wry smile came to the man's lips. "Forgive me, I did not realize that Chung Wu was one of our leaders."

Jiang pounded his desk with a fist, but the sound was almost inaudible. He struggled not to wince at the pain. "That is quite enough! For better or worse, you are the technical director. Now bring me up-to-date!"

"We have a little more to do, but most of the devices are in place. For that you can thank the fact that the Pacific Rim supplies most of the world's microchips—that, and the number of manufacturers we control or influence."

"Yes, yes, I know all that. But this thing is a ticking time bomb. If someone finds out what we're doing before we're ready . . ."

Zhu shook his head. "That won't happen. This is too well hidden, and the West isn't prepared. They are too naïve."

"They found out about our Y2K bug."

The man smiled. "I had nothing to do with that."

Jiang glared at him. "Do *not* try my patience! Let me remind you that the deadline can't be changed."

The smile took on the barest hint of a sneer. "I was the one who came up with the trigger date, if you recall."

"So, how much longer?"

The man paused. "A month—maybe a little longer."

Jiang exhaled audibly. "That's cutting it close."

"We'll make it."

"You better."

Zhu frowned.

"Something the matter?" Jiang asked.

"I hope we are prepared for the devastation this causes."

Jiang gasped. "You dare to question . . ." He couldn't finish.

His technical director shook his head. "No, of course not. Just a thought to the consequences."

"May I suggest you attend to your own duties."

The other nodded.

"You may go."

Zhu got up quickly and left. Jiang waited until the door closed, then slowly exhaled. He brought out his silk handkerchief and dabbed at the perspiration on his brow. He thought about the digital recorder in his coat closet. Were there others? Probably. He shook his head as he wondered who else might hear this conversation.

* * *

Paul Parker looked down on the floor of Blue Water Yachts' cavernous construction building from his office perched high up on one of the walls. He watched as the tall, heavyset man made his way between the yacht hulls, seemingly oblivious of the noise and chatter of the workers—clearly a man on a mission. *But what does he want to see me for?* Paul wondered. He watched as his visitor reached the tall steel stairs leading upward, then lost sight of him. Paul turned away from the long bay of windows and waited. Soon he heard heavy ringing footsteps on the steel catwalk outside his office. Two solid raps on the door.

"Come in," Paul said.

The door swung open immediately, and the man's round face peered in. He had serious brown eyes. Although he was clearly in his early middle years, his prematurely thinning brown hair seemed to suggest otherwise, not helped by the obvious tracks of hair transplants. After a noticeable pause, the man offered his hand.

"Mr. Parker, my name is Victor Yardel."

Paul shook his hand, noting the firm grip. "Yes, I know. The Agency phoned me you were coming. Please sit down." He motioned toward a bench seat near his desk while he dragged his swivel chair around from behind his desk. As the two men sat down, Paul noted that his visitor was more concerned with his groceries than with a StairMaster.

"Now, Mr. Yardel, what can a part-time researcher do for you?"

"Please call me Vic."

Paul nodded, although the offer didn't seem genuine. "OK, Vic, I'm curious why my research rates a personal visit from someone in the Directorate. It's all collected and analyzed there at Langley."

The man nodded. "I know how it's done. I've been with the Agency since I got out of school."

Paul gritted his teeth. "I'm sure you do. Well, what *can* I do for you?"

Vic furrowed his brow, which did odd things to his hair transplants. "Two things, actually. We've been curious about your Chinese source in Hong Kong. And we're concerned about this 'Project Dragon' in your reports.

"But let's talk about the source first. This is the same one who helped you take out the Y2K bug?"

"Yes," Paul replied cautiously. He shivered as he remembered how the sabotaged circuit breaker chips had almost brought down the North American power grid on the last day of 1999. Even now, very few knew how close the United States had come to complete economic break-down.

"We want to know about him—or her."

Paul shook his head. "Can't do that. This person is a friend of mine. He's willing to help me on an informal basis, but he doesn't want his identity known, especially with the new political reality in Hong Kong. Might not be good for his health."

"Hm, guess I see your—his—point. But, as you know, we like to grade our sources. We don't like to deal in 'Deep Throats,' if you know what I mean."

"You'll have to trust me on this. I've known the guy for a long time, and his stuff's good. He's never failed me."

Vic frowned. "Guess that will have to do. Now what about this 'Project Dragon'? Can you fill me in on that?"

Paul took a deep breath as he noted the intense interest in the man's eyes. "According to my source, Project Dragon is real bad news. It's supposed to have something to do with cyber terrorism—something that's coming straight from Beijing."

"I've read your reports," Vic said with visible exasperation. "What exactly are the Chinese working on?"

"That's all I've been able to find out. My friend isn't on the inside—obviously. But he has contacts, and they're all saying the same thing. The Chinese are planning some act of electronic terrorism against us, a follow up on the Y2K bug they planted." Paul paused. "Have any other researchers heard of it?"

The man nodded. "Yes. But they don't know any more about it than you do. This has our analysts baffled. Why would the Chinese do this? They have 'most favored nation' status; they're enjoying unprecedented economic growth, thanks largely to their economic ties with us. It just doesn't make sense."

"Well, regardless of whether it makes sense, they tried to do us in with the Y2K bug."

"The Beijing connection was never proved. The trail stopped with Lucky Real Estate Partners."

Paul shook his head. "No, several of the people involved are directly associated with the Chinese government."

"But we were never able to verify that, and since we know nothing of your source . . ."

"He's reliable!" Paul said with more heat than he intended.

"I'm sure he is. But you know we have to verify sources."

"Yeah, I know. So what do you think Project Dragon is?"

"We don't know."

"OK, then does the Agency think it's a real threat?"

Vic paused and for the first time seemed unsure. "Can't say. A few of the analysts are worried, but most think it just doesn't make sense, considering what it would do to China if they did such a thing."

"Well, I suggest we take this seriously. If it *is* real, wiping out vital computer systems would be a worse disaster than Y2K ever could have been."

"I'll include that in my report," Vic said as he got up.

* * *

"I'll get it," Hanna shouted as she hurried down the stairs. She rushed through the apartment entryway and opened the door. The last rays of a gorgeous May sunset silhouetted Paul Parker.

"Come in," Hanna said. "Glad you could drop by." She saw a grin light up his face, about equal parts chagrin and relief, it seemed to her. "Let's go back in the den. Russell will be down in a minute."

"Is Scott here?" Paul asked.

"No. He and Brian are studying over at the McCluskys."

"Good. I need to talk to you and Russell alone."

"About what?" Russell asked as he came down the stairs.

"Hi, Russell." The two men shook hands.

Hanna saw Paul's smile disappear, to be replaced by a look of deep concern. She and Russell sat down on the couch while Paul took the chair next to the coffee table.

"What we're going to say can't be repeated. I'm sure you know that, but I have to say it."

"We understand," Russell said. "This about your moonlighting?"

"Yes."

"I didn't think you were coming to sell us a yacht," Hanna said.

"Hardly." He paused. "Hanna, you told me a while back that you think the United States is vulnerable to cyber terrorism."

She nodded. "Yes, I believe we are. The experts are saying this is the next big thing. And not very much is being done to prevent it. It's not so much a matter of 'if' but 'when.'"

"Oh, I believe you. And from what I'm hearing, I suspect some sort of attack is on the way, and I think the target will be vital computer systems. But I'm having no luck finding out exactly what."

"There's a lot to choose from."

"That's what I figured. Hanna, what *are* the most likely targets? What would hurt us the most if we lost it?"

Hanna sighed. "Are we talking about the same source as before?"

Paul frowned. "Yep. The peace-loving leaders of the People's Republic of China, our most favorite of most favored nations."

"They don't give up, do they," Russell said.

"Not unless you stand up to them, and Foggy Bottom seems to have a problem with that—but don't quote me."

Hanna grinned. "I'm curious. What do the feds working inside the Beltway think of that term?"

He chuckled. "Foggy Bottom? I really don't know. I doubt they consider it a compliment. But getting back to my question. . . ."

Hanna thought for a moment. "Actually, we depend on quite a few computer systems. What would you like: the power industry, telecommunications, banking and finance, the air traffic control system?"

Paul nodded. "I know it's difficult. . . ."

"Difficult! It's impossible. There are probably hundreds of vital systems, and I bet not one of 'em is adequately protected—with the exception of military and high security systems."

"And we've had problems with a few of those as well."

"True."

A glimmer of a smile came to Paul's face. "Hey, we're talking about Hanna Flaherty here, not some pimply-faced geek who knows more about computers than he does about personal hygiene."

"Uh-oh," Russell said, "the gauntlet's down."

Hanna turned slowly toward her husband. "And what's *that* supposed to mean?"

Russell grinned. "Only that you can't resist a challenge."

Paul's smile faded. "Do you have any idea? Right now I don't have a thing to go on."

"Well, as I said, I think the power industry or telecommunications or one of our vital financial systems would be the most likely target. I don't know. If I had to guess, I'd pick the power utilities. We all saw what almost happened with the Y2K bug."

Paul nodded. "Makes sense. So how would they do it?"

"Either software or the programs etched inside embedded circuit computer chips."

"You mean like those circuit-breaker chips that Lucky Microelectronics slipped us?"

"Yes. And most of these chips come from the Pacific Rim, and a whole bunch come from China."

"OK. So what do they do?"

Hanna shrugged. "Come on like the mother of all computer viruses, would be my guess. I think they'd pick a certain trigger date. Then completely disable the devices the chips are in, destroying them if possible."

"They can do that?"

"In some cases. But disabling the device is enough. How are you going to fix a broken relay if there aren't any chips to do it?"

"And without the chips . . ."

"The system won't work," Hanna finished for him. "Unfortunately, lots of devices are completely dependent on a single chip."

"That's pretty grim."

"Yes, it is." She watched with concern as his expression took on a haunted look.

"What can we do?"

Hanna felt a tingle of fear. "Find the target before they can set it off."

"How?"

She shook her head. "I don't know."

* * *

Huo Chee Yong saw his friend approaching but gave no notice. Instead he got slowly to his feet and walked to the attendant and handed over his ticket. He boarded the Victoria Peak Tram along with a crowd of tourists, standing near the uphill side of the car. Out of the corner of his eye, he saw Zhu Tak-shing make his way to the other end. The tram operator released the brake. The car rolled backwards a few feet as the added weight stretched the cable that traveled up to the top and over the drive wheel before dropping back down to the sister tram on the adjacent tracks. Then up they went at the leisurely rate the English engineers had deemed appropriate. Halfway up they passed the other tram on its way to the bottom station.

Huo turned back and gazed at the panorama of Hong Kong and Victoria Harbor so far below. Modern buildings shot skyward in thin, angular shafts. He pondered the incredible wealth and poverty that abounded in the former British colony, a major commercial hub during the day and a refuge for the homeless by night. The tram stopped. Huo waited until most of the tourists were off, then stepped down and made his way along the well-tended path. After a few minutes he heard footsteps behind him. Huo took a narrow path that led away from the peak. He turned and saw his friend. The two men sat on a bench.

Zhu looked around, then leaned close. "I think I may be in trouble."

Huo's dread turned to fear. "What for?"

"I suspect my boss thinks I'm critical of our leaders." He pounded his leg with his fist. "Oh, I *am* critical, but I'm careful not to let it show. Or at least I try."

"Are you sure?"

Zhu shook his head. "Not positive. We were discussing the project, and he asked me if I was questioning our leadership. I denied it."

"Do you think he believed you?"

"That's what has me worried. He didn't have me arrested, which is a good sign. He knows how vital I am to Project Dragon. But maybe he's waiting until I'm done with my work. I don't know."

"What do you plan on doing?"

"Keep my eyes and ears open. I think I'll have some warning. At least I hope so. And, if it happens . . ."

"Yes?"

"Will you help me get out? If they come for me, a prison sentence is the best I can hope for."

"Of course I'll help."

"How can I reach you?"

Huo thought for a moment, then wrote on his business card and gave it to Zhu. "Call my beeper and leave one of *my* numbers. Doesn't matter which one, I'll know it's you. Then I'll meet you at this address within the hour."

Zhu nodded as he took the card. "Thank you."

6

HANNA READ THE FAX ONE MORE TIME, ALL FORTY-ONE pages of it, then let it drop to her desk next to Victoria Regina, her venerable laptop computer. Her puzzled expression softened as she watched the screen-saver's panoramic scenes segue from a towering thunderhead near Benjamin, Texas, to El Capitan hunkered under a light dusting of snow. Although less famous than its California cousin, Hanna much preferred the Guadalupe Mountains version. She nudged VR's mouse to make the screensaver go away. She heard the front door open and listened to the rapid steps up the stairs. She turned to see Russell come around the corner and enter her office.

"Hi, dear," she greeted him as she got up. "How was your day?"

He pulled her close and kissed her. Hanna grabbed him as he started to part. "Not so fast, pardner. I don't like getting shortchanged." He grinned and set about doing a more thorough job.

"That better?" he asked.

Hanna looked into his eyes, seeing the same pleasure she felt. "Yep."

"I aim to please."

Her eyes darted over his trim, athletic frame. "You do."

"So how were things at Roadrunner Consulting today?"

"A little slow—until this came in." She held up the thick fax.

He eyed the pages. "What is it?"

Hanna's puzzled expression returned. "An RFP for a prototype computer system from Singapore Shipping, Limited."

"Request for proposal? I didn't know you had any clients over there."

"I don't. Never heard of them."

Russell frowned in concentration. "So what do they want?"

"A freight manifest system for keeping track of cargoes from customer inquiry to delivery at the other end." She saw his look of concern.

"What do you think?" he asked.

She laughed. "That they don't need me. They'd be much better off with an off-the-shelf system than to have me write one." She tapped the fax with her finger. "But the day-rate sure is attractive—twelve hundred a day plus all expenses. Maybe they'd pay me to research and recommend a suitable package."

Russell smiled. "Could even be enough to pay for VR's next facelift."

"Hey, watch your mouth. Vicki's doing just fine. She's going to reign forever."

"Like her namesake?"

Hanna nodded. "You bet."

The phone rang, making both of them jump. Hanna picked up the portable and punched it on. "Roadrunner Consulting. Can I help you?"

"Ah, Ms. Flaherty, I presume," said the lightly accented voice suggesting a British connection.

"Yes, this is Hanna Flaherty. May I ask who's calling?"

"Yes, please forgive me. This is Gao Minqi, one of the managing partners of Singapore Shipping, Limited. Did you receive my fax?"

Hanna leaned forward in her swivel chair and reached for the document. "Why, yes Mr. Gao. In fact, I just finished reading it."

"Excellent. Does it look like something you could help us with?"

"I was going to phone you later. I appreciate the offer, but you can buy something off-the-shelf and be up and running in a couple of weeks. It would cost a whole lot less than what I'd charge. No point in reinventing the wheel, if you know what I mean."

"Thank you for your candor. I am aware of this, but we wish to have a system tailored to the way we do business. Off-the-shelf systems are, I think you say, 'take it or leave it.'"

Hanna laughed. "You have that right. Generic systems are capable, but you have to do things their way."

The man's laugh was clear despite the distance. "My point exactly. Does the project interest you?"

Hanna felt the attraction of the generous offer. Then she glanced up at Russell whose puzzled expression reeled in her expectations a little. "It's certainly an attractive offer, Mr. Gao, but I'd have to discuss it with my husband."

"Of course, I understand entirely. Would tomorrow be too soon to expect a reply?"

Hanna glanced at the fax, then over at Russell. "I think we can decide by then."

"Very good. I will look forward to your call. Good-bye."

"Good-bye."

Hanna punched the phone off and got up. "Wow. That would be some contract," she said with feeling. "Something like that would take a whole bunch of hours. And that day rate!"

Russell frowned. "Yeah, but would you have to go to Singapore?"

Hanna took a deep breath. "Yes, I probably would. I can do most of the grunt work here, but I'm sure Mr. Gao would require a face-to-face to be sure I understand the requirements."

Russell shook his head. "I don't know if I want my wife traipsing off to the end of the world."

Hanna felt the heat coming to her face. "I *don't* traipse, and Singapore *isn't* the end of the world."

"It's about as far away as you can get. Look at a map."

"Russell!" she said through clenched teeth. "This is a wonderful opportunity! We can use the money." She saw the hurt look in his eyes and looked quickly away.

"We're not hurting. My job provides a good income."

"I have a job too, in case you forgot!" She regretted the words as soon as they were out. She glanced at Russell, but he turned away. Hanna felt a momentary pang of conscience, but her irritation quickly buried it.

"No, I didn't forget," Russell said softly. "I'm proud of you Hanna, you know that. And it's not a question of whose job is more important. It's just that I think there should be some limits on our independence now that we're married."

Hanna felt the sting. "But I'm a *consultant.* I *have* to meet my clients, at least until I know what I have to do." She gave a nervous laugh. "Then they usually let me do what I want—as long as I deliver. Russell, I'm sure it would be a short trip."

She waited for him to respond, but he just stood there.

"Russell?" Hanna prompted.

"You know I don't dictate."

She looked down. "No, you don't. You're a wonderful husband. I love you."

He smiled, but she could tell it was forced.

"And I love you, Hanna." He paused. "I think we need to pray about this."

Hanna pushed the fax away with a sigh. "Yes, I think we do."

* * *

Hanna looked at the digital clock on her desk as she waited for Russell to get home. It had been almost exactly twenty-four hours since

Mr. Gao's phone call. Somehow she didn't feel right about traveling halfway around the world by herself, even if it was a rather nice bird nest on the ground.

The door opened and closed. Hanna got up from her desk and waited. Russell was smiling as he came through the door, but Hanna knew it was not exactly the real thing. The kiss, however, did not seem to have any missing parts.

"Hm, I think you meant that," she said when they parted.

"You know I did."

She looked in his eyes, pleased at the gleam she saw there. "Good."

The earlier tension returned. "Have you called Mr. Gao?"

"No, I was waiting for you to get home. I'm not going to accept the job."

"Thank you."

She grinned, thankful that the decision had been made. Hanna sat down at her desk and pulled the fax over. She punched the long string of digits into the portable phone and waited while a series of computers and satellites routed the call with a speed that surprised even her.

"Singapore Shipping," a female voice answered.

Hanna cleared her throat. "This is Hanna Flaherty of Roadrunner Consulting. May I speak to Mr. Gao Minqi?"

The distant voice seemed to brighten. "Yes, Ms. Flaherty. Mr. Gao said to put you right through. Just a moment, please."

"Thank you."

"Ms. Flaherty," Mr. Gao said a few seconds later. "Thank you for your prompt reply. I hope you have good news for me."

Hanna took a deep breath. "Mr. Gao, I appreciate your generous offer, but I can't accept the contract."

"Oh, I am sorry to hear that. May I ask why?"

"I wouldn't feel right about being away from my husband and family."

"I see. I understand the importance of family, and Singapore is not quite as close as, say, Tacoma."

Hanna laughed. "Not quite."

"May I make a suggestion?"

Hanna glanced at Russell. "Yes, I guess so."

"Perhaps there is a way we can make this work. Would you allow me to fly you and your husband to Singapore and put you up at a first-rate hotel—all expenses paid, of course. Think of it as a vacation. We could complete our business in a day or two. Meanwhile, you and your husband could enjoy the sights of Singapore. We have much to offer, I assure you. Would this make a difference?"

"I don't know. I wasn't expecting that." She saw Russell's look of concern.

"Please think it over. No need to decide now."

"OK, we will. But let me ask this: If I take the job, can I develop the system here?"

"Of course. In fact, Singapore Shipping has an office in Seattle. All meetings and demonstrations could be done there."

"I see. Let me call you back."

"I will await your call."

They said their polite good-byes. Hanna exhaled as she turned the phone off. She saw the questioning look in Russell's eyes.

"He wants us *both* to come—at his expense. Said to think of it as a vacation."

"Hanna. You *said* you weren't going to take the job."

"I know, but that was when I thought I'd have to travel alone. Doesn't this make a difference? Think what we could do with the money. We could buy a house. . . ."

She watched as he thought it over. At first it irritated her that Russell couldn't see how the new offer changed everything. But then an uneasy feeling crept over her. She dismissed it as tension.

"We don't need the money," Russell said at last. "I don't see that anything has changed, except that Mr. Gao is offering to pay for a chaperone."

"Chaperone, my hind foot! You're my husband. He's resolved our objection to my traveling alone. Wouldn't you like to see Singapore?"

"That's beside the point."

"Russell!" She watched as he set his jaw. They had had few serious arguments in their marriage, and Hanna was grateful that Russell was not a demanding husband. But she knew he rarely budged if he felt he was right.

"You really want this, don't you?" Russell said softly.

A whirlwind of thoughts made the simple question difficult to answer. The project intrigued her, and the pay was the best she had ever seen— by far. Even the thought of travel did not deter her. She found it difficult to meet his eyes. "Yes, I do."

He nodded. "OK."

"You sure?"

"Yes." He paused. "I'll see if Scott can stay with the McCluskys while we're gone. Shouldn't be a problem."

"Great," she said. "When can I call Mr. Gao back?"

"Well, I'm sure he's still there."

Hanna reached for the phone.

* * *

Paul Parker scooted his swivel chair closer to his desk and peered at his computer monitor. He maximized his Outlook application and clicked on the in-box icon. His eyes darted down the long list of E-mails. The first ten entries had unopened envelope icons indicating he had not looked at them.

"Come on!" he grumbled to himself. "I checked this. . . ." He stopped as he tried to remember when he *had* last checked his in-box. At first he thought it had been that morning, but he really couldn't remember. His mind drifted back to the previous day. After pondering, he finally decided it had been a while. He scanned down the new entries. Most were from Blue Water Yachts employees, while a few were from friends at church. Then he spotted a name he had not seen in a while.

"Wonder what David Ho wants?" he said as he double-clicked on the entry. He well remembered the wealthy Hong Kong customer. A window opened displaying the rich text message. He quickly scanned it, noting a whole series of attached graphics files at the bottom.

"Ah, the front office will love this." Paul read the document closely and displayed a few of the graphic files. Blue Water had sold David a 115-foot ketch eight years ago, without even a question about the price. The profits from a booming cosmetics business apparently made such things irrelevant. Paul couldn't remember a more sumptuously outfitted boat. The furnishings had cost almost as much as the basic yacht itself. Whereas the original design had called for two double staterooms and two double cabins, Mr. Ho had opted for a huge master bedroom with bath and sauna that opened onto a grand dining room with a crystal chandelier.

Paul played with the mouse as he thought. *I think we can handle this. Doesn't ask for a quote, just wants to know when we can do it.* Paul knew there would be no problem handling the requestecd conversion—not for *this* customer. It was just a matter of letting accounting know the good news.

Paul tapped in a polite reply, assuring David that Blue Water Yachts was ready to attend to his every need; Paul would take care of everything personally. He asked when Blue Water could expect the yacht and sent the E-mail winging its way across the wide Pacific. He noted that David wanted him to call as soon as possible. Paul glanced at his watch and saw it was almost noon. He did a quick mental calculation and decided that

David would not appreciate being called at four in the morning, no matter how concerned he was about his yacht.

That important business done, Paul leaned back in his swivel chair and turned so he could look down on the construction building floor. He tilted his Blue Water Yachts mug and sipped the strong black coffee as he watched workmen lowering the mast into a nearly complete twenty-meter yacht. He longed to be on the floor where he could supervise directly, but knew the construction foremen needed no help from him.

It was a cool, wet day outside, and that matched his mood. Nothing had changed since the previous day. He still had no idea how to uncover what he wanted to know—what Vic expected him to dig up. If Hanna didn't know where to look, *he* sure didn't. He took an impulsive gulp of his coffee and winced as the hot liquid burned all the way down.

His phone chirped, causing him to spill his coffee. He set the mug down on a report, marking it with a dark, round circle. He picked up the phone.

"Paul Parker. Can I help you?" He listened for a reply, but there was none. But he could hear noises in the background. He raised his voice. "Hello?"

"Mr. Parker?" a woman's voice said. Whoever it was sounded uneasy and irritated at the same time.

"Yes. This is Paul Parker. Are you calling Blue Water Yachts?" Somehow she didn't sound like a customer.

"Yes, I am. I'm here at Sea-Tac. Did you forget?"

Paul frowned and cleared his throat. "Ah, did I forget what?"

"That you were to pick me up."

Paul struggled for a halfway intelligent reply.

"Are you there?" the woman asked.

"Yes, I'm here. Who is this?"

It was her turn to pause. "Rachael O'Connor. Didn't Mr. Yardel tell you I was coming?"

Paul felt the knot of tension torque tighter. "You're with the CIA, Ms. O'Connor?"

"Actually it's Dr. O'Connor, but yes, I am."

"No, Victor *didn't* tell me." His mind quickly shifted gears. "Sorry about the mix-up, Ms.—er Dr. O'Connor."

"Please call me Rachael."

"OK, Rachael." He thought a moment. "I should be at the airport in about a half hour, depending on traffic."

"No, you don't have to do that. I can get a cab."

"No, stay there. It's awfully sloppy outside. I'll come for you." He paused and grinned. "We can both take this up with Victor later."

"Someone needs to."

"Right. See you in a little bit." He hung up, then realized he hadn't asked what terminal she was in. But she hadn't volunteered that information either. He finally decided they were both embarrassed and frazzled.

He grabbed his golf umbrella as he left his office. He clattered down the metal stairs, wondering why Victor had sent this lady doctor to Seattle.

* * *

Paul hurried into the terminal, pausing a moment to shake the rain off his umbrella before closing it. A quick call on his mobile phone to the terminal paging service had resolved the whereabouts of Dr. O'Connor. He hurried to the baggage claim area and looked around as he wondered what she looked like.

There were plenty of female travelers in attendance, he noted, most in sharp-looking business attire with expressions that matched. But which one was Rachael? Finally he spotted a short woman who seemed a little younger than himself. Her blue business suit announced a hard morning's travel in coach, as did her somber look. She was slightly heavier than most of the trim businesswomen around her, but not fat, Paul decided. The contrast between her serious brown eyes and her dark red hair surprised and intrigued him. She turned her head and saw him.

"Dr. O'Connor, I presume?" he said as he approached.

"That's me," she said with a glimmer of a smile. "But please call me Rachael."

She reached for his hand and lost her grip on the thin laptop she was carrying. The computer hit the floor with a clatter, springing the top open.

"Oh, no!" she wailed.

Paul stood with his right hand extended while Rachael stooped down. The strap on her shoulder bag slipped free. The large gray container hit the floor with a solid thump. Rachael tried to close the computer's top, but the latch was broken.

"Not again," she said as she got up. She finally saw his hand and shook it, almost dropping the laptop again.

"Oh, don't worry," Paul said. "We'll find some place to get it fixed. I know someone who can recommend a repair shop. In fact, she might be able to fix it herself."

"Girlfriend?"

He saw her clamp her mouth shut as if she regretted saying it. He couldn't help smiling. "Nothing like that. It's the wife of a friend of mine. She knows *everything* about computers."

Rachael frowned. "Yeah, and I know the rest."

"That could happen to anyone."

"With me it's a habit."

Paul looked into her eyes, trying to think of something reassuring to say, but nothing would come. Finally he looked down at the large suitcase beside her. "Well, let's get out of here. The Sea-Tac terminal isn't one of our better tourist attractions."

He reached for the handle, but she beat him to it. "Oh, I can get that." Her grip on the laptop started to slip.

"How about letting me carry one or the other?" Paul suggested.

Rachael looked at the computer, then down at the suitcase. "I guess that *would* be a good idea."

"May I get the bag?" He didn't move as she thought it over.

"OK." A glimmer of a smile appeared, nicely framed by her red hair. "Thanks."

Paul felt his face grow warm. He cleared his throat. "Shall we go?"

He tucked the umbrella under one arm and picked up the suitcase, noting the lady was not acquainted with traveling light. Rachael walked at his side, holding the laptop together with both hands. Outside he set his burden down and opened the umbrella. The rain had not slacked up.

"Is it always like this?" Rachael asked.

He grinned. "Sometimes it seems that way. Obviously this is your first visit to the Pacific Northwest."

"Yes. I grew up on Long Island and went to school in Washington, D.C. I've been to L.A. but never up here. This your home?"

They hurried through the crosswalk.

"I'm a transplanted Texan. But I guess Seattle's my home now."

"Texas? Horses and cows and six-shooters?"

He laughed. "Not a lot of those around Dallas where I grew up. Maybe a little farther west."

They reached Paul's black Firebird.

"Nice set of wheels," Rachael said.

He grinned. "Thanks. I like it." He unlocked the trunk and hoisted the bag into it, then opened the door for her. He couldn't tell if he was breaking a rule, but she got in without comment.

Paul drove through the garage and into the slanting rain. After paying the attendant, they were outbound from the airport exit.

"So why'd Victor send . . ." He stopped as his mobile phone chirped. He picked it up and punched a button. "Paul Parker," he said.

"Paul, this is Victor Yardel." His voice cut out for a moment, then steadied. "After thinking about our talk, I decided to send in a researcher to give you a hand. Her name is Rachael O'Connor. She . . ."

A sardonic grin came to Paul's face. "You're a little late, Victor."

"What?"

"She's already here."

"What?"

"You already said that. I just picked Rachael up at Sea-Tac. We're on our way into town as I speak."

"She was supposed to fly out tomorrow—which is why I was calling. She was scheduled to bring her relief up to speed today."

Paul glanced at Rachael. Her eyes held a strange combination of surprise and hurt. There was something about her expression that stirred him. A passing semi covered the small car with a whiplash of spray, bringing Paul's attention back to his driving.

"Paul?"

"I'm here."

"Thought you'd dropped out."

"No. Listen, don't worry about the mix-up. I'm sure coming out a day early isn't going to mean much in the grand scheme of things."

"No, I guess not. I just hate the lack of warning."

"Not a problem. Anything else I need to know?"

"Don't think so. Rachael can fill you in on the details."

"Fine."

"Call me if anything turns up."

"Will do. Bye."

He punched the phone off.

"What did he say?" Rachael asked as Paul returned the phone to his belt. Her eyes seemed to dread his reply.

Paul paused as he weighed his words. "Well, he said you were supposed to fly out tomorrow."

"Oh, that can't be," she said, her voice trailing off as if she weren't sure. She pawed through her purse until she found a slim book. She flipped rapidly through the pages, then stopped. "Uh-oh. I think I see what happened."

"Oh? What?"

She sighed. "Victor was telling me all this as we were walking to a meeting. I was trying to follow what he was saying, but I was preoccupied with my part of the presentation. I'd left my pocket scheduler in my office and didn't have a chance to write it down until later. I wrote the travel down on the wrong day."

"So, your replacement . . ."

"Is probably wondering why I didn't show up," she finished for him. She threw the scheduler back in her purse. "You probably think I'm a real klutz."

Paul kept looking straight ahead. "No, not at all." Even in his own ears it didn't sound convincing, which bothered him. He *wasn't* condemning her. He found her rather . . . interesting.

"That's all right. Everyone does."

Paul felt his heart going out to her. "Now why would you say that?"

"Because it's true."

He shook his head. "I think you're being too hard on yourself." He glanced at her out of the corner of his eyes and saw the look of discouragement. He ransacked his mind for something positive to say but came up with nothing. "Uh, Rachael?"

"Yes," came the sullen reply.

"We're approaching I-405. Where's the Agency putting you up?"

"Oh. Yeah, I guess that might help. All I know is it's an apartment in Bellevue." She pulled a folded envelope out of her purse and extracted a sheet of paper. "Here." She held it out to him.

He took a quick look. "OK, I know about where that is. We'll take 405 around."

The powerful car ate up the distance as the muffled wind and hissing tires punctuated the growing, uneasy silence. Paul considered several ways to break the ice but finally decided to wait it out.

"Paul?" she said finally.

"Yes?"

"Victor didn't tell me much about you—only that you used to be with the Agency, and that you're doing freelance research for us now. He said something about you building boats."

He rolled his eyes. "Yachts. And I don't build them. I started out on construction crews, but then I got into design and testing. I take our yachts out on their shakedown cruises."

"Sounds like an interesting job. Your company is Blue Water Yachts?"

He smiled. "That's right. We build the best."

"I'll take your word for it, since I don't know a boat from a yacht."

"You could learn. But getting back to business, I assume you know what I'm working on."

"Yes, cyber terrorism—end-of-the-world-as-we-know-it stuff."

He paused a moment. "I hope you're taking this seriously. We very nearly had a total collapse of the North American power grid in January of 2000. And according to my sources, the Chinese leaders aren't through with us yet."

"Not everyone in Langley agrees with that. The media are full of wild rumors, and conspiracy theories are as common as politicians' denials."

He grinned. "You have a sharp tongue, Dr. O'Connor."

She laughed self-consciously. "Sometimes gets me in trouble too."

"What's your take on Project Dragon?"

"I'm not sure. I find it hard to believe that the Chinese would do something so damaging to the world economy, especially since China is prospering. But I'm hearing the same rumors you are, and I'm inclined to think they're true. I believe they *are* planning something."

"OK. The question is, what?"

"I guess that's why I'm here."

"So it would seem. Where will you be working?"

"The Agency has set me up with an office in the Federal building in Seattle—a closet probably. I'll work out of there." She turned and looked at him. A grin appeared. "And with you, when you can take time off from tooling your boats around."

"Hm. I'll see if I can work you in."

"Thanks."

* * *

Paul punched in the international call and waited as it rang.

"Hello," a clear baritone said.

Paul grinned at the clipped British accent. "David. This is Paul Parker, Blue Water Yachts."

"Paul! I appreciate your punctuality. How are you?"

"Fine. Got your message around noon our time. That's quite a job order you put together. You want me to prepare you a quote?" He knew the answer to that but was determined to follow the rules.

"No need for that. Your company has always dealt fairly with me. And I know your work is absolutely top-drawer."

"We do our best. When shall we expect your yacht?"

The line remained silent for a few moments. "That's a bit of a sticky wicket, I'm afraid. That's why I wanted to talk to you. I'm afraid I've had to let my skipper go."

Paul's eyebrows went up. "Oh?"

"Yes, nasty business, but I won't go into that. I'm interviewing for a replacement, but this may take a while. Not a decision to make lightly, if you know what I mean."

"Yes, of course. So you're not sure when we can have the boat?"

"Paul, I'd like to ask a favor." The voice became less clipped and more strained.

"What is it?"

"Would you consider coming to Hong Kong and sailing it back?" David hurried on, "Of course I'd pay all expenses, and you remember what the boat's like. It's a dream to sail."

Paul took a deep breath and let it out slowly. One part of him wanted to say yes without a second thought, but it wasn't that easy. "Personally, there's nothing I'd like better, but I'd have to check with our management. I've got a lot going on right now, so I'm not too optimistic." He looked up at the ceiling as he thought of one particular task that such a trip would play havoc with.

"Please check with your management. Meanwhile, I'll call your CEO if you think that will help."

Paul gulped. "Whatever you think best."

"This is important to me."

"I know it is. Anything else you need right now?"

"No, I don't think so. I'll be in touch."

"Right. Bye David."

"Good-bye Paul."

Paul punched in an internal number, hoping he beat the Chinese businessman to it.

7

HANNA YAWNED AS SHE SAT ACROSS FROM RUSSELL IN THE dinning room of The Oriental, perhaps the most luxurious hotel in Singapore, just down the street from Raffles Hotel and across Marina Bay from Raffles Place itself. There, in 1819, Thomas Stamford Raffles, of the British East India Company, had stepped ashore on the island of Singa Pura to open a trading settlement to the Malay Peninsula. But right now Hanna was more concerned with jet lag and the need to be alert for her meeting with Mr. Gao Minqi.

"That reminds me of Palo Duro Canyon," Russell commented over the rim of his coffee cup.

Hanna blinked as her mental fog dissipated a little. "What? Watch your mouth, dude. I suppose you're wide awake after that never-ending flight."

"At least we were in first class."

She took another sip of the excellent coffee. "Yes, I have to admit that was nice. First time I've been up with the rich folks."

"Me too."

"You know, I could get used to first class—except when I think about what those tickets cost."

Russell nodded. "Mr. Gao didn't have to do that—or put us up in this hotel, for that matter. He must really want you to do this project."

Hanna's mind began to pick up speed. "Apparently so. Of course, his new system, if I agree to do it, will cost a whole lot more than this trip. But still . . ."

The waiter, in immaculate livery, approached with a silver tray. Hanna wondered what she was supposed to do, then picked up the cream-colored business card. His duty done, the waiter left.

"It's Mr. Gao's card," Hanna said.

As she turned in her chair, she saw a middle-aged Chinese man walking toward them. He looked about as tall as Russell. He had shining black hair, smoothly combed back, and friendly brown eyes. Hanna knew she would find no imperfections in his expensive western suit or gleaming shoes. She pushed her chair back, almost tipping it. She heard Russell get up.

"Please stay seated," Mr. Gao urged. "Finish your breakfasts. I apologize for interrupting, but I was anxious to meet you." He glanced at Russell. "Both of you."

Hanna felt at ease as she shook his hand. And his English was excellent, with a hint of a British accent. "Pleased to meet you, Mr. Gao," she said.

"The pleasure is mine," he replied. "And you must be Russell," he added as he reached across the table. The two men shook hands and traded greetings. They sat down, and Gao waved off the approaching waiter.

"I trust your flight was pleasant," Gao said.

"We were talking about that when you arrived," Russell said. "Thank you for the first-class treatment—and for paying my way."

"Don't mention it. Your wife is well-known in computer circles, as you know. I want the best working on our new shipping system, and I believe in treating people fairly."

"That brings up something I need to ask," Hanna said. "This is a big project—much more than I can do alone. I can do the demo system, showing design and functionality, but I'll have to put together a development team to crank out the system. Do I have a free hand in that?"

"Of course. If we come to an agreement, you may develop the system where and how you please. I leave all the details to you. As I mentioned, all demonstrations and deliveries will be at our Seattle office so no further travel will be required, in case you were worried about that."

Hanna saw the twinkle in his eyes. "Sounds wonderful," she said with obvious relief.

"Good. Now I want you and Russell to enjoy yourselves. Singapore has much to offer the tourist. I won't be monopolizing your time with business, I assure you." A disarming grin appeared. "However, a little work *is* required. Shall we adjourn to my offices?"

Hanna found the grin infectious. "Now that I've had my coffee, I'm rarin' to go."

"Rarin'?"

The man's puzzlement almost made Hanna giggle. "That's Texan for 'ready when you are.'"

The smile returned. "Oh, I see. Is there a dictionary I should consult?"

"I offer translations."

"Ah, then that's settled."

He got up and led them out through the glittering lobby. The heat and humidity hit Hanna like something solid the moment they pushed through the Oriental's front doors. Gao's chauffeur opened the door of the stretch Lincoln. The aroma of rich leather surrounded Hanna as she entered and sat down in the cool interior. Russell joined her while Gao took a jump seat. The driver closed the door. After a few blocks on Raffles Boulevard, he turned south. A few minutes later he parked at Clifford

Pier on Marina Bay, a short distance from Raffles Place. Gao led them to a waiting water taxi. The wooden boat was painted dark blue with a bright splash of red around the gunwales and white-rimmed eyes on the bows. The boat bumped lethargically against the pier, its auto tire fenders squeaking in protest. A half-dozen passengers waited patiently underneath the boat's low awning.

"I thought you might enjoy seeing Singapore from one of our bumboats," Gao said as they boarded.

Hanna followed their host to the back. As soon as they were seated, the deckhand cast off the lines and pushed the boat away from the pier with a boat hook.

"We're very close to where colonial Singapore started," Gao said. "However, things have changed a little since then."

Hanna looked at the shining steel towers all around them. "I'll say." It seemed almost western, until she considered the colorful bumboat they were riding in. Around the next bend they passed a long narrow Chinese boat, done up in garish reds, yellows, and greens. Hanna gaped at the fierce dragon head over the prow and the pagoda near the stern. She turned to Russell. He took her hand and squeezed it. *Not bad for a business trip,* she thought.

The boat chuffed along to the north toward Queen Elizabeth Walk before swinging west to enter the Singapore River. After passing under Anderson Bridge, they made a short stop at Boat Quay.

"This is the financial district," Gao said. "Many fine restaurants along here with every cuisine imaginable. Some of the finest nightclubs line these shores."

Hanna glanced at Russell and saw his brows arch. "We'll pass on the nightclubs," she said.

Their host looked a little surprised. "Oh. Whatever you think best."

"But the restaurants sound interesting," Hanna added.

"Best in Singapore," their host assured them. "And there are so many things to see."

"What would you recommend?" Russell asked.

Gao's smile returned. "I don't know where to begin. But, by all means, visit our National Museum and Art Gallery. Among other things the museum has the Haw Par Jade Collection, one of the largest of its kind. Also, the Botanic Gardens are magnificent. Started in the days of Queen Victoria, it features native trees, shrubs, and flowers arranged in the English style. And, if you would like something different, I recommend seeing Haw Par Villa—what we used to call the Tiger Balm Gardens."

"That related to the jade collection?" Hanna asked.

"Same family. The Par brothers made a fortune selling Tiger Balm Oil. They had a home here and in Hong Kong. With the profits they built Tiger Balm Gardens in both places and acquired their fabulous jade collection. The Tiger Balm Gardens are interesting."

"In what way?" Hanna asked.

"You will have to see for yourself. You won't be disappointed." He glanced at the shore. "Ah, this is Clarke Quay."

The captain brought the bumboat alongside the pier with a gentle bump against the fenders. The deckhand jumped out and secured the lines.

Gao led the Americans out of the boat to where his white limousine waited. "Fort Canning Park is a block in that direction," he said pointing. "Raffles built the British governor's headquarters there."

Hanna shook her head. "I did some research on Singapore on the Internet. All that history. And yet everything is so modern and clean."

"That is largely due to Lee Kuan Yew, our first prime minister."

"Yes, I know."

Gao sighed. "I realize we have lost a lot of our heritage, but I guess that's the price for economic success."

The comfortable limousine whisked them to a tall office building in the Orchard Road district. The chauffeur pulled into a reserved space in the parking garage and jumped out to assist his passengers. He then led them to an elevator, inserted a key, and saw them to the penthouse high above the city.

Hanna took Russell's hand as Mr. Gao escorted them into his spacious office. After seating them on a comfortable couch with a spectacular view of central Singapore, their host ordered tea.

Hanna saw the almost imperceptible tightness around his eyes, even though Gao's smile never wavered. *Ready for business,* she thought, something she understood. But she suspected the courtesies would be observed. It reminded her of the last few seconds before the rodeo bull rider is released from the chute.

A young lady entered with a silver tea service and poured tea into delicate china cups. She politely inquired about cream, sugar, and lemon, then left quickly. Hanna sipped the tea and found it excellent. Then she saw the glint in Mr. Gao's eyes and knew the moment had come.

"So, Ms. Flaherty. Does our business proposition interest you?"

Hanna slowly lowered her cup to its saucer, giving herself time to compose her thoughts. "My husband and I have discussed this at length."

The man nodded. "Very wise. And . . ."

"And we prayed about it." She saw him stiffen momentarily, then relax.

"I see."

"But, to answer your question, I accept your offer, provided I can develop the system back home."

Gao nodded. "Of course, that is already settled. How you execute the contract is up to you. I know your reputation. All I expect is results."

Hanna breathed a gentle sigh of relief but felt a hint of apprehension. Having agreed, she knew she had to deliver. She also knew the statistics on failed computer projects, not that it had ever happened to her.

Gao brought out a leather portfolio containing the contract and extracted a gold fountain pen from his pocket. "Shall we get the formalities over?" he asked. "The promised advance check is there in the side pocket. I'm sure you will find everything in order."

Hanna glanced at the check, her eyes widening at the number of zeros. "Quite in order," she replied as she wrote her signature with the heavy pen. "I expected 'check's in the mail,' to tell you the truth."

"And I believe in current accounts."

"I can see that." She slipped the check from its pocket and held it.

Gao took the portfolio, signed both copies of the contract and handed one to Hanna. "My information systems mangers tell me the functional overview we faxed you is complete. I've taken the liberty of scheduling a conference for you with them," he glanced at his watch, "starting about now. Please remain at ease. It will not take long. They will give you your detailed specifications. The rest is up to you. If you have any questions, my staff is available to you at any time."

Hanna smiled. "Thank you. I'm looking forward to working for you. As we say in Texas, 'preciate your business and aim to please."

He returned her grin. "And we are anxious to have our new shipping system up and running. This is a high-profile project, but I will try not to make a pest of myself. If I overstep, I suspect I will hear about it in ways impossible to misunderstand."

"I try to be polite to the one who pays me."

"Thank you." He stood and escorted Hanna and Russell to the door. "I'm afraid I have a pressing engagement. My secretary will escort you to the meeting. Afterwards my chauffeur will take you back to your hotel."

"Good-bye, Mr. Gao," Hanna said.

"Good-bye to you both." He shook both their hands as his secretary opened the door and waited. "I hope you enjoy your stay in Singapore."

* * *

By the third day Hanna decided she had seen and done enough. She sat on a bench inside Haw Par Villa watching tourists of all nationalities stream past, gawking at the garish statues and Chinese mythology dioramas. She glanced at Russell and saw that his usual smile had been replaced by a pensive look.

"So what do you think?" Hanna asked.

"This is one strange place."

"Haw Par Villa or Singapore?"

He laughed, but she could tell there was no joy in it. "Both, but especially this place. The Haw brothers made a fortune on Tiger Balm ointment, then built this monument to—I don't know what."

Hanna remembered the sign directing visitors to The Ten Courts of Hell, an attraction she and Russell had decided to skip. "I think it's safe to say it's not in honor of God, so it must be the other side."

"Right," he sighed. "The guy at the hotel called it 'Disneyland East.'"

"Eastern religions, perhaps."

"Yes." He stood and helped her up. They started walking toward the exit. "I did enjoy the Botanic Gardens," he continued. "Interesting the effect of the British on an Asian culture."

"I liked that too. The Brits *do* have their gardening down. Guess I really appreciate that because the Texas panhandle isn't noted for lush vegetation." She looked at Russell and squeezed his hand. "Not like where I live now."

"I'm glad you live where you live now."

She felt joy welling up in her heart. "Me too."

The red concrete walk rounded a corner revealing the pagoda exit. A bright red-and-white fence marched along one side of the path while fake stonework edged the other. They passed under the arch. Hanna glanced at the tiger over the lintel, then over at the statue of a fat bald man wearing an orange robe.

"Wonder what old Buddha's laughing about?" Russell asked.

Hanna sighed. "Probably about how easy it is to fool people."

"Unfortunately, I have to agree."

They took a taxi to the hotel. On the way back Hanna felt her mental gears changing. She was grateful for the new project. She saw the need for it and was confident she could deliver what Mr. Gao wanted—the prototype first, then the final product. And it was certainly her most lucrative work yet. A niggling thought tugged at the back of her mind, though. They didn't need this contract to survive. But . . .

"Russell?" she asked.

He turned. "Yes?"

"Do you think I did the right thing accepting this job?"

For a few moments he said nothing. "We discussed it; we prayed over it. I don't know what else we could have done."

"I know, but . . ."

"Cold feet?"

"I want to do it. It's an interesting project. And the pay is great. Russell, this is the biggest contract I've ever had." She looked at him, trying to analyze his serious expression.

"Are you comfortable about it?" he asked.

"Yes." The word jumped out. Then she had to look down. "No, not entirely."

"Well, that makes two of us."

"What should I do?"

"We're supposed to keep our commitments."

Hanna frowned as the taxi sped along the clean, orderly roads leading into the city. "Yeah. I know."

ORDINARILY, A VISIT TO THE SPRAWLING MANUFACTURING plant in Kowloon pleased Zhu Tak-shing, since it was his undisputed kingdom, if such a term were proper in the People's Republic of China. But this time was different. He fumed inwardly as he donned white coveralls, cap, and shoe covers. Jiang Ling went through the same routine as the two men prepared to enter the vast clean-room fabrication building. Workers came and went around them, seemingly unaware of the distinguished visitor. Jiang finished tying the laces on his shoe covers, stood up, and looked through the long bay of plate-glass windows.

"So this is where we make the devices?" he asked.

Zhu wasn't sure how much his boss knew. "This is one of the manufacturing sites. But there are many others throughout the mainland and among our Pacific friends. Actually, chip making isn't our main task here. This is our largest assembly plant. Here is where we put the final product together—the devices and controls that depend on our special microchips."

"And the testing?"

Zhu nodded. "Yes. Right here." A rare smile came to his lips. "Electronic manufacturers have always had the smoke test—powering up devices to see if they catch fire. Here that has special meaning."

His boss looked at him quizzically. "Do these things actually burn?"

"No. As you know, some of the circuits smoke on activation, and this failure can damage other circuits. But most of the chips quietly destroy themselves."

"And then?"

"Then the device is junk. It can't be repaired because all the spare parts have the same defect. Once past the trigger date, the circuits never work again."

Jiang looked about the cavernous building with its long assembly lines tended by swarms of technicians clothed in white. "You are quite sure this will work?"

"I am. We won't destroy everything, but that's not necessary. Anything over 50 percent will shut the rest down, and we'll manage that easily. They don't stand a chance; I'm positive of that."

"This better work. A lot depends on it." Jiang paused and looked into the other man's eyes. "You had better . . ."

Zhu felt sweat pop up under the cap covering his hair. "What?"

"Nothing," the other said. "I'm sure everything will go as planned. I have complete confidence in you."

"Shall we start with the microchip manufacturing lines?"

"Yes. I've never seen how it's done."

Zhu led his boss out onto the factory floor. He took his time as he explained each processing step, showing each high-tech machine. At the end of the line, he held up a large disk of layered and etched silicon.

"This is the final product, just before we cut the silicon into individual chips and mount them in cases."

Jiang peered closely at the tiny rectangular patches. "And this is what does it?"

Zhu nodded. "Yes. Each chip has date input. Once the trigger date is reached, it fails and never works again. It can't be repaired, and all the spares have the same defect. Without a functioning embedded circuit, the control itself won't function—period. It's back to the Stone Age."

"For them."

"Yes, for them. Our circuits have properly functioning chips."

"Which are not available to our enemies."

"That is correct."

"Excellent. Then you would say we are ready?"

Zhu took a deep breath. "Yes."

"Good. Then perhaps you could spare some of your valuable time to make a trip to Beijing."

Zhu tried to look surprised. "Now? Project Dragon is less than two months away."

"But you said everything is on schedule. Surely now would be a good time for a visit to the north." His right hand darted inside his coat. "I really must insist." He shook his head in mock sorrow. "I admire your brilliance, Zhu, but you really should watch your tongue. Our leaders are serious about receiving the respect they are due. After all, where would China be without them?"

"It seems you have the best of me."

"I believe I do. Please do not make a scene. It will only make things worse. Now come with me."

Zhu slipped a hand inside his lab coat pocket and pressed a button. All the sodium vapor lamps clicked off, leaving the factory floor in almost total darkness. The feeble glow from the emergency lighting at the exits was no match for blackness in the vast building. Zhu dropped down and lunged into Jiang. His boss gasped as he started to fall. A brilliant flash briefly illuminated both men. Zhu winced as the deafening blast caused his ears to ring. He sprinted away, hoping he could remember where the obstacles were. Twice more the gun went off, blind shots of desperation.

Zhu caromed off something and almost fell. He regained his balance and started out again, taking his direction from memory and one particular emergency light. If he could only reach it before . . .

"Turn on the lights!" someone screamed behind him.

Zhu felt a lightning bolt of fear race down his spine. He knew it was going to be close. He approached the light and felt around with his foot. He heard someone fumbling around nearby. It had to be the electrical distribution box. He had only moments.

His foot hit the handle. He dropped to his knees, expecting the light to expose him at any moment. He pulled up on the handle and felt around inside. Yes, there was the first rung. He turned and started down, hoping he wouldn't slip. He slowed as he neared floor level, gently lowering the cover knowing any sound would give him away. He winced at the abrupt light that lanced through the tiny crack. He lowered the cover the rest of the way.

Zhu paused a moment, half expecting a shout of discovery. There were plenty of shouts but nothing near. Soon enough someone would find this access shaft. He felt around until his hand closed on the heavy flashlight he had stowed on the concrete ledge. He pressed the button and panned the beam around, then down. For the first time he noticed the stench. He started down the ladder, coming ever closer to the black surface of the water. When he got close, he saw it was flowing sluggishly. He paused at the bottom, then jumped down.

The sewage came up to his waist. His skin crawled at the thought of the bacterial hothouse enveloping his body, seeking any opening to lay him low. He shuddered violently and almost dropped the light.

He shuffled off in what he hoped was the right direction. The gooey sediment sucked his shoe covers off, then tried to take his shoes as well. He leaned forward and tried to increase his pace, but it was like walking in molasses. Behind him he heard a muffled clang. He glanced back and saw a bright beam of light. They were coming down the shaft.

Zhu aimed the flashlight forward. Somewhere up ahead was his goal, a manhole leading to the surface, but he couldn't see it. The putrid stream flowed around him in the direction he had to go. He heard voices and the ring of shoes on metal rungs.

Zhu lunged forward, half diving into the raw sewage. The flashlight spun from his grasp and fell to the bottom. He looked down at the murky glow and thought about fishing for it. A muffled shout behind him ended that. He pulled himself through the water with powerful strokes, rolling his head to the side in a vain attempt to keep the vile stream out of his mouth. He coughed. The fear that drove him forward was the only thing that kept him from vomiting.

A powerful light illuminated the surrounding brickwork. The gunshot, when it came, was deafening in the confined space. Zhu saw the splash of the slug just ahead. Knowing the next one probably would not miss, he plunged beneath the surface and swam as hard as he could. He bounced off the bottom and scraped off some unseen obstruction. His lungs burned as he longed for a breath, even of the fetid air above his head. When he could stand it no longer, he thrust upward and into the air, gasping for breath. He heard three more shots, but only one came close. Again he dove down and thrashed toward his unseen objective.

Moments later his right hand plowed into something hard and unyielding. He stood up and felt with his other hand. It was a brick wall perpendicular to his path; he had reached the main sewer. He dared to hope as he groped around. He knew there was a manhole near this juncture, but his escape plan had assumed a flashlight and ample time to find the exit. He looked up. The barest glimmer of light shone from above.

His hand closed over a rough iron rung. He glanced toward the direction of the factory as he started up. A distant light bobbed and swayed as whoever carried it struggled to make it down the stream.

Zhu hurried up the ladder until he was directly under the cast-iron cover. Hoping no one was coming, he levered the heavy slab upward. It rolled away with a clatter. Zhu stepped out quickly and looked about. Street vendors and pedestrians looked his way for a few moments, then returned to their business. Zhu broke into a run, his shoes making loud squishing noises. He turned right at the first corner and continued his flight. His lungs burned, and his feet chaffed as his wet socks wadded up.

Zhu barely heard the shout over his labored breathing. He staggered to a stop and looked back, hoping it was not for him. The sight of two men in white coats buried that thought. One brandished a large automatic but was too far away to use it. But that wouldn't last.

Zhu struggled to keep down his rising panic. His eyes swept the nearby buildings, frantic for a place to hide. Twenty feet away he saw a small restaurant. He ran between two street vendors, knocking over a rickety table, scattering ivory carvings over the dusty street. The elderly proprietor wailed as the fugitive dashed past.

Zhu slammed open the restaurant's battered door, breaking the large glass pane. Patrons looked up, their chopsticks motionless over their bowls. In the back a cook scowled over the serving counter, a large knife resting on a duck carcass. Zhu burst through the swinging doors at the back without slowing down, knocking a waiter sprawling, covering him with the dishes on his tray. Zhu hit the greasy floor and almost fell. Behind him he heard racing footsteps followed by a shout.

Zhu slid to a stop and looked around. He spotted the back door and ran to it. Zhu twisted the knob and pushed but cursed when he found it locked. He heard a scream and the sound of something hitting the floor hard. A quick glance revealed one of his pursuers piled up under a table, his partner coming through the door with pistol drawn. Zhu hit the door with more strength than he thought he had. The flimsy wooden frame exploded into splinters.

He dashed out into the alley and looked around. Mounds of garbage all but blocked the narrow path back to the street. Zhu bolted for the open, thankful for his endurance. Down the alley he ran, dodging and hurdling the moldering refuse. A shot rang out as he neared the street. Brick dust from a nearby wall peppered him.

A door opened on his right. A startled man blinked at the sprinter. Zhu hesitated a moment, then ran up and shouldered the man aside. He stopped inside, whirled round, and yanked the heavy door shut. The latch engaged with a satisfying thud. Zhu felt momentary panic. He couldn't see a thing. Then he heard amplified voices followed by music. He was in a movie house. The door rattled. A moment later four muffled blasts sounded, causing a small circle of light to appear where one slug went all the way through the door.

Zhu turned and ran into the theater below the screen. He tripped on a step and fell sprawling in the aisle. Behind him he heard the rear door crash open. He scrambled upward on all fours, still unable to see anything except the splashes of color on the screen. Hearing scrambling footsteps closing in, he turned left into a row of seats. He crawled toward the other side as fast as he could, hoping he wouldn't run into anyone. Partway across he plowed into something. A woman screamed and jumped up.

Zhu leapt past, caromed off another dark shadow, and rolled into the far aisle. He heard his pursuers start across behind him. He could see dim shapes now. He glanced back and saw the rushing shadows were midway across the seating section.

Staying low, Zhu scurried up the aisle toward the front of the theater. A gun roared. The slug tore into the carpet close enough to feel. Zhu jumped up and raced for the front. Two more shots hit just behind him.

He dodged to the left and ran toward what he hoped would be the way out. Instead he found narrow stairs leading up. Having no choice, he took the steps three at a time, made a turn, and continued to the top. There he ran into a heavy door with no other exit. His breath came in ragged gasps as he pounded on the cold steel. Rapid footsteps sounded behind him.

The door opened a crack. Zhu yanked it open and ran inside, slamming it behind him.

The projectionist backed away. "What's going on?" he demanded.

"A gang's after me!" Zhu gasped. "Gambling debt! They're trying to kill me! Is there a way out of here?"

"Go away! I'm not involved!"

Zhu reached out and shook him. "Help me!"

The man pointed to a door in the corner.

Zhu ran over and opened it. Frantic pounding sounded on the door behind him. The projectionist cowered behind the projector.

Zhu jumped outside and shut the door as the first pistol shot rang out. He looked down the rickety ladder at the street two stories below, knowing he would never make it. Turning, he saw crude wooden steps leading up to the roof. That he could make, and it was the obvious choice. He rushed upward to the top, hunched over the parapet, and grabbed his still soggy coat. He squeezed hard, directing the filthy stream down the side of the building. Then he backed down until he stood on the wooden platform again. An abrupt crash told him his pursuers were now inside the projection booth.

Zhu slipped under the crude railing, gripped the deck, and swung underneath. There, as he had hoped, were the braces holding the structure up. He grabbed one and slid down it until he was against the side of the building. The door above his head banged open. Footsteps clattered about for a moment, then stopped. Zhu half expected to see a face peer around the platform edge, a sure death sentence if it happened.

"Look up on the wall!" one of the men shouted.

The sounds shuffled over to the side of the building. The platform creaked, and Zhu heard scrabbling sounds that diminished, then quit. He waited a few moments, then pulled himself up the brace, and peered upward past the platform edge. He heard distant shouts but saw no one.

Zhu pulled himself up, then raced down the ladder, hoping the noises from the roof masked his own. He reached the street and ran as hard as he could for the corner, expecting to feel a bullet in his back at any moment.

He turned right at the intersection and kept going. After two more blocks he allowed his pace to slow. He stopped a moment outside a restaurant and looked back. There were no signs of pursuit, but he knew that could change at any moment. He started off again with one thought: a phone call to Huo's pager.

9

PAUL GLANCED UP AT THE REARVIEW MIRROR. "SO, HOW was the trip?" he asked as he guided his Firebird away from Sea-Tac.

Hanna felt Russell's comforting hand around hers, but her vague feeling of unease had not gone away. "Singapore is an interesting place. Clean and modern, but . . ."

"Ruled by a heavy hand?" Paul suggested.

"Yes. And I found the British influence fascinating." She laughed. "It's so weird to hear a Chinese man speaking with a clipped English accent when you're expecting Charlie Chan at best."

"You see the same thing in Hong Kong. The former colonies are heavily influenced by their British heritage. Colonialism brought a lot of problems, but not all the effects were evil, despite what the PC people say."

"Americans have first-hand experience with that," Russell said.

"That we do," Paul agreed. "If I'm not being too nosy, did you take the contract?"

Hanna found, to her surprise, she did want to talk about it. "Yes, I did. But afterwards Russell and I felt uneasy about it."

"Oh? Why?"

"I don't know." A nervous laugh escaped. "We had words about it when I first got the offer."

"A fight? You two?"

"Not a fight, Paul. We don't have fights."

"A robust discussion," Russell interjected.

Hanna flashed her husband a hot look. "OK, it was a fight. I admit I *really* wanted the job. But we worked through it, and then the circumstances changed."

"I'm sure you prayed about it."

Hanna felt heat rising in her face. "Uh, not at first. But we did later. We finally decided to look into it, especially after Mr. Gao said he'd pay the way over for both of us—sort of like a vacation."

"I think you said the company was Singapore Shipping, Limited?"

"Yes. You familiar with them?"

"Heard of 'em. I know someone who could fill me in. What kind of system are you doing?"

"Complete shipping management system."

"Don't those things already exist?"

"That's what I told him. But he wants something tailored to their way of business rather than conforming to off-the-shelf software."

"His choice, I guess."

"Yep. He's signing the checks." Hanna's uneasiness drifted on to another concern. "Speaking of things cybernetic, how goes your research? Anything new?"

"A lot has happened, but no breakthroughs. Did I tell you about my CIA visitor?"

"No."

"Victor Yardel, CIA Directorate, came to see me. He's concerned, but I gather that our Langley folks are finding it hard to believe that the Chinese would attempt cyber terrorism."

"Even after what *we* found?"

"Remember, that was never resolved to their satisfaction. Oh, and something else."

"What's that?"

"Vic sent me a helper. Without asking."

"What's the new guy doing?"

"She. Her name's Rachael O'Connor."

"Irish?" Russell asked.

"Half. Her father is Irish Catholic, but her mother is Jewish. Rachael's a researcher, like me, and two shovels can dig up twice as much dirt as one. But so far we haven't found anything new."

Hanna sat up in the seat. "What's Rachael like?"

"What do you mean?"

"Let's have the details. For starters, is she single?"

"Ah, yes. She's single."

"And . . ."

"What else do you want to know?"

"This is like pulling teeth. What does she *look* like." She felt Russell start to squirm.

"That's kinda personal, don't you think?" he asked.

She turned and saw his obvious discomfort. "But this is important." She returned her gaze forward. "Paul, you don't mind, do you?"

He paused. "No, I guess not. You two are part of my church family. To start with, Rachael's about my height."

"That's nice. Go on."

"Brown eyes and red hair. I don't know how to describe her . . . figure."

"Take your best shot."

"Well, she's not like one of those skinny models."

"Good."

"And she's certainly not fat."

"Is she attractive?"

"You mean . . ."

"Yes, Paul. What do you think of her? As a woman."

He cleared his throat. "I don't know. I haven't known her that long."

"Do you find her pleasant?"

After a slight pause, "Yes."

Hanna settled back in the seat. "That's nice. Is she a Christian?"

"Yes, she is. We've talked about religion. I invited her to church on Sunday, and she accepted."

"Wonderful. I'll look forward to meeting her." Hanna waited for his reply, but he didn't.

* * *

Zhu looked back at the retreating Kowloon dock as the Star Ferry started on its journey to the island of Hong Kong. He had already called Huo's pager, so all he had to do was make it to the address on Bonham Strand. An army truck roared up to the terminal building behind him, and uniformed men spilled out, fanning out in all directions. Zhu felt an icy stab in the pit of his stomach. The noose was beginning to tighten. He watched for a few more moments, then started walking toward the Hong Kong side of the ferry.

Despite his appearance and smell, the other passengers ignored him, for which he was grateful. The squat vessel plowed through the wake of a departing freighter, then altered course again to avoid a large junk. Zhu squinted as he scanned the Star Ferry dock nestled between the Outlying Islands Ferry Pier and the Queen's Pier. He couldn't see any soldiers, but he knew that could change before the ferry pulled in. His stomach twisted into a painful knot as he watched the slowly approaching dock. Zhu shoved his way through the crowd as the ferry slid into its berth. The moment the dockhands opened the gates, Zhu dashed through.

He crossed Connaught Road, resisting the urge to run. Up ahead he saw a police car driving up a side street but without flashing lights. The driver seemed in no hurry. Zhu reached Des Voeux Road and stopped. To the right, several blocks ahead, an army truck crossed at Queen Victoria Street, and stopped, discharging armed soldiers, half going west on Des Voeux while the remainder began a slow march toward Zhu. His destination was now blocked, and he had no doubt as to their prey.

He turned with a vague thought about trying to go around when he saw a westbound double-decker tram approaching. The red vehicle ground to a stop and discharged passengers. He watched as those boarding stepped aboard. Making his decision, Zhu ran for the tram as it started forward, jumping up on the bottom step. He paid the fare and took the stairs to the upper deck. He walked to the rear and slid into a seat.

They crept ever closer to the troops. At the next stop Zhu sank lower in his seat as he peered over the sill at the soldiers less than twenty feet away. For a moment it looked like they would let the tram pass on through. Then a soldier stepped into the street and approached. Zhu waited until he boarded, then got up and started down the rear stairs.

The streetcar lurched forward. Zhu held onto the rail and peered forward, his head barely above the upper-deck floor. As soon as he saw the soldier coming up the forward stairs, Zhu darted the rest of the way down. He looked toward the east. They were now beyond the other soldiers and nearing the next stop. Zhu could hear the heavy footsteps above his head even as the tram's brakes began squealing.

He jumped down before the vehicle stopped and ran along the side up to the front. He pushed his way through those waiting to board and cut across the street expecting to hear a cry of discovery behind him at any moment. He cut through a side street and hurried along a zigzag path until he came to Bonham Strand. Zhu continued on until it turned from East to West before paying attention to the addresses.

A series of narrow shops, most with open fronts, lined both sides of the street. Slowing down, Zhu passed a produce store and one that sold electrical appliances until he found the place Huo had told him about. He peered inside one of the bamboo cages stacked up outside. Inside was a coiled python, which raised its head and blinked at him.

Zhu entered the shop. The owner looked up and, after a brief hesitation, nodded toward the stairs at the back. Zhu hurried upwards, entered the small, second-story room, and closed the door. He looked toward a sudden sound in the corner. In the dim light Zhu saw the shadow move. His earlier fear returned, sweeping away his feeble hope.

"Huo?" he asked.

"Yes," came the reassuring reply.

"I didn't know if you would come."

"I said that I would."

"Yes, I know. But if they catch you helping me . . ."

Huo came out of the shadows. "I understand all that. But you're my friend. I'm not going to let you down."

Zhu felt a glimmer of hope, weak and tenuous. "What can you do?"

His friend hesitated. "I'm not sure. How bad is it?"

Zhu shivered. "Very. With what I know, they'll stop at nothing to catch me. I barely got past two army patrols, one in Kowloon and the other here. And I'm sure this is just the beginning. They'll seal off all transportation, and then they'll search until they find me. You know how they are."

"Yes, I do. So we don't have much time."

"What can we do?"

"First of all, hide you. Then we'll worry about getting you out."

"Do you have someplace I can hide?"

"Yes. After our last meeting I thought it best to prepare. I fixed up a hiding place in one of our warehouses."

"But . . ."

"It isn't perfect, but it should serve until I can come up with something better."

While they waited, Huo brought out a large steel basin for his friend to bathe in. Zhu stripped quickly, relieved finally to be rid of his filthy clothes. He took great care and scrubbed hard using the harsh soap provided. Huo bundled up the reeking heap and laid out a complete change of casual wear. Done at last, Zhu got out, dried quickly, and dressed.

The two men waited as day turned slowly into dusk and finally darkness. Despite Zhu's impatience, Huo insisted on caution. At eight o'clock the shop owner appeared with a tray of steaming bowls of rice and fish. After a quick meal Huo got up and checked the door.

"Come on," he whispered.

They descended to the first floor where a single candle provided a feeble light. Huo led the way to the steel roll door and peered out through the grimy side window. Zhu jumped as he heard a sound behind them. He turned to see the shop owner approaching. The man unlocked the door and pulled on a chain. The fugitives ducked under when the door reached halfway.

Zhu felt a chill that had nothing to do with air temperature. He imagined a soldier hidden in every shadow as the shop door made its noisy way back down. The solid click of the padlock sealed them off from this temporary refuge. *How likely was it they would make it to the next one,* Zhu wondered.

Nightlife was in full swing in Hong Kong's Central District, with tourists and Chinese crowding the major thoroughfares. Zhu followed his friend's twists and turns as they worked their way through the pedestrian maze, angling toward the waterfront, avoiding the major roads as best they could. The press of humanity offered little comfort. Every shadow seemed to hide a sinister presence, every sound suggesting ambush. Zhu waited for the command to halt, enforced by the sharp click of a safety going off, but it never came. Street by cautious street they felt their way along until they were one block away from the warehouse they had seen together—how long ago?

The huge building stood out in stark contrast to the black skies overhead. Garish neon lights topped the buildings all around them, advertising trademarks known the world around. The warehouse lacked those, the only lighting provided by irregularly spaced mercury vapor lights. Huo took a quick peek around the harbor side of the building and immediately pulled back.

"What's wrong?" Zhu whispered.

"Someone's outside. Looks like a guard. Let's go this way."

They hurried to the warehouse's city side where they came to a ladder leading up to the roof. Without a word Huo started up. Zhu winced at the sound of shoe leather on steel rungs. He spun his head about. Not a sign of the guard. He started up behind his friend, feeling very exposed until he reached the top and stepped onto the flat roof. Huo extracted a large key ring, unlocked the padlock, and pulled open the roof entrance door. Zhu followed him in. The door swung shut, plunging the tiny space into inky blackness. A few moments later a narrow beam of light clicked on, seeming brilliant after the darkness.

"What if they find the unlocked door?" Zhu asked.

"Pray that they don't. I'll take care of it later."

The other turned and led the way down the steep stairs until he opened a door and led them out on the catwalk high above the warehouse floor. Only a few security lights were on. The vast room was silent except for the hum of the ventilation fans.

"Come on," Huo whispered.

They hurried down to the floor and over to a door in a corner. The whining rumble of multiple air handlers assaulted their ears as Huo opened the door and led the way over to one of the huge units. He bent down, turned two latches, and lifted the large panel away.

"Climb in," he ordered.

Zhu peered into the dark interior and stepped over the sheet metal threshold. Huo followed him in and flicked on a switch. A bare bulb came on, providing enough light for him to lift the panel back into place. It settled down with a solid thump. Huo turned the latches, locking them in.

Zhu turned slowly about. A cot lay alongside one of the steel walls, while a chemical toilet faced him in the opposite corner.

"Dried food," Huo said, pointing to some stacked boxes. "And bottled water."

"Where are we?" Zhu asked.

"Inside an old air handler. We upgraded the ventilation fans a few years ago. When we did, we no longer needed this unit. We scrapped the hardware but left the housing where it was. All I had to do was clean it up and bring in the supplies, cot, and toilet. The electricians never disconnected the power, so I didn't have to worry about that. All I had to do was install a light fixture."

"You did this? Just in case?"

Huo nodded. "Sounded like you might need it."

Zhu began to feel a glimmer of hope. "Glad you did. No one knows about this?"

"Oh, I'm sure some of our people know there's no air handler in here, but I did all this in secret. There's no reason why anyone should come looking in here."

Zhu nodded. "Thank you. This might work." He paused. "But what do we do now?"

Huo exhaled loudly. "I don't know. But let me ask you this. If you had an opportunity to escape to the United States, would you take it?"

Zhu felt a momentary twinge of distaste, more from indoctrination and his former job rather than reason. But who *was* his enemy? He wasn't running for his life because of anything the Yankee imperialists had done. He was fleeing from his own government. "Why do you ask?"

"I can't go into details, but I know someone who might be able to help."

"An American?"

"Yes."

"What would they want?"

"Probably what you know about Project Dragon."

"I shouldn't have told you about that."

"You didn't say much. You implied it was similar to the Y2K bug incident. You said it was very bad, that you weren't in agreement about our government doing it."

Zhu sighed. "Yes, I did."

"Sounds like perfect grounds for political asylum. I'm sure the American would give you a new identity and make it worth your while."

"Are you working for them?" Zhu saw his friend's hesitation.

"No, not anymore. But I have this friend, an American. I think he'd be willing to help."

Zhu's expression changed to a sneer. "For a price, you mean."

"I'm sure their government wants to prevent this. You, yourself, said this was an idiotic plan. Look what it will do to China."

"Yes, you are right. This is crazy." His face twisted into a sarcastic grimace. "But then I do not possess the forward-thinking wisdom of our great leaders. Perhaps *that* is the problem." He watched Huo's face, appreciating the concern he saw there—that and his loyal friendship over the years. If there was anyone he could trust . . . "Would you contact the American for me?"

"You are sure?"

Zhu nodded. "Yes. Please do it now. Believe me. Our government will stop at nothing. They'll kill me the first chance they get."

Huo glanced at his watch. "It's nearly seven in the morning in Seattle. I'll call as soon as I leave here."

"No, don't call. They might be monitoring the phone lines. Don't you have some other way?"

After a long pause, "Yes, I do. Leave it to me."

* * *

Paul jumped as the doorbell wave file played on his computer speakers. He clicked on the volume control icon and moved the pointer down a little. He hadn't decided yet whether he liked having this particular announcement for incoming E-mails, but he had to do something to help him remember to check his in box.

"Well, let's see what the postman left me," he grumbled.

He picked up his Blue Water Yachts mug and took a sip. He yawned as he set the coffee down, making him wonder if he was developing a resistance to caffeine. He grabbed the mouse and clicked on the Outlook icon. His eyes widened when the saw the sender was Huo Chee Yong.

Then Paul spotted the paper-clip icon. "With an attachment, no less. This must be serious."

He opened the E-mail and scanned it. Nothing remarkable there. It was a straightforward solicitation for business from Victoria Shipping, Limited. He received many of these in the course of a year, since Blue Water Yachts imported many of its supplies from Hong Kong. And they had used Victoria Shipping in the past, which is how he had met the man. But Paul knew from experience that the real message was in the attachment. The attachment extension identified it as a graphics file, and he knew it would display as such. But he also knew there was other information inside, double encrypted and nearly impossible to decipher.

Paul double-clicked on the file and waited while the Paint program loaded the attachment. He grinned as he wondered what the Wizards of Redmond would make of *this* version of their cybernetic Etch-a-Sketch. That it was highly modified was an understatement. Paul held down the Ctrl, Alt, and numeric Home keys, entered two different passwords, and hit Enter. The picture of a modern warehouse appeared. Paul pressed the Escape key, and a page of text replaced the graphic. He felt his mouth grow dry as he read the message.

> Paul,
>
> The director of Project Dragon asked me to contact you. The authorities are trying to arrest him for reasons I can't go into. Can you arrange political asylum for him?
> Without going into detail, I believe he has information vital to the security of your country.
> You can contact me in the usual way, but please hurry. The authorities will stop at nothing to prevent his escape. At present you are the only hope we have.
>
> Huo

Paul closed the program. This was hot. But how fast would Langley move? He felt a sudden chill. Or *would* they move? He remembered an earlier incident where the federal government's reaction time had been less than sterling. Where normal organizations used stopwatches to time events, he suspected Foggie Bottom preferred calendars, if they used anything at all. *That's enough grumping,* he thought to himself.

He jumped at the sudden rap on his office door. He looked around and saw Rachael enter, toting a laptop and a mischievous grin.

"My, what a sour expression," she observed. "Someone mess up on one of your boats—yachts?"

He felt that jolt of interest that had so surprised him the first time he experienced it. His frown turned into a smile as his eyes followed her every move. She placed her computer on the corner of his desk and scooted a chair closer. Those eyes. So full of life—and mischief. Then his mind drifted back to the E-mail, and his smile faded.

"Is something really wrong?" she asked as she sat down.

"That's hard to say. I just found out that the director of Project Dragon wants political asylum."

She looked startled. "That's great!"

"Maybe, but it's also dangerous, for this guy *and* my friend. Apparently the People's Republic of China considers this a case of high treason. My friend says they'll stop at nothing to eliminate the guy."

Her expression grew serious. "That means your friend is in danger as well, right?"

"Yep. We call it 'aiding and abetting.' I have no idea what Mao's acolytes call it, but I'm sure it doesn't put you in line for the keys to the Forbidden City. Last time I checked, Beijing didn't have a Human Rights R Us franchise."

"We're not supposed to meddle in politics." She said it with that smile he found hard to resist.

"*You're* not, but I think a part-timer has a little more leeway."

"Vic might see it differently." The smile faded. "Seriously, what are you going to do?"

"Contact Vic; see if he'll get the ball rolling on political asylum for this guy."

"Vic will want some confirmation. You know the drill: Is the source reliable? What happens if something goes wrong?—that sort of thing."

"The source is reliable," Paul snapped. "This is real, and it's the best chance of finding out where Project Dragon is going to strike. And if Washington stumbles around, we'll lose everything. And my friend will lose his life." He stopped when he saw the hurt look in her eyes. Guilt replaced his earlier anger. "I'm sorry, Rachael. I'm not mad at you. And I have no doubt you're right." He paused. "You're a remarkable woman, and I'm enjoying working with you." He grinned. "I'm glad Vic sent you."

"You weren't at first."

"Forgive me for that. It was a surprise, I admit. But I think we make a good team."

"Even if I am a klutz?"

"You're *not* a klutz." His eyes drifted over to the laptop. "Uh, they fixed your computer?"

"Nope, this is new. Wasn't economical to repair the one I dropped. They were able to copy over my files though. Thank goodness for small blessings. Now I think we were talking about my graceful ways?"

"Rachael. That could happen to anyone."

"I believe you said that when it happened."

"And I haven't changed my mind." He looked into her eyes, wondering how serious she was. "I mean it. You're too hard on yourself."

She cast her eyes down.

"I, um . . ." He started but couldn't finish.

Her eyes came back up. "What?"

"I enjoy being around you," he finally managed to stammer.

He watched for her reaction, wondering if he'd said the wrong thing. There were emotions there, but he couldn't decide what they meant. That, and he wasn't sure he was within the rules, as he understood them.

"Thank you, Paul," she said finally. "I enjoy your company as well. I guess we do make a good team, at that."

A sensation of joy welled up, surprising him. Then he thought about what he had to do, and his grin faded. "And this team member has something to do."

She started to get up. "I'll go down and get me some coffee."

"No, please stay. I want your opinion when I'm done."

"OK." She settled back down.

Paul placed the call. The conversation went almost exactly as Rachael had predicted, not that he was surprised. He replaced the handset with a sigh.

"It's almost like you wrote his script," Paul said. "Said he'd check into it, but I doubt he'll move very fast. He sounded awfully cautious to me."

"What's he want you to do?"

"E-mail my source and tell him the feds are working on it. Vic wants me to suggest that additional information might grease the wheels a little."

"You going to do that?"

Paul snorted. "I'll relay what Vic said, but I'll also recommend he play it close until I can give him some better assurances."

She nodded. "I think that's the right thing to do."

"You're siding with me?"

She smiled. "Hey, we're teammates, right?"

10

LATE THE NEXT DAY HUO MADE HIS WAY THROUGH THE crowded Hong Kong streets from his office at Victoria Shipping to the large warehouse near the harbor. He couldn't help noticing the large number of regular Chinese troops in the streets, each with a slung rifle. The intensity of the investigation surprised him. Even though he had expected this reaction, Hong Kong's history of relative freedom had lulled him away from the present reality. Now he was glad he had taken the time that morning to lock the warehouse's roof entrance.

Sudden movement up ahead caught his eyes. Huo craned his neck and saw an army squad searching a delivery truck. His blood ran cold as he watched the driver standing docilely on the sidewalk. Huo tried not to stare as he hurried past. Heavy boxes and crates crashed to the pavement as the soldiers rushed through their work.

Huo had not been to Chek Lap Kok airport, but he knew what he would find there. That would offer no way out, even with proper papers, which Zhu did not have. No, Hong Kong Island was sealed tight, with all entrances and exits governed by the People's Republic of China. Huo felt a wave of anxiety wash over him. Surely there had to be a way out.

He turned the corner and started up the street the warehouse fronted on. His heart skipped a beat as he saw a soldier jogging toward him, his rifle at the ready. It took every ounce of self-control not to turn and run. Huo continued on as the soldier approached. At any moment he expected the man to halt and hold him at gunpoint. But the soldier continued past without slowing down.

Huo breathed a sigh of relief as he hurried up the steps and entered the warehouse. He paused inside to make sure operations were completely normal. He knew at once that they were. The forklift operators roared across the concrete floor with their bulky pallets, loading cargo containers. Huo knew from the organized chaos that nothing was disturbing today's schedule. He sauntered across the floor, angling toward the equipment room in the corner. Once inside, he checked carefully to make sure he was alone. Only then did he approach the abandoned air handler.

"It's me," he whispered as he bent down to release the latches.

He heard no reply as he lifted away the panel. The dim light behind him revealed Zhu standing in a corner. Huo stepped in and replaced the panel. Only then did he flick the light on.

"Have you heard from your friend?" Zhu asked.

"Yes," Huo replied. "He says the request has been passed on to the CIA."

"Good. When will we hear something?"

"He said he would keep me informed. He warned me it could take a while."

"That's not good enough! They have to act now!"

"I understand, and so does my friend. He's doing everything he can, but these decisions are made at a higher level." Huo paused. "He asked if you could tell them anything about Project Dragon."

"I'll tell them everything—once I'm safe in the United States. But *nothing* until then. Make sure he understands that. And if they don't hurry, the only thing they'll get is their economy in smoking ruins."

"I will relay that, but my friend knows all this. Meanwhile, I think you are safe here for now." He hesitated. "And I am praying for your safety." Huo saw a complex expression come to his friend's face. It started out as irritation but slowly changed toward something softer.

"Thank you," Zhu said in a lower tone. "You saved my life."

Huo smiled. "You are welcome."

"And your concern for spiritual things is thoughtful. Misguided I think, but kind."

"We shall see."

"Yes. I only hope the Americans act before it's too late."

"I do too."

* * *

Hearing approaching footsteps, Paul glanced up and saw a familiar face glide past his office windows. Rachael smiled at him as she made straight for the door.

"Hi," she said. "I was on my way to the apartment, so I thought I'd drop by and see if anything new was happening."

He shook his head. "Haven't heard a thing from Vic or my contact. Didn't expect anything from Langley this soon, but I'm worried about my friend in Hong Kong. It's been almost a day."

Rachael pulled a chair up and sat down, placing her new laptop on Paul's desk with exaggerated care. "It's hard waiting, especially when you don't know what's going on. Maybe we'll hear something Monday."

"Hope so. But I plan to check my E-mail regularly this weekend. If the situation changes, I'll let Vic know."

"Good idea." Her look of concern changed to a smile. "I appreciate your inviting me to your church. I'm looking forward to Sunday."

Paul's throat tightened. "I am too. Say, Rachael. Some friends of mine, Russell and Hanna Flaherty, invited me—invited *us*—to their place tonight for hamburgers. I called your office right after I talked to Russell, but you'd already left. I mean, would you—I know it's short notice and all—but would you like to go? If you have something else planned . . ."

"Paul," she interrupted.

"Yes?"

"Do I get a chance to answer, or is this a monologue?"

"What?"

"Yes, I'd like to meet your friends."

"You would? Well, great." He glanced at his watch. "How 'bout I come by around six-thirty?"

"That will be fine." She pushed her chair back and reached for her laptop.

They both jumped when his computer speakers emitted a loud "bing-bong."

"What is *that?*" Rachael asked.

He grinned. "I have mail." He activated the Outlook window and felt a jolt of relief mingled with dread. "It's from Hong Kong." He opened the document and immediately double-clicked on the attached graphics file. After attending to the required security, the modified Paint program displayed the encrypted message. Paul scanned it quickly.

"What's it say?" Rachael asked.

"To hurry up. The defector's safe for now, but the government has things locked down tight. The guy won't tell us anything until he's safe. I don't blame him for that. Said we're toast without his help."

"He actually said that?"

"That's an accurate paraphrase. I'll relay this to Vic, but I doubt if it will make things go faster. Bureaucracies don't come equipped with accelerators."

"I can't argue that."

Paul tapped in a quick response, encrypted it, and sent it on its way to Hong Kong attached to an innocuous E-mail. Then he took his time composing an update for Victor. That done, he logged off the company network.

His anxious frown dissipated as he got up. "Walk you to your car?"

She smiled. "Thank you, Paul." She picked up her computer and, after a bit, offered it to him. "Carry my laptop?"

"Glad to."

"Thanks. Don't want to drop it."

* * *

Paul scratched his head as he stared into his closet. Dirty trousers and shirts made untidy heaps on the floor, not having made it to the cleaners yet. He grabbed a pair of tan Dockers, which had only been worn once before.

"Now, where's my brown belt?" he grumbled, pulling on the pants while trying to maintain his balance. Looking about the room, he spotted it draped across a chair in the corner. He grabbed it and threaded the belt loops. Rejecting his favorite blue shirt on suspicion of clash rather than certainty, he narrowed his choices to one with tan stripes and a solid off-white. He selected the cream-colored shirt, undid the cuff buttons, and slipped it on.

A glance at his watch told him he was running late. He tucked in his shirttail and hunted frantically for his tan loafers. Spotting them, he slipped his feet into them and headed for the bathroom without slowing down. He eyed his face, decided he could skip the shave and dabbed on an ample portion of Old Spice and patted it around. Rushing out, he grabbed his wallet and keys and went out the door.

The drive to Bellevue was pleasant and quick and at a speed reasonably congruent with the speed limit, at least as interpreted by the other drivers. He pulled up to the apartment complex only a few minutes late, but this still bothered his punctual nature. He jumped out of the car and rushed up the exterior stairs to the second floor, only slowing when he came to Rachael's door. He waited a few moments until he could catch his breath. Then he rang the doorbell.

For a few moments there was silence. Then he heard the sound of footsteps approaching. The lock clicked, and the door swung open. Although it was a cool day, it suddenly seemed warm as he saw Rachael smiling at him. It was more than he could take in at once. A jade-green blouse accentuated her dark red hair. Dangling silver earrings and a simple silver pendant were her only jewelry. Her jeans appeared new and seemed to fit her outgoing nature as well as her form. A whiff of her perfume completed the effect.

He cleared his throat. "Rachael, you look wonderful." He looked her over again and decided this was an entirely truthful statement. For a moment Paul thought his heart had slipped its timing, but the heat rising in his face assured him it hadn't.

She seemed pleased. "Thank you."

"Well, ah, ready to go?"

"Yes. Come in while I get my things." He followed her inside and waited as she disappeared into the bedroom. A few moments later she returned carrying a multicolored cardigan and her purse. They walked outside, and Paul closed the door. Rachael unzipped her purse and fished around inside. After several false tries she found her keys and pulled them out only to lose her grip partway to the door.

"Oops."

The keys hit the concrete deck with a clatter. Paul turned and bent down to retrieve them. Rachael stooped at the same time, and their heads collided with a solid thump. A stab of pain shot through Paul's skull as he stood back up, struggling to maintain his balance.

"Oh," Rachael moaned as she held her head.

"I'm sorry," Paul said. "Are you all right?"

She nodded as she dropped her hands. "My fault for dropping the keys. I am *such* a klutz!"

Paul knew she meant it, which bothered him. "No you're not. These things happen."

Her expression wavered between a scowl and an embarrassed grin. "If you say so."

He grinned. "I do. Shall we go?"

She nodded and returned his smile. "Stay where you are. I'm going to pick up my keys, so no sudden moves."

He laughed. "Wouldn't think of it."

She managed to hold onto the keys and lock the door. Paul watched her eyes as she turned back to him. After a moment's hesitation he held out his hand. She slipped her hand into his and walked with him to his Firebird. He held the door while she got in.

Paul found it hard to concentrate on his driving on the trip south from Bellevue. The weather was gorgeous for a change, with not a hint of rain in the forecast. But the weather wasn't the distraction; it was the person sitting beside him. They exchanged small talk as he negotiated the crowded highways to their destination.

"Nearly there," Paul said as he turned onto the exit ramp.

"Nice area."

"Yeah. This part is mostly apartments. Quite nice, but Russell and Hanna want to buy a house soon—especially Hanna. She's from West Texas, so she's used to the wide-open spaces."

"Oh?"

"If you ask her, she'll tell you all about it."

"I may do that. I'm looking forward to meeting the one who found that Y2K thing."

Paul pulled into the parking lot and drove into a visitor's slot. He jumped out, came around, and opened Rachael's door. He took her hand and helped her out. They walked hand-in-hand to the Flaherty's apartment and rang the bell.

Paul heard the squeaking of shoes on the entryway tile. The lock clicked, and the door flew open revealing Scott.

"Hi, Mr. Parker," he said, stepping back.

"Hello, Scott. I'd like you to meet Rachael O'Connor."

"Pleased to meet you, Miss O'Connor," Scott replied. After a moment he extended his hand.

She smiled and shook it. "I'm pleased to meet you, Scott."

He blushed. "Um . . ."

Paul could see the gears turning in the youngster's head. "What is it?"

The boy looked up at Paul. "Is this your girlfriend, Mr. Parker?"

"What?" Rachael said.

Paul felt the heat rising in his face and knew he was blushing.

"Howdy, Paul," Hanna said as she came in from the kitchen.

Scott looked up at Paul, then back at Rachael.

"Hi, Hanna," Paul hurried on. "Like you to meet Rachael O'Connor."

"Welcome to our home," Hanna said, shaking her hand. "Glad to meet you." She looked down at Scott. "I see you've met young Mr. Flaherty." She tousled his hair.

He smoothed it back in place.

"Yes, I have," Rachael said, a little stiffly.

"Did I miss something?" Hanna asked.

Paul tried a rather unsuccessful grin. "Perhaps we can go into the details later."

Hanna looked surprised and gave Scott a questioning look. He shrugged.

"Oh, OK," she said finally. "Come on in. Russell's out on the patio burning the burgers. I was working on the potato salad, chips, and drinks."

A horn honked outside. Hanna peered through the entryway window. "Mrs. McClusky's here, Scott. You ready to go?"

"Yeah." He ran back into the living room and returned with his back-pack. "See you guys later!" He made for the door as if on a marathon.

"Scott!" Hanna shouted.

He slid to a stop. "What?"

"Say good-bye to Paul and Ms. O'Connor."

"Oh, sorry." He turned to Paul. "Bye, Mr. Parker." Then he turned to Rachael. "Enjoyed meeting you, Miss O'Connor. Bye."

"Enjoyed meeting you, Scott. Hope I see you again."

"Oh, yeah. Well, OK. See you guys." And off he went.

The sliding-glass door rattled on its tracks. Russell came in with a large platter of hamburgers. "Chow's ready," he said as he disappeared into the kitchen. In a few moments he reappeared and headed for the entryway.

"Russell," Paul said. "This is Rachael O'Connor."

Russell smiled and shook her hand. "So nice to meet you. Welcome to Seattle."

"Thank you. Pleased to meet you, Russell."

He turned to Hanna. "Scott still here?"

"Nope. Fran picked him up a moment ago."

"Did he get to say hi?"

Paul tried to maintain his smile. "Oh, yes. He said hi."

"Good. Well, come on in. Food's ready—at least the meat is. Don't know how my able assistant is doing."

"Watch it, bub," Hanna said. She took a poke at him, but he neatly sidestepped it.

"Like I said, we're ready to eat."

Paul guided Rachael to the dining room table while Russell and Hanna finished bringing in the food. After they were all seated, Russell offered the blessing. Looking up, he started the platter of buns around while Hanna picked up the bowl of chips. Paul watched Rachael as she methodically prepared her hamburger. He looked down at his plate, noting the disorderly mound of lettuce, tomato, and patty. He shrugged, picked it up, and took a healthy bite.

Paul felt himself relaxing a little. The food took precedence over the conversation, but he couldn't help noting Hanna's interest in her guests. His mind drifted back to earlier conversations about life partners. He wondered what Rachael thought about all this. She looked up then and smiled at him. He stopped in mid-chew and grinned.

After desert Russell led the way into the living room. He and Hanna took side chairs. Seeing the intent, Paul guided Rachael to the couch. He sat down beside her, acutely aware of her presence.

"How are the vacation plans going?" Paul asked.

"They're beginning to shape up," Russell replied. "We have our reservations." He glanced at his wife. "We're about to continue the junior birdmen lessons that the Singapore trip interrupted."

"You and Scott making progress?"

"I'll let the resident aviatrix answer that."

Paul watched her deliver a silent but potent message toward Russell.

"They're coming right along." She looked toward Rachael. "I'm instructing Russell and Scott in hang gliding."

"You hang glide?" Rachael asked in surprise.

"Well, yes. It's a fun sport."

"Isn't it dangerous?"

Hanna sighed. "Not if you're careful. It's only flying, just with a lot less airplane." A glint came to her eyes. "Would you like to try it?"

"Ah, no. I don't think so."

"Hanna was hang gliding when she met Russell," Paul said.

"Really?"

"He's yanking on your leg," Hanna explained. "But, that is technically correct. I was hang gliding over Palo Duro Canyon when Russell called on my mobile phone. That's how I got involved in his Y2K project." She smiled at her husband. "And the rest, as they say, is history."

"Glad you decided to help us," Russell said, "for lots of reasons."

"Me too."

"One thing I've wondered," Rachael continued. "Paul told me the whole story, minus the hang-gliding part. How in the world did you find the booby trap in that circuit breaker?"

"It was a team effort—hard work and a lot of prayer."

Paul's mind flitted back to his latest E-mail from Hong Kong. "I've told Rachael about the unofficial advice you've given me concerning our newest problem," he smiled nervously. "It took a while for me to alibi the security aspect, but you *are* two of my sources. And I can't expect helpful answers if I don't tell you a little bit about what I'm working on. That's the way intelligence works."

Hanna smiled. "Sounds like you're still selling."

"It is a sticky problem," Rachael agreed. "Now that I've heard the whole story, I agree with Paul. I suspect our boss might have a problem with it, but then he's not on site right now."

Paul took a deep breath as he decided what he had to say. "Which brings us almost current. I got another E-mail today from my source in Hong Kong. The head guy on Project Dragon wants to defect, and he'll tell us all he knows if we grant him asylum."

"Did he say what the target is?" Hanna asked.

"No, and my friend made it clear we won't get anything until the guy's safe. And that's about all I can say."

"This is sounding more and more serious. What do you think will happen?"

Paul frowned. "My honest opinion is we'll fiddle around until it's too late. If the Chinese government finds the guy, he's history." He looked at Hanna. "Can you think of anything else we can do?"

"Without someone who knows, the only thing that might work is a nationwide investigation of vital computer systems. And that, of course, would require action by the federal government."

"So we're back to square one."

"Yep. Have you considered suggesting that to your boss?"

"Yes, and I probably will. But I don't expect a rapid response. And I get the feeling that whatever this thing is, it's going to strike soon."

"That's not very encouraging," Russell said.

"No, it's not." Paul shrugged. "But then we didn't think there was much hope with the Y2K bug either."

11

"THEY MAKE A NICE COUPLE," HANNA SAID AS RUSSELL closed the door. She peeked through the entryway window and watched as Paul and Rachael strolled hand-in-hand down the walk. "Don't you think?"

"I think some would call that being nosy."

She turned toward him. "I'm not being nosy. I'm interested. Don't you see it as romantic?"

He pulled her close. "I suppose that's up to them. But I know what *I* find romantic."

She saw that delightful twinkle in his eyes. "Oh? What's that?"

He pulled her into his embrace. She felt herself respond to him as he kissed her. Something like a spark seemed to leap across as their lips met. He pulled her even closer.

"That give you a clue?" he whispered, his voice husky.

"I think so," she said when she could catch her breath. "Explain it to me again."

"With pleasure."

Her pulse raced as he kissed her again. It was suddenly very warm, and when they broke, she had trouble catching her breath. She looked into his loving eyes, so happy that God had brought them together. She shivered in anticipation.

A questioning look came to his eyes. "Cold?"

She almost laughed. "Not on your life, pardner! Just wait til we get done with those dishes." She paused. "But that can wait, I suppose. I mean, if . . ."

"It's not *that* pressing."

She smiled sweetly. "You sure?"

"Get in there."

Russell flipped on the countertop radio as he entered the kitchen and started loading the dishwasher. Hanna spooned the leftover potato salad into a Tupperware bowl, put on the lid, and put it in the refrigerator. She vaguely heard the news come on at the top of the hour, but didn't really pay attention until she heard the announcer say "Hong Kong." She stopped and turned the sound up.

"At 11:00 A.M. Hong Kong time, government officials announced the sealing of all Chinese borders. The official statement cited the defection of an unnamed nuclear scientist. The new strictures were most apparent at Hong Kong's Chek Lap Kok airport where all departing passengers were subjected to extensive questioning. Airline officials warned travelers to expect long delays.

"More after this."

Hanna turned the volume back down. "What do you make of that?"

Russell filled the soap dispenser, closed the dishwasher, and turned it on. "Sounds like an excuse to lock down Hong Kong. It'll be a miracle if Paul's mystery man gets out of there alive."

Hanna frowned. "Yep. My thoughts exactly."

* * *

Paul sighed as he logged onto the Blue Water Yachts network. It had been a decidedly interesting weekend. He and Rachael had gone out to dinner on Saturday, and she had gone with him to church the next day. *That* he had enjoyed. But then there was the clampdown in Hong Kong; he knew what was behind that. He had checked E-mail several times, but there had been no answer from Huo.

The Outlook in box finally came up. Still nothing. He thought for a moment, then tapped in a quick message, enciphered it, and sent it on its way.

He picked up his coffee mug and went to his office windows. He took a thoughtful sip as he looked down on the construction building floor. Somehow the yacht hulls below seemed unimportant now. If Project Dragon were half as serious as he suspected, his company's line of business would soon be totally irrelevant.

Fifteen minutes later he heard chimes, announcing an incoming E-mail. He glanced at the in box. *That was quick,* he thought.

* * *

Hanna heaved a sigh of relief as she scanned her office. The five cantankerous UNIX computers were finally talking to one another without any sibling rivalry. She called it her IAN—itty-bitty area network, a mock-up of what she planned to install for Singapore Shipping, Limited. Now all she had to do was define the long list of Oracle database tables together with their keys and relationships. Only after this was done could she begin programming the client's user interface. A structured walk-through at Singapore Shipping's Seattle office would be her first milestone. Hanna had already assembled her prospective development team, but their work could not begin until the client signed off on the interface. She did not anticipate any problem with that.

She paused and looked out the window. Heavy rain clouds were rolling in from the west. It would be raining soon, she knew. Well, that matched her mood, she decided. As interesting as this project was, she had not been able to shake her negative feelings about it.

She jumped as the phone rang. She reached over and pressed the speakerphone button. "Roadrunner Consulting."

"Hi, this is Paul."

She brightened. "Hi, Paul. How was your weekend?"

He paused. "Anything particular you want to know?"

"Russell and I saw you with Rachael. Did she like our church?"

"Yes, she did."

"And . . ."

"And what?"

Hanna glared at the speaker. "Did you and Rachael have a nice time?"

"Ah, now we're getting down to it." He chuckled. "As a matter of fact, we did. I . . . I like her."

"Glad to hear that. Russell and I think you two make a nice couple."

"Well, I guess we'll see. But that's not why I called. I found out something you need to know."

"What's that?"

"I'm aware you're concerned about your new client. I asked my friend about Singapore Shipping—told him what you were working on."

"Oh? What did he say?"

"He's familiar with them, since they're in the same business. Doesn't know who owns them, but he did tell me one disturbing thing."

"What's that?"

"Singapore Shipping already has a computerized shipping system, strictly first-rate. He doesn't understand why they would be wanting a new one."

"Is he sure?"

"Yes. He's seen it himself."

She looked out the windows as the first large drops of rain began falling.

"Hanna? Are you there?"

"I'm here. What do you make of it?" She heard him sigh.

"I don't know. Since you and Russell are having second thoughts about the contract, I suggest you be careful." He paused. "I think you should at least consider the possibility this is tied in with Project Dragon."

"You mean to keep me busy so I can't help you?"

"Yep."

She frowned. "OK, I will. Anything else?"

"No, that's it. My friend didn't say anything about the potential defector. My guess is we won't hear anything until we can guarantee the guy asylum."

"Any news on that?"

"Nope. And I don't expect a breakthrough anytime soon."

"I hope that changes."

"So do I. Got to go now. Bye."

"Bye." She punched the button to terminate.

* * *

Paul looked around as he entered Rachael's office in the Federal Building. It wasn't the closet she claimed, but it wasn't very spacious either. And the furnishings probably hadn't been new in FDR's day.

"So this is where you hang out," he said.

"This is it. What do you think?"

"Not exactly a hole in the wall."

"Not much of a view."

He looked around. One thing he liked about his office was being able to look out on the construction floor, even if he couldn't see outside. "Guess windows would be too much to ask."

She shrugged. "This really isn't much different from my office at Langley, except my furniture there is a little newer." She smiled. "Please sit down, and I'll play the host for once. At least I do rate a guest chair."

She brought her desk chair around and placed it beside Paul's. He sat down. His eyes followed her as she joined him. He saw her look of concern.

"Anything new?" she asked.

He shook his head. "No, and unless somebody acts soon, Project Dragon is going to bring us down."

"And the defector will lose his life."

"Yes, and my friend as well, probably." He pounded his knee with his fist. "Sometimes I think no one in Washington is capable of making a decision."

"There's nothing we can do about that."

He took his time answering. "Maybe not."

"What do you mean? If Washington doesn't act, that's it."

He told her about David Ho's urgent request that Paul skipper his ketch back to Seattle for its shipyard overhaul.

"I hope you're not suggesting . . ." she began.

"I've thought a lot about this. We can't pass up this opportunity. I can get that defector out, *and* find out what Project Dragon is targeting. They won't be checking a rich man's yacht on its way to a shipyard."

"You don't know that."

"No, but they can't check everything. And believe me, Ho is well connected in Hong Kong circles. The Chinese government is careful about messing with the local big shots. All I have to do is get the defector aboard. Once we leave Chinese waters, we're home free."

The skepticism he saw in her eyes deflated his confidence.

"I doubt it will be that simple," she said. "And what about Vic? He'll have a cat if he finds out."

Paul struggled. "I plan to see he doesn't know about it until I'm back. Besides, all I'm doing is responding to my customer's request."

"Paul. You know that's not strictly true."

He tried a weak grin. "It mostly is."

"What does your boss at Blue Water Yachts think?"

"He was surprised at first. This is a little unusual, but I told him I'd always wanted to make a long cruise like this—which is true. I said I'd take part of the time as vacation." He saw her stiffen.

"You didn't tell him about the defector, did you?"

"Of course not. We'll take care of that little detail after I get back."

"Have you thought about how you're going to square this with Vic?"

"That I'm not sure. I'm hoping he'll arrange asylum so we can find out what the Chinese are into." He grinned. "By then, all the heavy lifting is done."

She put her hand on his arm. "I don't suppose I can talk you out of this." She said it almost in a whisper.

Paul felt his throat tighten. "This is something I have to do."

She nodded and looked down. "Please be careful. I don't want anything to happen to you."

"I'll be careful." He thought her eyes looked teary, but he wasn't sure. "I sent Vic an E-mail telling him I'll be on vacation. Think you can keep him from getting any wiser?"

"I'll try. Does your friend know you're coming?"

"I hope so. I E-mailed him with the bare details so he can plan accordingly. Haven't got a reply yet."

"You think things have blown up?"

"Don't think so. We would have heard something. The news reports are still yammering about the intense security in Hong Kong."

"So when are you leaving?"

"Tomorrow. I've got a nine o'clock flight to San Francisco. I leave there a little after 1:00 P.M. and get into Hong Kong at six-forty in the evening, the next day."

"International date line."

"Yep. Lose a day." He grinned. "But I get it back on the return."

She squeezed his arm. "Just be sure you get back."

Paul gulped. "I will."

* * *

Paul's troubling phone call echoed through Hanna's head as she guided her Explorer into a visitor's slot outside a new two-story office building that seemed to be made entirely of silvered glass. The incessant patter of the steady rain intruded as soon as she turned off the engine. She reached into the backseat and grabbed a large burnt-orange golf umbrella. She had given up on what Russell called "lady umbrellas" and had adopted his weapon of choice. Many asked about the unusual color, only to be informed that it was the only possibility for a University of Texas graduate.

She grabbed Victoria Regina and opened the door. A gust of wind blew spray inside the car as Hanna struggled to thrust the unwieldy umbrella through the crack and open it. Finally she stepped out and shut the door. She hurried across the parking lot, trying to avoid the deeper puddles. Once inside she closed the umbrella and approached a guard safely barricaded inside his kiosk. He consulted a directory and informed her that Singapore Shipping occupied suite 201. Hanna thanked him and took the wide, central staircase to the second floor. After a mental flip of the coin, she turned left and walked to the end of the corridor. There a bright gilt panel proclaimed "Singapore Shipping, Ltd.," with 201 underneath. After a moment's hesitation, she opened the door and went in.

A young lady looked up from the reception desk. "May I help you?" she asked.

"Yes, I'm Hanna Flaherty with Roadrunner Consulting. I have an appointment with Lau Jianguo."

The receptionist put through the call. A few minutes later a medium-height man came toward them.

"Ah, Ms. Flaherty," he said in heavily accented English. "So nice to meet you. I am Lau Jianguo." He glanced at the receptionist. "Is the conference room available?"

"Yes, Mr. Lau."

"Good. We will meet in there."

He led Hanna down the hall and opened the door for her. A massive table with attendant chairs dominated the room, taking up most of the floor space. A modest-sized white board hung on one wall, while a large teleconferencing set was placed in a corner.

"Thank you for coming out on such an unpleasant day," Lau said as he reached the head of the table below the white board.

"We have a lot of these," Hanna replied.

"So I am finding out." He sat down.

Hanna decided to take the chair at his left, putting the long row of windows at her back. "Your home is in Singapore?" she asked.

"No, Hong Kong."

"Oh. Well, when Mr. Gao E-mailed me about this meeting, I assumed you were from the home office."

The man smiled, but it seemed brittle. "Singapore Shipping has offices in most large ports. In fact, our Hong Kong office is the largest one we have. A lot more shipping goes through there."

"I see. Mr. Gao also said that all changes and approvals will come from you."

He nodded. "That is correct. We felt that would simplify the project."

"But don't you want your technical people to sit in?"

"Not necessary. I have a copy of the system specifications. Using that, I will review each milestone with you. Our specialists in Singapore will do their reviews as they install the components. With your reputation, we have no concerns about the final product."

Hanna thought this strange, but had decided long ago that the customer was always right, as long as he paid on time. "However you want to do it."

"Fine. Now how are you progressing?"

She gave a nervous laugh. "I just started. I've got the test UNIX network up and running finally."

He looked surprised. "Was that hard?"

"Irritating, more than anything else. Required a lot of tweaking."

"What is this 'tweaking'?"

She struggled not to smile. "Let's say you have to know where to give it a good poke."

His confused look did not go away. "I see. I take it everything is resolved to your satisfaction."

"Yes. Right now I'm working on the database tables and their relationships. After that I'll begin working on dummy versions of the user screens. Once you've approved the GUI—the graphical user interface—I'll bring in my development team to start cranking out all the subsystems."

"When do you think the, ah, GUI will be ready?"

Hanna thought for a moment. "Oh, in a week or so, I guess."

His eyebrows shot up. "That soon?"

"Well, yes. I don't mess around." She saw his look of confusion. "I work quickly."

"You obviously know what you are doing." He paused. "I hesitate to bring this up, but I have some changes for you."

"Changes? You mean you're *changing* the specification we agreed on?"

He held up his hands. "Yes, but there is no cause for concern. We will pay for every modification. But as Mr. Gao told you, we require a system tailored to our exact needs. While our original specifications were quite thorough, our information services people are requesting a few revisions."

Hanna struggled to bring her irritation under control. "Very well, what are they?"

He pushed a thick, bound document toward her. "Here is an updated system specification. All insertions and deletions are marked."

Hanna picked up the heavy book and flipped through it. Some data fields had been deleted and quite a few inserted. There were a few new screens, and some existing fields had migrated to different locations. Not too bad, she decided, but it would take a while to incorporate the modifications into the tables and revise the GUI accordingly. *And they* are *paying for it.*

"OK," she said finally. "I can handle this, but it will push back the approval of the GUI and the start of the development. It probably means the final delivery will be delayed."

"We understand completely. This is our doing, and we will cover all the extra expenses. Submit your progress invoices, and I will make sure they are paid promptly."

"Thank you." A nagging thought tugged at the back of her mind. "May I ask you a question?"

His expression seemed cautious. "Of course."

"I presume you are changing computer systems because the old one no longer meets your needs."

He nodded. "That is correct. We are making do with our existing software. We have been looking for a replacement for quite some time."

Hanna hefted the specification document. "I think you'll be pleased with this. Is there anything else we need to discuss today?"

"That is all I have. Have I answered your questions?"

"Yes. Time for me to get back to work."

They both stood at the same time.

"I'll E-mail you my progress report by the end of the week, along with an invoice."

"I will be looking for it. Again, thank you for coming out on such a dreary day."

"Not a problem," Hanna said as she edged toward the door. But that was not what she was thinking.

12

PAUL FOUND A PARKING SPOT AND PULLED INTO IT. AFTER
helping Rachael out, he opened the Firebird's trunk and pulled out his
laptop computer and a large, round canvas bag.

"That's an odd-looking suitcase," Rachael commented.

"It's called a seabag," Paul explained as he dropped the car keys into
her hands. "Feel free to use the car while I'm gone."

"Thanks, but I'll probably park it at my apartment." Her smile was
strained. "Hate for anything to happen to it. Besides, I've got the government car."

"Whatever you think best. Will you take my computer?"

"Sure you trust me?" she asked with a strained smile, as she made sure
she had a good grip on it.

"Yes. Besides, it belongs to the company. If you bust it, they'll get me
another one." He saw her eyes flash.

"If you're not careful, I'll bust it on you."

"I'll not say another word."

He hefted the seabag onto his shoulder and took her hand as they
started for the terminal. Inside, he checked his bag at the United counter

and found out where the San Francisco flight boarded. Relieving Rachael of the laptop, Paul pocketed his boarding pass and took Rachael's hand again. The warm softness did a little to melt away the gloom of foreboding that continued to build inside him. Ahead he saw a familiar face—two familiar faces.

"Russell. Hanna. What are you two doing here?"

"Couldn't let you get off without saying goodbye," Russell said as he shook his friend's hand. "Hi, Rachael. You seeing him off?"

"Yes."

Paul looked at her, seeing the obvious concern in her eyes. As the time to board approached, he wondered at his earlier assurance, all but drained away now. Russell and Hanna, although smiling, seemed reserved as well. *What have I gotten myself into?* Paul wondered.

"I was a little surprised by your call," Russell said as they walked toward the gate. "I mean, I didn't think you went out to pick up customers' yachts. Does this happen often?"

Paul thought about what to say and came to the conclusion that whatever cover he had was fading fast. "This is the first time I've ever done it." He paused. "Under different circumstances, it's something I'd *love* to do. And this particular customer is well worth it. He wants the best and expects to pay a fair price for it." He saw Hanna's penetrating gaze and knew he was in for it.

"So the real reason is a certain problem in Hong Kong," she said.

Paul tried a weak grin. "I cannot tell a lie."

They continued toward the gate in a somber silence, unaffected by the noise and bustle all around them. They found seats in the departure lounge and sat down. Paul found it hard to meet Rachael's eyes, seeing her deep concern. He swallowed, but it did nothing for the lump in his throat. Finally the gate attendant announced the San Francisco flight. Paul got up.

"Call when you get there," Rachael said.

Paul saw that her eyes were brimming with tears. He cleared his throat. "I will. Don't worry. I'm just going to get a customer's boat." He was sure that sounded as flat in their ears as it did in his.

Rachael nodded. Aware of his friends and the others at the gate, Paul felt heat rising in his face. He leaned down and kissed Rachael gently. Then again.

"Good-bye," he said. "I'll see you soon."

She nodded, and for one horrible moment Paul thought she was going to break down. "See you." She sniffed and reached into her purse for a tissue.

Paul glanced at Russell and Hanna and turned toward the gate. He reached into his pocket and pulled out a diskette. He looked at Hanna, then Rachael.

"There's a program on here that might come in handy."

Rachael dabbed at her eyes. "Give it to Hanna. The klutz wouldn't know what to do with it."

He extended it to Hanna. "If I send you an E-mail, it'll have an attached graphics file—picture of a yacht or something. This program will pull out the encrypted message for you. Also it will allow you to send me secure messages the same way. You'll have to create two passwords when you set it up."

Hanna took the diskette and eyed it critically. "Guaranteed unbreak-able?"

Paul grinned. "So they tell me, but you don't have to try and break it."

"Don't worry. I'll just use it if the need arises."

"It very well may."

He sensed a heaviness as he turned away, feeling the weight of their eyes until he was inside the jet way. A female flight attendant smiled at him as he boarded the aircraft. He made his way back to the business class section as if under a cloud.

* * *

Huo looked around the equipment room to make absolutely sure he was alone. The only sounds came from the warehouse floor behind him, muted sounds drifting through the heavy door. Huo undid the latches, stepped inside, replaced the panel, and flicked on the light.

"Where were you?" Zhu demanded in a hoarse whisper. "I expected you hours ago."

"It couldn't be helped. Government officials have been camped out in our office all day, asking questions, searching our records."

"Do they suspect I'm here?"

Huo shook his head. "No. I'm sure this is routine. They're searching all of Hong Kong."

"Did they say anything about looking in this warehouse?"

"No. But I imagine they'll eventually do it. It's obvious they're determined to find you."

"And they will eventually."

"Not necessarily. They can't dismantle everything in Hong Kong." Much as he wished to remain optimistic, he had to admit things did not look good.

"Is there any news from the Americans?"

Huo took a deep breath. "Nothing on political asylum. But something else came up."

Zhu scowled. "Unless it's a way out, I'm not interested."

"My friend is coming here."

"What? I thought you said . . ."

"I think he's coming unofficially."

"What good will that do?"

"We'll have to wait and see." Huo paused. "I know my friend wants to get you out; he's said as much. But he's having a hard time getting his government to go along."

"Well, whatever he's planning, he better hurry."

"We'll know soon."

* * *

Although it had been years since he had seen him, Paul recognized David Ho instantly. The man's height helped. He was taller than most Chinese and also taller than Paul. Paul sighed. He had to look up to *most* people, literally if not otherwise.

"Paul," Ho said. He hurried through the crowd.

"David, how are you?" Paul shook his hand, remembering the firm handgrip and friendly eyes.

"Fine. I trust you had a good flight?"

"Other than taking forever, it wasn't bad. Business class is sure a lot better than coach."

"You should have given me more warning. I would have bought you a first-class ticket."

Paul laughed. "Would it have made the trip shorter?"

Ho shook his head. "Alas, no. But we can discuss all this later. Are you hungry?"

"Well, they pretended to feed us. And I pretended to eat."

"I see. Another reason for going first-class. But all is not lost. I'll have my chauffeur take us to the Royal Yacht Club, and we'll have dinner there."

"Thank you. I appreciate it."

"Think nothing of it. May I have your baggage claim?"

Paul pulled out his ticket folder and removed the cardboard stubs. Ho turned and snapped his fingers. A young Chinese man hurried up. After a quick exchange of Mandarin, the man rushed off.

"What about customs?" Paul asked.

"Not a problem. My car is outside."

They left the terminal and got into the back of Ho's Rolls-Royce. Paul sank into the comfortable seat, savoring the pleasant scent of well-tended leather. The chauffeur pulled out briskly and soon had them out of the new airport and on the expressway linking Lantau Island with Hong Kong via several islands and Kowloon. It was nearly seven-thirty by the time they arrived outside the Royal Hong Kong Yacht Club.

"Have you ever been inside?" Ho asked as they walked up to the entrance.

"No, I haven't," Paul replied. "My other trips to Hong Kong were strictly business. Meeting with suppliers and shippers. Demanding customers, such as yourself, require us to do some serious shopping."

Ho laughed as he held the door. "Are you suggesting I am picky?"

Paul passed through into the spacious lobby. "In a word, yes."

"I am hurt to the quick."

Paul grinned. "I can see that you are." He paused and looked around at the glittering glass-front cases displaying legions of silver trophies. "Your members don't do badly, do they?"

"Indeed we don't. We take our racing very seriously." They passed by the old-fashioned bar. "Would you care to take the rough edges off your trip? Wonderful view of the harbor."

Paul looked inside. Many members sat at the long bar while others occupied tables near the large plateglass windows. "No thank you. I don't drink."

Ho seemed surprised. "Ah, well. I'm sure you are wise in refraining. Shall we proceed to the restaurant, then?"

"That would be much appreciated."

After a smooth transfer of folded banknotes, the waiter seated the two men at a choice center table. Paul scanned the tall menu and selected a deep-fried chicken dish. Ho selected the duck. The waiter returned a few minutes later with their salads and a large drink.

"Hope you don't mind," Ho said as he sipped from the tumbler. "It has been a hard day."

"How's the cosmetics business?"

"Couldn't be better. I seem to be supplying much of the munitions in the war against ugliness, and there's no armistice in sight."

"I guess that's good."

"It keeps me a paying customer of Blue Water Yachts."

"And on behalf of our president, I thank you."

Ho nodded. "Your company does excellent work. I depend on you."

For several minutes they said nothing. Paul concentrated on his salad while his mind raced over all the things he had to do—or try to do. He had to struggle to keep panic from gaining a foothold as he thought about what he was up against. The fact that he was inside the borders of a repressive government weighed on him, a government which could easily deny him exit on a whim.

"Is anything the matter?" Ho asked.

Paul forced a smile. "No. Just thinking of all the things I have to do to get your boat ready to sail."

"Don't you worry. You'll find *Sophisticated Lady* ready to sail anytime you're ready. I maintain her in tip-top condition."

"I'm sure you do. But sailing a boat halfway around the world is nothing to take on lightly."

"That is true. But your reputation precedes you. I know my boat is in good hands."

Paul tried to smile at this sincere compliment. But in the back of his mind, all he could think about was his friend, Huo Chee Yong, and the man who knew about Project Dragon.

* * *

Paul stroked his bristly jaw with his hand and yawned. A glance at the hotel's digital alarm clock told him it was almost 10:00 P.M. local time. He did the math and decided that 6:00 A.M. was an acceptable time to call. He punched in Rachael's number and waited.

"Hello," a not very alert voice said.

"Hi, Rachael. It's Paul. I had dinner with David Ho, and I'm checked into the hotel. He says the boat is almost ready to sail, so I think we'll be on the way back to Seattle in a day or two."

"That's nice."

"David is thorough. I need to check on the provisioning, and we may want to take some of the refit supplies back with us. It would save us using commercial shipping, not that David can't afford it. Oh, and I need to meet the crew. I want to take their measure, if you know what I mean." He smiled as she laughed.

"Sounds like a guy thing to me."

"Remind me to explain 'shipmate' to you sometime. At sea how well you do your job can make the difference between life and death. I trust David's judgment, but I also want to see them for myself."

"Will they feel the same way?"

"Oh, yes. They don't have a choice, but I want to put their minds at ease." In that moment he longed to put Rachael at ease as well, but he knew there was no way he could do that.

"I see."

"Well, I better let you go. It's late here, and I know you've got to get ready for work." He paused. "I miss you."

"I miss you too. Be careful, Paul. That's a long trip."

He swallowed the lump in his throat. "Yeah, it is."

He hung up. It would be a long trip. But what went before it worried him more.

13

PAUL BLINKED AWAY THE REMNANTS OF HIS JET LAG WITH
the aid of a second cup of coffee. His breakfast in the Luk Kwok restaurant had been excellent. Ho had dropped him off at the hotel at a reasonable hour, but Paul knew from experience that trips traveling west
were never-ending days. The fact that it was daylight the whole way did
not negate the thirteen-plus hours it took to get there. Added to this was
a long night spent tossing and turning. Paul sipped the strong brew, grateful for the caffeine's wake-up call to his weary body.

The Luk Kwok was a medium-priced hotel in Hong Kong's Wanchai
district, convenient to the Royal Hong Kong Yacht Club. The famous
name was a sham, however, since the contemporary hotel replaced the
original made famous in *The World of Suzie Wong.*

Paul glanced at his watch and saw it was a little after seven. He had
called Huo the previous night. His friend had seemed apprehensive but
agreed to meet at Hong Kong Park at seven-thirty. *Which makes it time to
go,* Paul thought as he pushed a tip under his plate and got up.

As the weather was clear and pleasant, Paul decided to walk. People,
mostly Chinese, jammed the sidewalks along Gloucester Road as he

followed the street westward toward the Admiralty district. Shops, stores, and restaurants jostled one another for space and the opportunity to sell their wares. Chinese signs alternated with those in English in a collision of cultures brought about by an empire that was no more but remembered by institutions deemed too valuable to discard.

Paul crossed over to Queensway and continued on to Cotton Tree Drive where he entered Hong Kong Park. He walked past Flagstaff House, former residence of British forces commanders, and followed the path to the rain-forest aviary. Inside, the humidity rolled over him like a hot, steaming towel. A cacophony of birdcalls assaulted his ears as he strolled along the paths amid lush tropical trees and bushes.

Finally Paul spotted a familiar face. He followed Huo at a distance, hoping he was not being obvious. A few minutes later found them in a dead-end side path with no one else around. Huo looked all around before approaching.

"Hello, Paul," he said, his voice almost inaudible over the bird cries. "How are you?"

Paul felt a chill despite the warm, moist air. "Hello, Huo. To be honest, I've been better." Then an unbidden thought came to his mind, and he had to smile. "But in light of eternity, I'm doing great."

Huo's strained expression changed subtly. "Ah," he said. "You are, of course, referring to our common Father."

"Yes, I am." He paused as he tried to bring his present troubles into perspective. "The end is not in doubt, but I'm not so sure about the in-between part."

"I understand. I hope you bring good news."

"A chance, maybe. I'm here to skipper a client's boat back to the U.S. If we can somehow get your friend aboard, I think we might be able to get him to safety." Paul saw a look of doubt cloud Huo's face.

"This is not an official operation?"

"No. The CIA doesn't know about it. I'm here on Blue Water Yachts' business." Paul paused as he considered what he could tell his friend. "I tried to get our government to grant political asylum, but I don't think they'll act in time. This is our best shot."

"It may not be enough. I don't think you realize how badly the Chinese want Zhu back. Hong Kong is a virtual prison. Your client, I assume, is well connected, but his boat will not be immune from search, assuming we can get Zhu aboard in the first place."

"And if we do nothing, they'll eventually get him anyway."

"True."

"And my country will suffer the effects of Project Dragon, whatever that is."

"Also true. So it's either this or nothing?"

"Right. Can you arrange a meeting with Zhu?"

"I don't know. It would be very dangerous. He is hidden in one of our warehouses."

"What if I come by your office? Victoria Shipping is handling several shipments for my company. It makes perfect sense for me to check on them while I'm in Hong Kong."

Huo nodded. "Yes, that might work." He glanced at his watch. "Shall we say, one o'clock?"

"Let's make it two. I have to meet with David Ho in a half hour to go over our sailing plans. I imagine we'll have lunch together afterward."

"So the cosmetics king is your client."

"That's him."

"Well, that may help. The government probably wishes to avoid angering him." He paused. "But that won't stop them from searching his boat if they suspect Zhu is aboard."

"I understand."

*   *   *

Hanna made a final change to the Customer table and released it to the tender mercies of Oracle. The database management system seemed satisfied with the modification, as the hard disk recorded all the ramifications.

Hanna glanced at the time display on the screen and saw it was almost 7:00 P.M. Scott was slaving away on his homework, or at least that's the impression he gave when she had passed his room earlier. And it seemed the maintenance manager for Western Washington Utilities had not reached the end of his day. But Hanna knew Russell would be home soon, or he would call.

A movement outside caught her eye. She looked through the blinds and saw a car turn into the drive. But instead of Russell's company Crown Vic, she saw it was one of the medium-sized "me too" cars. She wasn't sure which one, just a streak of gray.

Hanna gave her mouse some electronic aerobics, driving the pointer around the screen in mad swirls, as she tried to decide whether it was worth continuing with the table modifications for the Singapore Shipping system. What she really wanted to do was sit down to dinner with Russell and Scott. But there was this huge stack of changes she had to do before she could schedule the show-and-tell with her client.

The doorbell rang. Hanna got up, wondering who could be calling at this hour.

"Who's that?" Scott asked, sticking his head out into the hall.

"Don't know," Hanna replied, as she passed and started down the stairs. "We're not expecting anyone."

She hurried to the door, with Scott right behind her. She unlocked the door and pulled it open.

"Hi," Rachael said. "Can I come in?"

Hanna saw her look of concern. "Of course. Is anything wrong?"

She shook her head as she walked past. "No, not as far as I know."

"Have you heard anything from Paul?"

"Mind if we go up to your office?"

"I can take a hint," Scott said. He turned and thundered up the stairs and disappeared into his room. The door closed with a gentle click.

Hanna led the way upstairs and into her office. She closed the door and looked around. "Here, let me make a place here." She picked up a tall stack of listings and manuals and placed them next to the shredder.

"Thanks," Rachael said as she sat down.

"Anything I can help with?" Hanna offered.

"No, at least I don't think so. Paul hasn't called, but I don't really expect him to. There's too much chance the Chinese will get suspicious. If we hear anything, it'll probably be in an E-mail to you."

"That makes sense. How's the research going, or is that something you can talk about?"

Rachael fiddled with the strap on her purse. "Since you and Russell are sources, I can share some of what I'm doing." She rolled her eyes. "Actually, at present there's no security problem at all since there's nothing new. I think Paul's right. This guy in Hong Kong is probably our best shot—if Paul can get him out of there."

"I agree."

"Any ideas on what the Chinese are targeting?"

Hanna shook her head. "No. There are too many possibilities. With the circuit breaker Y2K bug, we lucked . . ." She stopped abruptly as she realized it had not been luck, although she only realized this later.

"You what?"

"I imagine Paul told you about what we went through in December of ninety-nine."

"Yes, he did. That's what worries me so. Those people will stop at nothing."

Hanna felt a sudden chill. "You can count on it." The muted sound of the front door opening drove through her thoughts like a wedge. "Russell's home."

Rachael jumped up. "Oh, I've got to be going."

"No, please stay and have dinner with us," Hanna said as she got up.

"Thanks, but I don't want to intrude."

"You're *not* intruding."

A knock sounded at the door. "Dad's home," Scott announced.

Hanna opened the door and saw his keen look of anticipation. "OK, pardner. Go order the pizza." He started to dash away. "Whoa!" He stopped and whirled around. Hanna turned back to Rachael. "What kind of pizza do you like?"

"Mushroom—with extra cheese."

"Me too. Scott, order a pepperoni for you and your dad and a mushroom with extra cheese for Rachael and me."

"OK." He turned and raced down the stairs as Russell was coming up.

"Don't I get a hello or something?" Russell asked.

"Be back in a minute, Dad. Gotta order the pizza."

Russell shook his head. "First things first, I guess."

Hanna's eyes followed him as he continued up the stairs and turned toward her office. She saw the unmistakable light in his eyes as he kissed her.

"How was work today?" she asked.

"I think the power will stay on for another day or two, if we're lucky." He turned to their guest. "How are you, Rachael?"

"I'm fine."

"Rachael's having dinner with us," Hanna added.

"Great. Glad you can join us. Maybe Hanna won't feel so outnumbered."

"I am *not* outnumbered."

Russell grinned. "I stand corrected." Then his expression grew more serious. "Heard anything from Paul?"

"No," Rachael said. "That's what Hanna and I were talking about. It's hard waiting."

Hanna saw the muted pain of remembrance in his eyes. "Yes, it is," he said.

* * *

"How was your lunch with David?" Huo asked.

Paul struggled to keep up with his friend as they pushed through the crowds near the warehouse. "The food was first rate. I don't think he knows anything but the best."

"How are the sailing plans progressing?"

"Quite well. David asked me for a departure date. He's got everything lined up. The crew is ready. The supplies are aboard, for the most part. I told him I thought we could sail tomorrow morning."

"What about weather?"

"Generally OK. There's a fairly severe storm near the Marshall Islands, but it's not bad enough to delay our sailing. I think it's impossible to transit the Pacific without running into at least one storm. We have a satellite phone plus all the latest navigational aids. I can plot a course that will avoid the worst of it."

"Going nonstop?"

Paul shook his head. "No. We'll stop at Honolulu for fresh provisions."

They stepped up to the warehouse door. Huo opened it, and Paul went inside. The American scanned the orderly rows of stacked merchandise awaiting shipment. A huge forklift roared past with a towering pallet of boxes wrapped in a clear plastic cocoon. No workers were nearby.

Paul leaned close. "There's no reason to delay the sailing, and David knows that. So we don't have much time to decide how we're going to do this."

"I understand," Huo said as he led the way to the equipment room.

He checked the room carefully, then released the latches and lifted away the panel. The light inside clicked on, and Paul at last saw a rather short, muscular man with glaring brown eyes.

Huo replaced the panel and said something quickly in Mandarin. Paul heard his name but understood nothing else. "Paul, this is my friend, Zhu Tak-shing," Huo continued in English.

"Pleased to meet you," Paul said, shaking the man's hand. "Wish it was in better circumstances."

"I wish it as well." He nodded toward his friend. "I understand your government refuses me asylum." Zhu's English was adequate but not as good as Huo's.

"That's not exactly true," Paul replied. "But it may take a while to get a decision."

"We do not *have* time!"

"Yes, I know. That's why I'm here."

"Huo tells me you are here unofficially. How can that help?"

"I'm here to sail a client's boat back to Seattle." He glanced at Huo. "If we can get you aboard, I think I can smuggle you into the U.S."

"There is still the problem of entering your country and keeping away from those who are after me."

"One thing at a time. Once we show my boss what you know, we'll have no trouble getting protection for you." Paul paused. "Is there anything you can tell me about Project Dragon?"

"No! You'll get nothing from me until I'm safe."

"I understand. I'd probably do the same thing in your place. A friend of mine says she thinks you have planted embedded circuits on us with computer viruses in them." Paul saw Zhu's eyes widen.

"I will say this and no more. We call it the Raptor Virus." He frowned. "But this idiocy was dreamed up by our government's leaders. I am completely against it."

Paul refrained from pointing out that Zhu had gone along with the operation. "Then we're agreed this is not in the interest of either country."

"Yes, of course. However, I'm told the people's leaders believe otherwise."

Paul turned to Huo. "I think I know a way we can get Zhu aboard."

"David's boat is not immune from search."

"I know. I've seen the army guards posted around the yacht club marina. They're checking everyone. But my company has ordered a lot of equipment for David's boat. Some of it is coming from Hong Kong, and we're using Victoria Shipping. I could take some of those things back on the boat."

Huo thought for a moment. "Like what?"

"Like the oven and hot tub. They come crated for export. I doubt the guards are going to take the trouble to rip through all that packing."

"But what if they do?"

"Let's send the oven first. We can hold the truck with the hot tub back. If the guards don't give us any trouble, we can proceed. Otherwise . . ."

"Back to the warehouse."

"Right. What do you think?"

"It might work. And if it does, that might be the end of it." He turned to his friend. "Want to try it? It's your life."

Zhu took his time. "I can't think of anything better. We wait until we see what happens to the oven?"

Paul nodded. "Yes. Of course, there's no guarantee they won't search the hot tub crate even if they leave the other alone."

"I'll take that chance. I want to try it."

Paul nodded, then turned to Huo. "How can I contact you if something goes wrong?"

Huo handed him his business card. "Go to a public phone. Dial my beeper and key in your number, but subtract one-one-one-one from the last four digits. I'll call you back."

"Good plan. What about zeros?"

"They stay zeroes."

"OK. Hope it doesn't come to this."

Huo nodded. "Me too."

* * *

Paul stood on the quarterdeck of the *Sophisticated Lady* and looked up the dock toward the quay. A workman drove a forklift toward the boat, a large crate held securely by the forks. Another man walked beside the lumbering load. Two armed guards watched, seemingly undecided on what they should do. Finally one of them stepped forward, his rifle held at the ready.

Paul raced across the gangway and jogged up to the soldiers. "What is the meaning of this?" he demanded.

"We have our orders," the man replied. He gave curt instructions in Mandarin.

The man on the forklift looked toward Paul. "He says we must open the crate."

"See here," Paul objected. "Are you aware this belongs to David Ho?"

The man seemed surprised but stood his ground. "I still must search it. My orders allow no exceptions."

Paul stood back as the workers removed the clear plastic wrapping, clipped the steel bands, and opened the crate to reveal a stainless steel oven.

"Have you any idea how much trouble you've caused us? Now we've got to repack and seal this so we can stow it aboard. We're sailing in the morning, and I don't have any time to spare. I'm reporting this to Mr. Ho."

"What seems to be the problem?"

Paul turned to see an army officer approaching. "Your men are interfering with my preparations for getting underway."

"Mr. Parker, I suggest you let us do our jobs." The man's smile was definitely lined with steel. "If you do not cooperate, I am afraid our government will have no choice but to deport you. Do you understand me?"

Paul gritted his teeth. "Yes."

"Very good."

Paul turned to the man on the forklift. "Go back to the truck and get the banding equipment and the export wrap."

The man nodded. He turned off the forklift and stepped down. Paul watched as he returned to the truck waiting on the quay. A truck farther up the road started, turned around, and drove away.

What now? Paul thought.

14

HUO CHEE YONG DROVE SLOWLY ALONG GLOUCESTER
Road, knowing Zhu was well aware of their failure. There was nothing to
be done now but return to the relative safety of the warehouse and contact Paul. Huo felt a sharp pain in his stomach as he realized how short
the time was. Paul was due to sail tomorrow, and it would be difficult to
change that. Huo inched along the gridlocked streets as the heavy traffic
added to his woes. Hoards of pedestrians crossed the street, filtering
around the intermittently moving vehicles. The army and police presence
was heavier than ever, giving the impression there was no place to hide.
Twenty minutes later Huo turned right and drove slowly toward the
warehouse.

The plan of offloading the hot tub crate on a loading dock dissolved
in an instant as Huo made his final turn. An army truck barreled toward
him from the opposite direction. It pulled up at the main entrance and
lurched to a stop. Armed soldiers piled out of the back and ran up the
steps. An officer climbed down from the cab and led them inside.

Huo considered stopping where he was, but decided it would be too
suspicious. Instead he continued driving slowly toward the parked truck,

feeling the army driver's eyes on him the whole way. Huo continued on, expecting to hear an order to halt at any moment. He knew that would be fatal for him and Zhu. But no order came.

Huo felt his pager vibrate and retrieved it from his belt. A glance at the readout told him it was a local number. Although he felt sure it was Paul, he realized he could not answer it now. First he had to find a hiding place for Zhu. But where? He wondered how long Paul would remain at the pay phone, but decided worrying about it did no good.

For lack of a better idea, Huo drove toward Bonham Strand West. He thought about returning to the snake shop but decided it would be too dangerous. Instead he kept driving as the streets continued to narrow. Seeing he could not go much further, he parked the truck. He waited a few minutes, but no one seemed interested in him. Then he got down, walked to the back of the truck, and raised the door. He clambered up inside and walked forward.

"Zhu," he whispered.

"Yes," came the anxious reply. "What happened?"

Huo started removing the clear plastic wrap from the crate. "Keep your voice down. The soldiers searched the oven crate. I was sure they'd search the one you were in."

"Where are we now?"

"Near the shop off Bonham Strand."

"What about the warehouse?"

Huo sighed. "That's where I went first. But an army patrol got there just as I drove up."

"Do you think they found the hiding place?"

"I think we have to assume they did."

"What about Paul Parker?"

"I think he beeped me, but I haven't had a chance to call him back."

"Let me out of here."

Huo cut the bands with some tin snips. "I'm working on it, but we have to be careful. The police and army are everywhere. It's much worse than when I took you to the warehouse." He pulled one of the cardboard flaps aside. He saw his friend blinking in the late afternoon light. "I'm going to call Paul, but I want you to stay in the truck."

"But . . ."

"Please trust me. I'll be back as soon as I can."

"What if they catch you?"

"Pray that they don't."

Huo jumped down and closed the rear door. He hurried toward the harbor, wondering if the authorities were looking for him as well as his friend, but decided this was unlikely. His spirits sank lower as he saw the number of soldiers patrolling even the out-of-the-way places in Hong Kong.

Finally he spotted a bank of pay phones as he neared Connaught Road West. He started toward them, but stopped as a police car turned the corner. The officers looked at him closely as they drove past. Huo almost ran as they slowed down, but the car continued along and turned at the next street. Huo hurried to the nearest phone, glancing over his shoulder to make sure the police had not returned.

He retrieved his pager and read the number. He inserted some coins, punched in the actual number, and waited as it rang. He heard a click.

"Huo?" a voice asked.

"Yes."

"Are you OK?"

"For the moment. I had to leave Zhu in the back of the truck. The police and army are everywhere."

"I know. And patrol craft are covering the harbor. I've never seen so many, and they're searching anything that floats."

"What can we do?"

"I don't know, but this is much worse than I thought. Even if I could delay the sailing, it wouldn't help. The government searches will only get worse."

"I agree, but we have to try something."

Huo waited for a reply, but all he heard was crowd noise on the other end. "Paul?" he said finally.

"I'm here. Listen, the soldiers aren't allowing anything on the piers without a thorough search, and there's no way a boat can make it past the patrol craft."

"So, it's impossible."

"I didn't say that. But the only way past I can think of is very dangerous."

"What is it?"

"Underwater."

"What?" Huo exclaimed, before he could check his reaction. "You can't be serious," he added in a lower tone of voice.

"If you've got a better way, tell me. I don't like it either."

"What are you thinking of?"

"Can you get us some scuba gear?"

Huo closed his eyes as he thought about it. "I think so. You can find anything in Hong Kong. It's only a matter of finding a dive shop and not getting caught."

"Amen to that."

Huo pulled a small notebook out of his pocket. "What do you want?"

"The most important thing is air. What we really need are a couple of Mares Azimuth rebreathers. If you can't find that, then get us some regular tanks and regulators."

"I'll find the Mares equipment," Huo insisted.

"Good. Then, wet suits, flippers, masks, underwater compass and depth gauge—make sure they're illuminated—a diving knife, and a couple of flashlights."

"OK. Anything else?"

After a short pause, "I think that's it; at least I hope so."

"Where do you want to meet?"

"How about at my hotel. I'm going to check out and haul my gear over to the boat. After I do that, I'll take a cab back and watch for you from the lobby."

"I'll come by after I have everything. I'll be in the truck."

"Good. See you then."

* * *

Paul shifted uneasily in the lobby chair. He checked his watch again, wondering if something had gone wrong. He had been sitting there since dusk, and it was now a little after nine. Several times soldiers had entered the hotel to check at the desk. Each time Paul had feared the worst, expecting to be identified by the clerk on duty. What they were checking for he didn't know, but it wasn't for him—at least not yet. He thought about waiting outside, but decided that would be even more suspicious.

Finally a familiar truck pulled up outside the hotel. Paul got up and walked outside. A nearly full moon stood high in the sky, providing more light than he cared for. After looking all around, Paul made sure it was Huo and climbed up into the cab's passenger seat.

"I was beginning to worry," he whispered as he closed the door.

"It took a while to find a Mares dealer. But I think I have everything you asked for." Huo pulled out into traffic.

"Good. Where is Zhu?"

"In the back of the truck and not very happy about it."

"What about the hot tub?"

"We dumped it. I didn't want it traced back to David Ho."

"Good thinking. The truck?"

Huo grinned. "I remember a few things from when I was on the CIA payroll. Don't worry. It can't be traced either."

"Just checking. Sounds like we're covered as well as we can be."

"I hope so. What next?"

"Take us some place where we can get down to the harbor without being seen. Keep us within about a mile either way of the Yacht Club."

"There's a condemned building near North Point that I think might work, assuming it's still there. It's built out over the harbor to the east of the Yacht Club."

"Is there access to the water?"

"I've never been inside, but I assume there is. Such buildings usually have a trapdoor or external stairs down to a landing."

"OK, let's try it."

Paul watched the dark harbor waters off to the left as Huo guided the truck past Causeway Bay. He felt the tendrils of fear burrowing deeper as he saw at least a dozen fast-moving craft racing about offshore. Brilliant shafts of light lanced out at intervals as the patrol boats inspected the ships and boats of Victoria Harbor. One thing was sure: A boat trip to Ho's yacht was definitely out of the question.

"Looks like an army truck coming toward us," Paul said.

"I see it. And this is where we make our turn."

"Hope they don't stop."

Huo slowed down. Paul felt the eyes of the other driver as the two trucks passed. The soldiers in the back sat in two orderly rows. Then they were past.

Huo followed them in the large sideview mirror. "His brake lights came on once, but he didn't stop."

"Think they'll come back?"

"Don't know. They're still going."

"This is our only chance. Let's do it."

Huo nodded as he pulled past a narrow street leading down to the harbor. He stopped and put the truck in reverse. "There won't be any room down there to turn around."

He rolled down the window and started a backing turn. "Watch that side for me," he said. "It's going to be tight."

Paul rolled down his window and cautiously stuck his head out. "I see what you mean. You've got about a foot on this side."

"I'll get less. Fold your mirror in."

Both men pulled the side mirrors in until they touched the doors. Paul saw the clearance between the truck and the shabby squat buildings dwindle down until only inches remained. The side of the truck gave an agonizing screech as it scraped against a steel pole attached to the side of a wooden shack with smashed windows. Huo slammed on the brakes.

Paul looked around. "Better pull up and try it again. We're up against a pole."

Huo pounded the steering wheel. "Won't do any good. We're almost touching on my side as well."

"What can we do?"

"Force our way past, unless you want to lug all that diving equipment down from up on the road."

"Do it."

Huo released the brakes and gently pressed the accelerator. The engine growled as the ominous scream of metal against metal started again. Paul expected the racket to draw some attention, but so far they were alone. He looked toward the street and saw normal traffic, but no interest in this narrow alley. Finally they were past, and the horrible noise stopped.

"I hope there's more room at the bottom," Paul said.

"I think there is. We'll know soon."

The alley did open up, revealing a tiny loading dock next to a structure that appeared ready to collapse. Huo stopped and set the emergency brake. Paul got out and hurried around to the back. The angular building blocked off the view of the harbor. The moon provided adequate illumination, welcome now, but Paul would have preferred a dark night for what they had to do. Huo raised the rear door. Zhu emerged from the inky shadows and stood over them.

"Start handing the equipment down," Huo ordered.

He grabbed a heavy tire iron and hurried to the building's rear door. After a few blows the rusty padlock crashed to the ground, complete with the hasp. Paul hefted one of the Mares rebreathers and started toward the door.

Huo flicked on a flashlight. "Here. Take this."

Paul entered the large room, stepping gingerly over the uneven, rough-hewn planks, feeling them give with a spongy resilience that suggested imminent collapse. A powerful smell, redolent of rotting fish, sewage, and bunker oil permeated the place. The sound of water lapping against pilings carried clearly through the chinks in the floor. Paul set the rebreather down. Zhu entered with the other unit and looked at Paul.

"Put it down over here."

The three men quickly unloaded the truck. After Huo pushed the shaky door shut, Paul squatted down and began going through the boxes. He lifted out the depth gauge and compass, noting the illuminated dials. He clicked off the flashlight. Silver beams from the moon came through the broken windows, providing enough light to see shapes.

"Did the dealer check out the Mares units?" he asked.

"Yes. He was very thorough. They are ready to go."

"Did he say what the endurance was?"

"Three hours at thirty meters."

"We won't be swimming that deep, so that should be plenty. I sure hope we won't be in the water for three hours." He turned to Zhu. "Are you ready?"

"What choice do I have?"

"Paul came here to help you," Huo pointed out.

"He came because his country fears what China might do."

"He's risking his life to get you to safety."

"If I have offended, I am sorry."

For a few moments the only sounds were waves slapping against the pilings.

"My friend, I hope I see you again," Huo continued. "But if I don't, I think you should know that Paul and Grandmother and I share something that is not yet yours."

"This is not the time," Zhu interrupted.

"That is up to you, but it explains why Paul would do something you don't understand. Think about it."

Paul felt a tightness in the pit of his stomach as he realized the time was near. He and Zhu stripped to underclothes and donned their wet suits. Huo helped them on with their rebreather units and handed them their masks and flippers. He then switched on a flashlight and searched the room.

"There's the trapdoor," he said. He went over and lifted it up. A wooden ladder led down into the water.

Paul strapped on the depth gauge and compass and tested his flashlight one more time. "I think I'm ready."

A muffled sound came clearly through the dilapidated walls.

"What was that?" Paul whispered.

"Sounded like footsteps," Huo replied.

Paul hurried to a boarded-up window near the door and peered through a crack. At first he could see nothing, and for a time the only sounds they could hear above the gentle waves was the traffic up on the road. Then Paul saw the glint of moonlight on polished steel. A series of shadowy shapes moved in single file along the alley approaching the truck.

"Looks like an army patrol," Paul whispered.

Huo opened the door and dashed for the truck.

Paul barely managed to keep from crying out. He watched in horror as his friend wrenched open the door and jumped in. The truck started, and the lights blazed on, revealing a line of startled soldiers. A moment later it was lurching toward the men with an intent that was obvious. A half-dozen rifles came up at once. Rapid gunfire split the night. Paul watched in horror as the truck roared on, the sounds of shattered glass and tortured metal mingling with angry shouts. Then the truck swerved and sideswiped a building, throwing splintered wood in all directions. The vehicle finally slid to a stop. For a few moments the headlights continued to light the alley. The soldiers continued firing into their target. One light winked out and then the other.

Paul tasted bitterness. He knew he would never see his friend again on this side.

15

"COME ON," PAUL WHISPERED. "THERE'S NOTHING WE CAN do for Huo."

He led the way to the open trapdoor and handed Zhu his flippers. "Hold on to these until we're in the water. Then slip them on. You go first, and I'll close the trap."

Zhu took the fins and started down the vertical wooden ladder. After several steps a wood slat broke. Zhu cursed as he fell down one rung.

"Be quiet," Paul said in a harsh whisper. "Hurry up."

Paul began his descent when there was room. He glanced toward the door, half-expecting gunmen to come crashing through at any moment. Every sense seemed ultra-alert as he lowered himself to floor level. Paul reached for the trapdoor and pulled it shut over his head.

He looked down. Zhu was in the water now, struggling to put on his flippers. Paul took the steps gingerly, keeping his feet to the outside where the rungs were attached to the side pieces. The bright moonlight carried a little under the building, revealing the rotting pilings. Paul was surprised they could hold the structure up at all. He continued down and lowered himself into the water. As expected, the temperature was pleasant, although the thought of what he and Zhu had to do was not.

Paul looked through the pilings toward the ship channel. He counted three rapidly moving boats within his limited field of vision and knew they had to be patrols.

"Got your flippers on?" Paul whispered as he struggled to slip his on.

"Yes."

"Good. Listen carefully. Swim to the last set of pilings, but stay inside the shadows. Then we'll dive and swim north for a hundred feet or so, then turn to the west toward the Yacht Club. Hold onto my hand, and whatever you do, don't let go. I'll be using the depth gauge and compass to guide us. Understand?"

"I do."

Paul handed Zhu the extra flashlight. "Hold on to this, but don't turn it on. If something happens to mine, we'll have a spare." He nodded toward the channel. "Besides the patrol boats, we've got to avoid shipping and obstacles in the water."

"What obstacles?"

"Sunken boats, rocks, assorted junk."

"What if we run into something?"

"Pray that we don't. But if we do, stop and back up carefully. I'll help you."

A cold chill ran down Paul's spine as he said a silent prayer that they wouldn't run into anything. He knew well the danger of getting tangled up in wreckage and drowning.

Paul helped Zhu with his mouthpiece and made sure his rebreather was functioning. They pulled their diving masks down and swam to the edge of the pilings. Paul pointed forward and took Zhu's hand. Together they submerged.

The murky water cut off all light after only a few feet. Paul propelled himself forward with his flippers. The backward pull on his left hand told him

Zhu was slow starting. Moments later they were together again. Paul planed down slowly until he reached ten feet, then continued on until he knew they were well clear. Then he turned due west and continued down to twenty feet. Since they had not hit bottom, Paul knew they would probably be OK since the water grew rapidly deeper as they intersected the ship channel.

Paul clicked on his flashlight, making sure its hooded beam was pointed slightly down. As he expected, all he could see was a few feet of murky green water that seemed alive with fine sediment. He knew the feeble beam could never penetrate to the surface under such conditions.

Paul heard the high whining buzz of a patrol boat. The sound rapidly grew louder, then drifted to the side before diminishing. They were approaching the channel. Paul tried to estimate five minutes, then made a thirty-degree turn to the left as he tried to skirt the channel and the anchorage that lay to the south.

When he could stand it no longer, Paul started angling toward the surface. Although he could hear the propellers of several patrol boats, none seemed near. He broached suddenly and looked around quickly. Based on the positions of the three nearest buoys, he knew they were actually inside the ship channel.

"What's the matter?" Zhu asked.

"Checking our position."

"How much farther?"

"A little over a half mile, I think."

The patrol boats were scurrying around the harbor like water bugs. One appeared headed their way.

"We're going down now."

Paul waited until he saw Zhu put his mouthpiece back in, then dove. Hearing the approaching propellers, Paul wasted no time in diving, this time to thirty feet since he knew the water was deeper. The boat whined overhead very close and continued on toward the east.

A deep thrumming sound began to superimpose upon the high-pitched whine of the patrol boats. Paul couldn't tell where the sound was coming from, but he knew what it was. It had to be a freighter, and the increasing sound level indicated it was approaching. But Paul didn't know if the ship was coming from the east or west. He knew they should be out of the channel by now, but the currents might have thwarted him, or the ship might be outside the channel. Either possibility could be fatal.

The monstrous thudding grew ever louder until Paul was sure the ship was right on top of them. He turned sharply to the left toward the shore and started angling down. He kicked his flippers with all his might, grateful that Zhu was keeping up. Still the sound grew louder.

Paul saw the ship's hull just before they ran into it. It was sliding to the left like a moving wall. He thrust out the flashlight to fend them off. The encrusted metal knocked it from his grasp. He watched as the light spun away into the murky depths. Inky blackness descended. The propeller beat drew even closer. Paul turned frantically to the left, paralleling the ship's course, then kicked hard to try to get out of the way. But the powerful suction was pulling them back in. Paul angled downward, knowing that if they went through the propeller, that would be all.

The turbulence grew even worse. Paul sensed the huge, curving blades slicing through the water toward them. Down they went, toward an unseen bottom. A roiling current, full of bubbles, flipped him over, and something brushed against his upper right arm. Then it was past, and the relentless pounding began to recede.

Paul wanted to examine his arm but dared not let go of Zhu. He didn't feel any pain, but he knew that would come after the shock wore off. He struggled to bring his breathing under control as he guided his companion toward the surface.

Paul broke the surface and looked around. He looked up and saw the white stern light of the freighter that had nearly run them down.

"What happened?" Zhu shouted.

"Hold it down," Paul ordered. "That ship was outside the channel."

"You're going to get us killed!"

"I said shut up!"

The dark shape beside him lapsed into silence.

"We're still alive," Paul whispered. "We still have a chance. Do you have that flashlight I gave you?"

Paul heard a splash and saw a dark object sticking out of the water. He took it. "Thanks. Ready to go?"

"Do I have a choice?" Zhu grumbled.

Paul felt anger supplanting his earlier fear. "You know the answer to that."

He quickly dove to thirty feet and turned a little more toward the shore to stay well within the anchorage area. But this, he knew, held its own dangers, except running into a moored ship was certainly less dangerous. Still it was something he wanted to avoid if he could. Paul knew from their brief time on the surface that the Yacht Club was about a quarter mile away. He flicked on the flashlight and again saw the murky green globe of light that revealed almost nothing.

Paul began to slow as fatigue took its toll. His right arm ached. He felt anxiety rising up inside as he thought of all they had to overcome and the likelihood of failure. As his mind worried over this, he thought he saw a slightly darker shadow off to the left. Zhu clamped down hard with his hand. Paul arced around to the left and ran headlong into a steel object. It took a few moments to recognize the object for what it was: an anchor chain.

An urgent upward pull told Paul that Zhu wanted to surface in a hurry. Without any real choice Paul followed him upward as he listened for patrol boats. He could hear multiple high-speed whines, and one sounded quite close. He considered trying to keep Zhu under but decided he wouldn't be able to.

Paul saw the moon's glimmering reflection on the surface and wondered at the dark patch directly overhead. He hit something hard that had a slimy covering which in no way lessened the impact. Water flooded his mask as the impact shoved it off his face. Blinded, Paul almost dropped the light and Zhu's hand as the other struggled to get loose. Paul yanked hard and pulled Zhu back.

Paul surfaced with a great whooping cough. Nearby spluttering told him Zhu was having his own problems. Paul reached out and felt a curving steel object standing three or four feet out of the water. Recognition dawned. They had hit the anchor chain for a buoy and had come up under it.

"Get me out of here!" Zhu shouted.

"Quiet!" Paul looked up and saw the towering black shape of a ship, its anchor chain attached to the buoy. At the rail stood two sailors, pointing down at the water and talking rapidly.

Paul looked away reluctantly. He could hear the patrol boat's engines clearly now, and it was very close. A spotlight clicked on, backlighting the buoy.

"Dive!" Paul whispered. "A patrol boat is on the other side of the buoy."

"I can't. I lost my face mask."

"Close your eyes! I'll guide you."

"No!"

Paul saw the boat's bow pass into view. He placed his flippers against the buoy and pushed away as hard as he could, clamping down on Zhu's hand as he did. The other came away. Paul glimpsed the men standing in the boat as he started down. Muffled gunshots sounded on the surface accompanied by sounds like angry bees as the slugs penetrated a few feet into the water. Splashes sounded, which he knew had to be divers, proved moments later when the water overhead turned a murky green as they flicked on powerful flashlights.

Paul dove ever deeper, grateful that Zhu was still with him. He glanced at the illuminated depth gauge and saw the indicator pass twenty, thirty, and finally forty feet. There he leveled out and turned toward the Yacht Club. Looking back, Paul could no longer see the glow from their pursuers, but knew they had to be close. His heart pounded as he swam as hard as he could, oblivious of whatever might be in their path. He kept up this pace for as long as he could, until fatigue finally forced him to slow down. Knowing they had to be approaching the shore, Paul started angling upward.

Judging by the propeller noises, none of the boats were extremely close. He guessed the one they had encountered had stopped to pick up the unsuccessful divers and had not picked up the trail again. Paul said a silent prayer for that. But where were they? He felt certain their course was about right, but he had no idea how close they were.

He flicked on his flashlight and again saw the amorphous green glow. A few seconds later he saw a round hump ahead and a little below. A rock. They were near the bottom. Paul angled up a little more and slowed down. Again the bottom appeared, this time as gently undulating ooze. He turned off the light and started up.

A few moments later his head broke the surface. There, under the cool white glow of the moon, slumbered a forest of hulls and masts. Less that a hundred yards away stood the Royal Yacht Club marina. Paul felt hope grow as he turned toward the open harbor behind him. He could see four patrols plying the waters, but fortunately none were close.

He dropped Zhu's hand. "We're almost there," he whispered. "Follow me."

A few of the boats in the marina sported navigational and cabin lights, but most were dark. Mercury-vapor lights marched down the numerous piers and slips, augmenting the moon's generous lighting. Paul scanned until he saw the familiar silhouette of the *Sophisticated Lady*. He swam toward it, alert for signs of detection from the shore. But everything seemed peaceful.

He carefully approached the yacht, looking for signs of a deck watch. He had not inquired whether the crew did this in port but felt it was unlikely. Nearing the stern, he saw the ladder he had rigged earlier was still in place. Reaching it, he slipped off his flippers and motioned for Zhu to do likewise.

Paul led the way, pulling himself wearily out of the water, supporting the cumbersome rebreather with his shaky legs. He stepped over the rail and down onto the boat's stern.

"Where's the crew?" Zhu whispered as he came aboard.

"In the crew's quarters, I hope. Follow me."

Paul hurried over the teak deck to the ladder leading down. He tiptoed down and stopped when he reached the dark companionway. The only sounds he heard were the soft taps of harbor water dripping on the deck. He flicked on the light and walked aft a short distance. He felt around behind a fire extinguisher and retrieved a key.

"Where does that lead?" Zhu asked, pointing to a door further aft.

"Engine room."

"That where you're going to hide me?"

"No, I think you'll be safer in my cabin. You'll stay in there until we're in international waters."

Paul led the way forward past the ladder and unlocked a door on the port side. He pushed it open and turned on the light. After Zhu entered, Paul closed and locked the door. His large seabag rested on the single bunk.

"Strip out of your gear and wet suit," Paul ordered. "There are some clothes in the closet." He pointed toward a door in the corner. "Head's in there. We can take a shower after I ditch all this."

Zhu began unbuckling the rebreather. Paul took his off and peeled off his wet suit. He examined his arm and found a shallow cut oozing blood. Thankful it was not worse, he got towels for them and hurriedly dressed. He then grabbed the two rebreathers, opened the cabin door, and peered out.

"Where are you going?" Zhu asked.

"Taking our diving stuff up on deck."

"I'll help you."

"No, you stay inside. I'll be back for the suits and flippers."

Paul stepped out into the companionway and struggled up the ladder with the cumbersome breathing rigs. He made one more trip for the wet suits, flippers, and his face mask. He tied all these together, along with a spare anchor, and struggled down the stern ladder with the unwieldy load. He lowered it gently into the water and watched as it sank out of sight. He then tossed the depth gauge and compass after them. Returning to the companionway, he turned off the light, entered the cabin, and twisted the dead-bolt lock.

"You shower first," Paul said. "After that we can turn in. I told David we'd shove off at eight."

Zhu nodded and disappeared into the cramped head. Moments later Paul heard the water running. He felt a deep weariness stealing over him as he sat in the desk chair, waiting his turn. After Zhu got out, Paul hurried through his shower, dried off, and applied a Band-Aid to his arm. After dressing, he opened the door and came out. Zhu was sitting at the desk watching him.

Paul opened the wardrobe and pulled out two blankets. "You take the bunk. I'll bed down on the deck."

"But this is your cabin."

"I'll be fine. Believe me, I've experienced much worse." He set the alarm clock for six-thirty. "Once we're at sea, you can shift to the master's cabin."

Zhu nodded and prepared to turn in.

Paul spread one blanket over the carpet and waited until Zhu was in the bunk. He then turned out the light and sprawled on the deck. He pulled the other cover up and in moments was asleep.

16

HANNA FORCED HERSELF TO USE SHORTER STRIDES TO match Rachael's more sedate gait as they made their way among the cubicles toward the agent's office. Even after a restless night Hanna was beginning to have second thoughts about requesting a meeting, especially on short notice.

"After you," Rachael said, as she held the door open. "We can sit at my desk, or we can sit at my desk."

Hanna smiled. "Nice to have a choice." She placed her bulky laptop on the edge of the desk.

"That's some computer," Rachael remarked as she brought her desk chair around front.

"VR is my faithful companion." She opened the lid.

"VR?"

"Didn't Paul tell you? This is Victoria Regina. She's been my main laptop for quite a few years now. This is what I was using when we discovered the Y2K bug."

"*Queen* Victoria?"

"The same. I maintain her myself, so I expect her to reign forever."

"I see." Rachael paused. "Your call surprised me."

"Yes, I suppose it did. But I'm concerned."

"Worried?" Rachael suggested.

"Worried," Hanna agreed. "I didn't sleep very well last night. I'll feel a lot better when we hear that Paul's on his way back. Any news?"

Rachael shook her head. "He called me after he got to the hotel, but nothing after that. I don't suppose you've gotten any E-mail."

"No. I would have called. I've been thinking of sending him one, but I didn't want to without checking with you. Do you think it would hurt?"

"I don't see how it could. Paul's the only one who can decipher it." She sighed. "And I'd like to know how he's doing."

Hanna hesitated. "He's quite special to you, isn't he?"

Rachael looked down and nodded. She blinked rapidly and reached for a tissue from a box on her desk.

Hanna patted her hand. "Hang in there. What say you compose a note to Paul—something like, 'Hi, having a wonderful time, wish you were back here.'" She saw her attempt at lightness had missed its mark a little. "Or whatever you feel like. Here, let me open up an Outlook message for you." She did so and pushed VR to Rachael.

Rachael thought for a few moments, then began her composition, taking her time as her fingers deliberately clacked out her message. Five minutes later she was done.

"Close it if you want," Hanna said. "I don't have to see it."

"No, go ahead. I don't mind."

Hanna pulled the laptop around until she could read the screen.

Dear Paul,

Hanna and I are concerned about how things are going, especially since the situation is so tense in Hong Kong. We hope you will be on your way back soon.

Have not heard a word from Vic, so I hope your mission is successful. I am hitting a brick wall on my research. Hanna tells me she has nothing new to report.

If there's anything we can do, please let us know. I miss you.

Rachael

"Think I should take out the last sentence?" Rachael asked. "He's probably got enough to worry about."

Hanna shook her head. "No. I think you should send it as is. Ready for me to pack it up?"

"Yes."

Hanna opened Paul's program, encrypted the message, and placed it inside the graphics file of a yacht on Puget Sound with the Blue Water Yachts logo superimposed. Then she keyed a bogus message from the company reminding him to check on the price of teak in Hong Kong. After attaching the graphics file, Hanna attached a line to her mobile phone and sent the message.

"You made that look like it's coming from Blue Water Yachts?" Rachael asked.

"Yep."

"How'd you do that?"

"Trade secret."

Rachael laughed in spite of the situation. "Something the klutz wouldn't understand."

"No. This is part of my stock in trade, not that I spend a lot of time spoofing E-mail addresses. But I know how to do it if I have to."

"Well, that's done. What time is it in Hong Kong?"

Hanna glanced at her watch. "Let's see. A little after 9:00 A.M. here—just after one in the morning."

* * *

The insistent buzzing finally wiggled its way through the cobwebs of sleep. Paul forced his eyelids open to identify the obnoxious sound. He groaned as reality replaced the fantasy of dreamland. The alarm clock's brilliant digital readout announced the time: 6:30.

This was all he could see in the blackness of the windowless cabin. Paul groaned as he stretched his legs and felt the pain that went with unaccustomed stress and hard exercise. He rolled over on his side, threw aside the blanket, and struggled to his feet. He wobbled there for a few moments as he fought for equilibrium. Paul took a few stiff-legged steps and flicked on the lights. He turned to see Zhu blinking up at him.

"Time to get up," Paul said. "I've got to make sure the crew is ready to sail. And I expect David Ho will be down to see that his pride and joy is in good hands." He paused. "I need to make a quick check around the boat. After that, I'll drop by the galley and bring you something to eat."

"Thank you," Zhu said, wiping the sleep from his eyes. He looked up at the American. "I appreciate what you did for me last night."

Paul felt a stinging sensation come to his eyes. "I couldn't have done it without Huo." He watched as Zhu's eyes dropped to the deck.

"I know. He was a very good friend. He and his grandmother . . ."

Paul waited for him to continue, but he didn't. "Huo said you knew his grandmother. How was that?"

"She saved my father's life. And she was my grandmother as much as she was Huo's."

Paul smiled. "Huo and I talked many times about her—and Miss Jones."

"You know about all that?"

"Yes. Huo and I belong to the same Lord." He saw the other's look of irritation.

"I guess I should have known."

Paul nodded as he understood. "So you and Huo have discussed this before."

"Many times."

"I see. Well, I have work to do before we sail. I don't think the crew will bother my quarters, but lock the deadbolt after I leave. I'll bring you back something to eat."

Zhu nodded.

Paul pulled his ditty bag out of his seabag and retreated to the head for his shave. He lathered up and guided the razor about his face more or less on autopilot. He finished without significant damage, brushed his teeth, and examined his reflection in the tiny mirror. He had looked better, he decided. Suddenly the desire to be underway on a course for home was almost overpowering. He splashed on aftershave and stepped back into the cabin.

Zhu was already dressed. Paul hurriedly pulled on a fresh set of khakis, a short-sleeved shirt, white socks, and a pair of deck shoes. Finished, he walked to the door and unlocked it.

"There's extra shaving gear and a toothbrush in the head. Need anything before I go?"

Zhu shook his head. "No."

"OK. Don't forget the lock."

Paul opened the door a crack and listened. Hearing nothing, he opened it wider and peered out. No one was about, but the companionway light was on, so the crew had to be stirring. *They better be,* Paul thought. *We've got a busy day ahead of us.*

Paul made his way forward to the galley. Tang Wanbao, the first mate on David's crew, looked up from the table, a cup of hot tea in his hand. Paul sensed the man's reserve, as his brown eyes seemed to measure and analyze.

"Good morning," Paul said. He longed for a cup of strong, black coffee, but there wasn't any. He set about making a pot, knowing he would need it. "Are we ready for sea?"

"We are," the man answered.

Paul poured grounds into the filter, set it in place, and poured the water. A narrow black stream began flowing into the glass pot. He turned around and attempted an engaging smile.

"Good. I'll be glad to get underway."

"Will Mr. Ho come before we leave?"

"He said he would. I can't imagine him not seeing his boat off."

"Nor I."

Paul opened the refrigerator and looked in. There, where he had left it, was a bag of sweet rolls he had gotten at a small market, part of the provisions he had purchased during his preparations for sailing. He stuck one in his mouth and grabbed another. He saw Tang looking at him oddly.

"I'm hungry," Paul said, biting off a chunk.

He hurried back to his cabin, his hands full with the rolls and his coffee. He paused outside the cabin door and made sure he was alone before knocking quietly.

"It's Paul," he whispered.

The lock clicked, and Zhu pulled the door open. Paul handed him a sweet roll and closed the door.

"The first mate was in the galley, so that's all I could bring. I can go back later."

"This is fine," Zhu said, keeping his voice low.

"Want some coffee—or tea?"

"Tea, I think."

"I'll get you some." Paul glanced at his watch. "But first, I have to inspect the boat before David gets here. He'll ask if we're ready to sail, and he won't accept hearsay. Need anything else before I go?"

"No."

"OK..."

Paul stopped as he heard footsteps approaching. Several sharp raps sounded on the door.

"Mr. Parker," came his first mate's voice.

"Yes?"

"There is an army officer on deck. He says he must speak with you at once."

Paul felt a sudden chill. "What about?"

"He did not say, but he was most insistent."

"Very well. I'll be right up."

Paul listened as the footsteps retreated. He pointed to the head. "Go in there. After I'm gone, lock the door." He saw fear return to Zhu's eyes.

"What..."

"There's no time for questions. Just do it."

Zhu frowned but did as he was told. Paul left the cabin and looked around the deserted companionway before walking to the ladder leading up to the quarterdeck. He paused and looked up at the blue rectangle of sky framed above him, deceptive in its peacefulness. He walked up the steep steps slowly, turning at the top toward the port side.

There on the quarterdeck stood a Chinese officer with four soldiers standing behind him and another two on the dock. Tang Wanbao stood to the side, looking like a sailor expecting a storm. The five crewmen were huddled together on the starboard side a little forward of the mizzenmast. They traded guarded whispers as they waited to see what their skipper would do. Struggling for a look of righteous indignation, Paul approached.

"I'm Paul Parker, skipper of the *Sophisticated Lady.* You wished to see me?" He did not extend his hand.

"Ah, Mr. Parker," the officer said, his eyes critical and uncompromising. "It was not a request. The harbor master informs me you plan to sail at oh-eight hundred."

"That is correct."

"Then I must have my men search this boat before you leave."

"What!" Paul said, louder than he intended.

"Mr. Parker. Need I remind you that you are subject to laws and regulations of the People's Republic of China? If you interfere with my duties in any way, I shall be forced to arrest you."

Paul struggled to regain his composure. "I am well aware of that. We will, of course, comply with your orders. But I've been told this boat has been searched twice already."

"And it will be searched again," the officer said, with a confident smile. He barked an order in Mandarin. The four soldiers turned and faced forward.

Paul felt the first tendrils of panic. "You are aware that this boat belongs to David Ho?" He thought he saw a fleeting look of doubt in the officer's eyes, but the iron resolve returned quickly.

"Of course. However, all Chinese citizens are subject to government regulations—even those corrupted by the scourge of capitalism."

Paul looked around at the skyline. "The people of Hong Kong seem to have done fairly well under this scourge."

The officer's eyes became very hard. "I could arrest you for that. But I will overlook it for now. You and your first mate will accompany us on the search, but your crew will remain on deck."

"Very well." Paul beckoned to Tang. "Tell the men to stay topside." He turned back to the officer. "Where do you want to start?"

"Forward. Open everything, and let me warn you that I am familiar with the construction of yachts."

Paul extended his hand forward. "Shall we get it over with?"

He led the way below deck and forward to the master suite. From there, they proceeded aft. The officer did indeed understand yachts because he missed nothing. Paul's sense of dread increased the closer they got to his cabin. *After all the toil and danger, and the loss of a good friend, are we to fail at the last moment?* he wondered. He wracked his brain for any ploy that would prevent the discovery but to no avail. Finally they arrived.

"Your quarters?" the officer asked.

Paul nodded. "Yes."

"Open it."

Paul pulled out his key and inserted it in the lock. As he turned it, he felt no movement of the bolt. *It's not locked!* he thought as he struggled against panic. He pushed the door open and stood to the side.

"Not a lot of room in there. I'll wait out here."

The officer gave the order. One of the soldiers went inside and searched while his commander watched from just inside. It didn't take long.

"We are almost done," the officer said as he came out into the companionway. "The engine room is next, I think."

Paul felt his blood run cold. He knew that was where Zhu had to be hiding. This was it. He cleared his throat. "Yes."

He led the way to the door and waited. Up on deck he heard muffled shouts and rapid footsteps. Paul turned toward the ladder leading up and saw a set of legs pumping hard as someone started down. David Ho reached the bottom and turned until he saw the search party. He stormed aft, his eyes locked with those of the officer.

"What is the meaning of this?" he demanded.

Paul watched as serious doubt came into the eyes of the accused.

"I am under orders to search your yacht."

"It has already *been* searched! Two times! Did you find anything?"

"No."

"Then why are you bothering my crew a third time?"

"My orders are most explicit."

"I can get you a new set of orders. Would you prefer serving our country in Tibet, perhaps? I have friends who can arrange it."

"But . . ." The man's objection hardly qualified as one, so subdued and low was its tone.

David's fierce expression moderated a little. "I know you are only trying to do your job. But believe me, you do not have the big picture. Leave us in peace. My skipper and crew are supposed to be preparing to take my yacht to Seattle for an overhaul. They need to be about their duties."

The officer hesitated, then pointed to the engine room door. "I have not finished my search."

David glared and clinched his fists. "And exactly how much do you lack?" he asked, his voice deceptively calm.

"The engine room and the compartments aft."

"So you have already been through most of it. And what have you found?"

"Nothing."

"Do you really expect to find anything in the engine room?"

The man hesitated.

"Do you!" David thundered.

"No. But . . ."

"Get off my boat!"

The officer's eyes darted to Tang, then Paul, and finally back to David Ho. He nodded and gave an order. The soldiers turned and filed toward the ladder. As soon as the last disappeared, the officer turned, with what remained of his dignity, and made his exit as well.

David's glare slowly dissolved as he turned back. "Paul, I'm sorry. This whole thing about the defector has made our officials . . ." He paused, and his eyes flicked over the first mate. "They are naturally sensitive. But enough is enough. Are you ready to sail?"

Paul took a deep breath as he began to relax a little. "I was about to do my final look around when this happened. But I know Mr. Tang has made his inspections. He says we're ready for sea."

David nodded. "Good. But as skipper, you'll want to make your own tour, I'm sure."

"Yes."

"Well, don't let me keep you from your duties." He handed Paul a thick envelope. "Here is a copy of all the sailing papers, properly executed, and sealed." He made a face. "Give a bureaucrat a stamp, and he thinks he has ascended the throne."

Paul laughed as he took the documents. "I think that's a universal problem."

"Probably. I'll go topside and wait for you."

"Well, I've already seen everything below decks."

"Except the engine room," Tang said.

"I'll do that after I stow this." He hefted the envelope.

David started toward the ladder.

"I'll meet you forward in a few minutes," Paul told his first mate.

Tang followed the owner up to the main deck.

Paul waited a few moments to make sure he was alone, then hurried back to the engine room door. He turned the handle and pushed it open a crack.

"It's me," he whispered.

He flicked on the light and looked down the steep ladder. He descended slowly, looking all around the cramped compartment. A large diesel engine for propulsion occupied most of the space, with other spots allotted for the generator, air-conditioning compressors, electrical distribution panels, and pumps. But nowhere did he see Zhu.

"You can come out now," Paul whispered.

He heard a rattle near the generator that seemed to be coming from a damage control locker. Paul hurried over, turned the handle, and opened the narrow door. Zhu blinked at him in the sudden light.

"I thought I would be safer down here," he said as he stepped out.

"Turns out you were right. They insisted on searching the boat again. They looked in my cabin, but Ho chased them off before they could get down here."

"That was close."

"Amen to that. But I think you better go back to my cabin. We still have to get out of Hong Kong, and I don't want the crew knowing about you until we're in international waters."

"Are we ready to leave?"

"Yes. Now I've got to go topside and check the rigging with the first mate."

Paul hurried up the ladder and looked into the passageway. Finding it clear, he motioned Zhu to hurry. Paul waited until he saw the cabin door close, then went up on deck.

He couldn't have asked for a more gorgeous day. Victoria Harbor nestled under Hong Kong's mountains, capped by cobalt blue heavens above. Stately white clouds sailed toward the horizon in no hurry to get there. A gentle breeze from the northeast ruffled the water in the marina, providing a more pronounced chop out in the harbor. All in all, an excellent day for sailing.

He and Tang made a quick but thorough tour of every significant part of the standing and running rigging. As he expected, Paul found the material condition excellent and far superior to that of most yachts that are ready for a yard overhaul.

He returned to the proud owner.

"Well?" David asked.

"The *Sophisticated Lady* is ready for sea in all respects," Paul reported.

The businessman sighed. "As I expected. Then I will go ashore and commit my yacht to your care."

"I'll take good care of it."

"I know you will. Godspeed."

Paul shook his hand, remarking on how strangely British the last comment sounded.

"Thank you, David. I take that literally."

"What?"

"'Godspeed.'"

This seemed to fluster him. "Perhaps it is best to cover all bases, as you might say."

"Maybe one base is enough."

"Keep me posted," David said as he turned and stepped onto the dock.

"That I will."

Paul joined Tang in the cockpit. "Start the engine."

The first mate adjusted the throttle, turned the key, and pressed the starter button. The engine turned over a few times then started, settling down to a smooth rumble in seconds. Paul saw that the wind would set them off the pier.

"Cast off all lines," he ordered.

Tang relayed the orders. Two of the crewmen dashed about, receiving the lines as they were cast off by the dockhands. The yacht began to drift away.

Paul felt the familiar thrill of sailing return as they were officially underway. He glanced toward Tang while watching the yacht's movements carefully.

"Reverse, slow."

The first mate engaged reverse and moved the throttle up slightly. The propeller took hold, and the boat began to gain sternway. Paul turned the wheel slightly to port to stop the starboard drift toward the adjacent pier.

Once they were well clear of the piers, he turned the rudder fully to port and watched as the stern went directly into the wind and beyond.

"Secure the engine," Paul ordered. "Man the sails, main and mizzen first."

Tang gave the orders. Towering triangles of white soared to the tops of the main and mizzen masts. The sails flapped, then filled, propelling the yacht forward. The *Sophisticated Lady* was under full sail toward the islands to the west. Paul adjusted course once to avoid a Kowloon-bound ferry and again to pass a junk that was on the same outbound course. Paul counted five patrol craft speeding about the harbor. His heart rate increased as one roared close beside the yacht. The other skipper observed for a while, then veered off.

Paul's expert eye traced the curves of the sails, noting the mizzen and main were slightly out of trim. Tang issued orders before Paul could say anything.

He knows his stuff, Paul thought.

He tried to relax. They were underway for international waters with perfectly good papers for doing so. The rest of the cruise should be almost like a vacation. But Paul knew he really wouldn't feel comfortable until they entered the Strait of Juan de Fuca.

17

A FEW HOURS LATER PAUL BEGAN TO BREATHE EASIER. HE
had turned the *Sophisticated Lady* south at Kennedy Town and sailed
downwind through Sulphur Channel. Rounding the western head of
Hong Kong Island, Paul set the large ketch on a beam reach driving
through the East Lamma Channel between Lamma Island and Aberdeen.
The wind remained fresh and steady from the northeast. The yacht made
excellent headway as it plunged smoothly through the gentle South China
Sea swells.

Paul grinned despite the fact that they were still in Chinese waters and
could be boarded at will. He worked the wheel with the skill born of
many years' experience, countering each force vying to turn him aside
from his chosen course. He loved the feel of the rolling deck under his
deck shoes as the yacht heeled over to starboard.

"You know what you're doing," Tang observed.

Paul eyed the man, knowing the compliment was sincere. "Thank
you. I've been sailing for a long time. I take it seriously."

"That's obvious."

"And I know a competent first mate when I see one." Paul nodded to the two crewmen who were tending the running rigging under Tang's watchful eyes. "And you have a sharp crew."

"Mr. Ho demands nothing less than the best."

Paul nodded. "I am well aware of that."

Each plunge of the bow threw prismatic salt spray into the air to be carried aft. Bright points of light glinted off the waves as they formed millions of mirrors to catch the sun's rays. And each minute of sailing time carried them closer to international waters and home.

"Care to take the helm for a while?" Paul asked.

"My pleasure," Tang said, taking the wheel.

Paul hurried below and paused at his cabin. He looked around. A distant clatter told him the cook was busy in the galley. He saw no sign of the off-duty crewmen. Paul knocked softly before unlocking the door. Opening it, he found it apparently empty, as expected. He stepped in, locked the door, and turned on the light.

"It's OK," he whispered.

The door to the head opened, and Zhu came out. "How long do I have to hide in here?"

"At least until we're in international waters. But I'd prefer to wait until Taiwan is abeam. I wouldn't put it past your government to board us on the high seas."

"I don't *have* a government," Zhu grumbled. "That's why I'm here."

"I'm sorry about that."

"Are you?"

"Yes, I am."

Zhu shrugged. Paul could see he was worried, which was understandable.

"How long until we are past Taiwan?" Zhu asked.

"Depends on the winds and weather. But I estimate around 10:00 P.M. tomorrow."

"That's a long time to stay in here."

Paul felt heat coming to his face. "I imagine this cabin is a little more comfortable than a cell in Beijing."

Zhu glared for a few moments, but Paul could tell the point had been made.

"Yes, it is."

Paul opened his closet and pulled out an aluminum case and his laptop computer.

"What's that for?" Zhu asked.

"I'm going to check my E-mail."

Paul unlocked the door and opened it a crack. Seeing no one, he went out and hurried up on deck. He hauled his gear back to the cockpit where he saw Tang's inquiring eye.

"Hold a steady course," he ordered. "I'm going to check in with my company."

Tang nodded.

Paul opened the aluminum case and lifted out the satellite phone. He set up the antenna, rough aimed it, plugged together all the components, and ran a wire to his laptop modem. After several attempts he got the antenna locked in on the satellite.

"How about that," he mumbled to himself.

Paul keyed in the long-distance number of his Internet service provider and hit the enter key. Moments later he was logging in. A diminutive chime sounded from the tiny laptop speakers.

"Well, well, I have mail."

He clicked on the Outlook in-box icon and saw it was a message from his company asking him to check on the price of teak in Hong Kong. Attached to the message was a graphics file. Making sure Tang could not see the screen, Paul double-clicked on the file. A window opened up displaying a luxury yacht with all canvas spread. After entering the required keystrokes and entering both passwords, he slowly read the message.

So, they're not getting anywhere, he thought. Well, that was about to change, assuming he could get the ungrateful Mr. Zhu back to the U.S. safely, and the man decided to cooperate. Paul looked at the last line. *She misses me.* He felt a stinging in his eyes that had nothing to do with the sea spray.

* * *

Jiang Ling got up from his desk, turned, and walked to the windows overlooking Hong Kong Harbor. He scanned the shore until his brown eyes found the Hong Kong Royal Yacht Club. All around stood a forest of masts, sprouting from the boats belonging to wealthy Hong Kong businessmen. Like it or not, those rich men were now answerable to Beijing. That this made them nervous, Jiang did not doubt. He held up the report his secretary had given him earlier. *Could David Ho be involved in this mess?* he wondered, *or was he being used?*

He jumped as he heard the muted rap on his massive wooden door. Jiang hurried back to his desk and sat down.

"Come in," he said.

His secretary opened the door. Outside stood a People's Liberation Army general whose expression seemed a strange combination of puzzlement and fear. He walked over the carpet as if it were a minefield until he stood a respectful distance from the desk.

"I am General Chow," the man said in a subdued voice. "You sent for me?"

Jiang eyed the report. "Yes, I did. I have been told that you are in charge of our security operation to find the defector Zhu."

"Yes, I am."

"This man your men killed last night near North Point—Huo Chee Yong. According to your report he worked for Victoria Shipping."

"That is correct."

"And Mr. Huo has handled shipping for a Mr. Paul Parker, who works for Blue Water Yachts in Seattle—the *same* Paul Parker who interfered with our previous project."

The general nodded.

"Shortly after your men killed Huo, a harbor patrol craft sent divers into the water at a point on a line between North Point and the Royal Yacht Club. Two sailors on a freighter said there were two men in the water."

"Yes, but . . ."

Jiang struggled to contain his rising anger. "Yes, *what*, General? Were the government's instructions concerning the defector in any way unclear to you?"

Chow cleared his throat. "My orders were perfectly clear."

"So Mr. Parker knew Huo, and Zhu knew him as well since Victoria Shipping has handled shipments for us from time to time. Tell me General, does what I am saying suggest anything to you?"

The man stiffened. "Not until we identified Mr. Huo and started checking into his background. Mr. Parker is here at the request of Mr. Ho to sail his yacht back for a scheduled overhaul."

Jiang slammed his fist on his desk. "After all this bungling, you had one more chance to get Zhu. Your men were searching David Ho's yacht just before it sailed. You had Paul Parker and Zhu Tak-shing in your grasp, but you let them slip right through your incompetent fingers!"

"Mr. Ho interfered with our search."

"You are under Mr. Ho's command?"

"No, of course not. But the man has friends in high places. He could have caused a lot of trouble."

"Not if you had arrested Zhu and that meddling Mr. Parker!"

"But we do not know if Zhu is aboard—not for sure. We had already searched most of the boat by the time Mr. Ho got there."

"You did not search it all. Your man admitted that." Jiang rapped the paper on his desk.

"No. But all the evidence is circumstantial. We have no positive proof that Zhu is aboard."

"Oh, he is on board, General." Jiang glared at the man. "And since you have failed us, we will be forced to take other steps to capture the traitor." He nodded toward the door. "You may go, General."

Jiang waited until he was alone. Then he placed his call to Beijing.

* * *

Paul glanced toward the north. Although the coast of China was over the horizon, it wasn't all that far away, and the yacht's eastern course meant the proximity would remain for many more hours. He shuddered at that oppressive thought as he opened Notepad to compose a message.

> Hanna, please relay this to Rachael. We are underway for home. We left Hong Kong a little after 8:00 A.M. local time. Everything is fine, so I recommend preparing for our arrival.
>
> At the present time I expect to pass south of Taiwan around 10:00 P.M. tomorrow; however we could have delays due to weather. There's an unstable air mass over the western Pacific, and it's moving toward the South China Sea.
>
> My sailing plan calls for one stop in Honolulu, which we should reach in two or three weeks, depending on winds and weather. We need to ask Vic what he wants to do. Tell him the defector's name is Zhu Tak-shing, and he requires asylum or it's no go. I'm convinced he's the key to Project

Dragon. Tell Vic to get a move on because I don't think we
have much time left.

And please tell Rachael I miss her too.

Paul

He read it over carefully. He considered deleting the personal message
but decided he could trust Hanna with it. He wanted Rachael to know
how he felt.

Paul saved the note and inserted the encrypted version inside a graphics file of a Blue Water Yachts promotional flyer. That done, he composed
a simple "wish I was there" note, attached the encrypted message, and
clicked on the send button. A quick mental calculation told him it was
nearly 7:00 P.M. in Seattle.

Paul unplugged the modem line. He stared at the satellite phone for
a while, the urge to phone Rachael almost overpowering. But he
decided it would be best to wait. Besides, the message conveyed everything he wanted to say, omitting the grim details that were still painfully
fresh.

He wondered if the Chinese agents had connected Huo to Zhu and
himself. If not, Paul knew it was only a matter of time. The fact that the
Sophisticated Lady was officially in international waters probably offered
little protection if the People's Republic of China decided to act on their
suspicions. *But would they?* he wondered. He scanned the expanse of blue.
They were alone on this particular part of the South China Sea. He
looked up at the gathering clouds. Finding them wouldn't be easy if the
weather got sloppy. Even in excellent weather it would be difficult, unless
their course were known. Paul made a note to deviate from their planned
track when they got past Taiwan.

He shut down the phone and packed it up.

* * *

Rachael tried to relax as she listened to the closing chords of Bach's *Toccata and Fugue in D Minor,* marveling at the musical genius who had created it. It had always amused her that the piece often showed up in horror films. Did the directors see Bach as a mad composer, or was it because the piece was in public domain?

She jumped as her secure phone rang. She got up and turned down the volume on the CD player and picked up the receiver.

"Hello," she said.

"Rachael, this is Hanna. I just got an E-mail from Paul."

Her friend's words hit her like a sledgehammer. "What? What did he say?"

"He was rather guarded. He's on his way, and the defector is on board. His name is Zhu Tak-shing. Paul expects to arrive in Honolulu in two or three weeks. Said that Vic better get started on whatever he has to do to grant the guy asylum."

Rachael sighed. "That may take some doing, but I'll start working on it. Anything else?"

There was a slight pause. "Yep. He says he misses you too."

"Too?"

"Uh-huh. As in 'also.'"

Rachael felt the tears coming and could not stop them. Her shoulders shook as she sobbed noiselessly.

"Rachael?" Hanna asked.

A cry broke free as she struggled to breathe.

"Rachael, are you OK?"

"Yes . . ." She walked to the kitchen and got a tissue. She dabbed at her eyes. "I mean, no. I've been worried sick the whole time Paul's been gone."

"But he's on his way home. And he has the defector. I think you can relax now."

Rachael blew her nose. "I hope so. I guess this bothered me more than I knew."

"That's understandable. Do you want me to come over?"

"No, I'm all right. Besides, I've got to get busy. There's a certain bureaucrat in D.C. that needs a fire lit under him. If we don't get Mr. Zhu political asylum, then all Paul's work is for nothing."

"I hear that. Let me know if I can help."

"I will."

"We'll be praying."

"Thanks."

Rachael hung up and thought for a moment. It was a little after ten in Washington. She considered trying Vic's mobile phone but knew he didn't always carry it. She punched in his pager number. When she heard the tone, she keyed in the number of her secure phone.

Rachael walked slowly to the CD player. She listened for a while to the muted tones of Bach's *Fantasy and Fugue in A Minor,* then pressed the stop button. She returned to her reading chair and sat down. She was glad Paul was on his way home, but her relief was tempered when she thought of how long a trip it was—and what could go wrong. She closed her eyes. *Come on, Vic,* she thought. *Call me back!*

18

RACHAEL JUMPED AT THE SUDDEN CHIRP. SHE PICKED UP the receiver on her secure phone. "Hello, this is Rachael."

"I hope this is important," Vic said, his irritation evident. "I'm at a reception for a German trade delegation."

Rachael took a deep breath as she considered how to bring her boss up to speed. "It's important. We've got a breakthrough on Project Dragon." All she heard was silence.

"Vic? Are you there?"

"I'm here," he said slowly. "What sort of breakthrough? Your last report said you weren't having any luck."

"Paul has found a Chinese defector who knows all about it."

"Paul's on vacation."

"Not exactly."

"Oh? Then where is he?"

"He went to Hong Kong. Right now he's on a yacht sailing east toward Taiwan. He has the defector with him."

"What!"

Rachael winced at Vic's sudden shout.

"The man's name is Zhu Tak-shing. I gather he was high up in Project Dragon."

"You mean he actually went and *got* this guy?"

"There didn't seem to be any other way."

"I won't have it! He had no authority to do that!"

"He's bringing back a yacht for his company, at the request of the owner. He decided to bring back Mr. Zhu while he had the chance."

"Don't give me that! He's freelancing, and you know it."

"But . . ."

"Can you tell me he had the owner's permission to do this? And does the Chinese government know about it?"

"Well, no. But Vic. If we don't get a breakthrough on Project Dragon, and soon, we're going to be thrown back into the dark ages."

Rachael listened as the silence drew on. "Vic?"

"Where's he going with this guy?"

"Paul's sailing the yacht back to Seattle, but he's stopping in Honolulu. Vic, we need to arrange political asylum for Mr. Zhu. He won't cooperate with us unless we do."

"He could be a crackpot, for all we know. I'm not sticking my neck out for some guy who'd rather live in America than China. We have no assurance he knows anything about Project Dragon—or that Project Dragon really is cyber terrorism, for that matter."

"My research says it's real. So does Paul's, and I know other researchers at Langley agree with us."

"Not all of them. I do read the summaries, you know. I still can't believe the Chinese would really do something like this."

"But they did it once before!"

"Calm down. We've been through all this before. Show me some proof, and I'll act."

Rachael struggled to regain her composure. "Unless we grant asylum, he won't cooperate."

"Then that might be a problem."

"Vic!"

"Tell you what, I'll have some agents meet with the guy when they get into Hawaii. If he can give us something to go on, maybe we can proceed. But it's up to him to convince me. Anything else?"

"No, I guess not."

"OK. Do you have any way to contact Paul?"

"Yes."

"Tell him he has some explaining to do."

"I will. Bye."

The line clicked, and the dial tone came on.

Rachael waited a few minutes as she struggled with her anger. Then she called Hanna and told her what Vic had said.

"That guy doesn't like to change horses, does he?" Hanna asked.

Rachael snickered in spite of the situation. "Vic *is* rather hidebound, if that's what you mean."

"Yep. Maybe we should put a burr under his saddle blanket. Might make the other horse look a little better."

"What sort of burr did you have in mind?"

"I don't know. Get the Chinese to act prematurely—something to confirm what they're planning. Let me think on it."

"OK. Could you get a message off to Paul, tell him what Vic said?"

"I will."

"Thanks. Bye."

Rachael replaced the receiver. She closed her eyes as her thoughts spanned the wide Pacific. She longed to see the one she . . . What did she feel about Paul? She wasn't sure. But she knew it was strong. And she knew it was growing. "Paul, where are you?" she moaned.

* * *

Hanna encrypted the concise message, stored it inside the picture of a roadrunner on her letterhead, and sent the E-mail on its way. Then she tilted back in her swivel chair as she pondered what she might do. If she only knew what the Chinese were targeting. She heard the front door open. *Another long day at work,* she noted, as she listened to the hurried footsteps on the stairs.

Russell stuck his head inside the office. "I'm home."

She turned toward him and got up. She smiled but somehow couldn't chase away her preoccupation.

"Is something wrong?" he asked as he kissed her.

"Hi, dear. I got an E-mail from Paul a little while ago."

"Good." He paused. "It *is* good news, isn't it?"

"Oh, yes. He's on his way back, and he's got the defector with him. I called Rachael, and she brought Vic up-to-date."

"Ah, I think I catch the drift. Vic's still balking."

"Big time."

Russell shook his head. "Well, we can't do anything about that."

"Maybe." She saw suspicion come to his face.

"What's that mean?"

"Nothing. I was thinking out loud."

"Hanna?"

She heard his rising concern. "I'm just thinking—really."

"Oh, Scott had dinner over at the McCluskys. Do you want to go get him, or should I?"

"I'll do it," he said. "Do we need anything while I'm out?"

"No. I'll fix us something to eat while you're gone. Pizza OK?" She saw his eyes light up.

"You bet." He paused, and a glint came to his eyes. "Homemade or delivered?"

"That depends on whether I can hide the boxes or not. Now be gone."

"Yes, ma'am."

He kissed her and left for their bedroom. A few minutes later he dashed downstairs and out the door.

She turned back to her large-screen monitor and stared at the Windows NT desktop, what she called her gateway to the world. She scooted the mouse pointer around the screen as she contemplated the problem. She didn't know what the Chinese were targeting, and she had no power to act if she did. *But do the Chinese know that?* she wondered. What she had done in December 1999 had certainly surprised them. If she could get them to react, Rachael's boss would have to do something, wouldn't he? She thought about what America would be like in economic ruins. That some foreign country would do that—on purpose!

She gritted her teeth, switched to Outlook, and clicked the New Mail Message button. She selected Lau Jianguo's E-mail address, tabbed down to the subject line, and keyed, "I see you." One more tab placed the cursor in the message box. After a slight pause, her fingers flew over the keyboard, typing two terse sentences.

> I know what you are planning! It didn't work in January 2000, and it won't work now!

Hanna read the subject line and then the message. She stared at it as the cursor hovered over the send button. She jabbed the left mouse button with more force than was required. The message box disappeared, and for a moment she saw a count of one in her outbox. Then that disappeared. The message was on its way. For a while she felt good. Then she began to wonder if she should have thought it over.

* * *

Jiang tried to remain calm, but it was difficult. His boss in Beijing had assured him that military liaison would be set up immediately. That had been over an hour ago, and every minute took the traitor and that American farther from Chinese waters. If Zhu got away, the cost would be beyond counting. Even though he had been expecting it, he still jumped when the phone rang.

He grabbed the receiver. "Yes?"

"Mr. Gao is on the line for you," his secretary said.

Jiang frowned. "I wasn't expecting him. What does he want?"

"He did not say."

Jiang sighed and punched the blinking button. "Hello."

"Mr. Jiang, we have a problem."

Jiang's frown grew deeper. "What do you mean?"

"Ms. Flaherty knows what we are doing."

"That's impossible!"

"She sent Lau an E-mail."

"Your watchdog in Seattle?"

"Yes. She said she knows what we are doing and that it won't work. She made a reference to what we tried in 1999."

Jiang traced Victoria Peak with his eyes as he pondered what to say. "Was that all?"

"Yes."

"Something else has come up. I need you in Hong Kong as soon as you can get here."

"What? I'm a busy man. I can't leave right now."

"It is not a request. You have been with Project Dragon from the start, and I need your help."

"I don't understand."

"Zhu has defected."

"*What!*"

"Paul Parker was in Hong Kong picking up David Ho's yacht. We believe Zhu is a stowaway."

"Wasn't Parker involved in . . ."

"Yes," Jiang interrupted. "And I have *not* forgotten."

"How did Zhu get past all the checkpoints?"

Jiang gritted his teeth. "That is not the point! I will take care of Zhu and Parker. Right now, I am more worried about Hanna Flaherty. She is outside my control."

"But what can she do? Zhu assured us no one can find the Raptor Virus unless they know where to look. There are billions of embedded circuits."

"It was impossible for anyone to discover the defective power circuit breakers we planted, but she did it. My brother, Wu, underestimated that woman. I am not making the same mistake."

"I think you are overreacting."

Jiang saw another light start blinking on his phone set. "You forget your place," he snapped. "I expect you in Hong Kong as soon as you can get here. Meanwhile, I have other things to take care of."

He punched the blinking button, disconnecting Gao. "Yes?"

"Admiral Pang, here. I received orders to call you."

Jiang sensed the man's confusion. "Yes. I require military liaison for a sensitive project—your ears only."

"I understand. How may I help you?"

"A traitor left Hong Kong this morning around eight on a yacht."

"Who?"

"You have no need to know. The boat's name is *Sophisticated Lady,* belonging to David Ho."

"Ho is involved?"

"Admiral, I suggest you confine yourself to the mission."

"Yes, sir."

"My secretary will be faxing you the yacht's sailing papers shortly."

"Do you want me to board the yacht and arrest this traitor?"

"No, Admiral. I want you to sink them. There is to be no trace whatsoever."

"Sir?"

"Do you understand what I said?"

"Yes, of course."

"Then carry out your orders." Jiang slammed down the receiver.

* * *

Paul held the *Sophisticated Lady* on a steady course of 95 degrees true. He and Tang had settled on a four-on, four-off watch at the helm. His first mate had finished his watch at four and was below getting some sleep. *It would be a long crossing,* he thought.

The wind continued fresh from the northeast, and although clouds were piling up, there was no sign of a storm. But Paul sensed one coming, and he knew it could appear without much warning. A glance at the chronometer told him it was almost 5:00 P.M. They had been underway for nearly nine hours. In the old days he would have had to take a celestial navigation fix or estimate his position. However, the Global Positioning Service (GPS) receiver gave their position within several hundred feet. The *Sophisticated Lady* was 95 miles from Hong Kong and still quite close to the China coast, although in international waters. He frowned in his frustration. There was no way to speed their flight to safety.

* * *

The pilot of the Chinese Harbin H-5, snug under his bubble canopy, scanned the sea below when holes in the clouds permitted. A copy of the venerable Russian Ilyushin Il-28 bomber, the H-5 found service primarily in the Chinese maritime patrol. Ahead of the pilot was the bombardier. Nestled inside his World War II style greenhouse nose, he had the best seat in the house. A third crewman manned the twin twenty-three-millimeter cannons in the tail.

The pilot felt uneasy about his orders but knew they had to be followed. What really puzzled him was what threat an unarmed yacht posed to the People's Republic of China. But that was not for him to decide. So far their only sighting had been a freighter en route to Hong Kong. They were using a standard search pattern, which meant they were seeing a lot of nothing. And if the weather continued to deteriorate, they would see even less.

"I have a contact," the bombardier said over the intercom.

"Where?" the pilot asked.

"Dead ahead. I caught a glimpse of sails through a hole in the clouds."

The pilot hesitated as he pondered what to do. His orders were to get a positive identification, then sink the boat without allowing them to get off a distress message. This would probably be impossible, but the orders didn't list that as an option. Sink the wrong boat, and the military would hang him; and if a warning got off, the same would happen. He contemplated ignoring the contact but decided he couldn't really do that. He pulled the throttles back and pushed the bomber into a shallow dive.

"Did you get a course estimate?" the pilot asked.

"I estimate 100 degrees."

The pilot glanced at his compass: 180 degrees due south. He began a slow turn to the right until the compass read 270. He held that course as the bomber began descending through the scudding cloud layers. Minutes later they broke through into clear air, miles behind their target. The pilot racked the plane around into a tight turn and settled on a course of 100 degrees at 50 feet off the choppy sea. The overcast was almost complete now.

"Look sharp," the pilot commanded. "I want a positive ID on the first pass. If that's our target, we will begin our bombing run immediately."

"Roger," the bombardier replied.

The pilot strained his eyes searching for a speck on the horizon, which would become a yacht. He pulled the throttles back farther to give himself and the bombardier more time.

"There it is!" the bombardier announced. "Off to the left a little."

"I see it." The pilot turned until the growing dot was centered in his canopy. He dropped even lower until the bomber was skimming the wave tops. It seemed to take forever to close within a mile, but the last thousand feet went by in a blurred flash.

"Did you get it?" The pilot asked.

"Roger! *Sophisticated Lady!* That's it!"

"Stand by for the bomb run!" the pilot ordered.

* * *

Paul leaned to the side as he looked forward over the sharply heeling deck. The yacht sliced through the seas with precise pitching motions, throwing fine spray with each plunge. The northwesterly wind gusted in over the port bow, carrying away all sounds from astern. For this reason Paul had no advance warning of the bomber's approach.

He jumped as the sleek silver shape screamed past below mast height level. Raw fear stabbed every nerve as he watched the bomber accelerate in a climbing left turn. He recognized the markings instantly. The Chinese maritime patrol had found them. The smell of kerosene was almost overpowering as the yacht sailed through the plane's exhaust trail. Paul followed the bomber as it flew to the north and made a sharp 180 to head back in. There was no doubt what the pilot intended to do.

"Ready to jibe!" Paul bellowed at the crew.

The two sailors ran to the winches. Paul watched as the bomber came straight at them. The bomb bay doors snapped opened. Paul's heart thudded in his chest. Closer and closer the plane came, until Paul could see the bombardier hunched over the bombsight.

"Jibe-ho!"

Paul spun the tiller all the way to the right. The *Sophisticated Lady's* rudder took hold, and the bow came around to the right smartly. The apparent wind shifted from over the port bow to over the port quarter and finally from astern. The crew cranked the winches frantically, pulling the main and mizzen booms back in. Finally the wind started coming in over the starboard quarter and got behind the sails, throwing them over onto the port side. The crew reversed their cranking to let the booms out on the new tack. Paul centered the helm on a downwind run before the wind and ordered the crew to let the sails out further.

He glanced back and saw the bomber banking hard, trying to maintain aim. Two olive drab cylinders dropped away from the open bomb bay and seemed to fall in slow motion. Paul could tell they were falling a little to the side and aft. *But was it enough?* he wondered.

"Hit the deck!" he ordered.

The crewmen did as ordered. Paul fell prostrate and closed his eyes. The two explosions merged into one deafening blast. The boat's stern lurched upward, and a wall of water thundered down accompanied by the stench of cordite. Paul lifted his head and squinted forward. He caught a glimpse of the bomber as it roared past in a tight right turn.

Tang charged up on deck as Paul got on his feet.

"What's happening?" the first mate demanded, his eyes wide in fear.

"Patrol craft attacked us!" Paul yelled, his ears still ringing. He looked past Tang and saw Zhu at the top of the ladder. The man hesitated, then finally came out on deck.

Tang followed Paul's eyes and saw the stowaway. "Who are you?" he demanded.

Paul turned and searched the sky frantically. "Belay that! The bomber's coming around again!" He followed the silver shape as it made a broad turn to come in from the northwest. The pilot was flying much slower now.

"He's going to take his time on this one," Paul told his first mate. "Ready to jibe!" he bellowed at the crew.

The two men began cranking in the sails.

"Jibe-ho!" Paul ordered, spinning the wheel all the way to port.

The yacht swung swiftly around to port and through the wind again. The sails swung over, and Paul settled in on a beam reach driving hard toward the southeast.

"What . . . ?" Zhu began.

"Not now!" Paul snapped. "Go below until this is over!"

"No! I'm staying up here!"

Paul glared at him. "I don't have time to argue! Stay out of the way!"

Tang leaned close. "What are you going to do?" he asked Paul.

"Start to reverse course before they drop. But right after we come about, immediately reverse course again to the previous course. Will you give the orders?"

"Yes. Get them to change their aim, then turn back after they're committed."

Paul nodded. "That's the idea, but it's going to take split-second timing." Paul glanced toward the ladder leading down and saw the cook near the top with the other two crewmen right behind. "Get those men below!"

Tang barked the order. The three faces disappeared.

The clouds grew heavier as the ceiling continued to drop. But Paul knew it would not prevent the attack. Around came the bomber, this time much slower. He watched as the plane approached. The bomber grew larger and larger as it aimed at the yacht's broad, white side. Time seemed to stand still. Paul longed to throw the helm over but knew their lives depended on waiting for the right moment. The bomb bay doors popped open. Still Paul waited.

"Now!" he bellowed as he cranked the wheel all the way over to port.

Tang gave his orders.

The *Sophisticated Lady's* rudder bit in hard, and the bow swung rapidly around to the northwest. In moments they were around on the new tack. As he expected, the plane angled a little to the west. Paul waited two more seconds then cranked the wheel back to starboard. The yacht's bow obediently curved back around through the wind, regained the port tack, and finally settled in on the former course. The bombs fell away. Paul watched as they both landed behind them.

The jet pulled into a tight bank. Paul knew the pilot was assessing the damage—and probably cursing. After a few moments the bomber disappeared into the thick clouds.

"Is he giving up?" Tang asked.

"I think he's out of bombs." Paul replied. He worried momentarily about the twin twenty-three-millimeter cannons in the Harbin's nose, but when the plane did not reappear, he figured the pilot was radioing for orders and reporting the *Sophisticated Lady's* position. That was bad news, he knew, as it opened them up to attack by aircraft, surface ships, and submarines.

Paul brought the yacht back to its original base course.

Heavy raindrops began to fall out of the dark clouds. Soon a squall would be upon them. The light continued to fail as dusk approached.

Tang glanced at the stowaway, then turned his attention fully on Paul. "We need to talk," the man said. It was not a question.

"Yes, I suppose we do," Paul agreed.

19

PAUL'S MIND RACED AS HE HELD THE *SOPHISTICATED LADY*
steady on course. *Was that the end of the attacks?* he wondered. He thought
of the thousands of miles of open sea until they reached Hawaii. They
were still very much in the South China Sea, which China regarded as
theirs, international waters or not. One thing was sure: He did *not* want
to return to a Chinese port.

"Who is this man, and what is he doing here?" Tang demanded.

"That is none of your business!" Zhu said.

"It is very much my business! Let's start with stowing away. I know you
don't have Mr. Ho's permission to be aboard his yacht. And you have
most certainly violated the exit regulations of the People's Republic of
China."

Zhu remained silent.

Tang turned to Paul. "You do know this man, don't you?"

Paul nodded. "Yes."

"Please explain."

"Under the circumstances there's not much I can say, beyond what you
already know. The man is a stowaway, and since he's not listed in our

sailing papers, it's logical to assume he doesn't have permission to leave China."

"That's not good enough."

"It will have to do for now. I doubt we're done with your naval forces."

"That is easily taken care of. Radio Hong Kong and tell them we're returning to port."

"I wouldn't advise that."

"And why not?"

Paul's eyes bored into the man. "Your government will have lots of questions for you! I doubt you will be able to convince them you didn't know about the stowaway. They are a little on the suspicious side, shall we say, when it comes to situations like this." Paul saw that the first mate understood. The sudden fear in his eyes was real.

Tang hesitated. "I can explain."

"Don't give me that! It wouldn't work, and you know it. At the very least you'd lose your job with David. And the government would be looking over your shoulder for the rest of your life. Do you really want that?"

"I need to think it over."

"You do that. And in the meantime we have to plan on how we're going to keep from being blown out of the water." Paul looked up into the gathering storm. "This weather should give us a breather, but it can't last forever."

Tang glared at the stowaway, then went below.

"What are your plans now?" Zhu asked.

Paul eyed the compass as he thought about how long it would take to reach Hawaii. The grim reality began to sink in. "I don't know," he said with a sigh. "With Huo's death, I suppose this was inevitable. But we don't have any option but to continue on."

"What will they do?"

"Send out more patrol planes—plus surface ships and subs probably."

"All that?"

"You know how badly they want you."

"But the ocean is big. They can't search it all."

"That's true enough. But they know exactly where we are now. Assuming they don't find us tonight, the search box won't be all that large by morning. We're not exactly speed demons. Add to that the fact they know where we're going."

"What about another port?"

Paul hesitated. "I've been thinking about that, but our options aren't all that great. We're closest to Taiwan, but I don't want to get wrapped up in politics between Taiwan and the mainland."

"What about the Philippines?"

"That's a possibility, but our relations with them aren't the best. Guam is probably our best shot, but Japan might do, or even Australia. But if the Chinese find us again, all this will be wishful thinking."

Zhu looked around at the rapidly darkening sky. "I am going below."

"I think that's best. When I get off watch, I'll unlock the master's suite. You might as well be comfortable while we wait and see how this works out."

Zhu turned and went down the ladder.

Paul considered calling Vic on the satellite phone but decided to wait for nightfall with its welcome shield of darkness, which would make attack less likely.

* * *

In the gathering darkness Eddie Zanders ran a hand through his curly black hair as he stared at the Kaohsiung storefront in disbelief. At twenty-seven he was still learning how to measure the unexpected against the yard-stick of eternity. He clinched his teeth in irritation, relieved his wife, Barbara, wasn't with him. She had her own challenges, he knew, struggling to make the cramped apartment into a home. He had made a quick survey with her, noting all the things they would have to work out with the landlord. The "honey-do" list was becoming formidable.

Only last week the Zanders had completed their missionary training in T'aipei. Many times Eddie had wondered at his wisdom in accepting this call. After four years in seminary, the couple had spent another two intense years in learning the intricacies of Taiwanese and Mandarin Chinese while they worked with another missionary couple. Eddie knew he hadn't mastered either language, but at least he could make himself understood, and the Chinese usually didn't laugh at what he inadvertently said.

A week ago the Zanders had relocated to the coastal city of Kaohsiung. After a long search, Eddie had finally found a storefront building that was large enough (barely) and within his meager budget. The only problem was, the former tenant had not removed all his property from the building. Stacks of empty snake cages obscured much of the narrow sidewalk.

Eddie maintained a cautious distance from the cages. He assumed they were empty, but he wasn't sure. He pulled on a rusty chain, and the steel roll door went up with a noisy clanking. Inside he saw the actual front: broad plateglass windows that still proclaimed the former tenant's wares and the double glass doors. Eddie entered the store proper and felt around for the light switch. The lights came on, revealing more cages along with tall rows of wooden shelves. He sighed. All these leftover fixtures would have to go before he could begin to convert the space into a rudimentary church. Then he smiled as he realized this was just one more thing to overcome. He and his wife had a place to live, and they had a church building. Many missionaries didn't have that much. *Yes*, he thought. *This will do nicely. All it takes is a little work.*

Eddie's original plan had been to sweep out the store and decide where he wanted the rear wall built to enclose a small kitchen, office, and bathroom. But he had to have the old fixtures cleared out first. He randomly pulled out drawers, half expecting to find dreadful things. But they were all empty, with only faint odors of esoteric smells remaining. He looked around a little longer, then decided to return to the apartment to help Barbara.

* * *

Paul maintained the yacht's eastern course. He glanced down at the dimly lit instruments noting it was nearly eight, the end of his watch and the beginning of Tang's. He heard footsteps on the ladder and saw a dark shape emerge.

"Tang, is that you?" he asked.

"No—Zhu. We must talk."

Paul felt his earlier fear return. "OK. What's on your mind?"

The man came close. "I heard the crew talking in the galley. They are very upset."

"Was Tang with them?"

"He was."

"What do they want?"

"I only heard a little bit. They told Tang they wanted to return to Hong Kong, but he explained why this wasn't possible."

"Did he convince them?"

"I'm not sure. They weren't happy, but I think they understood the problem."

"Anything else?"

"I don't know. I didn't want to get caught, so I turned around and came up here."

"Thanks for the warning."

Zhu didn't reply. Paul wondered what was going through his mind but decided to wait him out. It took several tense minutes.

"What can you offer me, Mr. Parker?" Zhu asked at last.

"Political asylum in exchange for what you know about the Raptor Virus."

"But you said the CIA did not send you. And you told Huo that you were having trouble arranging asylum."

Paul took a deep breath. "Things are different now, don't you think?"

"Are they?"

"I think so. Based on what you know, I can't imagine our government refusing you sanctuary."

"But you don't know, not for sure."

Paul hesitated. "No, I don't. But as soon as Tang relieves me, I'm going to contact my boss at the CIA and see what he can do for us."

"Make sure he understands. I will not cooperate unless your government takes care of me."

"I know that. I'll do everything I can."

Rapid footsteps sounded on the ladder.

"Mr. Parker," Tang said, approaching. "I must see you in private."

"Whatever you have to say will have to be in front of Mr. Zhu. He's staying right here."

"He is the source of our trouble."

Paul's anger flared in an instant. "The source of our trouble is the idiots running your government!" He paused as he struggled for control. "I'm sorry—truly sorry—for what happened, but it wasn't my doing."

"This gets us nowhere. What will you do for me, Mr. Parker? What will you do for the crew? They wanted to go back to Hong Kong until I explained what would happen."

"You were wise in talking them out of it."

"We shall see. Now, please answer my question."

"Under the circumstances I think you and the crew qualify for asylum the same as Mr. Zhu."

"You think? You don't know?"

Paul felt sweat pop out in his armpits. "I don't have that authority. But I believe my government will grant it—to all of you. This is the best hope you've got."

"I could take over and sail this yacht to some port far away from here."

"Yeah, right! Commit mutiny, steal a rich man's yacht, and run away from the peace-loving rulers of your country who will have you shot on sight. That sounds real appealing."

Paul watched the dark shape standing before him, wondering what he would do. The moments stretched on as the *Sophisticated Lady* plunged through the heavy swells. He tensed, half expecting a lunge at any moment.

"I hope your government is reasonable," Tang said finally.

Paul cleared his throat as the tension began to drain away, along with his energy. "I hope so too. Are you ready to take the watch?"

"I am."

Paul stepped back and allowed him to take the wheel. "Good. I'll call my boss now. The sooner we get started, the better off we'll all be."

"I hope so," Tang replied.

Paul returned to his cabin and got the satellite phone. With Zhu's help he set it up near the cockpit. He aimed the antenna. He decided to try Vic's home number, hoping he was not already on his way into Langley. It was 7:00 A.M. in Washington, and Paul knew his boss was not an early riser. He punched in the number and waited as it rang. On the fifth ring the receiver clicked.

"Hello," came the reply.

"Vic. This is Paul. I need your help."

There was the slightest of pauses. "Paul! What do you think you're doing? Rachael told me what you did! I'll have your head for this!"

Paul felt his anger returning. "We can talk about that later, but right now I'm in danger of being blown out of the water!"

"What?"

"You heard me. The friendly PRC folk just dropped four bombs on us. Luckily the pilot's aim wasn't all that great, or I'd be calling you from a life raft."

"Stop right there! This is your own fault! If you hadn't . . ."

"I don't have time for this, Vic! The point is, I've got the guy who knows all about Project Dragon with me . . ."

"But . . ."

"And we're going to be dead meat unless you do something, and quick! The PRC patrol bomber almost sank us! Believe me, they're going to keep it up until they kill us all unless you do something!" Paul listened as silence came over the clear connection.

"I don't know what I can do," Vic finally said in a more subdued tone.

"Let me help you. Get on the spook phone to the Defense Department and tell them to get these guys off our backs."

"But . . ."

"Listen, Vic. Rachael knows about this, and so does Hanna Flaherty. This is going to get out eventually, and if you leave us hanging out to dry . . ."

"Rachael can't say anything. This is classified."

"Maybe, but Hanna sure can. And she's not very bashful, as I'm sure you know."

"You told a civilian about this?"

"Hey! I'm a civilian."

"But you're part-time CIA. You know the security requirements as well as I do."

"Yes, I do. But Hanna is a source, and you know how that works. Experts can't work without information."

"But you didn't check with me about this."

"We can work that out after I get back. Which brings me back to the reason for this call. I need you to get the defense boys on the stick, and I mean now! It's night where I am, but I fully expect another attack in the morning. If we don't get help, we're dead." Paul felt his stomach knot up as he waited.

"I'll see what I can do," Vic said finally.

"I appreciate it. And one other thing . . ."

"What's that?" Vic snapped.

"Political asylum for Mr. Zhu Tak-shing. He's the Project Dragon guru."

"You sure he's the real thing?"

"As sure as I can be. It'll be easy enough to prove once we get back, but without an agreement he won't cooperate."

"I'm not buying a pig in a poke," Vic said, but without force.

"Trust me on this. He knows. Why not get the wheels turning?"

"I'll check into it after I contact DOD."

"Fine. I appreciate it. Oh, one more thing. We're going to have to do something about the crew on this boat. We can't turn them over to the Chinese; you know what they'd do to them."

The phone remained silent.

"Vic? Are you there?"

"Yes. You're just full of little surprises for me, aren't you?"

"I am sorry for the trouble. I didn't expect this would happen, but it did."

"OK, OK. But I'm not done with this. Tell me your position. No, hold that for the military. What's your course?"

"We're in the South China Sea west of Taiwan. I expect to be in the Luzon Strait south of Taiwan by tomorrow night, if the PRC don't get us. My sailing papers give Honolulu as our first port of call; however, I'm changing that to Guam."

"That sounds best. The sooner we get this over, the better." Vic's sigh came clearly over the phone. "Keep me posted. I've got a lot to do."

Paul gave him the satellite phone number and disconnected. Dark thoughts churned in his mind as a series of disasters played themselves out in soundless fury. So many things could go wrong. But then a quiet peace stole over him, strangely contrasting with the disturbed seas. Nothing could happen to him that God did not already know. Paul knew that he might be dead in the morning, but that wasn't the final end.

"Do you want help with this?" Zhu asked, his voice jolting Paul back to the present.

"What? Oh. No, I'm expecting a call back. But you can go below, if you want. You can have the master's suite, but I think you'd be better off staying in my cabin."

"I will stay with you."

"OK. I'll be down after a while."

The dark shadow turned and disappeared down the ladder. Paul glanced back at Tang. The first mate was keeping his watch in silence as he maintained the prescribed course. Paul longed to call Rachael. Even though it was around 4:00 A.M. her time, Vic would be calling her soon anyway. But Paul knew he couldn't take a chance on blocking a call from the military. How long he would have to wait or what command would call, he had no idea.

20

THE OVERCAST MADE THE NIGHT VERY DARK. PAUL looked back at the cockpit. The ghostly glow of the instruments cast a faint illumination on Tang's impassive face as he steered the large yacht. Paul glanced at his watch. It was after 10:00 P.M. and still no answer. He checked the satellite phone and saw the communications link was still up. *How long does it take to get the military to respond?* he wondered, not for the first time. *What if Vic has decided not to involve them? What if the director has put a lid on things?* He tried to remain calm, but it wasn't easy. He jumped as the phone chirped. Paul grabbed the handset.

"This is Paul Parker!" he said in a rush.

"Mr. Parker, this is Captain Bob Ingram, commanding officer of the USS *John Stennis*. I am holding some rather strange orders in my hands. Top secret orders. They say I am to offer you every assistance. Can you fill me in?"

"Yes, I can. I'm the skipper of the *Sophisticated Lady* out of Hong Kong bound for Seattle. Near dusk today we were attacked by a twin jet PRC bomber, and I'm convinced more attacks are coming."

"Sounds like a Harbin H-5. Any damage?"

"Not as far as I know. They made two passes. Dropped two bombs each time."

"I see. What is your present location?"

"Wait one," Paul said. He hurried to the cockpit, noted the GPS read-out, and returned. "We're at 116 degrees, 28 minutes, 12 seconds east and 21 degrees, 51 minutes, 5 seconds north."

"Are those GPS coordinates?"

"Yes, they are."

"Good. What's your course and speed?"

"Ninety-six degrees true at ten knots presently."

"What does your boat look like?"

"Ketch-rigged yacht, white hull, 115 feet long. Presently in one piece."

The officer laughed. "Let's see if we can keep it that way. Mr. Parker, *Johnny Reb*'s at your disposal. My orders come right from the top, as I'm sure you know."

"Johnny Reb?" Paul asked in surprise.

"The *John Stennis* is named for the late Senator Stennis of Mississippi."

"Oh. Well, I certainly appreciate your help."

"Glad to be of assistance. We left Yokosuka, Japan, at sixteen-hundred hours bound for Pearl Harbor, but we've turned around and are making over twenty knots in your direction."

Paul felt his heart sink. "So, you're what—about fourteen hundred nautical miles away?"

"About."

"So when can you give me some cover?"

Captain Ingram paused. "It will be a while. You're beyond the range even of my S-3 Vikings, and they have pretty long legs. But I'm trying to get us a P-3 Orion out of Kadena, Okinawa."

"Captain, I don't want to sound ungrateful, but I fully expect a PRC come-as-you-are party around dawn."

"Believe me, I understand. I'll report this up the line. Anything else I need to know right now?"

"No, except please hurry!"

"Roger that! I presume I can reach you at this number."

"Yes, or by radio. We're monitoring the emergency frequencies."

"Let's stick with the satellite phone, since it's a little more secure."

"OK."

"Hang in there, Mr. Parker. I'll get to you as soon as I can."

The phone clicked and went dead. Tang's watch was more than half over. Paul considered going below, but he knew he couldn't sleep before he came on at twelve. Maybe he could catch some shut-eye when Tang took the four-to-eight. But probably not, because eight was well past dawn. Weariness stole over him as he fetched a folding aluminum chair and sat down beside the phone to wait.

* * *

Rachael sipped her coffee as she sat in her apartment kitchen. She had been up since five, after a restless night and little sleep. It was almost six. Too early to go to work, and she wasn't sure she was going in today anyway.

She jumped when the secure phone rang. "Hello?"

"This is Vic." He sounded tired also. "Just wanted to let you know that the Navy is sending an aircraft carrier to help Paul out."

Rachael felt an icy chill in her spine. "Help him out of what?"

"A Chinese patrol plane attacked them several hours ago."

"Oh, no! He's not hurt, is he?"

"No, no. He's fine. The bombs missed."

"Oh, thank God. How soon will the Navy get there?"

"That's a little bit of a problem. The carrier's patrol planes won't be in range for about another day."

Rachael reached for the box of tissues as the tears came. "But what if the Chinese attack again?" she managed to ask.

"Take it easy. The military's working on it. The carrier captain has asked for a long-range patrol plane, and they'll have one in the air as soon as they can get a crew in."

"Thank you."

"We're doing everything we can." He paused. "Rachael, I'm still mad about what Paul did, but if this defector is the real thing . . ."

"He *is* the real thing," Rachael interrupted.

"Let me finish, please. I'm well aware of your opinion, and for what it's worth, I think you may be right. We'll see when we can get them into a port somewhere. Now I've got to go. I'm late for a meeting."

"I understand. You'll let me know what's happening?"

"I will. Bye."

"Bye."

Rachael thought it over and decided she had to call Hanna. She picked up the phone and dialed.

* * *

Paul waited until after eleven, then placed the call he wanted most. The line clicked after the first ring.

"Hello," came a familiar voice. Paul felt a fresh surge of energy.

"Rachael, this is Paul."

"Paul! Thank God you called! Are you all right?"

"Yes. Did Vic contact you?"

"Yes, and he told me what happened. What are you going to do?"

"The best I can. The captain of the *Stennis* said it would be a while until they're in range. But he's trying to arrange a long-range plane."

"Vic said one would be on the way as soon as they can get a crew."

"Good. I guess the military's serious about this. Did he say anything about Mr. Zhu?"

"Yes. I believe Vic's coming around. He'll probably recommend political asylum."

"I'd like him to be a little more positive than that."

"Me, too."

"Well, I need to hang up. I'm expecting a call from Captain Ingram."

"I understand."

Paul swallowed a lump in his throat. "You don't know how much I wanted to hear your voice. I . . ."

"What?" she asked.

"I miss you."

After a few moments she replied. "I miss you too, Paul."

After he disconnected, Paul sat by the satellite phone until nearly twelve as he tried to sort out his thoughts. His fears about what the new day would bring played tag with his deep longing for Rachael. Although he was still convinced that going to get Zhu had been the right thing to do, he hated the consequences. Finally he got up and went below. Minutes later he and Zhu were back on deck, Paul for his watch and Zhu to watch over the phone.

* * *

The Chinese Kilo submarine pitched and rolled in the heavy seas as it cruised along barely submerged. The diesel engines thudded away, faithfully recharging the sub's batteries and providing power for the electric drive motor.

The captain frowned, but it wasn't because of the uncomfortable motion of his boat. He looked over the shoulder of his navigator at the South China Sea chart. He stroked his stubbled chin as he pondered his orders, received an hour ago when the Kilo had reached periscope depth to start snorkeling to recharge the depleted batteries.

The orders were clear enough. Proceed to the coordinates provided by the Harbin H-5, locate a large white-hulled ketch, and sink it. *But, why?* the captain wondered. He would carry out his orders; there was no question of that. But that would require an uncomfortable transit, requiring a series of submerged sprints at seventeen knots followed by a few hours snorkeling to recharge the batteries. Diesel boats did not have the luxury of unlimited submerged runs that were available to nuclear subs.

"Stand by to surface," the captain ordered.

At his command, high-pressure air poured into the ballast tanks, and the Kilo bobbed to the surface like a cork. The captain ordered the snorkeling secured as the powerful diesels switched to the normal intake manifold for air.

"All ahead flank! Come left to one-seven-zero."

He grabbed a stanchion as the sub took a violent roll to starboard. Loud crashes accompanied by fervent curses revealed improperly secured manuals and equipment. A wry grin came to the captain's face, despite his concern about his orders. His crew were not used to this, since they spent most of their time in the calm depths. He wondered how long it would be before seasickness claimed its first victim.

* * *

At 11:51 P.M., the aircraft commander taxied onto the active runway at NAF Kadena, Okinawa, and pushed the power levers forward. The heavily loaded P-3C Orion began its lumbering takeoff roll down the active runway while the copilot monitored the readouts. The runway lights came toward them, slowly at first, then in a blur as the plane jounced along on the uneven surface. Reaching flying speed, the venerable Lockheed sub-hunter rotated and lifted into the unstable night air. Moments later it flew into the low overcast.

"Who turned out the lights?" the commander asked, to break the tension.

"Wasn't me, Skipper," his copilot replied with a laugh. He was a young lieutenant and newly assigned to the P-3 detachment at Kadena. "Maybe the base CO forgot to pay the electric bill."

The aircraft commander nodded. "Yeah, that's probably it. What can you expect from an Air Force operation?" He scanned the instruments and found, as he expected, that all readings were nominal. The bird was ready, and hopefully the crew were as well.

"Skipper?" the copilot asked.

"Yes?"

"What do you make of our orders?"

"Locate a 115-foot ketch and provide surveillance for the officer in tactical command aboard *Johnny Reb*. Attacks possible from PRC patrol aircraft, surface units, and subs. Sounds pretty routine to me."

"Skipper!"

The commander steadied the aircraft as they entered severe turbulence. "We carry out our orders, mister. We give Captain Ingram some eyes and ears and await his commands. That's all we need to know."

"Yes, sir."

Not that the commander did not wonder. But fifteen years of naval service had taught him what he could question and what he couldn't. And top secret orders—orders that were restricted to him, his copilot, and the relief pilot—were not the kind you questioned. Later they would know more—maybe. Meanwhile, it was onward through the murk.

The P-3 reached cruising altitude and droned on toward its destination as the crew monitored their duty stations. A little over two hours later the commander caught an unmistakable whiff of coffee.

"Are you gents awake up here?" the flight engineer chief asked. "Brought some coffee from the galley."

The pilot turned and took the thick mug. "You sure this is safe to drink, Chief?"

"Yes, sir. You won't find any better in the Chief's Mess."

"That's what I was afraid of. Did you put any salt in it?"

"Navy coffee's got to have a little salt, sir. You know that."

"If you say so." He took a sip. It was strong and hot, and he noticed there was a hint of salt. Still he could feel his earlier weariness dissipating as the caffeine began to take hold. "Not bad."

"Thank you, sir. What's the scoop on what we're looking for?"

The commander knew they were on station now, allowing him to brief the crew. "You know the classification of our orders."

"Yes, sir. Heard they were 'you'll know when you get there.'"

The pilot laughed. "You know the drill, Chief. But we're on station now. Tell the crew we're looking for a large ketch-rigged yacht, white hull—the *Sophisticated Lady* out of Hong Kong. A PRC bomber tried to sink them at dusk today—yesterday, I mean."

"What? An unarmed civilian boat?"

"That's right."

"Why?"

"I don't know. But we're to locate them for *Johnny Reb*. What happens after that is up to the officer in tactical command."

"Sounds like deep stuff, sir."

"Roger that." He flipped the intercom switch. "TACCO (tactical coordinator), Flight, anything on the radar?"

The response was clear in his earphones. "Flight, TACCO. Not a thing, Skipper. But a boat that size is hard for the radar to paint with the seas running so high. You thinking of going down for a look-see?"

"You're reading my mind. Let's see if we can pick them up on the low-light television."

"Roger that," the TACCO replied.

The commander turned back to his flight engineer. "All systems go, Chief?"

"Yes, sir. We're ready when you are."

The pilot pulled the power levers back and started the P-3 on a steep descent toward the sea below. The hissing sound of the slipstream became a roar as the aircraft's airspeed neared the red line. The altimeter unwound rapidly. The pilot pulled out when the radar altimeter read five hundred feet. The windshield might as well have been painted black as he brought the plane around to a heading of ninety-six degrees true.

He keyed the intercom. "Sensor three, Flight, see anything?"

"No, sir," the low-light TV operator replied. "We're still in the clouds."

The pilot continued a gentle descent, keeping his eyes on the radar altimeter. He felt sweat break out in his armpits as the instrument indicated two hundred feet above the angry waves.

"Flight, sensor three! We're out! I can see the water!"

"I was beginning to wonder if the clouds went down to the deck," the pilot remarked as he leveled out. "Any contacts?"

"No, sir. Swells and chop all the way to the horizon."

"OK. We're probably to the east of them. This weather's probably holding them up. Coming around to two-seven-six. Keep a sharp lookout."

"Yes, sir."

The copilot turned his head. "We could miss them entirely if they deviated just a little from their course."

"That's what standard search patterns are for," the commander replied. "We'll find them."

A few minutes later. "Flight, sensor three. Contact, sir, zero-one-zero relative."

"Is it the *Sophisticated Lady?*" the pilot asked.

"I see two sails. They're coming toward us, but I can't tell what kind of rig yet."

"Roger. Altering course to port. Get a good look when we go by."

"Aye, aye, sir."

* * *

Paul steered as much from feel as sight, as the dark overcast night swallowed up all else. But the compass and GPS readout told him his course was steady, despite the heavy seas. The *Sophisticated Lady* handled well. Paul grinned in spite of his worries since he knew the design and construction were beyond reproach. He wondered at this thought a moment, but decided that it was the truth rather than pride.

Scanning the instruments, he saw it was a little after two in the morning. He sighed. Tang wouldn't relieve him until four. He cocked his head to the side, wondering if he really heard something or if his imagination was playing tricks on him. A tense knot formed in his stomach as he strained to hear. The faint whining sound grew louder, but he couldn't see a thing. The sound increased in volume until it swept past to starboard. Paul had no idea what it was except that it was a turboprop. He hoped it was a Navy P-3. He listened for it to return. A few minutes later the unseen aircraft flew over going in the opposite direction, this time directly overhead.

"Guess they can see us," Paul muttered to himself. "Whoever *they* are."

* * *

"There they are!" the low-light TV operator reported.

"You sure?" the commander asked.

"Yes, sir. Saw the name on the transom: *Sophisticated Lady.* That is *some* boat."

"Glad you like it. Keep a sharp lookout."

"Aye, aye, sir."

The pilot grinned as he switched radio frequencies. He spoke to the duty communications officer on the *Stennis* and told him whom he wanted to speak to. A few minutes later a tired-sounding voice came through the earphones. "Snoopy One, this is Quarterback," Captain Ingram said. "Report, over."

"Quarterback, Snoopy One. We've found your boat and are awaiting your orders."

"Roger, Snoopy One. Your orders are to maintain contact until I can get my birds in range, which will be a while. Meanwhile, set up sonobuoy screens to the west and north. If you pick up anything or if you get any surface contacts, let me know immediately."

"Aye, aye, sir. Any instructions on rules of engagement?"

"Release of weapons is authorized if you are attacked. This is subject to change as the operation progresses. How long can you remain on station?"

"Around eight hours, sir. But another P-3 from Kadena is scheduled to relieve us around oh-nine-hundred."

"Very, well. Carry on. Quarterback out."

"Aye, aye, sir. Snoopy One out."

* * *

Paul never saw the dawn, but he knew exactly when the unseen sun had appeared above the horizon. Exhaustion hung over him like a shroud. It was around 7:30 A.M., and he would be taking over for Tang soon. Paul sipped hot coffee from his mug, wondering if caffeine would be able to keep him awake for four hours.

Zhu sat beside him. The satellite phone had been silent since Paul had talked to Rachael. He had to struggle not to let thoughts of her call him away from his present duties. His life, and the lives of all aboard, might depend on what he did today. A sudden adrenaline surge perked him up, but the effect would not last long.

Paul knew the *Stennis* should be within twelve hundred nautical miles by now, almost within range of its S-3 Viking sub-hunters. And Captain

Ingram had said he was trying to get a long-range patrol craft. Help was near; Paul could feel it. But it wasn't here yet, and a lot could still happen.

"Are you hungry?" Zhu asked.

Paul jumped in surprise. "Yes," he admitted. "But I don't have time now. I've got the watch in a few minutes. Why don't you go below and see what's in the galley."

Zhu got up. "I'll bring you something."

Paul nodded. "Thanks. I appreciate it. And how about a thermos of coffee."

"I will have the cook fix it."

Paul watched as Zhu made his unsteady way to the ladder, pausing a moment as the yacht shuddered its way through a deep trough, sending flying spray aft. Steadier now, he hurried down the steep steps.

Paul jumped as the phone rang. He grabbed the receiver and clamped it to his ear to keep out the moaning wind. "Paul Parker, here."

"Mr. Parker, this is Captain Ingram. I'm calling to let you know that we've had a P-3 Orion over you since around oh-two-hundred this morning."

"I know. I heard it."

"That one will be on its way back to Okinawa at around ten-hundred hours. So far there are no contacts near you, either on the surface or under."

"Captain, the PRC are not done with us. I can guarantee that."

"Well, that's what we're here for. That's all I have for now. I'll keep you posted."

"Thanks, Captain. We appreciate it."

"Roger. Out."

The connection went dead.

21

JIANG LING GLANCED AT HIS WATCH AND SAW IT WAS almost 1:00 P.M. He paced the luxurious carpet while his mind flitted between two sore problems. The first was the traitor Zhu. The failure of the patrol bomber was now ancient history, and Admiral Pang's report on the submarine had not been much better. The Kilo was in transit to the assumed position of Ho's yacht, but its sedate surface speed made that a long trip, even though no great distance was involved. The deteriorating weather eliminated the Harbin H-5s since they lacked the sophisticated equipment the American planes carried. And finally, the Admiral could not use surface craft because Jiang's boss was concerned about alerting those who constantly spy on China.

The other problem was Hanna Flaherty. The more Jiang thought about Gao's comments, the more convinced he became that she knew. *How* she knew, he had no idea, except she had discovered their earlier plot, against all odds. And she had been responsible for his half brother's death. Jiang didn't know what he desired more: to make her pay for Wu's death or to keep her from ruining his plan—the plan for elevating China to its proper place among the nations.

The intercom buzzed on his desk. Jiang hurriedly sat and pressed the button. "Yes?"

"Mr. Gao to see you," his secretary replied.

Jiang straightened his suit coat and buttoned it. "Send him in." He struggled to bring his raging thoughts under control and regain his composure.

The door opened, and Gao Minqi entered, his suit bearing only a suggestion of air travel. Jiang stood.

"Ah, and how was your trip?" he asked politely.

"Most pleasant," Gao replied with a respectful nod. "Cathay Pacific offers an excellent service to Hong Kong. I have used them often, and I am most grateful the airlines no longer land at Kai Tak."

"Yes, Chek Lap Kok is certainly an example to the world—and a much safer airport, to be sure."

Jiang's secretary entered with tea, served them and left. The two men observed this modernized ancient custom with polite conversation, a sharp contrast to their tense expressions that revealed what was to come. Both cups descended to their respective saucers at almost the same time.

Jiang regarded his guest. He knew Gao was a sharp businessman, *but how would he do in this unusual task?* he wondered. "What are your thoughts on the Flaherty woman?"

"Very capable," Gao replied. "Even though our contract was intended to keep her away from our project, our people did check her credentials thoroughly. She knows what she's doing." His smile turned wry. "If Lau's specification change slowed her down, it wasn't much. I think it best not to underestimate her."

Jiang nodded. "My thought as well. I well remember what she did to Chung Wu."

"A most regretful event."

"And one that will not be repeated."

"So where do we stand?"

"The operation against Ho's yacht continues. The attack by our patrol bomber failed, but we have a sub on the way to intercept. We will succeed. I am more concerned about Ms. Flaherty. I have decided that you and I will go to Seattle to make sure this detail is taken care of."

"But . . ." Gao began, obviously shocked.

"Regretfully, this is not a matter for discussion. I have already contacted Mr. Lau, and he is expecting two senior businessmen from Singapore Shipping. We will leave as soon as we have taken care of the troublesome Mr. Zhu."

"As you wish. What are your plans, then?"

"Ms. Flaherty must be removed from the picture permanently. I see no other way."

* * *

The captain of the Chinese Kilo submarine clutched the bridge railing as his boat plunged through the angry swells and chop of the South China Sea. The wind blew salt spray aft every time the bow pitched up from a trough. He breathed in the fresh air, such a welcome relief from the pungent odors below deck, where the usual smells of diesel oil and sweat mingled with that of vomit. He shared the cramped space on the sub's sail with the officer of the deck and the lookouts.

A noisy pop sounded on the bridge speaker. "Captain, we are picking up radar transmissions bearing one-nine-two, probable U.S. patrol aircraft."

The captain jabbed the transmit button. "Are they painting us?"

"Unlikely, sir. The signal is weak, and we would be hard to pick out of these heavy seas."

"What aircraft type?"

"Probably a P-3, sir, or possibly an S-3 if a carrier is nearby."

The captain felt a fresh jolt of adrenaline. The last thing he needed was to tangle with an aircraft carrier. "Very well. Bridge out."

His mind raced. Soon he would have to go below and confer with the navigator. The radar bearing, in all likelihood, gave him the yacht's position, assuming the base course reported by the Harbin H-5 had been accurate. But the patrol plane could prove to be a deadly barrier in approaching the target. He knew he would have to submerge to avoid radar detection, but that meant dropping his speed from ten knots down to seven, the best the Kilo could do while snorkeling to recharge the batteries. And he had to run the diesels for another half hour before the next submerged sprint at seventeen knots.

The captain looked to the south where he knew the Navy patrol craft was lurking. "Clear the bridge!" he ordered. "Dive!"

The diving claxon sounded as the bridge crew hurried down through the hatch below.

* * *

"Flight, TACCO," the tactical coordinator reported. "Probable sub contact. We're getting weak passive returns from that last line of sonobuoys we dropped. Bearing is roughly three-five-zero, range unknown. Sensor One thinks it's a Kilo, and so does the computer. Could be one of the ones Russia sold the Chinese."

The pilot smiled. The cat had finally gotten a whiff of the mouse. "Very good. Close or far away, what's your best guess?"

"I think it's close—has to be if it's a Kilo. You know how quiet they are."

"Roger. Is he north of the line?"

"Yes, sir. Otherwise we'd have picked him up on the previous drop. Want me to ping him?"

"Negative. I want to get closer before we let him know we've spotted him. Stand by for another drop."

The pilot brought the large aircraft around in a tight turn. They flew north, turned west, and dropped a series of sonobuoys in a diagonal line across the contact's assumed course. After each one hit the water, it lowered a hydrophone on a long line.

"TACCO, Flight. Hear anything?"

"From all over the place! We must be right on top of him. Ouch!"

"What happened?"

"Loud noise, Skipper. Sounded like someone hit one of the hydrophones with a hammer. There it is again! The phone's making a scraping sound along with banging every few seconds. I've never heard anything like it! There's a swishing sound. Oh no!"

"What now?"

"One final bang and the hydrophone went dead. Skipper, are you thinking what I'm thinking?"

The pilot's grin grew very wide. "You don't suppose that Kilo ran into a hydrophone?"

"Be willing to bet on it, Skipper."

"Roger that. OK, light him up. He knows we have him."

"Aye, aye, sir."

* * *

The Kilo captain winced with every muted thud as the object, whatever it was, made its way down the sub's bulbous hull. Since he knew a Navy patrol craft was in the area, he had to assume they had blundered into a sonobuoy hydrophone. He cursed, but then realized it didn't make all that much difference. He knew there had to be other buoys around him, which were even now transmitting his machinery sounds back to the plane. A Kilo might be quiet, but all subs made some noise.

"Captain, we're being pinged," the sonar operator reported.

"Where?"

"Multiple sources in line, port and starboard."

"Very well." There were sonobuoys, and now they knew exactly where he was. He considered slowing from his submerged sprint and trying to sneak away, but decided against it. He understood it was unlikely the Americans would attack, as long as he didn't fire a weapon. The Kilo had every right to be in international waters. However, he also knew that American ASW personnel could be complete and utter pests.

* * *

"Flight, TACCO. Got a good fix on him. He's steady on course one-nine-five. We painted him good, but he doesn't seem to care."

"Roger. If we could stick a mic in his face, he'd probably tell us he's on a peace-loving mission in international waters. Give me his position and keep an eye on him."

"Have it for you in a moment, Skipper."

The copilot looked over. "What next?" he asked.

The pilot began a broad turn. "Report his position to *Johnny Reb.* Then take his picture with the MAD (magnetic anomaly detector) gear and keep him pinned down with the sonobuoys." His grin turned severe. "And if he acts ugly, pop him."

"I heard that."

* * *

Paul finally went below at 2:00 P.M. and threw himself into his bunk without taking off his damp clothing. For a few minutes his raging thoughts kept him awake. Then utter exhaustion stole over him, and he was out before he knew what had happened.

It was a dreamless sleep, one interrupted what seemed minutes later by a loud knock at the cabin door. He rolled over and forced his eyes open. For a few moments he was not sure where he was. Then it all came flooding back.

"What is it?"

"Time for your watch," Zhu reported. "Tang sent me down."

Paul groaned as he levered himself up. "I'll be there in a minute." He rubbed his eyes as sheer exhaustion threatened to claim him.

He got up and stumbled out into the passageway. He could tell that the weather was worse. The pitching and rolling were more pronounced, but nothing beyond the capability of the boat. He arrived on deck and looked around. The clouds were lower. Paul estimated the ceiling at a little over a hundred feet, not a whole lot higher than the masts. And the waves were higher.

"Are you ready to relieve me?" Tang shouted from the cockpit.

"Yes." Paul hurried over and stood beside the first mate. "Anything new?"

Tang shook his head. "The weather is a little worse, but we expected that. Course and speed are as before."

"Very well. I relieve you."

He took the wheel as Tang stepped away and hurried below. Paul scanned the instruments, noting the heading and the GPS coordinates, which had not changed all that much from his previous watch. He sighed. Sailing trips were not fast under the best of circumstance. He looked up. Zhu was sitting beside the satellite phone.

"You can go below," Paul shouted above the wind. "Bring the phone back here where I can reach it."

Zhu nodded. He got up and started carrying the satellite phone and its stand back toward the cockpit. He was obviously exhausted.

Paul looked forward. For a few moments he did not understand what he was seeing. Then his blood ran cold as he realized what it was. A gray wall of water was sweeping toward the yacht, a wave at least forty feet tall.

"Look out!" he shouted at the crew. He saw the two men turn forward. They both dashed back to the mizzenmast and locked arms around it.

Paul turned back to Zhu. He could see the man would never make it below in time. "Grab something!" he shouted, pointing forward. "That wave's going to hit us!"

Zhu dropped the phone and looked forward. He fell to the deck in front of the cockpit console and held on. Paul waited until the last moment then turned the *Sophisticated Lady* directly into the wave. The bow plowed into it with an explosion of spray. Tons of angry water swept aft as the boat pitched up, following the wave's lofty contour. The satellite phone crashed to the deck and started sliding aft. Paul ducked low behind the console as the waist-high torrent roared past, drenching him. He sputtered and spat out seawater. The yacht reached the crest, leveled, and started down the far side. The bow plunged deep into the following trough, sending another cascade of water back.

The danger past, Paul resumed the former course. His heart sank as he looked about the deck aft of the cockpit. The satellite phone was gone.

Zhu stood up, his waterlogged clothes clinging to him. "What was that?"

"Rogue wave. Sometimes happens in bad weather—a wave two or three times higher that the average."

Zhu shook his head. "I am going below."

"Go ahead. There's nothing more you can do up here for now."

Zhu disappeared down the hatch.

Losing his only secure means of communications reduced Paul to the yacht's radio, a very public medium indeed. He doubted if Captain Ingram would use it except in an emergency.

* * *

The aircraft commander tried to hide his irritation as he approached the open bomb bay of the replacement P-3C. This was the third patrol crew, and they had been scheduled to use Snoopy One, the first aircraft.

But the flight engineer had written up that aircraft when he discovered a bad oil leak on the number three engine. The only available replacement had been a plane scheduled for a training exercise, which meant that the torpedoes had dummy warheads.

"How does it look, Chief?" the pilot asked as he stooped down to see into the bay.

The flight engineer turned and shook his head. "Afternoon, Skipper. Besides missing warheads, these torpedoes have been recovered and reused a lot. Look at all those dents and scratches."

The ordinance man continued checking the torpedoes and pulling the pins.

The flight engineer looked disgusted. "Well, now you can drop them, for all the good that does. Don't we have time to load up the real thing?"

"Wish we did. But our orders say we launch immediately. If we delay, we could lose that Kilo. Let's get a move on."

"Aye, aye, sir."

* * *

Captain Bob Ingram ordered the S-3 Viking launched. He sat in his chair on the port side of the bridge while his officer of the deck conned the carrier. The stubby twin-jet sub-hunter shot down the starboard catapult and into air. Moments later it entered the overcast and disappeared. This much-prized aircraft was affectionately called a Hoover by naval aviators because of the distinctive sound made by its turbofan engines. The S-3 would be joining the search in a little over two hours.

The captain of the *Stennis* frowned. The P-3 currently on station had the Chinese Kilo under close surveillance. The sub was less than fifty miles from the yacht on a direct line to intercept. Bob knew what his opponent planned, but the rules of engagement didn't allow a first-strike option. And striking second would leave the yacht, and all aboard, at the bottom of the South China Sea. Operational orders instructed Captain Ingram to see the vessel safely to its destination. But how?

* * *

The captain of the Kilo grabbed the handles of the attack periscope and folded them down. He pressed his eyes against the rubber shield and walked around in a tight circle, scanning for surface and air contacts. His ears popped as a wave momentarily covered the snorkel, forcing the diesel engines to draw air from inside the sealed boat. Then the wave passed, and the air pressure returned to normal.

"All clear," he announced. He trained the scope forward. "Emissions?" he bellowed.

"Still picking up the airborne radar."

The captain expected that. The sub-hunters had been on top of them the entire time. With the target known to both, it wasn't that hard. What worried the captain was the possibility the P-3 would attack before the Kilo could approach close enough to shoot. He didn't think the other would shoot first, but he wasn't sure.

"What's the battery state?" he asked.

"Approximately 50 percent, Captain," the officer of the deck reported.

"Very well. Down scope."

The mirror-surfaced periscope slid back into its well. The captain waited impatiently for their next seventeen-knot submerged sprint. Maybe then he could shake the pesky sub-hunter.

* * *

The P-3 aircraft commander glanced at his windshield, then back down at the instruments. They were in solid clouds, and the windows might as well have been painted gray. It was a little after 6:00 P.M., and they were newly on station. The pilot selected the tactical radio frequency.

"Quarterback, this is Snoopy Three. We are ready to relieve Snoopy Two."

"Snoopy Three, this is Quarterback. Roger. Check in with Snoopy Two. No further orders. Quarterback out."

"Snoopy Two, this is Snoopy Three. What have you got for us?"

The pilot made hasty notes as the other aircraft commander provided a thorough brief. That done, the other P-3 turned for home.

"TACCO, Flight. You get all that?"

"Roger, Skipper. We have the Kilo on the last line of sonobuoys Snoopy Two dropped, but it's time we dropped another screen. I'll have the coordinates for you in a bit."

"Roger. Is he still on the same base course?"

"Affirmative. He's heading for that yacht straight as an arrow. No question what he intends."

The pilot gritted his teeth. "Get me those coordinates."

"Aye, aye, sir."

The sub-hunter came around and dropped a line of sonobuoys across the submarine's projected course, then resumed its orbit between the Kilo and its intended prey. The pilot tried to relax, but this wasn't possible. *How absurd,* he thought. *I know what that jerk's going to do, but I can't do a thing about it!*

"TACCO, Flight. What's our friend doing?"

"Skipper, he just finished snorting. I think he going down for another high-speed run."

"Keep on him!" The aircraft commander said, louder than he intended.

"Roger that. Skipper, I think he's going to try to evade. He's turning right, maintaining seven knots. I'm not sure, but I suspect he's going to dive as deep as he can."

"Thermocline?"

"Affirmative. Our last BT (bathythermograph) drop showed one at 150 feet. But we can follow him by dropping the hydrophones below that, unless he's real determined."

The pilot knew that could well be the case, and the odds were the Kilo would give them the slip if that's what he wanted to do.

"Roger. Track him as long as you can, then come up here. We have something to discuss."

"Aye, aye, sir."

A few minutes later the TACCO entered the flight deck and came up behind the pilot. "We just lost him. He merged with the bottom, and that was that."

The pilot gave a derisive laugh. "Don't know what he thinks that will get him. We know where he's going. He's sure not going to fire on a sailboat skimming along the bottom. We'll stick a fence in front of him, and when he goes past, we'll have him."

The TACCO cleared his throat. "I'm with you that far, sir. But then what do we do?"

"I don't know," the pilot admitted. "I sure wish those were live torpedoes in the bomb bay."

"Yes, sir, I do too."

* * *

The Chinese captain maintained his outward appearance of calm, but he knew the dangers they faced. This part of the South China Sea was relatively shallow, well within the diving limits of the Kilo. They were close to the bottom now, in order to evade. But if they ran into something, it could easily spell disaster. And there was still the problem of sneaking back to attack the yacht. That would require at least one more snorkeling run.

He watched the clock, timing his next turn.

* * *

"What's your best guess?" the P-3 pilot asked.

"He was headed almost due east when we lost him. He won't stay on that course long because it's taking him away from his target. He'll turn back on an intercept course once he thinks he's lost us. He'll probably stay low and slow for a while, but eventually he's got to come back up to periscope depth in order to attack."

"And he'll have to sprint in order to close, and that will require one more snort."

"That's the way I see it."

"OK. What do you suggest?"

"Three possibilities as I see it. He can set a direct course for the boat, or he can alter slightly toward the east or west to try to evade."

"And hope we lay our sonobuoy lines in the wrong places."

"It's the only hope he's got."

"Right. Well, *Johnny Reb*'s Hoover will be here in a few minutes. I'll have them lay lines to the east and on the direct course. We'll put down the western sonobuoy barrier."

"Sounds good to me, Skipper. How long will the Hoover be on station?"

"Not long. They're at about max range from the carrier."

"Too bad," the TACCO muttered. "They've got live torpedoes."

"Yep. Well, let me know when you've got the line plotted."

"Aye, aye, sir." The TACCO turned and left the flight deck.

The sub-hunter flew lazy orbits above the storm-tossed seas as the crew prepared for the next drop. The flight engineer left the flight deck and returned a few minutes later with mugs of hot coffee.

"Coffee, gents?" he asked. He handed one mug to the commander and the other to the copilot.

"Thanks." The pilot took a sip. "That's got *some* authority, Chief."

"Figured we need to be alert."

"Well, this should do it."

"Glad you like it, Skipper." He left once more to get a mug for himself and the relief pilot.

The pilot's earphones crackled. "Snoopy Three, this is Hoover One reporting on station."

The pilot smiled. "Hoover One, this is Snoopy Three. Glad you're here. How's business?"

"It's picking up," the S-3 pilot replied with a chuckle.

"Roger that. The Kilo gave us the slip. We will be laying down three sonobuoy lines to reacquire. Hoover One will handle the eastern and center lines. Snoopy Three will take the western one. Stand by for a brief by our TACCO."

"Roger. Hoover One standing by."

* * *

The Kilo captain decided it was time. "Ahead flank!" he ordered. "Make your depth one-seven-five. Come left to one-two-zero."

His face remained impassive, but inwardly he was pleased with the crew's response to his orders. The sub made a sweeping turn to the left on a bearing that would bring them in on an eastern approach to the yacht. The captain knew that detection was possible now but not terribly likely. The thermocline above them would hide what little noise the sub was making, at least from listening devices near the surface. When they had to come up for snorkeling, however, that was a different matter.

The captain watched the clock and acknowledged each report on the state of the batteries. Each three and a half minutes brought them one nautical mile closer to their target. Finally the batteries reached near depletion.

"Ahead slow," he ordered. "Periscope depth."

A few minutes later he ordered the communications mast raised.

"Captain!" came the excited report. "I have two airborne radars!"

"Are you sure?"

"Affirmative. There must be a second patrol plane on station."

The captain frowned because he suspected the second plane was from a carrier. This could be very bad news. He knew he had to attack soon. He ordered snorkeling to begin. Those batteries had to be fully charged.

* * *

"Snoopy Three, this is Hoover One. We're bingo on fuel."

The P-3 pilot keyed his mic. "Roger, Hoover One. Thanks for your help. Snoopy Three out." He switched to the intercom. "TACCO, Flight. The Hoover's on the way home. How does it look back there?"

"Flight, TACCO. We're monitoring all three barriers. Nothing yet."

"Think he can sneak past?"

"It's possible, but unlikely. He's got to snort one more time."

"I hope you're right."

The pilot monitored his instruments as the sub-hunter orbited north of the yacht. He began to wonder about their tactics as the minutes became hours. But it was not until after 8:00 P.M. that he heard what he had been waiting for.

"Flight, TACCO! We've got weak signals from two buoys in the eastern screen! It's him!"

"You sure?"

"As sure as I can be. He's snorting. Wait! He just secured."

"Do you have a fix on him?"

"Only approximate. He's definitely within torpedo range of the yacht, but I doubt he's picked up the target on periscope, or he'd have fired by now. The darkness and sea state are working against him."

"How long until he gets a visual on the yacht?"

"Hard to say. Could be any time."

"Very well." The pilot focused on the black windshield as he tried to imagine what the Kilo's captain was doing. Every second brought those on the yacht closer to violent death. There had to be some way to at least divert the sub. Then he remembered something about the P-3's radar system.

"Sensor Three, Flight. On my mark shift to high PRF (pulse repetition factor)."

There was a slight pause. "Flight, Sensor Three. Roger. Shift to high PRF on your mark. Standing by."

The aircraft commander rolled the P-3 out on a course of zero-one-zero. "Mark!"

"Flight, Sensor Three. Radar on high PRF."

* * *

"Fire-control radar lock-on bearing one-nine-five!"

The Kilo captain whirled around, his hands still gripping the periscope handles. "Can you identify?"

"Negative, Captain. Just a bearing. Must be a surface contact beyond our sonar range."

The captain knew he had only moments to act. A lock-on by a fire-control radar meant a missile would soon be on its way. He cursed his bad luck as he ordered a crash-dive at flank speed with a sharp turn away from the target. And that, at the moment, was all he could do. He looked up at the steel hull over his head, wondering if he had acted in time. If not, they would all be scattered over the bottom of the South China Sea in short order.

* * *

"Flight, TACCO! We're picking up cavitation sounds on multiple buoys. It's definitely the Kilo, and he's diving."

"Do you have a positive fix?"

"Affirmative. He bought it. He thinks a missile's about to ruin his whole day."

"It won't fool him for long. He'll be back up after he gets over his scare."

"We'll be waiting for him."

The pilot instructed Sensor Three to change back to normal PRF, then switched off the intercom. He glanced at his copilot. "Yeah, we'll be waiting for him all right. But we don't have so much as a wet firecracker to drop on him, even if we had permission to fire."

"I feel sorry for those guys on that yacht," the copilot replied.

"Me too. Guess I better let Quarterback know." He switched to the tactical net. "Quarterback, this is Snoopy Three."

"Snoopy Three, Quarterback. Go ahead."

"We have the Kilo localized, sir. We spoofed him with our radar on high PRF. He thought he had a missile coming at him. He crash-dived and is presently evading."

There was a pause. "Is the Kilo within firing range?"

"Affirmative."

"Snoopy Three, Quarterback. Weapons release authorized. I say again, weapons release authorized. Confirm. Over."

The pilot felt his pulse rate increase. He rocked back against the headrest as he wished for live torpedoes.

"Snoopy Three, this is Quarterback. Reply to my last. Over."

The pilot keyed his mic. "Quarterback, this is Snoopy Three. Our bird was scheduled for a training exercise. We're carrying practice torpedoes."

The radio link again went silent for a few moments. "You have *no* live ordinance?"

"Affirmative."

"Very well. Do the best you can. Quarterback out."

"Quarterback, Snoopy Three. Roger. Out."

The pilot glanced at his assistant. "Say it!" he grumbled.

"Do our best?" the other asked. "With what?"

The pilot flipped on the intercom. "TACCO! Grab a chart and get up here!"

"Flight, TACCO. Aye, aye."

Less than a minute later the tactical coordinator entered the flight deck carrying a marked-up nautical chart. He came and stood behind the center console.

"You've got it!" the pilot ordered.

"Roger," the copilot replied.

The aircraft commander grabbed the chart and looked up at the TACCO. "OK, where's he going to come back up?"

"That's hard to say, Skipper."

"Take your best shot. Show me."

"Right about there, sir." The nonflying officer pointed to a spot not far from the Kilo's last known position.

"OK. Plot me an approach from the north—standard torpedo drop."

"Sir, we're loaded out with practice torpedoes."

"I'm aware of that, Lieutenant! Just get back there and do it."

"Aye, aye, sir. Recommend we also drop another line of sonobuoys."

"Granted. Now hop to it. That Kilo's not going to stay down for long."

The TACCO took his map back and hurried off the flight deck.

* * *

The Kilo crept along at periscope depth with the communications mast barely above the surface. After the captain determined that the only radar signal was coming from the sub-hunter, he ordered the mast lowered. A suspicion began to grow in his mind, but he could not be sure the

P-3 had been the source of the scare. And if there were a surface combatant out there, they could be in grave danger.

The captain had still not sighted the yacht, but he knew he would soon. And his torpedoes would handle the rest.

* * *

"Flight, TACCO. I have him."

"Roger. I need a firing solution."

The pilot looked down at the display set up by his TACCO. He guided the P-3 lower until the aircraft reached fifty feet. They broke out of the low cloud deck above an angry sea. The pilot opened the bomb bay and selected two practice torpedoes. At the aiming point he mashed the pickle, and the torpedoes fell away.

"Flight, TACCO. I have the torpedoes. Both are running true and normal."

"What's the sub doing?"

"He just heard them. He's diving. Wait, he launched two noisemakers."

"Are the torpedoes going for them?"

"Negative. Didn't fool 'em a bit. They're diverging to come in from the side. If those were real, it would be a sure kill."

"Wish they were."

"The first fish has shut down. Should be floating to the surface now. Skipper!"

The pilot winced at the sudden shout. "What's happening?"

"Something's wrong with the second torpedo! It's still running! The Kilo has kicked into high gear, and he's heading right at the yacht!"

"Do you think he's sighted them?"

"I doubt he's had the opportunity with how busy we've been keeping him."

"How long till impact?"

"Any time now. Wow! Rang him like a bell! Bet that gave them a thrill. Wait! Skipper! That torpedo is still running! It bounced away, circled around, and is coming in again. Whoa, there it goes again!"

The pilot mentally tuned out the intercom chatter as he tried to visualize the situation below. As annoying as the practice torpedo was, it would eventually stop, and ramming the Kilo's sturdy hull wouldn't do any permanent damage. And when the sub skipper figured that out . . .

"TACCO, Flight. Where's the Kilo now?"

"Several hundred yards from the yacht on a collision course."

"And the torpedo?"

"Stopped a few seconds ago."

A thought sprang to the pilot's mind. He almost dismissed it, but the more he thought about it, the more hopeful it sounded. It might work, he decided, if the skipper of the yacht was on his toes.

"TACCO, Flight. Commence dropping flares on my mark. Stand by."

"Flight, TACCO. Roger. Standing by."

The pilot took one last look at their position. "Mark! Keep punching 'em out until I tell you to stop!" He turned the wheel and started the P-3 into a tight orbit above the two boats.

* * *

Paul and Tang stood side by side in the cockpit as the yacht plowed through the heavy seas. The American had decided not to go below after hearing the second patrol craft earlier. Something was definitely up, and he thought he knew what, since the boat was a sitting duck for a submarine, even in bad weather. Earlier he had seen the navigational lights of a patrol plane dip below the clouds, although it had been too dark to tell what it was doing.

A brilliant light flashed on to the north. Paul winced and shielded his eyes. He squinted as he scanned the restless waves, now clearly visible. He heard the nearby engines of the patrol plane, but it was up in the clouds. He looked in the direction of the sound. A few moments later a thin shaft poked above the surface less than a hundred yards away. Paul felt the icy tingle of fear.

"Sub!" he shouted, pointing.

They were on a near-collision course, but the Chinese captain had apparently not seen the yacht as yet. Paul knew he had a chance to do something about this deadly intruder, but only one chance.

"Brace for collision!" he shouted.

Tang relayed the order in Chinese.

Paul spun the wheel to the left. The yacht began a ponderous turn to port coming into the wind. The vessel began to slow as the sails started flapping. They were almost to the periscope. Paul lost sight of it as it crossed under the bow. The yacht lurched as its hull scraped along something unseen. Then it was over. Paul looked over the starboard rail and got a brief glimpse of the periscope, bent over at a ninety-degree angle. Then it disappeared under the waves.

Racing footsteps sounded below decks. A moment later the two off-duty crewmen raced up the ladder followed by the cook and Zhu.

"What happened?" Zhu demanded, his eyes wide with fear. "There's a hole up front! We're sinking!"

"I'll handle damage control!" Tang shouted.

"Right!" Paul agreed. "I'll get off a distress signal."

Tang went below, taking all the men except one to tend the sails. Paul looked forward. They were dead in the water, headed directly into the wind. He directed the crewman to brace the mainmast boom out to the side. The head wind filled the sail and began to give the yacht sternway. Gauging the moment, he ordered the man to knock away the brace.

Paul cranked the wheel hard against the left stop. The yacht made a ponderous backing turn and stopped. The wind blew in over the port side and again filled the sails. The boat was again underway, but Paul knew the damage below was grave. They were already down by the head, and the handling was becoming sluggish. His next decision was not hard. Taiwan offered the closest port of refuge.

22

PAUL STEADIED THE WHEEL AS HE HELD THE *SOPHISTICATED Lady* on a port tack with a course of oh—seventy-five degrees true. Kaohsiung, Taiwan's largest port city, was their only choice for refuge. He tried not to think of what Tang, Zhu, and the crew were going through with damage control, but he knew it would be a desperate fight to keep the yacht from sinking. Paul noted with increasing alarm that they were down by the bow, and the boat was sluggish in lifting out of each trough. If they had to abandon ship, he didn't hold a lot of hope for their survival as the storm continued to gather strength.

Paul selected the emergency frequency and lifted the mic. "Mayday, mayday, mayday. This is the skipper of the *Sophisticated Lady* out of Hong Kong. We are badly damaged and sinking. Request assistance. We are under sail, heading for Kaohsiung, Taiwan, as nearest port. Over."

He turned up the radio's volume, but all he heard was static. He wondered if the communications room on the *Stennis* had heard him. Paul was sure they had but thought it unlikely Captain Ingram would reply. The carrier was too far away to help, and the international situation had become uglier with the necessity of pulling into what China considered a renegade province. *And politics rules,* Paul thought in irritation. But then he remembered that ultimately this was not so.

"*Sophisticated Lady,* this is Kaohsiung harbormaster. Identify yourself, and give me your position. Over." The man's English was heavily accented but understandable.

Paul wiped the driving rain out of his eyes and squinted at the GPS readout. "This is Paul Parker, skipper. Our position is 21 degrees, 42 minutes, 48 seconds north, 119 degrees, 59 minutes, 11 seconds east. We are currently 59 nautical miles from Kaohsiung. Over."

"Will you abandon ship?"

"Cannot say at this time. Damage control is in progress, but we are down by the head. If we can't patch the hole, we are going down."

"Understand. I am dispatching a patrol vessel at once. What was source of your damage?"

Paul thought that over, wondering what he should say. "We collided with another ship," he said finally.

"Does the other vessel need assistance?"

"Negative. Other vessel continued on course and is no longer in sight."

"I see. Inform me if your condition changes. I will require a full report when you enter port."

"I understand. Thank you. *Sophisticated Lady* out."

"Kaohsiung harbormaster out."

* * *

Zhu pushed his way through the flooded passageway, dragging the mattress from Paul's cabin. The water was above his waist now, the level definitely higher. Thankfully the lights were still on.

"Hurry!" Tang shouted, sticking his head out the forward cabin.

Zhu pushed the waterlogged mattress ahead of him until he got to the open door. Tang grabbed it and turned to the crewman who waited with the timbers and wedges. Zhu looked inside and saw seawater surging in through the hole. Then the yacht sluggishly climbed the next wave. Water poured out of the jagged opening.

"Stand by with the brace!" Tang shouted.

He centered the mattress over the damage. One of the crewmen placed a slab of plywood against the mattress while another wedged it in place with a beam anchored against the far bulkhead.

Tang held it in place while other braces were shoved into place and secured. "Get a pump down here!" he ordered.

The crewman nearest the door struggled down the passageway against the drag of the waist-high water.

"Think it will hold?" Zhu asked.

"I hope so. I don't want to abandon ship in weather like this."

A few minutes later the crewman returned with a submersible pump. He turned it on and lowered it into the water.

Tang pointed to two men. "Watch the patch!" he ordered. "If it starts to slip, one of you hold it in place. The other, come for me. Understand?"

They nodded.

Tang turned to Zhu. "We must report to Mr. Parker."

*　*　*

Paul heaved a sigh of relief as he saw the pump hose spouting a long stream of water. Moments later he saw two dark shapes come up from the ladder.

"Did you get it patched?" he shouted over the shrieking wind.

Tang and Zhu struggled for their footing as they approached.

"The patch is in place!" the former shouted to make himself heard.

"But I don't know how long it will hold. If it carries away, I don't know if we can do it again."

"Did you set a watch?"

"I did. They'll come for me if something happens. Did you reach anyone on the radio?"

"Yes. The Kaohsiung harbormaster is sending out a patrol boat." Paul watched the man's face in the eerie glow of the instrument lights. Tang was not happy.

"That seals my fate," he said slowly. "I certainly cannot return to China now, not after entering Taiwan."

"I've asked my boss to arrange for asylum in the U.S."

"So you have told me, Mr. Parker. But can you guarantee it?"

"I'm sure they'll grant it, especially after all that's happened."

"You did not answer my question. Can you guarantee it?"

Paul paused. "No, I *can't* guarantee it. But I believe it will come through."

"I hope so, Mr. Parker. I certainly hope so."

Paul felt his energy draining away, now that the immediate danger was past. A fog of exhaustion crept over him. "You ready to take the watch?"

"Yes."

"I'll be below if you need me."

"It will be a while until the water is pumped out."

"I don't care."

He handed over the wheel and staggered toward the ladder. All he could think of was getting out of the storm and finding some place to lie down. He paused at the ladder and looked down. The passageway light revealed nearly a foot of surging water. A plastic food container drifted back, struck the ladder, and continued aft. A moment later the yacht plunged into a trough, and the water flooded forward revealing the deck.

Paul hurried down the ladder. Zhu came down and stood beside him. The water came rushing back as the boat rode up the next wave.

"Where are you going?" Zhu asked.

"I don't know. There's nothing dry in my cabin, that's for sure." He turned aft. "The engineering spaces should be OK."

He led the way to the watertight door and waited until the water retreated with the next wave. "Hurry!" he said, as he opened the door.

Zhu went through. Paul followed him and closed the door. The ship's equipment appeared untouched by the earlier ordeal. Except for the noise from the generator, the space was a pleasant respite from the chaos caused by the damage forward. At least it was dry.

"This will have to do," Paul said. He picked a space beside the diesel engine and sprawled on the deck. A moment later he was in a deep sleep.

* * *

Captain Bob Ingram, commanding officer of the USS *John Stennis,* sat in his bridge chair and stared out into the dark as his ship plowed its way through the storm toward Taiwan. Rain pelted against the broad plateglass windows. The huge ship's motion was only moderate, but Bob knew his escorting ships were having a rough ride in the high seas.

He had already sent off the top-secret report on the battle, if you could call it that. So far there had been no reply. Communications had informed him of the intercepted mayday from the *Sophisticated Lady.* Under the circumstance, he couldn't reply to it, and that irritated him. But orders were orders. Unless something else happened, Captain Ingram expected orders directing him to resume course for Pearl Harbor. Meanwhile, the *Stennis,* now traveling at a more comfortable twelve knots, maintained its heading toward Taiwan.

* * *

Jiang slammed the receiver down. He looked out his office windows, watching as the sheets of water blurred the nighttime lights of Hong Kong. Large raindrops rattled against heavy panes.

"Admiral Pang reports our sub is damaged and returning to port."

"What happened?" Gao asked.

Jiang waved his hand dismissively. "It is complicated. While the sub was evading a patrol plane, the yacht rammed him. He lost the periscopes and sustained some other damage. The captain decided he could not continue the attack."

"What about Ho's yacht?"

"Damaged, apparently. Our navy picked up a distress signal. Kaohsiung is sending out a patrol boat. That's where Parker is heading."

Gao shook his head. "This is bad." He paused. "What do we do now?"

"Send agents to Kaohsiung for Zhu." He regarded the businessman closely. "But you and I are going to Seattle. We still have the troublesome Ms. Flaherty to deal with."

* * *

The two agents cleared security with ease and made their leisurely way to the Cathay Pacific counter at Hong Kong's Chek Lap Kok airport. There they checked in for the 9:30 P.M. flight to Kaohsiung, Taiwan. The attendant was a little flustered. The flight had been cancelled earlier because of weather but then unexpectedly reinstated and rescheduled for a 2:00 A.M. departure. The fast-moving storm system was expected to pass their destination by then.

The men thanked the young lady. They were not at all surprised at the flight's reinstatement. They took their boarding passes, picked up their carry-on baggage, and went to the departure lounge.

* * *

It was nearly 9:00 A.M. by the time Paul made the final turn in Kaohsiung Harbor and started his approach to the dock. Although his watch had been over at eight, he decided that docking was his responsibility, especially considering everything that had happened.

The Taiwanese Navy patrol craft had reached them around one that morning. Since the weather had been moderating and the patch seemed secure, Paul had decided he and the crew would remain aboard the yacht. But it had been a comfort knowing help was there if need be. The rain had finally stopped, and the winds had moderated. A light gray overcast shielded them from the sun. The forecast promised clearing weather.

Paul eased the throttle back on the diesel. The patrol craft had guided them into a naval base and given them docking instructions over the radio. Paul recognized security precautions when he saw them.

"Stay close to me," he whispered to Zhu.

"I will," Zhu replied.

The yacht made a port-side approach to the dock at a shallow angle. Waiting until the right moment, Paul cranked the wheel full left and engaged reverse, moving the throttle forward to stop forward movement and bring the stern in.

"Stand by all lines!" he ordered.

Tang relayed the order and watched as the two crewmen threw the nylon lines to the dockhands.

Paul shifted the engine into neutral and watched. The yacht's remaining momentum bled off, and the vessel gently kissed the bumpers hanging down along the dock. Under other circumstances Paul would have been pleased with this maneuver. A glance forward told him Tang was impressed. *For what* that's *worth,* Paul thought wearily. The dockhands made the yacht fast, then lifted a gangway into place.

A Taiwanese naval officer hurried aboard. Paul stepped forward to meet him.

"I'm Paul Parker, skipper of the *Sophisticated Lady*. Thank you for coming to our assistance."

"You are welcome. . . ." the officer began.

Paul interrupted. "If you could arrange transportation to a hotel for me and my crew, I would appreciate it. We're exhausted."

"But I must have your report."

Paul wasn't an expert on Taiwanese Navy uniforms, so he took a guess. "Lieutenant, I'll be glad to do that later, but can't it wait? Have your men examine the yacht, if you like. We're not going anywhere until the hull is repaired."

"But . . ."

"Look, this yacht belongs to Mr. David Ho." Paul saw the look of surprise. "You have heard of David Ho, I'm sure."

"Well, yes, of course."

"I'm sure Mr. Ho would appreciate it if you would extend us this courtesy. As for me, I work for Blue Water Yachts in Seattle. We built this boat. We were on our way to Seattle for a refit when this happened. Mr. Ho can confirm all this for you." He could see the man wavering between duty and practicality. "Listen, Lieutenant. We're really beat. How about taking us to a hotel, let us get some rest, then we can give you our report—say over dinner as my guest. It would be a lot more comfortable."

The young man smiled. "Under the circumstances, that sounds reasonable." He turned and gave an order. "If you will follow me?"

Paul picked up his seabag and walked over the gangway with Zhu at his side. Tang and the crew followed along behind. The naval officer led them to a minivan and opened the door for them. Paul, Zhu, and Tang got in the seat behind the driver while the crew squeezed into the back. The lieutenant got in beside the driver and gave him directions.

Paul looked at the sprawling city without much interest. The trip was mercifully short. The driver pulled up at the entrance to The Ambassador Hotel on Min Sheng 2nd Road and stopped. Paul stepped out, and the crew gathered around him. The Lieutenant hurried around the back of the van and signaled to a following car. Two sailors joined him.

"I think you will find this acceptable," the officer said, waving toward the inviting doors.

Paul led the way inside and up to the registration desk, where he set down his seabag.

"May I help you?" a young man asked, his tone indicating he thought not.

"I sure hope so," Paul said. "I'm Paul Parker, representing Blue Water Yachts, Seattle, Washington. I'm the skipper of the *Sophisticated Lady* out of Hong Kong, Mr. David Ho's yacht." He saw recognition in the man's eyes. "We were nearly shipwrecked last night. Your navy escorted us to Kaohsiung."

"I see," the clerk said, with a little more enthusiasm. "If I could have a card, I will be happy to proceed with your registration."

Paul handed him his company's American Express card. A few minutes later he signed for four adjoining double rooms. He turned and found the lieutenant waiting.

"I shall be here at, shall we say, seven?"

"That will be fine," Paul agreed.

"Good. Meanwhile, my men will remain outside your rooms. I regret the inconvenience, but until we have your full report, I have no choice."

"I understand. I will see you at seven."

The officer brought his heels together, nodded, and left.

* * *

The agent returned to the rental car and got in. "They have checked in," he told his partner.

"Did you see Zhu?"

"Yes, he is with them. However, two sailors went up with them and didn't come down."

The other agent frowned. "That is not good. Call Mr. Jiang. I'll watch the hotel."

"Yes."

The man got out and hurried down the street.

* * *

Paul led the way to the elevator lobby, trying to ignore the open stares of the other guests. His mind raced as they went up to their floor and found their rooms. He opened the door and looked around at Tang. "Take care of the crew. I'll phone David." He paused. "I'll start working on what we talked about earlier. OK?"

"I understand." Tang turned to the crew and gave them their instructions.

Paul and Zhu entered the room.

"Well, this is certainly nice enough," Paul said after he looked around. "You can have the bathroom first. I've got some phone calls to make."

"Concerning my . . ."

"Yes!" Paul snapped. As soon as it slipped out, he regretted it. His mind spun with all that he had to do. "I'm sorry. Yes, my first call is to the one who can help you." He paused. "I can't go into specifics with him until later, you understand?" Paul pointed to his ear, then around at the walls.

After a short pause, Zhu nodded. He picked up his bag and disappeared into the bathroom. Paul plodded over to a table near the window.

He searched around until he found some hotel stationery and a pen. Doing the math, he found it was a little after 9:00 P.M. in Washington. He punched in the Sprint access number followed by Vic's mobile phone number and Paul's account and PIN number. The phone began to ring. Paul sent up a silent prayer he wouldn't get voice mail.

"Hello," Vic answered.

"Vic, this is Paul."

"Paul!" Vic shouted. "Where are you! Just what do you think you're doing?"

Paul winced. "Did you get a report from Captain Ingram?"

"Yes, of course I did. But there weren't any details. Are you on a secure phone?"

"No, I'm not. I'm at the Ambassador Hotel in Kaohsiung, Taiwan— along with the yacht's crew."

"I see." His boss's tone was a little less strident. "I'll send someone around for you."

"I appreciate it."

"Is there anything else you can tell me now?"

"Some. We collided with another vessel which knocked a hole in our hull. I sent out a mayday, and the Taiwanese Navy sent out a patrol boat to escort us in. By the way, I have to make a report to them this evening. They've posted two sailors outside our rooms to make sure we stay for the festivities."

"OK, OK! I'll work on that as well. Don't talk to the Taiwanese until you've made your report to us."

"How soon will you send someone by?"

"As soon as I can! I'll start on it as soon as I get off the phone."

"OK. Have you thought about what we discussed earlier?"

"We'll talk about that later. Good-bye."

"Bye."

Paul sat back in the chair. He glanced toward the bathroom and saw the door was ajar. A few moments later the shower started. Paul pulled David Ho's card from his wallet and closed his eyes as he tried to compose what he would say to the businessman about his beloved yacht—and other things. He punched in David's private number and waited.

"David Ho."

"David, this is Paul Parker."

"Paul, where are you?"

"I'm afraid I've got bad news. We collided with another vessel and had to pull into Kaohsiung for repairs. There's a hole in the bow, and some flooding. I'll do a thorough inspection later, but I'm sure repairs will not be a problem. I'll have the hull patched at a shipyard here, but we'll do the heavy-duty work in Seattle."

"What is going on? The police told me you are using my yacht to smuggle a traitor out of the country."

"I'm sorry, but I can't talk about that."

"But . . ."

"David, I think you know me pretty well."

"Yes, I do. I have the highest regard for you."

"The feeling is mutual. I owe you a full report, but I'd like to call you back later, if that's OK."

There was a slight pause. "Well, I suppose so. How about the crew?"

"They're OK. I'll see that they're taken care of."

"Good. Then, I will await your call. Good-bye."

The line clicked. There was one more call to make, the one that came first, as far as Paul was concerned. He punched in the number and waited as it rang.

"Hello?"

"Rachael. This is Paul."

"Paul! Where are you? Are you OK?"

He paused. "Has Vic called you recently?"

"No, not since that plane attacked you."

"A lot's happened since then, but I can't go into details. We're in Kaohsiung, Taiwan. The crew and I are OK, but David Ho's yacht has a big hole in it that has to be patched."

"Will you be coming home from Taiwan?"

"I don't know. I'll be talking to Vic later on today. After that, I'll call you back. I'll be able to talk then."

"Oh, Paul. I've been *so* worried."

He could tell she was close to tears. "I'm sorry. But I'm all right now." He paused. "I've spent a lot of time thinking about you on this trip. I've missed you so much."

"I miss you too." She sniffed.

Paul felt his throat constrict and his eyes start to sting. "I'll talk to you later. Bye."

"Good-bye."

He replaced the receiver. He longed for sleep and regretted the drudgery of a shower and shave. He was tempted to sprawl on one of the beds in his current filthy state, but knew he couldn't. Finally Zhu finished and came out.

"Is it arranged?" he asked as he dried his hair with a towel.

Paul got up and pulled a pair of underwear and his shaving gear out of his seabag. "He's sending someone to pick me up. I need a secure phone to discuss your situation."

"I see."

"Don't worry. This will work out."

Paul entered the steamy bathroom, set his things down, and turned on the shower. He quickly stripped and stepped under the hot spray. He lathered quickly, washing away the accumulated grime. He could not remember a shower feeling so good.

It took a few moments for him to recognize a new sound, barely audible over the noise of the shower. He turned off the water and listened. Someone was knocking frantically at the door. Paul wrapped a towel around himself and went to the door, leaving wet footprints in the carpet. He looked out and saw one of the sailors.

"What do you want?" He snapped.

"The man with you. He leave your room."

Paul spun around and swept the room with his eyes. He felt his heart sink. Zhu was, in fact, gone.

23

ZHU RACED DOWN THE EMERGENCY EXIT STAIRS, HOPING the sailor behind him would not fire. He made the final turn and saw the first-floor door before him. The clatter of heavy boots told him he did not have much of a lead. Zhu crashed through the door and found himself in a corridor. He ran along it until he reached the lobby. Startled guests gawked at him as he dashed for the front doors.

Zhu went through and out onto the street without slowing down. Traffic was heavy under the gray skies. He chanced a look behind. The sailor emerged from the hotel, but he was definitely falling behind. Zhu scanned the sidewalk ahead, looking for police. So far he didn't see any. A pedestrian several hundred feet away stopped momentarily before dashing for a car parked at the curb. The man jumped in and pointed.

Zhu's blood ran cold. They had to be Jiang's agents. Zhu cursed as he realized there had been plenty of time for his old boss to locate them. He should have bolted immediately. The car screeched away from the curb and roared toward him.

Zhu looked all round. He was less than fifty feet from a narrow alley. He ducked into it, running as hard as he could. His lungs burned as he gasped for air. He heard the car turn in behind him and start accelerating. About halfway down, a delivery truck blocked the alley as men unloaded boxes. Zhu ran as hard as he could, not daring to look behind as the car bore down on him.

The deliverymen stopped, attracted by the noise. Zhu reached them, shoved his way through, and continued toward the next street. He heard the car slide to a stop with an angry scream of rubber. A gunshot rang out. A puff of brick dust on a wall marked the impact. Fresh adrenaline coursed through Zhu's veins, enabling him to increase his breakneck pace as he weaved back and forth. Two more shots. One he didn't see, but the other he heard whiz by his right ear.

The other end of the alley seemed impossibly far off. He glanced at the doorways as he passed them but dared not stop to try one. He could hear a clatter behind him. Zhu risked a glance back. Jiang's agents were running after him, but the attempt to shoot him had cost them some distance. Zhu reached the next street and looked around. A delivery truck pulled away from the curb on the far side of the street. Zhu dashed across and jumped up on the rear bumper. He looked back at the alley. The two agents looked around frantically, but no taxis were in sight. One started running after the truck, but soon gave up.

Zhu stayed on the truck for over a mile. Although he saw no sign of pursuit, he couldn't be sure. He knew Jiang would simply send more agents from Hong Kong, men who would have impeccable papers, which he did not. It would only be a matter of time until they found him. And then . . .

Zhu jumped down when the truck stopped at a light. Right now what he needed was a place to hide, any place until he could think this through. He turned down a narrow street to get off the busy thoroughfare and eyed each shop as he passed it. About midblock he saw one that looked familiar, but it took him a moment to realize why. The store sold snakes, among other things. Stacked cages stood before the plateglass windows.

He remembered his first hiding place in Hong Kong, the one Huo had arranged. This brought back thoughts he wasn't prepared to deal with. He still didn't understand why his friend risked his life for him. Zhu looked at the store again. This shopping district looked a lot different from Bonham Strand in Hong Kong. Without really knowing why, he approached the double glass doors and went inside.

Zhu looked down the narrow aisles and saw there wasn't any merchandise. *Possibly this is a new store, not yet open for business,* he thought. He heard a banging noise near the back. He glanced over his shoulder to make sure he wasn't being followed.

"Is anyone here?" Zhu asked, as he approached the back.

The hammering stopped. His next words froze in his throat as he saw the man was a westerner, the last thing Zhu had expected to see.

"Can I help you?" the man asked in Mandarin.

A westerner who speaks Chinese, Zhu thought, his surprise complete. "You are an American?" Zhu finally asked.

"Yes. My name is Eddie Zanders." His smile was friendly and open. "If I can in any way assist you, I would be most happy to do so."

Zhu noted the heavy accent and formal style, but how many Americans took the trouble to learn Chinese? "I . . ." he began. *What could he tell this man?*

"Yes, go on."

Zhu longed for another option but couldn't think of any. "I need a place to stay."

"Can you tell me why?" Eddie asked after a slight pause.

"Some people are after me. I . . . I owe some men a gambling debt that I cannot pay. I am afraid of what they will do if they catch me."

"I see. I don't know. What did you say your name was?"

"Zhu Tak-shing."

"Mr. Zhu, I am here on a visa issued by Taiwan. They could deport me if I got involved with anything illegal."

"I am at your mercy! Let me be plain. These men will kill me if they can. You are the only hope I have." He watched as the American thought this over. He fully expected to be turned down. It's what he would do under similar circumstances.

Eddie Zanders nodded. "I will give you sanctuary."

Zhu bowed. "I thank you." His thoughts snapped back to Hong Kong and what seemed ages ago. Huo had not refused him either.

The American grinned. "How are you with a hammer?"

"What?"

"I'm working on where you'll be staying. I'm taking the shelves down so I can build a wall."

"Oh. Yes, I will be glad to help." Zhu looked around and spotted a small table in the corner. A delicious aroma drifted over from some small cardboard boxes.

"Are you hungry?" Eddie asked.

Zhu's stomach growled. "Very much so. I have not eaten in a long time."

"You are welcome to share my lunch. We can take a break early." He brought over two chairs. They sat down, and his host promptly bowed his head. "Thank you for this food, heavenly Father. Bless it as we partake of your provision. And heavenly Father, I ask that you would protect Mr. Zhu from those who seek him harm. In Jesus' name I pray. Amen."

Only then did Zhu spy the heavy book with a black cover. His eyes traced the gold Chinese characters. *I should have known,* he thought.

"Mr. Zanders, may I ask what you are doing in Taiwan?" he began.

Eddie smiled. "I am a Christian missionary." He swept a hand about the cluttered room. "And this is going to be the church." He opened one of the cardboard boxes. "Fish," he said. He pushed it toward Zhu along with a set of chopsticks. He opened up other boxes revealing rice, rolls, and sauces. "And I have a thermos of tea we can share later."

Zhu watched his host pick up some chopsticks and was surprised to see he was quite proficient. Zhu had to struggle not to eat ravenously. All too soon the small boxes were empty. He regretted there was not more, until he remembered he was sharing a meal intended for one. Not only that, he had eaten over half of it.

"I thank you," he said when they were finished.

"You are welcome."

Zhu forced an embarrassed smile. "Shall I help you with your church?" *How have I gotten into this?* he wondered.

"I would be most grateful."

* * *

Paul almost smiled. It never ceased to amaze him how fast the federal bureaucracy could move, if certain executives wanted it to. But it *did* take concerted effort. Fortunately, Vic was one of the "movers and shakers."

Paul sat down at the desk in a borrowed office and waited for the promised call. It was a little after 2:00 P.M. in T'aipei. Vic's agents had arrived a few minutes after the irate Navy lieutenant, much to Paul's relief. After a heated exchange the Americans had left with Paul and Ho's crew. Then a borrowed Taiwanese Navy helicopter had whisked them to the capital of Taiwan. Paul was bone weary, having slept only an hour on the trip to T'aipei.

He frowned as he struggled not to nod off. What had happened to Zhu? Why had he run? Paul thought he knew the answer. The man apparently didn't trust the CIA.

Paul jumped when the phone rang. "Hello," he croaked as he picked it up.

"OK, what happened?" Vic demanded, getting right to the point.

Paul sighed. "I dictated a complete report after I got here. It's already been faxed to your office."

"I'm holding it in my hands. What about Zhu?"

"I can't add anything. All I know is he ran out while I was in the shower. I don't think he believed we would grant him asylum."

"But I said we would."

Paul struggled to keep his temper. "You weren't very clear on that, or at least that's the way it seemed to me. I can see why Zhu would have his doubts. And we are talking about high stakes here." He paused. "What are you planning to do now?"

"I have men out looking for him. I'm working on a cover for the attacks. Zhu will not be mentioned. The Taiwanese are cooperating but keeping a low profile. The last thing they want is to crank up the ranting machine on the mainland."

"I can understand that. What about Ho's crew? They can't go back to Hong Kong under these circumstances."

"I know, I know! I'm arranging asylum for them. They'll stay in T'aipei for a few days, then we'll fly them into San Francisco for processing. But Mr. Zhu better turn up."

"I hope he does."

"I want something a little more positive than that!"

"What do you want me to do?"

"Come home. There's nothing more you can do there. I have you booked on a United flight to San Francisco leaving at 2:00 P.M. tomorrow. Then a 10:50 A.M. flight to Seattle arriving at 12:53, if you believe flight schedules."

"Thanks. How much can I tell David Ho? He knows about the stowaway."

"Use your best judgment. You know what's covered by security. The less said the better."

"OK. Anything else?"

"No. See you when you get back."

"Right. Bye."

Paul hung up and immediately dialed David Ho's private number.

"David Ho here."

"David. This is Paul. I'm calling from T'aipei."

"Oh, what are you doing there?"

"I really can't go into that. What happened to us is covered by my country's security regulations. But I can say this: If you are thinking this might be related to the difficulties we had before sailing, you wouldn't be far off."

"I see. And perhaps there might be more to that than meets the eye."

"You are most perceptive, David."

"I have lived in Hong Kong all my life. Did you have a chance to examine my yacht?"

"I intended to, but circumstances forced me to come up here. I talked with Tang earlier, and he gave me a complete rundown on the damage."

"You can rely on what he says."

"I know. I'll be calling the president of Blue Water Yachts tomorrow before I leave. He'll arrange for a shipyard in Kaohsiung to patch the hull and check for other damage. After repairs are complete, I'll return to sail it back to Seattle."

"I appreciate that, Paul. That takes a load off my mind."

"I promised."

"Yes, you did, and I knew I could depend on you."

"I appreciate your understanding."

"We will say no more about it. Have a nice trip back."

"Thanks."

Paul hung up the phone. All he could think about was finding a place to stretch out, but there was one more call to make.

Rachael answered after the first ring. "Hello."

"Rachael, this is Paul."

"Paul! Where are you?"

"T'aipei. Vic had us flown up here from Kaohsiung. I'm flying to San Francisco tomorrow and then to Seattle."

"Oh, I'm so glad. I'll meet you at the airport."

He grinned in spite of his fatigue. "I was hoping you would. I'll be on the 12:53 P.M. United flight. I don't know the number."

"I'll be there. Will Mr. Zhu be coming back with you?"

"Zhu's bolted. Apparently he didn't trust us to take care of him."

"You mean you've been through all this for nothing?"

Paul had to struggle not to slide down into depression. "Vic has agents out looking for him, and the Taiwanese are cooperating. We may find him."

"I hope so."

"I do too. I'll see you when I get back."

24

Paul felt his spirits lifting as he left the jet way and looked about. Then he saw Rachael, and her beaming smile was all he wanted. She started toward him tentatively, then broke into a run. He dropped his seabag and wrapped his arms around her. He felt an electric tingle as their lips met, and he fully realized how much he had missed her. They were both breathless when they parted.

"I'm so glad you're back," she said.

He held her head against his chest, smiling as he smelled the scent of her hair. "Believe me, I'm glad to *be* back." He felt a tightening in his throat. "There were times I wondered if we'd make it."

"Oh, Paul!"

"It's over now," he sighed. "Except I lost Zhu."

"You didn't lose him. He ran."

"Same difference. He's gone. And unless we find him, we'll never find the Raptor Virus."

"You did the best you could. And it's not over yet. It hasn't struck yet—whatever it is."

"No, but I don't think we have much time left." He picked up his seabag.

"Any more luggage?"

"Nope, and I'm ready to see Sea-Tac in the rearview mirror."

Rachael's purse slipped out of her hands as she opened it. "Oops!" It landed on the floor, scattering the contents. "Oh, no!"

Paul squatted down and helped her scoop up the various objects.

"The klutz strikes again," she grumbled.

"I'm not listening to that," Paul said. He glanced at her and saw she was blushing.

"Thank you," she said.

He smiled. "You're welcome. You're talking about someone who matters very much to me." Her blush grew even more pronounced.

"I'll try to keep that in mind." She grabbed a set of keys. "Here! That's what I was looking for in my own inimitable way."

Paul pocketed his car keys. He held Rachael's hand as they took their time walking out to the parking garage. He put the bag in the trunk and helped Rachael into the Firebird. Soon they were exiting the airport.

"What are we going to do now?" Rachael asked, once they were on the way to Bellevue.

"Keep on looking. Meanwhile, I've got to get back to my day job. And my boss will want to know what happened to Ho's yacht and what Blue Water Yachts is going to have to do about it. Of course, there's a limit to what I can tell him."

"Will that cause a problem?"

"No. He knows about my moonlighting for the CIA, and he's fairly supportive. But he's probably worried about making David Ho mad."

"Is he mad?"

"David? Not exactly. He's concerned about what happened to his yacht, of course. But he trusts me. He knows I'll take care of him."

"But what about the damage? Who'll pay for it?"

"That I *don't* know. The friendly folk of the People's Republic of China are responsible for it."

"Because you were helping Zhu escape."

"That's right. So I don't know what will happen, except the PRC won't pay. David will probably end up footing the bill, but I think I'll see if Vic will kick in."

"Think he will?"

"We'll see," he chuckled. "Wonder how he'd document *that* on his expense report?"

"Entertainment?"

Paul glanced at her. Then they both laughed. Paul reflected on how comforting it was to have someone he cared about to share his troubles with. And he had a lot to share on this particular difficulty.

* * *

Zhu awoke with a start. He heard the rattling noise and for a few moments didn't realize where he was. Then he remembered as light began filtering in through the dingy front windows. The steel roll door reached the top with a loud thump.

Somehow Zhu had made it through the previous day, helping the American missionary dismantle the shelves. He had decided against telling him how tired he was, as that would only have invited more questions.

Zhu got up from the cot and started dressing. He heard the missionary's gritty footsteps approaching from the front of the store.

"Good morning," Eddie said, as he rounded the end of the half-demolished shelves. "I hope you were comfortable last night."

"I slept well."

Eddie placed a large sack on the table. "Barbara, my wife, cooked this for you," he said as he pulled out each item. "Hope you like it."

"Thank you. I am sure I will." He sat down and reached for some chopsticks. Then he looked up at his host. "Did you wish to pray?"

Eddie sat down and prayed over the food. Zhu listened without interest, then began his meal. The missionary poured them both some hot tea.

"I appreciate your help," Eddie said as he sipped from the cup. "We got a lot done yesterday."

Zhu glanced around the back of the store. "Yes, but there is still much to do."

"It will get done."

Zhu wondered at Eddie's confidence, and that brought out another question. "Why are you doing this?" he finally asked.

"Helping you?"

"Yes. But also why are you here? Why did you leave America?"

The missionary laughed. "I'm not sure I can explain. Do you know anything about Christianity?"

The memory of Huo and his grandmother came in on Zhu with a near-physical force. "Yes. I . . . I had a friend who was a Christian, as was—*is* his grandmother." In his memory he could see her loving eyes. He cleared his throat. "So I am acquainted with what you call the gospel."

Eddie nodded. "I see. But this means nothing to you."

"No, it does not," Zhu said, sharper than he intended. He looked at his host, afraid he had offended. But all he saw was concern, very similar to what he remembered about Huo's grandmother.

"All I can do is agree with your friend," Eddie said. "What he told you is true, but what you do about it is up to you. No one can decide for you." He paused. "But I would like to say this: I think God is after you."

Zhu shivered and spilled his tea. "Perhaps we can discuss this later." That wasn't what he wanted to say, but somehow he could not be rude to this man.

"Perhaps." Eddie got up. "Finish your meal. I'm going to check on our work."

* * *

Paul sipped from his coffee mug as he faced the office windows above the construction floor. He had considered taking the day off to get his body back in sync with Seattle time but decided he couldn't. Instead he had compromised by coming in at nine in the morning. He had not checked his E-mail, but did see a terse note from the CEO of Blue Water Yachts. "See me ASAP!" it said in red ink. Paul sighed. He had already decided to interpret "ASAP" loosely. There were things he had to do first.

A few minutes later he saw Rachael, Hanna, and Russell enter the building and start across the floor. For a few moments Paul's mind detached itself from his worries as he watched Rachael. Despite what she thought of herself, she was quite graceful, he decided. Paul started for the door when his guests reached the steel stairs.

"Come in," he said, ushering them in.

"Thank God you're back!" Hanna said. "Rachael told us what happened. What are we doing about it?"

Paul shook hands with Russell. "Please sit down." He waved toward the bench seat while he and Rachael sat in side chairs. "You mean what is the CIA doing." He glanced at Rachael. "Not much. Vic chewed on me—again. This has caused quite a stir in Washington, but the Directorate folk apparently can't decide what it all means."

"What does it take?" Hanna asked. "Your friend murdered, that underwater escape with Zhu, and then they try to sink the yacht—twice. What more do they want?"

Paul struggled against discouragement. "Those who doubt the Raptor Virus still aren't convinced. And added to that, unless we can find Zhu and get him to cooperate, we still don't know what the target is."

"He may turn up," Rachael said. "I'm sure he doesn't want to end up with his former buddies."

"You got that right. Let's hope he comes to his senses."

"Isn't there something else we can do?" Russell asked.

"I don't see what," Paul replied. He saw Hanna wince. "Something the matter?"

"Ah . . ." She glanced at Russell. "I did something you need to know about. I sent Lau Jianguo an E-mail telling him I knew what they were up to."

Russell turned to her, his eyes wide. "You did *what?*"

"Well . . ." she replied, taking her time. "I decided that we had to do something. Paul and I were suspicious that this Singapore Shipping job was to keep me from looking into the Raptor Virus. And . . ."

"Why didn't you tell me?" Russell demanded.

She looked down. "With everything that was going on, I forgot."

"Did Lau reply?" Rachael asked.

"No, he didn't. Now I'm beginning to wonder if our suspicions were correct."

"That contract sure looks like busywork to me," Paul reminded her. "What better way to keep you out of their hair—assuming they're connected with the PRC plot."

"Yeah, but I've seen companies do funnier things. Singapore Shipping could have decided to ditch their existing software, despite Huo's thinking their shipping system was first-rate."

Paul rocked back in his chair. "Lau's lack of response suggests you were on target."

"Not necessarily. It's a weird message. Maybe he didn't know how to reply."

"That's possible, I guess." Paul paused. "I wish you hadn't done it."

"Me too!" Russell said, obviously irritated.

"I'm sorry, dear," she replied.

He shrugged. "Well, it's done now. I hope nothing bad comes of it."

"I'm sure we all do," Paul said.

"What now?" Hanna asked.

Paul sighed. "Sit here and wait. We can't do anything until Washington acts."

"Or we find Zhu," Rachael added.

"That is a happy thought." He paused. "Which brings something else to mind. My friend, Huo, was a Christian. But Zhu isn't, despite hearing about it for years. Then he saw his friend die for him. I tried to talk to him, but he wasn't interested."

"Are you thinking God is after him?" Hanna asked.

"Don't know. But I've sure wondered about it."

"All you can do is plant the seed," Russell said.

"Yeah," Paul said. "And in the meantime, I guess it's back to the day job." His expression soured. "I've got to meet with our CEO sometime today. He'll want an explanation of what's happened and what Blue Water Yachts will have to do about it."

"Do you think we should postpone our vacation?" Hanna asked.

"What? Oh. Your trip to Big Bend. I'd forgotten."

Hanna grinned. "You have been sort of preoccupied lately."

"You might say that. I'd say, go. But just in case, let me have your itinerary, in case I need to contact you." He smiled. "Not that that will happen."

"I'll E-mail it to you," Hanna said.

"Fine. Hope you all have a wonderful trip. Going to do some hang gliding?"

She glanced at Russell. "You bet! We wouldn't miss that for the world."

Paul cocked an eyebrow at Russell. "That so?"

"As a matter of fact, it is," he admitted. "Scott and I are really taking to it. Big Bend sounds like a wonderful place to fly."

"When do you leave?"

"On Tuesday. We'll be getting ready on Monday."

Paul's smile turned wry. "Enjoy it, folks. I've already *had* my vacation."

*   *   *

Hanna turned about in her swivel chair as she surveyed the office of Roadrunner Consulting. Reserving Monday to get ready for their trip had been a good idea, she decided, since it involved more than throwing a few clothes in a suitcase. It was already midmorning, and she hadn't made a dent in her to-do list. And Russell had not returned from having the oil changed in her Explorer. Hanna smiled. He had been all too ready to do that in exchange for her helping him with his packing. *Men might be from Mars,* she thought, *but their home-away-from-home is the hardware store.*

Scott raced by on his way to the stairs.

"Whoa, pardner!" she shouted.

The frantic footsteps stopped, and a few moments later he peeked around the edge of the door. "Yes?"

"Where's the fire?"

"I'm going to the kitchen to get something to eat."

Hanna glanced at her watch. "We had a big breakfast, and I'll be fixing lunch as soon as your dad gets back."

"But I'm hungry *now,*" he pleaded.

Her eyes narrowed. "You all packed and ready to go?"

"Um, not exactly."

"Have you started?"

"No. I thought you were going to help me."

"I said 'help,' not 'do.'" She smiled. "Tell you what. We'll work on it together after lunch, OK?"

"Yeah." He started to move away, then stopped. "Can I still get something to eat?"

"OK, but don't spoil your appetite."

"I won't."

The stampede resumed. Hanna listened as the sounds diminished.

Hanna turned back to VR and retrieved the Outlook draft of their trip itinerary. She scanned it carefully, then sent it to Paul. Then she clicked on the print icon. The network printer began to whir as it printed a hard copy.

The doorbell rang. She got up, grabbed the E-mail, and hurried downstairs. Scott already had the door open by the time she reached the entryway.

"Delivery for Hanna Flaherty," the uniformed young man said. "Sign here." He extended the clipboard.

"I can't sign for that," Scott said. "It's not for me."

"Look kid, I've got a lot of deliveries to make. It doesn't make any difference; just sign it."

"Can I help you?" Hanna asked, coming up behind Scott. She placed the E-mail on the table by the door.

"I hope so, ma'am. Package for Hanna Flaherty."

"She doesn't like that," Scott said.

The young man's look of irritation changed to confusion. "Doesn't like what?"

"Being called 'ma'am.'"

Hanna struggled not to smile as she reached for the clipboard. Then she saw the long, bulky package. "I don't remember ordering anything. What is it?"

"Ma'am—uh, Ms. Flaherty, how would I know? Please!" He pointed to the signature line.

Then she saw the shipper: Cascades Hang Gliding and Paragliding. "Ian," she said thoughtfully. "What in the world would he be sending me?" She signed.

The deliveryman took the clipboard and hurried off. Hanna and Scott carried the box inside and left it in the entryway.

"You gonna open it?" Scott asked.

"Nope. I'm gonna call a certain Aussie first." She picked up the portable phone and punched in the store number.

"Cascades Hang Gliding and Paragliding," a familiar voice said.

"Ian, what did you send me?"

"Hanna, old sport. Meant to ring you about that, but it slipped my mind. Have you opened it?"

"No. Thought I'd call you first. Now what gives?"

"Steady, mate. It's something for you and Russell to try—if you want to. It's a tandem glider from Brazil, called a Neko."

"Oh? I've seen tandems, but never tried one." She laughed. "Never knew anyone I wanted to fly with—until Russell, of course."

"Right you are. So you and Russell will give it a go? I'm thinking of carrying them, and so I'd like to hear from an expert."

"Tell you what, I'll look at it. Then I'll talk it over with Russell."

"That's bonzer."

"No promises."

"I understand. Ring me up when you get back."

"I will."

"What is it?" Scott asked after she hung up.

"It's a tandem hang glider. Two people fly it rather than one."

"Cool! Can I try it?"

"We'll see. First I have to discuss it with your father. We were planning on taking the trainer and my glider. If we take the tandem, we'll have to leave mine here."

"I think it would be so cool if you and Dad could fly together."

"I could go for that. Meanwhile, I need to start rattling some pans. I know some men folk who are gonna want some chow. Right?"

He grinned. "Yeah."

* * *

Jiang scanned the crowded arrival lounge. It was late Monday night, and the delay in San Francisco had not improved his disposition—that and the long eastward flight. He had slept some on the plane but did not feel rested. Finally he spotted Lau Jianguo. Jiang and Gao Minqi made their way through the chaotic crowd with single-minded determination.

"Welcome to Seattle," Lau said as he shook hands with the two men. "I hope your flight was pleasant."

"The Cathay Pacific flight was excellent; however a gate change in San Francisco almost made us miss our United connection."

Lau nodded. "Unfortunately, that is commonplace. Shall I take you to the hotel?"

"No, your offices. I know it's late, but we have a lot to do and not much time."

"As you wish. May I have your claim checks?" Lau turned them over to another man to handle. "I have a car waiting outside."

Jiang's mind raged during the entire trip to the office building. All he could think of was eliminating this threat to Project Dragon—the most dangerous they faced. He thought briefly of the traitor Zhu, but knew he had to leave that to his agents in Taiwan. What he *could* do, and what he *would* do, was take Hanna Flaherty out of the picture—permanently. He vowed he would not fail, as his brother Wu had.

Jiang followed Lau into the large conference room, taking the chair at the head of the table. Gao sat beside him while Lau stood by the door. Soon two men in dark suits joined them, and Lau closed and locked the door. Although Jiang had never met them, he had read their dossiers on the flight over. Both were from Shanghai and quite proficient in their trade. He felt a brief chill.

Jiang looked toward Lau. "You may begin. Bring me up-to-date."

Lau hesitated, clearly uncomfortable. "Nothing has changed. Following your instructions, I changed the specifications on the shipping system; however this did not slow Ms. Flaherty down. She remains on schedule, which could allow her time to look into other things."

"I know that!" Jiang thundered, pounding the table. "It was *my* idea to keep her busy in the first place. And it was up to *you* to make sure the diversion worked."

Lau nodded. "If I have offended . . ."

"I don't have time for this! There is still a chance, but we must act at once. Tell me again about the message. Is there nothing new?"

Lau shook his head. "Regrettably, no. Ms. Flaherty sent me an E-mail saying she knew what we were doing and that it wouldn't work. I included the complete text in my last report."

"Yes, yes. You did not reply to her E-mail?"

"No. Without instructions from you, I dared not do such a thing."

"And there has been nothing more from her?"

"There has not."

Jiang made his decision. "You have the weapons and vehicles I requested?"

"Yes."

"Very well." He glanced at his watch. "We strike at four tomorrow morning."

25

"IS THIS IT?" JIANG ASKED, AS LAU PULLED THE MERCEDES sedan up to the curb.

"That's their apartment," Lau replied, pointing.

The dashboard clock read 03:57. They seemed to have the night to themselves. There was no traffic, and they hadn't seen anyone for several minutes. A white Chevy Suburban pulled up behind them, and its lights blinked out. An icy chill raced down Jiang's spine. There was no turning back now.

"Let's go," he said, as he opened the door and got out.

Lau and Gao joined him on the sidewalk. One of the agents held a large, angular object. The other reached inside his coat and pulled out a Glock nine-millimeter automatic and checked to make sure it was ready. He flicked the safety off. Both men donned bulky, low-light goggles. Jiang nodded.

The two men ran for the apartment's front door while Jiang, Lau, and Gao stood back. One of the men placed a heavy bar against the door and extended the base against the concrete walk. He pumped the handle rapidly, forcing the vertical bar inward. The dead-bolt lock groaned; then the door crashed inward as the wooden jamb gave way under the relentless pressure. Both agents were through the door, guns drawn, before the door hit its stop. Jiang hurried inside with Lau and Gao.

Jiang's heart pounded as he waited in the pitch-black darkness of the entryway. He heard his men racing up the stairs, but couldn't see a thing. A crash sounded, followed immediately by a second. Jiang waited for the gunshots, but they didn't come. Another crash sounded. Jiang struggled against the urge to call out. The clatter of objects being thrown around drifted down and finally stopped. Two dark shapes materialized out of the shadows.

"There is no one here," one of the men said.

"That can't be!" Jiang said, louder than he intended. "What did you find?"

"They are gone. The beds are made."

Jiang felt a chill more intense than the previous excitement. He turned slowly, unsure what to do. *This was to have ended the problem, once and for all. But what now?* he wondered.

"Ransack the apartment," he ordered. "Make it look like a burglary."

The two agents ran back upstairs. Jiang approached the open door and peered out. Everything was quiet for now. He turned and saw a white glimmer, illuminated by the dim light streaming through the doorway. He approached and saw it was a sheet of paper sitting on a table. He picked it up, but couldn't read what it said. The men returned carrying two bulging sacks.

"Come on," Jiang said.

The last agent out pulled the door shut, hiding the damage as much as he could. Jiang got in the front of the Mercedes while Gao slipped into the back.

"Back to the office," Jiang ordered as Lau got in and started the engine. He waited until they were well clear, then flicked on the overhead light. "Well," he said. "It seems Ms. Flaherty was kind enough to leave us an itinerary." He turned to Lau. "Do you have a description of their cars?"

"I do. They have three, a large company car, a Mustang, and her Explorer."

"They'll probably take the Explorer. Can you identify it?"

"Yes."

"Good. This may work out yet."

* * *

"Need some coffee, pardner?" Hanna asked as she observed her husband at the wheel of her Explorer. He seemed alert enough, but looks could be deceiving. Those eyelids didn't seem quite as perky as they had been when they had first entered I-90.

"Yeah, I think I do." He flicked a glance her way and grinned, a strange sight in the ghostly light of the instrument panel. "You guarantee that stuff?"

"Made it from Grandmother's secret recipe. I think it would eat its way through a tin cup."

"Good thing we've got mugs."

She found the travel mugs and made sure she had the red one since the blue one was hers. She filled it from the thermos and handed it to him. Russell took a cautious sip.

"Whoa, I see what you mean!" he gasped.

"There, now those eyes are open. Let me know if you want some more."

"This should do me for a while."

A face appeared between the front seats. "Can I have some?" Scott asked.

Hanna turned and tousled his hair. "This isn't recommended for junior aviators. How about some Coke?" She could tell he was considering a protest as he smoothed his hair back in place.

"OK, I guess. But that smells good. Couldn't I try a little bit?"

Hanna looked at Russell. "Sounds like a question for old-man Flaherty."

She saw the flicker of a grin even in the dim light. He offered his mug to Scott.

"Eew," Scott said. "In my own cup, please."

Russell's grin changed to a laugh. "Please fix Mr. Fastidious up with a sterile cup. He might get a germ or two from Pops."

"Dad!"

"Cool it, you two." Hanna took Scott's Chuck E. Cheese cup and poured a little coffee into it.

The boy took it and sniffed. Then he tilted the cup up very slowly. Hanna heard the cautious sip. Then Scott lowered the cup as slowly as he had raised it, and his scrunched-up expression told the story.

"How was it?" Hanna asked.

He coughed. "Gross! How can you guys drink that stuff?"

"It takes getting used to," she admitted. "But after a while, you get to like it." She saw his doubt. "Trust me."

He settled back in the seat. "Where are we?"

"We're nearing Easton."

"How much farther to Billings?"

Hanna sighed. She knew a recurring theme when she heard one. "A long way. Remember when we discussed this before we left?"

"Yeah," he admitted, with obvious reluctance.

"We decided to change our plans and make the trip to Hereford in two days rather than three. That's why we left so early. But this way we can have an extra day in Big Bend, after we see the Davis Mountains and McDonald Observatory. Isn't that worth a couple of long days at first?"

"I guess so."

"Hang in there."

A little after seven, Scott announced he *had* to have some breakfast, despite the fact that they'd eaten something before they left, and Hanna had packed ample snacks. Bowing to the inevitable, Russell pulled off at the next stop offering food services. They would not reach Spokane on schedule, Hanna saw.

* * *

The big Suburban roared down I-90. It was seven-fifteen, and they would be in Spokane in less than an hour. Jiang knew they were well over the speed limit, but they had to chance it if they were to catch up with the Flahertys. Lau kept a sharp watch as he maintained the relentless pace. Jiang scanned each car they overtook, looking for Hanna's Explorer, hoping they would find it before reaching Butte.

* * *

It was almost 6:30 P.M. when Paul's phone rang. He pushed his computer keyboard away and punched the speakerphone button. "Blue Water Yachts, Paul Parker. Can I help you?"

"Paul, glad I caught you in. This is Jim McClusky."

"Hey, Jim. How are you doing?"

"We've got a problem. The Flaherty's place was broken into. I went by after work and found the door busted. I just now got done with the police."

Paul sat up straight. "What happened?"

"The police say it was a burglary. Quite a bit of stuff is missing. They ransacked the place pretty bad. I have a friend who's in remodeling. I'm having him fix the front door."

"Have you called Russell and Hanna yet?"

"No. I'll call them at the motel in Billings."

"Jim, let me do it," Paul said after a moment's thought. "There's something else I need to discuss with them."

There was a slight pause. "Something related to cyber terrorism?"

How do I answer that? Paul thought. "I really don't know. I guess it could be, but I suspect I'm letting my imagination run away with me. There're no reason to believe it's more than the police are saying."

"Whatever you think best. Give them my best, and tell Russell everything's under control. No need for them to cut short their vacation. They can fill out the insurance papers when they get back."

"I will. Thanks."

"And give my best to Rachael."

Paul felt the heat creeping above his collar. "Ah, I'll do that. Bye."

He punched the button to disconnect. He thought about going home, but decided he might as well get caught up on some of his neglected paperwork, although it was hard to concentrate. Finally he gave up around 7:00 P.M., hoping the Flahertys had arrived at their first stop. He pulled the revised itinerary across his desk and dialed the number for the motel in Billings.

"Big Sky Motel," the voice in the receiver said.

"Have the Flahertys checked in?" Paul asked.

"Yes, they did, a few minutes ago. I'll connect you." The line clicked, and the number rang.

"Hello."

Paul sighed with relief. "Russell, how are you?"

"Tired, but OK." He paused. "Is everything all right?"

"Not exactly. Your apartment was broken into. Jim found it and called the police."

Russell groaned. "What happened?"

"The police say it was a burglary."

"Are you thinking it might be something else?"

Paul rocked back in his chair as he pondered that. "No, I believe that's what it was—more than likely. After what I've been through, I think I'm jumpy; however it's probably wise to consider it might be tied in with what I'm working on."

"But Hanna's not doing anything on your project."

"Yes, but she did send that E-mail. We have no way of knowing if Singapore Shipping is involved, but if they are. . . ."

"Yeah, yeah. I see what you mean. Well, we'll turn back in the morning."

"No, don't do that. No point in ruining your vacation. There's really no reason for you to be here. Jim's made the police report, and he's getting someone to repair your door. Just notify your insurance company and take care of the details when you get back. If they want to send an adjuster by, we can let him in."

"But . . ."

"Look, you're almost halfway to Texas. This can wait for your return."

"I guess so. But what . . . what about the other?"

"I don't believe there's a connection. I don't see how there could be. An attack against me, I'd understand. But not this."

"I guess you're right." He managed a halfhearted laugh. "I know two people who would be mighty disappointed if we interrupted this trip."

"Then don't do it."

"OK. We'll call you from Hereford."

"Do that. Give my best to Hanna and Scott."

"I will. Bye."

Paul punched the disconnect button. He frowned as his mind refused to let go of the incident. He hoped he was right. But if not, he knew it was in God's hands.

*　*　*

Jiang scowled at the nearly empty parking lot in front of Butte's Copper City Motel. It had been easy enough to find, given the Flaherty's detailed itinerary. But their Explorer had not shown up, and it was almost ten. Of course, he knew there could have been car trouble or some other emergency. *But how likely was that?* he wondered. Much as he regretted the necessity, he finally decided to ask at the office.

"Keep a watch," he said finally. "I'm going to check on them."

Lau nodded.

Jiang got out and walked across the wide concrete drive and into the tiny office. A middle-aged man came in from a back room when he heard the door chime.

"Can I help you?" he asked with a smile.

"I hope so," Jiang replied. "I was supposed to meet some friends here—Mr. and Mrs. Russell Flaherty. I was wondering if you had heard from them."

Jiang could see doubt in the man's eyes. "Well, I don't know. I don't like to give out information like that."

"Oh, I quite understand. But they gave me their itinerary." Jiang pulled a folded sheet from his pocket and extended it. "I'm just concerned something might have happened, that's all."

The man examined the paper, then looked down at his register. He ran a finger down the entries for that day.

"I guess it's OK. Ah, here it is. Yep, they had a reservation for tonight, but they cancelled it."

"What? Did they say why?"

The man looked back up. "Nope."

Jiang struggled not to let his anger show. "Well, I guess . . . I guess I made a mistake. Thank you."

The clerk nodded.

Jiang left and returned to the Suburban.

* * *

"OK, pardner, up and at 'em," Hanna said as she shook Scott. "Time to hit the road."

The motel's cheap alarm clock said 3:14. Hanna reflected on the fact that she wanted to go back to bed herself. She glanced at Russell. He was staggering toward the bathroom, but she couldn't swear his eyes were open.

"Leave me alone," Scott moaned, as he turned over and pulled the covers up.

Hanna jerked them off. "Come on. We've got a long way to go today."

Seeing resistance was futile, Scott groaned and swung his legs over the edge of the bed and stumbled to his feet.

"Atta boy," Hanna encouraged. "Get dressed. You can have the bathroom as soon as your dad gets out."

He started dressing. Hanna started packing as she waited for her turn. After Russell and Scott finished, she rushed through her makeup routine with the depressing thought that it probably showed. They ate breakfast at a small twenty-four-hour restaurant and got on the road a little after four. Though this would be the longest leg of their trip, it was comforting to realize that they would be spending the night at her folk's home in Hereford.

Russell took the wheel while Hanna navigated and helped in keeping Scott occupied, something she found she enjoyed rather than being a burden. They rolled through the darkness and into the dawn as they followed I-90 into Wyoming, taking I-25 at Buffalo. Although Russell wanted to make Cheyenne for lunch, Scott's stomach overruled, and the Flahertys pulled off near Wheatland.

After lunch Hanna took over, and soon after Scott fell asleep. I-25 took them, ever so slowly, to Cheyenne and finally into Colorado. Hanna felt the long hours taking their toll as she struggled to stay alert. Towns appeared regular as clockwork on the straight highway. Finally they were past the sprawl of Denver. Passing Castle Rock, Hanna looked down at the dash clock. It was 2:25 P.M.

"You doing OK?" Russell asked.

"Pretty good. Mind pouring me some coffee?"

He filled her blue mug and handed it to her.

"Thanks," she said as she took a sip. "I know we're supposed to be on vacation, but my mind keeps going back to Zhu—wondering why he ran, where he is, and what he's doing."

"You mean finding out what the Raptor Virus is?"

"Yes, that. But also what Paul said about his resisting Christianity."

"Well, would you like me to pray about it?"

She felt her spirits lift. "Yes. Would you?"

* * *

Zhu turned the corner and entered a familiar street, although he couldn't remember how he got there. Heavy fog swirled about him, but it was beginning to burn off. He was in Shanghai, and it was as he had remembered it, every detail sharp and clear. There was the apartment building, an ugly gray monstrosity squatting among so many others exactly like it. He hurried along, anxious to see a familiar face. He entered the building and ran up the steps to the second floor. There he paused at the door. Somehow he couldn't bring himself to knock.

"Come in," a strong masculine voice said.

The recognition hit him like a sledgehammer. His heart pounded as he tried to decide what to do. *This can't be,* he thought. *You're dead!* He opened the door and looked in. A thin man stood by the window, looking out. Then he turned and looked Zhu in the eye. It was Huo Chee Yong.

"Grandmother and I have been waiting for you," Huo said.

Zhu turned his head and saw her sitting in a chair across from Huo.

"Yes, come in," she said, standing up. "I have longed to see my other grandson. Come here."

Zhu did so, seeing again those deep brown eyes of the one who loved him so. He felt the tears coming as he embraced her. "I've missed you, Grandmother."

"And I have missed you." She looked up into his eyes. "But you are always in my prayers, so I think we are closer than you suppose."

Zhu turned to his friend. "I don't understand," he said, his voice choking. "You're dead. I saw you die."

Huo's smile was relaxed and serene. "No, I am not dead, as you can see." Then a look of concern came to his eyes. "But you are, unless you change."

"That's right," Grandmother agreed.

"But . . ."

"You know what I'm talking about," Huo said. "Think it over. There's help if you ask for it, but it's up to you."

Thunder sounded in the distance. Fog poured through the open window and began filling the room. Huo and Grandmother began to grow dim. For a while longer he saw their shadows, then they were gone.

The thunder came again, louder this time. Zhu's eyes popped open. His heart was pounding so hard he wondered if he was having a heart attack. Then he saw the light filtering in through the steel roll door and realized where he was. He shivered as he remembered the reality of the dream. He couldn't recall one more vivid, and this one had not faded after awakening. If anything, it seemed even more real.

"Good morning," Eddie said as he approached. "I hope you slept well. I've got . . ." He stopped. "Is anything wrong?"

"No!" Zhu answered quickly.

"Are you sure?" Eddie asked as he set a bag of food on the table. "You look upset."

All Zhu wanted was for Eddie to leave him alone. But his anxiety, rather than subsiding, only increased. He considered confiding in the missionary but immediately rejected the idea. But the thought would not go away. He finally realized he wanted to talk to someone, and who else did he have?

"I brought your breakfast," Eddie said. "Are you hungry?"

"Yes." Zhu made his decision. "I . . . I had an unusual dream." He sat down at the table, and Eddie joined him.

"Oh? Would you like to talk about it?"

"Yes, I think I would."

Zhu described the dream and its vivid impact on him. Then, like a knot unraveling, he told Eddie what had happened to Huo. He described how he had really come to be in Kaohsiung, omitting only the details of his work for the Chinese government. He watched the American's eyes, expecting horror or shock, but all he saw there was deep concern. And that reminded him of Huo and Grandmother. *What is it with these Christians?* he wondered.

"You've been through a lot," Eddie said, shaking his head.

"Are you mad at me?"

"What? For misleading me? No, I'm sorry about what happened to you—and for the loss of your friend. Can I do anything to help?"

"I don't see what." Zhu looked Eddie in the eye. "Have I got you in trouble with the Taiwanese?"

"I don't know. That's secondary to helping someone who's in need. But I think God is trying to get your attention. Huo talked to you about him, as did Grandmother and Paul Parker. Do you really think it was by chance that you stumbled into a missionary when you needed help?"

The answer to that question shouted inside Zhu's head, but he couldn't face it—not now. He couldn't deny what the American was saying, but to give in was too hard. But the pressure inside would not go away. A separate consideration nagged at him as well. He realized he could not go along with what the Chinese government was doing with Project Dragon. Although he didn't trust the American government, he decided that not acting was no longer an option. But what could he do? Whatever his decision, he knew it would be very dangerous.

"I don't really know," he said finally.

26

SCOTT HAD AWAKENED AROUND COLORADO SPRINGS AND
had not gone to sleep since. Hanna had driven this route many times on
her way to Colorado ski resorts. She never tired of the rugged beauty of
the Rocky Mountains. Scott was suitably impressed with Pike's Peak's
towering majesty over Colorado Springs and Hanna's description of the
cog railway that went to the summit. Russell drifted off to sleep south of
Pueblo and didn't wake up until they were approaching Trinidad. There
I-25 began a series of tortuous twists and turns as it fought its way up
Raton Pass and down into New Mexico.

Hanna turned off the interstate at the junction with highway 87. They
ate dinner at the Dairy Queen and got three Blizzards to take with them.
Russell took the wheel and pulled into a filling station east of the junction. He stopped on the right side of the gas island and got out.

Hanna looked out the driver's side window at a huge motor home that
blocked her view of the highway. She watched Russell as he began to fill
the tank.

* * *

Jiang had decided to spend the night at Butte. Although nagged by the thought that the Flahertys might have cancelled their trip, he thought it unlikely. Since the intercept had failed, the next possibility would be in Hereford, unless they spotted the Explorer before then.

Jiang read the approaching sign, then consulted his map. "Get off here," he ordered. "We take highway 87 to the east."

The big Suburban began to slow as Lau took his foot off the gas. The town of Raton nestled under the foothills to the west, bathed in the warm tones of late afternoon sunshine. Lau pulled up to the stop sign, turned left, and accelerated briskly.

Jiang scanned the cars they passed. He stared at a motor home parked in a filling station, wondering absently what it would be like to travel that way.

* * *

Hanna heard something in the backseat.

"How much farther?" Scott asked.

Hanna turned and saw the restlessness in his eyes. She reached out to muss his hair, but he jumped back in time. "We're on the home stretch," she replied. "It's a little over two hundred miles to Amarillo."

"How close is that to Hereford?"

"Why you can hit Hereford with a cow chip from there."

He made a face. "Eew, gross."

She grinned. "Gotta admit we've got enough ammo around those parts."

"Seems like we've been driving forever," Scott said as he sat back in the seat.

"I know. This part isn't much fun. But tomorrow we'll visit with my family, maybe get in some horseback riding."

"Can we?"

"Don't see why not. Then the next day we'll be camping in the Davis Mountains."

"Aren't we going to San Antonio first?"

"Your dad and I discussed that while you were asleep. We decided it would be more fun to get on with the camping and hang gliding."

"All right!"

"Thought you'd like that. We'll come back through San Antonio on our way back. Gotta show you and your dad the Alamo and the River Walk."

"Way cool!"

Russell finished and got back in. "Next stop: Hereford."

"Drive on, pardner," Hanna said.

She smiled as she got comfortable in her seat. An hour and a half later they left the Land of Enchantment and entered the Texas panhandle at Texline. The last vestiges of twilight faded to black as they followed highway 87 through Dalhart. At Dumas they turned south on 287. Less than an hour later, Hanna saw the lights of Amarillo on the horizon. As they reached the city limits, she reached for her purse.

"Think I'll phone my folks," she said, as she began rummaging around. Not finding her mobile, she flicked on the overhead light. But though her purse contained many things, her phone wasn't among them.

"Do you have my phone?" she asked.

Russell glanced over. "No. Isn't it in your purse?"

"Doesn't seem to be." She turned. "Scott, have you seen it?"

"Not today. Didn't you take it out of your purse at the motel?"

Hanna closed her eyes as she remembered. "Yes, I was going to call my folks after we heard about the break-in. Then I decided to wait until we got to Hereford. I bet I left it on the bedside table." She felt her irritation mounting. "Electronic technology is my stock in trade, and I do something like this."

"Take it easy," Russell said. "We'll call the motel tomorrow. I'm sure we can get them to ship it to us."

"That's not the point. I brought it along for the convenience, in case we had car trouble or something."

"I'm sure we won't need it. Now relax."

The humor of the situation began working on her irritation. "That an order?" she asked.

"No, ma'am," Russell said with a chuckle. "A loving suggestion."

She smiled finally. "Hm, that sounds interesting." She felt her pulse quicken. "Did you have anything particular in mind?"

He cleared his throat. "We'll see." He slowed as they entered downtown Amarillo.

Hanna turned around. "We're about an hour from Hereford," she told Scott.

"Cool," he said with a yawn. "I'm tired."

"Well, it won't be long now."

＊ ＊ ＊

"There it is," Jiang said, pointing to the large ranch-style house. He had printed an Excite map from the itinerary before leaving Seattle and was pleased to find how accurate it was.

"I don't see her car," Lau said, as he pulled up to the curb across the street and stopped.

"We probably beat them here," Gao said from the backseat.

"Quite likely," Jiang agreed.

A car turned onto the street behind them. The glow from its headlights grew as it approached.

"Drive on!" Jiang ordered.

Lau put the Suburban in gear and drove off. Jiang turned around and looked out the back windows. The car turned into the Sidwell's drive.

"It's their Explorer," he said.

"What do we do now?" Gao asked.

What Jiang wanted was to end the problem now, since they had finally caught up with the one who jeopardized Project Dragon. But it would be dangerous to attack in town.

"We wait," he said. "We'll take them after they leave."

"How long will they be here?" Gao asked.

"One day. Then they drive to San Antonio. And between here and there we will have plenty of opportunities."

* * *

Hanna hugged her mother, then turned to her dad.

"Glad you're here," Curtis said as he hugged her. "Your mother about wore out the floor with her pacing."

"I did not," Carol said.

He shrugged and turned to Russell. "Welcome," he said, shaking his son-in-law's hand. "How was the trip?"

"Long and tiring."

Curtis nodded. "That's a far piece." He looked around. "Where's Scott?"

A car door slammed. Hanna saw what he had in his hand. "Forgot your Game Boy, huh?"

"Yeah."

"Hi, Scott," Curtis said.

Scott shifted his game to his other hand and shook hands. "Hello, Mr. Sidwell."

"Welcome to Texas. I know some fat ole horses that need some exercise. Suppose you could help me with that tomorrow?"

"Yeah! That would be cool!"

"Good. Well, you go on in while your dad and I get the bags."

"I'll help," Hanna said.

"Git," her father ordered. "I reckon Russell and I can manage."

"Hm." She stood there for a moment as she considered an objection, then went inside with Scott.

She looked around the living room as the relaxed comfort of her parent's home surrounded her and began to draw away the tension of travel. After nineteen hours on the road, she did not plan on getting up early.

* * *

After an all-too-short night, Carol made early rounds to wake her guests for breakfast. Hanna peered at the clock radio on the bedside table. Well, she had to admit, seven o'clock wasn't all that early, but it felt like it. She turned to Russell and saw from his bristly face and squinted eyes that he felt the same way. Then the aroma of coffee and bacon drifted in from the kitchen. Soon the Flahertys were on their feet and dressing.

After breakfast, Curtis and Scott rounded up Hanna and Russell. Hanna's dad drove them out to the ranch in his four-door pickup. He saddled the horses and led them out through the pasture for a morning's ride. Travel weary, Hanna was quite content to spend some leisure time in the saddle. The hours passed as pleasantly as she expected.

Hanna heard leather creaking and turned. Russell was standing up in his stirrups. He saw her and slowly sat down.

"Saddle sore, pardner?" she asked sweetly.

"Oh, no. Just stretching my legs." His smile was less than perfect.

"Uh-huh," she replied, not buying a bit of it. Hanna nodded across the pasture. "Your son seems to be having a good time." Scott was chasing a calf that took every opportunity to head back to its mother. Curtis remained close to the boy, making sure the fun stayed in bounds.

"Yes, he is. Your dad is sure nice to him."

Hanna shrugged. "As far as Mom and Dad are concerned, they've got a new grandkid. I suppose you saw what Mr. Scott got for breakfast."

"Uh-huh. And he put it all away, too." Russell shook his head. "Wish I could still eat like that."

Hanna turned her head and narrowed her eyes. "You don't do so bad yourself." She paused as her eyes did a quick inspection. "However, it doesn't seem to hurt your physique any. Must be your exercising." She saw his sheepish smile and loved it.

"Uh, thanks," he said. "You look pretty fit yourself, gal."

It was drawn out, but the accent wasn't even close. She adjusted the brim on her hat. "You from around these parts, cowboy?"

The Boston Irish returned. "Not exactly, lass."

"Didn't think so." She glanced at her watch. "Almost noon. We better head for the barn before Mom sends out a search party."

Russell shifted uneasily in the saddle. "Sounds good to me."

* * *

Zhu had struggled with his decision all of the previous day, not helped any by the disturbing claims of Christianity. More to the point, the examples of his dead friend, and Grandmother, and Paul, and this American missionary gave him no rest. It was only after a miserable night that he finally came to a decision. Zhu was waiting for Eddie when the roll door clattered up in the morning.

"Would you do something for me?" Zhu asked, as Eddie came through the front door.

"I will if I can. What is it?"

"Call Paul Parker in Seattle and tell him I'll cooperate."

"That's all?"

"Yes. He'll know what to do. And please do it now. There's not much time."

"OK. I'll have to do it from my apartment. I don't have a phone line in here yet. Do you want to talk to him?"

Zhu shook his head. "No. It is not safe for me to leave here. Agents of my . . ." He paused. "Chinese agents are after me. I was running from them when I found your church. Be sure you tell Paul that. If you don't reach him at home, try Blue Water Yachts in Seattle."

Eddie nodded. "I'll be back in a little bit."

* * *

Paul yawned as he took a sip of coffee from his Blue Water Yachts mug. It was after 4:00 P.M., but his day still had a ways to go. He had cleared a lot of his backlogged paperwork, and the company president seemed placated. At least Paul hadn't been fired. He still had the problem of getting David Ho's yacht back to Seattle, but that wasn't pressing—yet. Right now there were more important problems. He checked his Outlook in-box and found, to his relief, that he had no new messages. His phone rang, and he picked up the receiver.

"Blue Water Yachts, Paul Parker. Can I help you?"

"Mr. Parker, this is Eddie Zanders. I'm a missionary in Kaohsiung, Taiwan. Zhu Tak-shing asked me to call you."

Paul sat bold upright, suddenly alert. "Do you know where he is?"

"I gave him sanctuary in the church I'm building. He said to tell you he's ready to cooperate—that you'd know what to do."

Paul's head spun. "Yes, I do. Tell him I'll get right on it. And be careful. He's in great danger." Paul hesitated. "Eddie, you might be as well."

"I understand. And Zhu said to tell you Chinese agents are after him."

"He's seen them?"

"Yes."

"OK. Give me the address of your church."

Paul wrote it down as he mentally ticked off all the things he had to do.

"I have it," he said when Eddie finished. "Tell Zhu to stay there. I'll have someone there as soon as possible. And thank you."

"You're welcome. I think I see the Lord's hand in this."

Paul grinned. "I think you're right. Stay by your phone. I'll call you right back."

"OK. Bye."

Paul punched in Vic's office number from memory, hoping he was still in. He waited impatiently as it rang.

"Victor Yardel."

"Vic, this is Paul! We've got a breakthrough! Zhu's turned up in Kaohsiung, and he's willing to cooperate."

"How'd you find him?"

"He ran into a missionary. Please, Vic, we've got to move on this. Chinese agents are after him. We need to get him out of there immediately." There was a slight pause. Paul sent up a silent prayer.

"OK. Do you know where he is?"

Paul gave him the address.

"Got it. Get back to your missionary friend, and tell him help is on the way."

"OK, I'll do that."

"Good. FYI, I'll have Zhu brought into McChord Air Force Base in Tacoma. I'll call later with the details."

"Great. Thanks, Vic."

"That's what I'm here for. Bye."

The line went dead.

Well, Paul thought, *Vic can make a decision when he has to.*

He called Eddie back with the news.

* * *

"That's all he said?" Zhu asked. "Help is on the way?"

"Yes. I don't think we'll have to wait long."

Zhu laughed sarcastically. "We will see."

In the distance he could hear a siren, but that was not at all uncommon in that sprawling city. But as he listened, it grew louder. Less than a minute later an ambulance pulled up in front of the shop-cum-church and stopped. Three Emergency Medical Technicians jumped out of the back, ran inside, and hurried to the back. Zhu's heart pounded. Were they sent by the Americans, or was this the end? One of the men approached and reached inside his uniform.

"Mr. Zhu Tak-shing?" It wasn't really a question. The man opened his wallet and displayed an ID card printed in Chinese and English. One line jumped out at him: "Central Intelligence Agency."

"Yes," Zhu managed to croak.

"Please come with me."

"Where are you taking me?"

"To Tacoma, Washington. Other agents will meet you there, including Paul Parker."

Zhu nodded. He started for the door, but the agent grabbed him by the arm.

"Please," the agent said. "Let us do our job." He waved at one of the real EMTs who hurried forward with the wheeled stretcher.

Zhu turned and saw Eddie standing back. He felt a tightness in his throat. "Thank you for everything."

Eddie came forward and shook his hand. "On behalf of the Lord, you're welcome. Will you do something for me?"

A tight smile came to Zhu's face. "If I can."

"Remember what we talked about. Remember your friend and Grandmother."

Zhu nodded, unsure he could speak. "I will," he said finally.

One of the EMTs took him by the arm and helped him onto the stretcher. His assistant pulled up the blanket and fitted an oxygen mask over Zhu's face. Zhu started to struggle, then realized what it was for. The three men rolled their patient out to the waiting ambulance. Zhu looked up through the clear plastic mask as the men locked the stretcher into place. A few moments later the ambulance was shrieking its way through downtown Kaohsiung.

27

ZHU STEPPED DOWN FROM THE HELICOPTER, KEEPING HIS head low. He ran out from under the rotors and turned. The CIA agent stood beside him, obviously determined that his charge get where he was going. The Taiwan Air Force helicopter immediately lifted off, peppering those on the ground with fine grit. Zhu squinted until the blast subsided. Before the clatter of the aircraft faded, he heard the whine of jet engines approaching. A gray, four-engine C-141B transport turned off the taxi-way and approached. The huge craft made a lumbering right turn and stopped. The whine lessened as the near-side jet engines shut down. A door near the cockpit opened, and an officer in a green flight suit jumped down and strode toward the two men.

"Mr. Zhu Tak-shing?" he asked as he approached.

"Yes," Zhu replied.

"I'm Lieutenant Colonel Denton. My orders are to transport you to McChord Air Force Base in Tacoma. Are you ready to leave?"

"I am."

"Very well. If you will follow me, we're cleared for immediate departure."

"Yes, Colonel."

He followed the Air Force officer to the door and stepped up after him. Zhu turned and looked out. The CIA agent was still standing there. One of the crewmen closed and locked the door.

"Mr. Zhu," said the pilot. "You'll be riding with us on the flight deck."

Zhu turned all around the vast, empty aircraft. "I'm the only one on board?" he asked.

The pilot's blue eyes glinted. "The only passenger. You obviously have better connections than most generals. This way to the flight deck. We really *are* in a hurry."

Colonel Denton strapped him into the jump seat behind the command pilot's position. Zhu watched as the officer resumed his seat and put on his earphones and boom mic. After starting the two port engines, they were soon rumbling down the long taxiways while Taiwan Air Force fighters waited for them to pass. Without a pause the pilot guided the heavy transport onto the active runway and pushed the four power levers forward. The engine whine became a scream. The empty aircraft accelerated quickly to takeoff speed. Soon they were at cruising altitude.

"You've got it," Colonel Denton told his copilot. He turned in his seat. "Mr. Zhu, we'll be flying nonstop to Tacoma with inflight refueling. It's more than fifty-two hundred nautical miles, so our flying time will be about twelve hours. My ETA for McChord is around ten-hundred hours on Friday. You're free to move about the flight deck, but please don't touch anything. Any questions?"

Zhu shook his head. "No, Colonel. I appreciate your help."

"We're here to serve." He grabbed a paperback novel and turned to the copilot. "Junior, I'm goin' back to the can. Try to keep us right side up."

"Yes, sir," the young captain said.

* * *

Hanna glanced at the speedometer. It was a hair over seventy, but she decided to leave the speed control where it was. It was already eight o'clock, and her plan to leave early had been completely thwarted by her mother, who insisted on cooking a hearty breakfast for the travelers. They were south of Springlake on highway 385, and Russell was occupied with navigation.

"Did you know we're only a few miles from Earth, Texas?" he asked with a grin.

"Yep," Hanna agreed. "We're also close to Muleshoe, Bovina, Lazbuddie, and Circle."

He shook his head. "Why all the unusual names?"

"With the state being so big, we were running low on respectable names by the time we got to west Texas."

For a few moments he only looked at her. "Uh-huh. I don't think I'll pursue that." He looked down at the map. "Next big town is Littlefield. Is that where we would have turned if we were going to Abilene and San Antonio?"

"Yep. But aren't you glad we're going to the Davis Mountains first?"

"Yeah!" Scott said, suddenly appearing between the seats.

"Yes," Russell added. "I don't know which I'm looking forward to more: McDonald Observatory or hang gliding."

"Hang gilding," Scott said.

"OK," Russell said, "but the visitor's center closes at five. So we better do that first."

"But . . ."

"There'll be plenty of time for hang gliding," Hanna reassured him. "We'll be in the Davis Mountains for two days, and three more in Big Bend."

"Well, OK."

Hanna flicked her eyes over the rearview mirror. Then she took a longer look. "Russell, a white Suburban has been following us, hanging way back. I first noticed it after we left Dimmitt."

Russell turned around. "They're probably traveling in the same direction." He faced forward again. "You're not getting paranoid, are you?"

Her memory went back a few years. "After what we went through, it's hard not to be."

"And what just happened to Paul."

"Yeah."

"Why don't you slow down. Then they'll pass us, and we can stop worrying about it."

"OK." She tapped the brake to turn off the speed control, putting her foot back on the gas when the speedometer reached 50. "That should do it. Isn't anyone out here can stand movin' this slow."

Russell looked back.

"What's going on?" Scott asked.

"Don't know," Russell replied. "Hanna thinks that Suburban might be following us."

"Really?" Scott turned.

"They're still hanging back," Hanna said, her voice rising. "They caught up a little when I slowed down, but then they backed off. Russell, I'm getting worried. The traffic's light. What if they're after us?"

"I don't see how they could be."

Hanna heard the doubt in his voice. She knew he wasn't sure. "What should I do?"

"Pull over and let them pass."

She felt a surge of relief mixed with fear. *That should do it,* she thought. *But what if it is the Chinese?*

She checked her mirrors. One car was coming toward them. That and the Suburban were the only other vehicles in sight. Hanna took her foot off the gas and started braking hard. She pulled onto the wide shoulder and stopped.

"What're they doing?" she asked

"Slowed down a little, but they're still coming."

* * *

"Get ready!" Jiang screamed.

The two agents opened cases and pulled out their Uzi submachine guns. Checking to make sure rounds were chambered, they flicked the safeties off and waited.

"Pull up behind them!" Jiang ordered. He turned around. "Kill them all! Make sure!"

The two men nodded.

"There's a car coming toward us," Lau announced.

Jiang turned back around and cursed. "Drive on. We'll turn around after the other car passes."

Lau kept his speed at 40 as they neared the Explorer.

Jiang watched the approaching car. Finally he recognized what it was and cursed again.

* * *

The Suburban drove past. Hanna looked but couldn't see anything through the deeply tinted windows.

Hanna's eyes moved to the northbound car. "It's a state trooper," she said, as the black-and-white car came toward them.

The car made a sharp U-turn and came up behind the Explorer. The trooper got out, put on his hat, and came up on the driver's side. Hanna rolled down the window and looked out.

"Howdy, folks," the officer said, touching the brim of his hat. "Any trouble?"

Hanna hesitated. How in the world could she answer that? Chinese agents *might* be after them? The more she thought about it, the more ludicrous it sounded. "No, officer," she said finally. "We pulled over for a bit."

The man nodded. "Just checking. You folks have a nice day, now." He walked back to his car and got in. Moments later he drove off to the south. Hanna pulled out behind him and accelerated up to 70 and found that was what the trooper was doing. It was comforting to see the black-and-white car in front of them.

* * *

Jiang struggled to regain his composure. He had seen the trooper stop behind the Flahertys and get out. When the officer drove off to the south, Jiang had expected the worst. For several miles he had expected to see flashing lights, but nothing happened. Then he relaxed a little when he considered that the Flahertys couldn't really know they were being followed.

"What do we do now?" Lau asked as he looked into the rearview mirror. "That police car is still between us and the Flahertys."

Jiang's mind raced. He consulted the map and saw they were nearing Littlefield. "Since they're going to Abilene, they'll turn on highway 84."

"Are you sure?"

"Yes, I'm sure!" Jiang snapped, throwing the map down. "It's the most direct way. Find some place to hide outside town. When they come past, we'll take them.

After reaching south Littlefield, Lau turned left on the entrance ramp to U.S. 84. When they were well clear of town, Jiang began scanning the flat farmland. Finally he spotted a semi pulled off on the shoulder, with triangular markers indicating a breakdown.

"Slow down!" Jiang ordered. He looked up into the cab as they passed. "Pull over! The driver's gone for help. Back up as close to the truck as you can. We'll be invisible from the other side."

Lau braked hard and stopped on the shoulder. He threw the shift lever into reverse and backed the Suburban until his rear bumper was inches from the truck.

"Now we wait," Jiang said.

* * *

"Is that the highway we would have taken to Abilene?" Russell asked.

"Yep. Down 84 to I-20."

"Where are we?" Scott asked.

"Outside Littlefield," Hanna said. "Next big town is Levelland." Her eyes flicked over at Russell. She knew something had to be rattling around in his mind. "Out with it," she said finally.

"How apt," he said.

"It *is* kinda flat around these parts."

"How long till we get to the Davis Mountains?" Scott asked.

Hanna did a quick calculation. "We'll be there a little after one."

* * *

Jiang's anger mounted with each passing minute. They had been waiting in front of the stalled semi for more than a half hour and still no sign of the Flahertys.

"Where are they?" He grumbled.

"Maybe they stopped to eat."

Jiang looked at his watch and saw it was a little after nine. "Not this early. Let's go. Find a place we can turn around. We're going back."

Lau started the Suburban and pulled back onto the highway. A few miles later he found a crossover and turned around. Jiang watched the opposite side carefully but saw no sign of the Explorer. They took the exit for highway 385.

"Turn left," Jiang ordered when they reached the junction.

"Where do you think they're going?" Lau asked as he completed the turn.

Jiang's eyes flicked over the itinerary. "The Davis Mountains. They've decided to go there first. It's the only thing that makes sense." He struggled with his inner doubts. Was he right?

* * *

Paul held Rachael's hand as they stood on the ramp at McChord Air Force Base. If Vic objected to this inter-service fraternization, he didn't say so. Besides, he was rather involved with Colonel Brining, the base commander. The two men were standing off to the side.

A gray C-141 turned off a taxiway and trundled toward the four people waiting on the ramp. It came straight in and stopped a hundred feet away. The whine from the engines dropped rapidly as the pilot switched them off. The side door opened, and two men stepped down on the concrete. An Air Force officer walked toward them with long strides, matched by the civilian at his side.

The pilot saluted. "Lieutenant Colonel Denton reporting as ordered, sir. This gentleman with me is Mr. Zhu Tak-shing. My orders are to deliver him to you."

"Well done, Colonel. I'm Colonel Brining, base CO." He nodded toward Vic. "Actually you're delivering Mr. Zhu to Mr. Victor Yardel of the CIA."

"Thank you, Colonel," Vic said, shaking the pilot's hand. "You've done your country a great service."

"We're here to serve, sir." He turned back to Colonel Brining. "Colonel, I'll report to Base Operations as soon as I secure the aircraft." He saluted the base commander and hurried back to his plane.

"Welcome to America, Mr. Zhu," Vic began. "I have arranged political asylum for you. We can go over the details on our way back to Seattle, but I'm sure you'll approve."

"Thank you, Mr. Yardel." Zhu turned to Paul. "But most of all, thank you, Mr. Parker. I appreciate everything you did for me."

"You're welcome. I'm glad it worked out."

Zhu's eyes flicked back to Vic. "There is something we must discuss immediately," he continued. "You are wise to worry about the Raptor Virus. It is scheduled to strike your telecommunications network in a little over a week. You must act immediately."

"That's worse than we thought," Paul said.

"What can we do?" Rachael asked.

"I can provide a list of the sabotaged parts," Zhu replied. "You need a team to get samples of each one. I can show you what to correct. After patching the defect, you can copy them onto replacement parts and distribute them. It won't be easy, but it can be done."

"We need Hanna back," Paul said to Vic.

"Agreed. Where are they?"

"They're going to Abilene and San Antonio today."

Vic turned to the base commander. "Colonel, I think we may need your help in bringing the Flahertys back here."

"Shall we retire to my office?"

Vic and Colonel Brining took his staff car while Paul, Rachael, and Zhu got in the government car the agents had driven from Seattle. Paul started the engine and followed the staff car.

"Mr. Parker," Zhu said. "Forgive me for running away."

Paul hesitated, not knowing exactly what to say. "I forgive you," he said finally. He wondered at Zhu's tone of voice. The man really did sound contrite, as well as grateful. *What had happened?* he wondered.

They made the trip to base headquarters quickly.

28

"WHAT DID HE SAY?" RACHAEL ASKED AS PAUL HUNG UP THE phone and glanced at his watch.

"Curtis said they're headed for McDonald Observatory today."

"They changed their itinerary again?"

"Sure did."

"What about Hanna's mobile phone?"

"I'll try it, but coverage isn't so hot down there." He punched in the number and got a recording. "No good." He turned to Vic. "We have to do something. They were planning on camping in the Davis Mountains and in Big Bend."

"Colonel, can you help us out?" Vic asked. "We need these people back ASAP."

"Yes, sir. I can get a Pave Low helicopter out of Laughlin Air Force Base in Del Rio. It's a little over two hundred miles from there to McDonald."

"Do it."

* * *

Jiang struggled with his frustration as he studied the map. Although he hoped the Flahertys were on their way to McDonald Observatory, he was far from sure. They obviously didn't feel obliged to follow their itinerary since they had already deviated from it twice. If the observatory *were* their destination, that helped, since only two roads went there. State highway 118 dropped down from Kent, while 17 went from Toyahvale to Fort Davis, where it met 118 east of McDonald. From 118, Spur 78 traced a lonely trail up to the top of Mount Locke.

Jiang gripped the armrest as the heavy Suburban rounded a tight curve, tires squealling. Lau gripped the steering wheel with both hands, struggling to maintain control. Highway 118 opened up a little. They had a little over fifteen miles to go.

"Faster," Jiang ordered.

Lau accelerated up to 85.

* * *

The Air Force Captain looked down on the desolate landscape as his Sikorsky MH-53J Pave Low helicopter approached the Glass Mountains near Marathon, Texas. His copilot monitored the flight instruments while the two enlisted flight engineers watched over the powerful General Electric turboshaft engines. Two aerial gunners rounded out the crew, responsible for manning the two 50-caliber machine guns and the 7.62-mm minigun.

Ahead lay the Davis Mountains and McDonald Observatory. There, hopefully, they would rendezvous with the civilian VIPs, then return to Laughlin Air Force Base.

Why this required top secret orders, the captain did not know. But his squadron CO's last words had been most emphatic: "Bring them back ASAP, and don't let anything stop you!"

* * *

Russell took his foot off the gas as the Explorer entered a curve in the Davis Mountains.

Hanna turned toward the backseat. "We're almost there, pardner," she informed Scott.

"Cool. Where is it?"

She started to point but froze as she saw a light-colored car through the rear window. Her blood ran cold.

"Hanna?" Scott said, his voice rising. "Is something wrong?"

"I'm not sure." She turned to Russell. "Do you see that car following us?"

"Yes. Noticed it a couple of minutes ago. Whoever it is seems to be in a hurry."

"I think it's the same car that was following us earlier."

Russell stared into the rearview mirror for a few moments. "Are you sure?"

"No, but it is a white car or at least light colored. And they're really moving. Russell, I'm scared. What if it *is* them? We're miles from help."

Russell stepped on the accelerator. The Explorer screeched around a tight curve. "I don't think we can outrun them."

The next few minutes proved this true. The distance between the two cars steadily decreased. Hanna's eyes darted around as they topped a hill. Then she looked back. The following car was hidden by the rise.

"Stop!" she shouted. "See that gully? Drive down it until we're behind that ridge. We'll be hidden from the road."

Russell stomped on the brakes and brought the Explorer to a tire-screeching halt. The pungent odor of burning rubber drifted inside. Russell engaged four-wheel drive. He turned off the road and drove along the dry creek bed. The car bounced and lurched as they crunched over the dry brush.

"Any sight of them?" Russell asked.

"Not yet," Hanna replied. "But hurry. They'll be topping that hill any time."

Russell pressed the accelerator harder and fought with the steering wheel, trying to avoid the worst bumps and holes. Finally they reached the ridge. He turned in behind it and stopped.

Hanna and Russell jumped out at the same time. A rear door opened, and Scott joined them.

"Back inside!" Russell ordered.

"But, Dad . . ."

"Do it! We may have to leave in a hurry!"

Scott did as he was told.

Hanna joined Russell as they hurried toward the edge of the ridge. She could hear the racing engine of the approaching car.

"If they go past, we can return to Kent," Hanna said.

"Yeah," Russell agreed. "But will they keep on going?"

Hanna and Russell ducked behind a yucca plant. The white Suburban topped the hill and swept down the short straightaway. For a while the car continued its breakneck pace, but started to slow as it approached the next curve. Finally it stopped.

"Go on!" Hanna urged in a whisper.

"It's not going to work," Russell said.

"What do we do?"

He shook his head. "I don't know. They're definitely following us. Since we disappeared, they know we have to be off the road somewhere."

"You think they've got four-wheel drive?"

"Suburbans come either way, but I'd guess they do. Which means we're going to have company as soon as they spot where we left the road."

Hanna looked down at the tracks in the dirt. "They'd have to be blind not to see that."

Russell looked toward the Explorer. "OK, we'll wait until they're near, then beat them back to the road."

"Which way then?"

"We're closer to McDonald than Kent. Our best chance is to beat them to the top. What do you think?"

She nodded. "I agree."

They peered through the yucca's saber-sharp leaves as the Suburban backed slowly down the road. Two men scanned the roadside through the open windows. Hanna shivered as she saw the sinister black object the man in back was holding. The car stopped. The engine roared as the driver turned the wheels sharply and started into the desert brush.

"Go back to the car," Russell said. "I'll be there in a minute."

Hanna hesitated a moment, not wanting to leave her husband, then hurried back. She opened the door, got in, and looked back through the rear window. Russell remained behind the yucca for a few more moments, then came racing back. He wrenched open the door, jumped in, and cranked the engine. It caught at once. Russell slammed the car into gear and stood on the accelerator, fighting for control as the rear end fishtailed. The suspension bottomed repeatedly as the rugged vehicle pounded through the brush and over the hummocks.

The Suburban rounded the ridge behind them. "Here they come!" Hanna shouted. "Hurry! They're shooting at us!" She glanced at Scott. "Get down on the floor!"

He ducked down.

They roared over a small hill and flew through the air, plowing through a large yucca. Russell cranked the wheel hard to the left as they cleared the ridge. He turned toward the road but found his way blocked by a deep ravine. He turned toward the way they had come in. The ridge provided temporary shelter.

"They're coming around the end!" Hanna said.

Russell angled for the road, skirting the ravine as closely as he dared. A heavy slug blasted through Hanna's window and exited through the windshield, showering them with tiny shards of glass. Rounds slammed repeatedly into the side, banging the car like a drum.

"Get down!" Russell ordered.

Hanna sprawled out on the seat, looking up at her husband. She winced with each impact. A bullet pulverized a side window in the back, spraying the interior with glass.

The Explorer bounded onto the pavement, tires screaming as Russell floored the accelerator. Several more bullets slammed into them. Then the firing stopped.

"What happened?" she asked.

"They've lost sight of us temporarily. But that won't last long."

Hanna sat up slowly. "Can we beat them to the top?" she asked.

He shook his head. "No. They hit our radiator." He pointed to the steam rising from the back of the hood. Hanna could see a ragged hole near the front.

Hanna held on as Russell turned onto Spur 78. They roared past a deserted parking area and continued up the road leading to Mount Locke's summit.

"We're not going to make it," Russell said. "The temperature gauge is already redlined, and we've got over a mile to go."

Smoke poured out of the back of the hood, accompanied by an ominous clattering noise. Hanna looked out the back. "They're about a half-mile back! There must be *something* we can do!"

"I don't know what. We're all alone on the road."

The pounding racket grew ever louder. Hanna knew it wouldn't be long now.

"Hey!" Russell shouted. "There's a turnoff!"

"Where does it go?" Hanna asked as she turned back around.

"Don't know. It climbs that hill on the right. Think we should try it?"

"Do it! We're dead if we stay down here."

"OK."

The dirt trail paralleled the road before curving to the right as it climbed the hill. Russell took the rutted path without slowing down. The Explorer lurched and bounded alarmingly as they roared upward toward the summit. Russell selected four-wheel drive. The car lurched along, the engine screaming in protest. Finally it quit, and they slid to a stop.

"That's it!" Russell shouted.

Hanna jumped out and pulled Scott's door open. "Head for the top!" she ordered.

He dashed past her. She and Russell ran over the rise to find Scott standing at the edge of a cliff.

"It's an overview!" Hanna said, out of breath. "That must be a hundred-foot drop!" She stopped and turned. "Russell! Get the gliders!"

"We don't have time. They'll be here before we can set them up."

"It's the only chance we've got!"

Hanna ran back to the smoking Explorer. Russell caught up as she was reaching for the rooftop carrier. She unstrapped one glider and pulled it down. Russell freed the other, and they started back up the hill. Hanna chanced a backward glance. The Suburban was almost to the turnout with the Explorer in plain view. They hauled the gliders over the crest to the precipice.

Russell threw down the tandem. "You and Scott set these up! I'll be back in a bit."

"Where are you going?" Hanna demanded.

"Just do it!"

He dashed off and disappeared down the hill. Hanna turned and saw Scott looking at her.

"You heard your dad. Get busy."

He fell to his knees and started undoing the straps. Hanna worked on the tandem while trying to ignore the roar of the approaching car.

* * *

Russell raced toward the ruined Explorer. Below, the Suburban slowed for the turnoff, tires screaming. A dark shape appeared in a rear window. The soft "plops" of a silenced automatic drifted upward. A lethal trail of impacts stitched its way up the hill. Russell wrenched the door open and dived into the front seat as several slugs slammed into the car. He turned on the ignition, stomped on the brake, and yanked the gearshift into neutral. Then he jumped out and rolled. He peered cautiously over a mound of dirt.

The Explorer started rolling backwards toward the approaching Suburban. The driver slammed on his brakes and started backing up. The two cars collided and locked bumpers. A frantic attempt to back away failed. Finally the driver turned sharply to the left and broke free. But the smaller SUV blocked the trail. Four men got out and started up.

Russell jumped to his feet and raced up the hill. Behind him he heard their crunching footsteps growing louder. Near the summit Russell spotted a large boulder. He got behind it and pushed until he saw stars. The boulder moved a little then stopped. Russell shoved again, straining with every muscle. The boulder lurched, then started rolling. It rolled into a rut and started bounding toward the road below.

Russell took a cautious look. One of the men cried out as he spotted the menace. Two of the agents took refuge behind a boulder against the hill while the other two slipped over the slope on the other side. The boulder bounced past and hurtled into the Explorer, which deflected it away from the Suburban. Then it reached the road and continued downhill. The men scrambled out of their hiding places. Russell whirled around and ran.

* * *

Hanna checked Scott's hang glider and his harness. She saw the fear in his eyes.

"Good work," she said in an attempt to reassure him.

"Where's Dad?" he asked.

"We have to trust him to God," she replied as she snapped her harness to the tandem hang glider. She sent an arrow prayer for his protection.

She turned when she heard running footsteps, breathing a sigh of relief as she saw Russell appear over the rise.

"Come on!" she shouted.

"Get Scott airborne!" he ordered.

Hanna turned. "You know what to do," she told the boy.

Scott looked over the edge and gulped. "Yeah," he said.

"OK. Remember, fly directly away from the mountain. Understand?" He nodded.

"Good. Your dad and I are right behind you."

Hanna stood upright, shouldering the weight of the tandem hang glider she was strapped to. Her heart was in her throat as she watched Scott run toward the edge as hard as he could. The glider dropped alarmingly after Scott jumped off, then recovered as he struggled for control.

"Let's go!" Russell shouted as he put on his harness. "They're right behind me!"

"Strap in."

He connected his harness to the glider.

"OK," Hanna said, "back up for the takeoff."

They turned around. One of the gunmen reached the top, followed immediately by his companion. Both brought their automatics up at the same time.

"We don't have time!" Hanna said. "Jump!"

They turned back and ran for the edge of the cliff.

Muted gunfire sounded behind them as they fell into space. The wind roared in her ears. Hanna pushed the control bar forward, guiding them away from the cliff face. A hole appeared in the wing fabric near the right tip.

Hanna angled to the left a little as the distance to the mountain increased. Ahead Scott turned and looked back.

"Keep going!" Hanna shouted.

The boy resumed his former course.

"We need to catch up," Russell said.

"Right." Hanna pulled back on the bar. The tandem hang glider picked up speed, but also fell below Scott's level. The boy did a series of S turns and dropped down beside them.

"What now?" Russell asked.

"I think we can turn back to the south now." She turned her head to the side. "Follow us," she told Scott. He nodded.

Hanna pushed the bar to the right. The glider made a graceful turn to the left. The ground below fell away from the mountain in graceful valleys and hills, a beautiful combination of dark greens and browns. Tall yuccas and century plants stood over the hearty brush, accentuated by stands of stunted trees. Hanna looked back at the cliff, now several hundred feet above them. Four dark shapes stood there, looking down at them. Hanna shivered, grateful they were out of range.

"Ground's coming up fast," Russell said. "Are we going to have to land?"

"Unless we can find a thermal." She felt a solid bump as they entered slightly warmer air. "Speaking of," she added, starting a gentle spiral to the left. A glance at Scott showed he was following.

The rising air currents lifted them higher and higher, buoyed up by the sun-warmed earth below. Soon they were above their launch point and spiraling higher. Several minutes later they were higher than the observatory.

"Think we can make it to the visitor's center?" Russell asked.

"Not yet. We need a few hundred feet more. We'll probably lose the thermal once we start for the observatory."

"Hey!" Scott shouted. "Those guys are going back to their car!"

Hanna looked around. The agents reached their Suburban and got in. Soon they were back on the road leading to the visitor's center. The parking lot was almost deserted.

"Great!" she grumbled. "Now what? Those guys can park up there and wait us out."

"We could land at the base of the mountain."

"Yeah, but then we'd have to hike out. And they'd probably be waiting for us."

The Suburban reached the top and parked near the exit road. Hanna heard a heavy thumping sound and looked toward the east. About a mile away, a large military helicopter was making an approach to Mount Locke. Looking down, she decided they had enough altitude to reach the parking lot.

"What's that?" Scott asked.

"Our way out!" Hanna shouted. "Turn for the observatory!"

The Suburban raced away as the Pave Low began its ponderous approach. The rotor blast washed over the parking lot, kicking up dirt and trash.

"Follow me!" Hanna shouted. "We can't let them get away!"

She pulled the control bar back and began a fast descent toward their landing zone. The helicopter touched down, and one of the crewmen jumped out and ran for the visitor's center. Several S turns later Hanna rolled out on their final approach. Nearing the ground, she pushed the bar forward as far as she could. The hang glider stalled, and they ran it out. Scott landed beside them.

"Over here!" Hanna shouted, as she got out of her harness.

The crewman turned around, obviously surprised to see three civilians appear out of nowhere. He hurried back to the helicopter and met them at the door.

"Are you the Flahertys?" he asked.

"That's right."

"We have orders to take you back to Laughlin Air Force Base. You're wanted back in Seattle, pronto."

"Glad to see you guys," Hanna said. "But there's something else you've got to do first."

"What's that?"

"Enemy agents were trying to kill us. They're on the way down the mountain right now."

"Get in."

One of the flight engineers got the Flahertys strapped into seats. The pilot started the engines and lifted off. A few minutes later the Pave Low descended to the road and started hovering. Hanna jumped as one of the gunners fired a short burst on a machine gun. Then the helicopter landed, and the other gunner opened the door and stepped down.

"They decided to give up," the flight engineer said with a wide grin. "Don't think they cared for the odds."

A few minutes later the five Chinese agents boarded the helicopter, their hands tied behind their backs. Hanna gasped as she recognized Gao and Lau. One of the other men glared at her on his way to the back.

29

"SO, THIS IS WHERE YOU DID IT?" ZHU SAID AS HE LOOKED around the large lab at Western Washington Utilities.

"This is it," Hanna agreed. "We had the defective chips flown in here, fixed them, and shipped them back out. Of course, the problem's a little different this time. And without your help there's no way we could have found it in time. We're just too vulnerable to cyber terrorism."

"That, unfortunately, is true."

"How are you going to fix the defective chips?" Rachael asked.

"That part's fairly simple," Hanna replied. "We copy the defective chip over to a blank, then make the deadly branch a no op."

"Could you say that in English?"

"Past a certain date, each chip has an instruction that jumps to the subroutine that destroys the circuit. We'll change the date-compare instruction to what's called a 'no operation.' This makes it impossible to execute the routine that does the dirty work."

"That's it?"

"That's it. With the feds handling the notification and logistics, all we have to do is fix one of each type chip. After that, we copy the fixed version as many times as necessary and send them out. There's a lot to do, but we should get done in time."

"So now's the lull before the storm," Russell said.

"Yep."

Zhu looked toward Paul. "This is most remarkable. Considering all that has happened, I am surprised to find myself here."

"Perhaps there is more at work than you are aware of," Paul replied.

"You refer to your beliefs?"

"I do, the same as Huo believed. The same as everyone in this room believes, except you. Have you thought about what I said?"

Zhu gave a short laugh. "I have. The missionary in Taiwan said he thought God was after me."

"Think about everything that's happened. Is it chance or plan? Seems clear enough to me, but only you can decide."

"Yes. That's what he said."

Hanna saw Paul and Rachael holding hands. *That's working out nicely,* she thought. She reached out and took Russell's hand. He gave her a reassuring squeeze. She smiled in contentment, so thankful for the life partner God had given her.

She looked over at Zhu. She thought she knew how that particular battle would turn out.